Richard Owen, Charles Davies Sherborn

The Life of Richard Owen

Vol. 2

Richard Owen, Charles Davies Sherborn

The Life of Richard Owen
Vol. 2

ISBN/EAN: 9783337083816

Printed in Europe, USA, Canada, Australia, Japan

Cover: Foto ©Raphael Reischuk / pixelio.de

More available books at **www.hansebooks.com**

THE LIFE

OF

RICHARD OWEN

BY HIS GRANDSON

THE REV. RICHARD OWEN, M.A.

WITH THE SCIENTIFIC PORTIONS REVISED
BY C. DAVIES SHERBORN

ALSO AN ESSAY ON OWEN'S POSITION IN ANATOMICAL SCIENCE
BY THE
RIGHT HON. T. H. HUXLEY, F.R.S.

PORTRAITS AND ILLUSTRATIONS

IN TWO VOLUMES—VOL. II.

LONDON
JOHN MURRAY, ALBEMARLE STREET
1894

CONTENTS

OF

THE SECOND VOLUME

CHAPTER III

1857-59

CHAPTER IV

1860-61

CHAPTER V

1862-64

CHAPTER VI

1865-68

LIST OF ILLUSTRATIONS

IN VOL. II

PROFESSOR OWEN

CHAPTER I

1855-56

The Phœnix—The Crystal Palace at Sydenham—Juror of the Universal Exhibition at Paris—Knight of the Legion of Honour, 1855—Superintendent of the Natural History Department of the British Museum—Death of his Sister, Grace Owen—Cardinal Wiseman, Dr. and Mrs. Livingstone, 1856.

In the year 1855 Owen's work ' On the Archetype and Homologies of the Vertebrate Skeleton' was translated into French and appeared under the title, ' Principes d'Ostéologie comparée ; ou, Recherches sur l'Archétype et les Homologies du Squelette vertébré.'[1] The publication of his lectures on the ' Comparative Anatomy and Physiology of the Invertebrate Animals' reached a second edition. Before the beginning of his Hunterian course, he gave a lecture to a large audience at the Royal Institution on ' Anthropoid Apes.'

The subject chosen for the Hunterian Lectures this season was ' Fossil Remains ;' but before delivering them Owen gave as an introduction to

[1] Paris : J. B. Baillière, 1855.

the subject three lectures in the Theatre of the
Royal College of Surgeons explanatory of Hunter's
MS. essay ' On Extraneous Fossils.' In relation
to this course Owen remarks : ' The palæontological is now the only department of the museum
which has not been systematically elucidated in
this theatre, to the extent at least of the time at my
command. . . . It will be observed that Hunter,
in his general collection, illustrates the three ways
in which the anatomy of animals may be broadly
and philosophically followed out.

'There is a series of organs in their mature
state, traced from their simplest to their most complex conditions, as in the first division of the
physiological series.

'There is a series of the progressive changes
or stages in the development of each organ in the
embryo and fœtus of different species, as, e.g., in
the second division of the same great series.

'There is, thirdly, a series of entire animals, occasionally dissected to show the general collocation
of their organs, and arranged, as in the physiological series, in the ascending order, commencing
with the more simple forms and proceeding gra-
dationally to the Mammalia and to Man.

'The Council of this College has confided to
me the making of the catalogues of these exemplifications of animal structures, and of the methods
by which those structures may be studied. And
those catalogues have been completed and published

with one small exception, relating to the vertebrated province of the series arranged according to
the classes of animals. . . . In the session of last
year I concluded the series of lectures in which the
animal organisation was treated of according to
the classes of animals, beginning with the lowest
and ending with the highest. . . . .

  ' Now John Hunter had not neglected the field
of anatomical inquiry presented by fossil organic
remains.   He lived to publish little respecting
them.   The scientific world probably first became
aware of the fact that he had paid any attention
at all to them when Hunter communicated to
the Royal Society of London, in 1793, his paper
on the fossil bones presented to that Society
by His Most Serene Highness the Margrave of
Anspach. . . . Those men accustomed to think,
who heard or read that paper, would recognise in
it the mind of the great Master.   It is characterised by the same broad views and acute insight
into the phenomena under review, by the same
unexpected illustrations, which only a wide em-
brace of facts could have suggested, by the same
bold excursions into fields stretching away far
beyond the immediate subject of the memoir, which
peculiarly mark all the papers from Hunter's pen.

  ' In those letters which are introduced into the
life of John Hunter prefixed to Palmer's edition
of his works, scarcely one of them omits a recommendation to Jenner to secure for his correspon-

dent and revered teacher, Hunter, whatever fossil remains might fall in his way.'

Owen was evidently regarded more or less, all through his life, as legitimate prey to the numerous inquirers as to the nature and habits of such monsters as the cockatrice, the phœnix, and the bunyip (this last monster being an imaginary creature which hailed from Australia, whose skull turned out to be merely that of an embryo sheep). He has left a description of his interview with an Oriental personage who had come to inquire about the phœnix.

On April 15 he writes : ' A grave Oriental with his interpreter were ushered into my study, as I was preparing my lecture. After due salaams and the visitors seated, the interpreter stated that they were from the Turkish Embassy in order to ask my opinion of the phœnix ; whether I believed there had ever been such a bird, and what was the last scientific intelligence regarding it. Of course I told them nothing was known beyond old tradition. The Turk then took from an inner recess of his vest a crimson velvet case, which contained a most beautiful ladle, the handle of carved coral and gold, jewelled, the bowl of a kind of fine horny material, half rose colour and half cream colour, united at an angle. This, with a few similar ladles, had been in the Sultan's jewel-house for many centuries, and was held to be made—the bowl—out of the beak of the phœnix. My opinion was respectfully requested as to whether such was the case, or, if not, from what bird's beak the bowl had been made.

'After some research in the museum I found the head and beak of the bird which must have yielded such a bowl as that of the Sultan's ladle. The bird is a very rare one, a native of Ceylon, and called the "Helmeted Hornbill," or *Buceros galeatus.* Sir Joseph Banks had presented a specimen of it. The head and beak were brought into my study and handed to the Oriental. He examined it very deftly, comparing the beak with the bowl, and then exclaimed with astonishment and reverence, "God is great! That surely is the bird!" I took a large sheet of paper, and wrote a brief certificate of the nature and country of the bird from which the Sultan's ladle had been made, and gave it to the Turk, requesting the interpreter to write down the name and titles of the individual to whom the precious article had been entrusted. It was as follows: "Mohammed Abu Said, Chief Spoon and Ladle-maker to the Commander of the Faithful."

'So much for the phœnix.'

On April 20 Owen attended the opening ceremony of the Crystal Palace, which had been removed to Sydenham. It is thus described in the diary:
'To London Bridge about eleven. Babbage in our carriage; crowd tremendous. We kept together till fairly in the Palace. R. could not find his

ivory ticket when he left home this morning, and
the official at the turnstile would not let him in,
in spite of Babbage offering to prove his identity.
At last Babbage found some person of importance who recognised R. at once, and so we got in
finally. We saw the Queen, Prince Albert, and
the Emperor and Empress of the French file
past as they walked along the gallery; the
Empress, having gone a little way, sat down on
a chair, and we afterwards heard that she found
it so comfortable that Prince Albert gallantly
bought it on the spot and presented her with it.
The upper gallery was not open to the public, to
prevent crowding on the light spiral staircase.
Mr. and Mrs. Charles Darwin there; we walked
about a bit with them. The Honourable Artil-
lery Company also there in full force; the officers
of R.'s old corps seemed delighted to meet him
again. Home about eight.'

The following extracts are also taken from
the diary :—

'*May* 11.—R. dined with Lord Ashburton.
He met the Duc d'Aumale there, who was
pleasant in manner and evidently knows something of fossils. There were present Thomas
Carlyle, Mr. Thackeray, Lord Stanley, &c.'

'*June* 5.—About three o'clock there came in
Landseer and E. W. Cooke, hot, weary, and
luncheonless. They had been to a private view
of J. J. Chalon's pictures, which are to be sold, and

had missed their train. Cooke has all the enthusiasm of a child over the trees, shrubs, and flowers in the garden. Landseer enjoyed them as much, but was quieter. They were never tired of looking at the pictures in the dining-room, but had to go off early to a dinner of Academicians at the Star and Garter.'

On July 16 Owen started for Paris in order to perform much the same services for the Universal Exhibition of 1855 as he had done for the Great Exhibition of 1851 in London. On the resignation of Prince C. L. Bonaparte he was appointed Chairman of the Jury (XI.) on 'Prepared and Preserved Alimentary Substances.' This, of course, included wines. Some half-dozen of his letters are preserved, but as the proceedings are somewhat similar to those described at the time of the Great Exhibition the following extracts may suffice :—

'*July* 18, 1855.—I have attended a meeting of the Institute, and, oddly enough, the learned body was engaged in discussing my merits, amongst others, relative to a vacancy in the list of eight foreign members. At present, I am a " corresponding member " only, like Lord Brougham, Brewster, &c.'

'*July* 27, 1855.—[Milne Edwards] lives now in Cuvier's old house, and many pleasing recollections and associations arose on entering the well-known door. The general arrangement of the

old dwelling—its subdivision into many small
rooms—is much as it was ; the fittings and furniture in a gayer Parisian style. . . . The morning
occupations of our jury are curious and various,
each one well adapted to its end, but performed
amidst a scene of gesticulation and action and a
Babel of seeming altercation which renders the
result, when we come afterwards coolly to sum
up the notes, surprising to me.   Take the following as an example : Time, 7 A.M. ; subject,
Wines of Austria ; scene, Grande Exposition, in
a small whitewashed chamber with a skylight ;
a table with green cloth, and books, papers,
writing materials ; another with rows of bottles of
wine, corkscrews, &c.   Hampers of wine on one
side of the room.   President and two or three
members of jury in green velvet *fauteuils* ; three
experts seated in a corner of the room with a tin
pail before them, each with a silver chalice like
a Highland quaigh, and a small napkin.   The
Austrian Commissioner and the representatives
of the several wine-growers ; a man in green and
silver uniform to uncork ; a grinning negro to
serve the wine to the tasters ; a worthy ' blouse '
to hand and take back the sample-bottles.   Commissioner calls out the number and vintage-year of
the sample.   A juryman enters it in a ruled book,
the uncorker uncorks the bottle ; the grinning
negro pours a little into the pail, then fills the
chalice.   Each taster agitates the wine, carries it

to his nose, draws it slowly into his mouth, rinces and spurts it out into the pail; then the three interchange knowing remarks in a low tone, their heads together, and bawl out a number, 3, 6, 10, as the case may be, indicative of their verdict as to quality. The same entered by secretary of jury and vouched by president. After each trial the expert wipes his chalice and recommences. After five or six trials water is served to each, with which he rinces out his mouth and chalice, then wipes his tongue with his napkin. The trial recommences : Number and vintage of bottle called ; clack goes the cork ; black Hebe bottles up the sparkling ruby or gold-coloured wine in the silver chalices ; sniffing, rincing, smacking of lips, and all goes into the pail. Two of our experts are *décorés*, and their jovial fellow is bearded like the pard. Strange and outlandish are the shapes of the bottles, and quaint their labels, from Hungary and Bohemia. As the tasting progresses, the din of discussion waxes louder and fiercer. Any peculiarly fine wines are submitted in *petits verres* to the jury ; the progress is from the ordinary to the *recherchés* ; most delicate and *aromés* were some, and more especially the concluding sample entitled "Tokay-Essence, du Cru de Monak, du Comte George Andrassy." It was grievous to see the amber-coloured, sparkling Tokays liberally added to the now almost brimming pailful of the mixture of all the choicest wines of the Austrian Empire.'

'*July* 31, 1855.—You may expect me home any day after the receipt of this. . . . The Prince [C. L. Bonaparte] drove me in the Bois de Boulogne yesterday, after the Institute, and called upon one of his brothers [Pierre], to whom he introduced me. In the evening I played two games of chess with the Duke of Brunswick (the Diamond Duke), and won one.'

On August 3 Owen returned from the 'Exposition Universelle' 'with an opinion of the French,' as he writes, 'raised to a high degree in respect to their abilities and disposition.' For his services given to the Exhibition the Emperor of the French created him a Knight of the Legion of Honour, but the decoration itself did not arrive till Christmas.

On Owen's return from Paris, his wife went to Wirksworth for rest and change, and the Professor wrote her (September 13) the following doleful account of his domestic experiences during her absence :—

'Cook was seated in a chair, bending herself double, shedding maudlin tears, and complaining of great pain. Of course there was nothing to be done before getting her to bed. When Sister E. had helped her to undress and got her covered up, I went upstairs. She was knocking her head about the pillow, bewailing her fate ; maundered about how her uncle loved me and how she loved you, and, when I asked her some professional questions, said she would speak the truth. I assured her I had not doubted it ; but when she said she had taken nothing but a drop of tea, I thought it had left a most uncommon odour of gin and peppermint. Thereupon I gave her a composing draught and took away her candle, and of course she is quite well this morning. . . .' 'She took herself off last night,' he says in a letter of the 15th, 'with a restoration of robustness and voice which would have been miraculous if the prostration and pangs of the previous evening had been real.'

In September, Owen had another visit from Prince C. L. Bonaparte, who brought with him his daughter and son-in-law, the Comte and Comtesse di Campello. In this month an entry in the diary states that Owen made the acquaintance of Staunton, the famous chess-player, with whom he played several games of chess, 'at which he came off with some credit, considering.'

On October 2, 1855, Owen writes to his sister Eliza :—

'I dined yesterday at St. Bartholomew's on the occasion of the opening of the Medical Session. I was placed at the right hand of the chairman at the dinner, and on that of the President of the Hospital in the grand old hall at the introductory address, and was called upon to

return thanks for the visitors, which included
most of the distinguished medical men in town
who had been students at the Hospital.   In
short, my reception was very gratifying to me.
It happened to be just thirty years that day
(October 1, 1825) when I first made my entry as
a strange shy pupil in the Hospital yard and first
listened to good old Abernethy's introductory
lecture.   It was just twenty years since (in the
progress of my development) I gave my first
lecture as Professor of Comparative Anatomy at
the Hospital (the first they had had in that
science), so I had some topics that raised con-
genial sentiments in many who had been pupils
at and before my day. . . .'

In another letter, dated November 4, Owen
writes :—

'I don't know whether I told you I had
enjoyed a holiday accompanying the Duke of
Cambridge and Colonel Liddell shooting in the
Park.   The Duke is a fine tall man in the prime
of life, wearing the large and full beard and
moustaches which he let grow in the wars.   He
chatted very freely with me in the intervals of the
shots, chiefly putting questions after the family
manner : asked how I went to town, the times of
the trains, the cost of the season ticket, &c. . . .
On Thursday I went to see, by invitation, the
photographs of the Crimea shown by gaslight;
they marvellously exemplify the power of that

application of science to obtain graphic records of a campaign.'

Before the close of the year 1855 Owen issued his 'Catalogue of the Fossil Remains in the Hunterian Museum,' 4to, but he never completed it ; for, to use his own words, 'the "Catalogue of the Fossils of the Hunterian Museum" passed out of my responsibility and care when I accepted the office of Superintendent of the Natural History Department of the British Museum.'[2] This office was generally understood to have been created expressly for Owen. There is no doubt that he owed his appointment, to a great extent, to Lord Macaulay, with whom he had as yet but the barest acquaintance ; and with reference to this, Macaulay's letter and the explanations accompanying it may be quoted from his 'Life,' by his nephew, Sir George Trevelyan. He says :—

'Long after Macaulay had abandoned all other public business he continued to occupy himself in the administration of the British Museum. In February 1856 he wrote to Lord Lansdowne with the view of securing that old friend's potent influence in favour of an arrangement by which Professor Owen might be placed in a position worthy of his reputation and of his services. The circumstance which gave rise to

[2] The completion of the concluding volume was entrusted to Professor John Morris.

the letter was the impending appointment of
Signor Panizzi to the post of Secretary and Principal Librarian to the Museum. "I am glad of
this," writes Macaulay, "both on public and
private grounds. Yet I fear that the appointment will be unpopular both within and without
the Museum. There is a growing jealousy
among men of science which, between ourselves,
appears even at the Board of Trustees. There
is a notion that the Department of Natural
History is neglected, and that the library and the
sculpture galleries are unduly favoured. This
feeling will certainly not be allayed by the
appointment of Panizzi, whose great object,
during many years, has been to make our library
the best in Europe, and who would at any time
give three mammoths for an Aldus."'

Macaulay then went on to propose that,
simultaneously with Signor Panizzi's nomination
to the secretaryship, Professor Owen should be
constituted Superintendent of the whole Department of Natural History, including geology,
zoology, botany, and mineralogy. 'I cannot but
think,' he says, 'that this arrangement would be
beneficial in the highest degree to the Museum.
I am sure it would be popular. I must add that
I am extremely desirous that something should
be done for Owen. I hardly know him to speak
to. His pursuits are not mine; but his fame is
spread over Europe. He is an honour to our

country, and it is painful to me to think that a man of his merit should be approaching old age amidst anxieties and distresses. He told me that eight hundred a year, without a house in the Museum, would be opulence to him. He did not, he said, even wish for more. He seems to me to be a case for public patronage. Such patronage is not needed by eminent literary men or artists. A poet, a novelist, an historian, a painter, a sculptor, who stood in his own line as high as Owen stands among men of science, could never be in want except by his own fault. But the greatest natural philosopher may starve while his countrymen are boasting of his discoveries, and while foreign Academies are begging for the honour of being allowed to add his name to their list.'

On May 26, 1856, Owen received the appointment that Macaulay had suggested, with a salary of 800l. a year.

But before the final arrangements were completed he confesses to have felt very unsettled, as there was some uncertainty connected with the nature of the appointment, and from the number of suggestions which were brought forward he was apprehensive of considerable delay. As his connection with the College of Surgeons had ceased, he had no more Hunterian Lectures to give, but filled up a good deal of the time in giving lectures elsewhere at various places. He

also took the opportunity of attending some of
Faraday's at the Royal Institution. In describing
one of these lectures, which took place in January,
he says : ' The Prince of Wales and Prince Arthur
there. They seemed much interested, and sat on
chairs, with a footstool, as their feet did not reach
the ground. Faraday in great force—on Metals.
Gold, silver, &c., were rolled into long ribbons.
The theatre crowded.'

At another lecture ' Faraday explained the
magnet and strength of attraction. He made us
all laugh heartily ; and when he threw a coal-
scuttle full of coals, a poker, and a pair of tongs
at the great magnet, and they stuck there, the
theatre echoed with shouts of laughter.'

On January 8 Owen accompanied Sir Joseph
Paxton to Coventry, where, he says, 'there was
a deputation to meet us. Bells ringing, &c. Gave
lecture on " Ruminants " at 8.30 in an old hall to
a crowded audience, which was largely composed
of the ribbon-weavers—men and women—watch-
makers and so on, all very attentive : a good
many open-mouthed listeners.'

On April 13 Owen went to Manchester,
where he gave a course of four lectures, and then
to Liverpool, where he also gave a short course.
' At my first lecture at Liverpool,' he writes to
his wife, ' the managing committee had Haydn's
overture to the " Creation " played by a good
orchestra, whilst the audience was assembling in

the great hall. All went off satisfactorily. The only cloud is the news of sister Grace's serious illness.'

As soon as Owen was able, he went to Lancaster, and spent some time with his sister; but she never rallied, and her death occurred soon afterwards. He had the greatest affection for all his sisters, and deeply felt the loss of this one, who was the youngest. He had a portrait of her painted, and in his last illness it was placed where he could easily see it, and he then would often talk about her. He was, however, not able to stay long in Lancaster, but was obliged to hurry back to London to lecture at the Royal Institution on May 2 'On the Original Cattle of Great Britain,' and also to give a lecture at Richmond on the 5th of that month.

On May 22, 1856, Owen writes to his wife, who was travelling in Germany with their son, that he had a seat on the Judge's bench for one day of the Palmer trial. He says: ' His advocate, Serjeant Shee, began at half-past ten, and I left him speaking at half-past three; he did not conclude his address till half-past six! A course of lectures rolled into one! The main points were an attempt to show that the prisoner had no motive for killing his friend, but the reverse; and that the deceased had died of ordinary convulsions. Some parts of the speech able; a few, touching and eloquent. He has a

bad habit of beginning his sentence too loud, and
dropping his voice too much at the close, and
drowning the last and most important words of the
statement by a violent thump on the table.   I
augur that the defence has nothing to offer to bar
a conviction ; but one cannot reason upon law
as upon anything else.'

On May 26 Owen was formally appointed
Superintendent of the Natural History Department of the British Museum, and entered upon
office on June 8 ; but as his work in connection
with the museum is fully detailed in another
chapter, we need not dwell on it here.

It is somewhat surprising that he makes
hardly any mention in his letters of the important
change which this new appointment made in his
mode of life.   A brief note about 'taking office
at B.M. on Monday,' and 'after seeing Panizzi a
few more forms to be got through, all to be ended
by Saturday, when at twelve o'clock I make my
first bow to the Trustees and receive my formal
installation,' are the sole references to the occurrence.   A little later on he remarks (July 26,
1856) :—

'Willie regards the British Museum as a very
superior position, chiefly, I believe, because, just
beneath my window, a sunburnt, rough-voiced
sergeant musters and turns out with the guard
every two hours. . . . Look out for the next
number of Blackwood and riddle me out my con-

tribution thereto. I had a very flattering note from Mr. Blackwood on sending me proofs of the light little article I amused myself some time ago by penning. . . . The College responded to my resignation by a letter acknowledging my long and valuable services, &c., in the usual official terms.' The document in question was a letter forwarded to him from the Secretary stating that at a meeting of the Council of the College of Surgeons on June 12, 1856, a resolution was passed, to express "the great regret of this Council at the loss of the services of a gentleman who has been so long connected with the museum, and who has earned so wide a reputation, &c., and of their gratification that the cause of his resig- nation is his appointment to an important office connected with the same department of science in the British Museum."'

Amongst the letters with reference to this appointment which Owen received, the following from Professor A. Sedgwick may be quoted :--

Norwich : June 20, 1856.

'My dear Owen,—. . . I trust that your move to the British Museum is for your happiness. If God spare your health it will be a grand move for the benefit of British science. An *Imperator* was sadly wanted in that vast establishment.

'Ever yours,
'A. SEDGWICK.'

The following entry in the diary will show that with his work at the British Museum Owen still kept up his musical interests :—

'*July* 13.—Mr. Ella, Madame Hallé, Signor Piatti and his wife and the two Hallé children, spent the day here very pleasantly. Mr. Hallé could not come, being laid up with a sore throat. Madame Piatti is small and fair and an accomplished musician. She and her gifted, quiet husband played some duets in the dusk of the evening, Piatti playing on R.'s beautiful " cello." [3] They gave us tickets for Hallé's morning concert on the 17th.'

On August 5 Owen travelled with his wife to Bedford, where he gave a lecture on fossils found in that county. 'We dined with the Mayor,' Mrs. Owen writes, ' who made a speech after the lecture. Hoped Professor Owen's presence and lecture would incite the people of Bedford to set up a museum of their own, and so on.' After leaving Bedford, Owen went on to the meeting of the British Association in Cheltenham, and then travelled up to Scotland, where he was the guest of the Duke of Argyll at Murray Castle, Inveraray, stopping at Lancaster on the way, to leave his wife with his sisters there.

While at Inveraray he wrote them a long account of the beauties of the scenery of that district. Leaving on the 26th, he stayed a few

[3] By Foster.

days in Perthshire, and then went on to Dundrum, 'near Burns's country,' where he rejoined his wife. They returned home on September 5.

The article contributed to ' Blackwood's Magazine,' to which Owen refers in his letter of July 20, was signed *ENNΩ*, presumably an anagram for *O N*, and was entitled ' A Visit to Selborne.' This was an account of a visit which he paid to Thomas Bell, who was then living in Gilbert White's old house.

Professor Owen was keenly anxious to add to the collection of fossil bones at the British Museum, and many of his friends who were on the look-out for specimens were in the habit of communicating with him at once as to opportunities of purchase. These communications he evidently looked upon as a personal favour to himself, as the following letter which he wrote to Dr. Falconer[1] will show :—

British Museum : Oct. 10, 1856.

' My dear Falconer,—It is most kind of you to have thought of me and my peculiar interest in the dentition of mastodon whilst you were at Darmstadt. . . . It's unlucky that the grant for this year was exhausted by the grand Dinornis collection of Mr. Walter Mantell (come and see the skeleton of the *Din. elephantopus*, which I have just had set up). But the specimen of the *Mastodon longirostris* is one we ought to have ; and I will do my best to have it purchased with-

---

[1] Kindly communicated by Professor Prestwich, F.R.S.

out delay. . . . Have you thought of the ' Swiney Professorship?' It is just the occupation or amusement that would suit you, and do you good.

' I was glad to hear from old Kaup, one of the worthiest of men.

> ' Ever yours,
>
> ' RICHARD OWEN.'

On November 28 Owen writes to his sisters to tell them of the death of an old friend, and continues :—

' Yesterday, singularly enough, I was an hour by the sick bed of another friend, at his special request—Lord Ellesmere. I fear he has not the strength to fight through his present attack. The Duke of Argyll called on me to acquaint me with Lord Ellesmere's illness, and to tell me that he had expressed a wish to see me. I went directly after Museum hours to Bridgewater House, and was immediately admitted on sending in my card. The half-lit halls looked like dark unexplored caverns ; the noble owner of all on a pallet in a small closet-like room, which seemed like a recess on one side. His fine features and expressive eyes bespoke sickness and suffering. I talked on a variety of topics, with intervals of quiet, until the Duchess of Sutherland and the Duchess of Arygll entered. . . . That morning (yesterday) I breakfasted with Mr. Henry Taylor, and met Lord Monteagle and a very interesting party. . . .

London is the place, after all, for interchange of thought.'

In this month Owen ' met Cardinal Wiseman at a dinner party at a neighbour's house.'

In a letter to his sisters he says :—

' The Cardinal was attended by two priests, and there were two or three others of different rank, including the pastor of their small chapel at Mortlake. A very handsome dinner : about half a dozen ladies. The Cardinal astounded me by his attire ; it was a spectacle to behold, and, as you know I was always fond of scarlet, it was quite pleasant to have his Eminence opposite me at the table. He wore a close-fitting Eastern tunic and tights, of purple edged with crimson, fitting close to the throat and at the wrists, Turkish fashion ; short lace ruffles at the wrist, a close white stock round the neck, covered by the ribbon of an Order. Below the tights appeared the crimson silk stockings, shoes, and large rich buckles. Over his dress he wore a rich stiff crimson cloak, with a broad embroidered margin, without sleeves, attached round the neck by a broad embroidered band. A large jewelled gold cross was suspended by a long enamelled chain, and rested on his comfortably prominent stomach. On his crown was a shallow round scarlet skull-cap. He made an excellent dinner ; contrasting it, however, with one he had assisted at, at the Bishop of Malines', in his route through Belgium, and which lasted four hours. The Cardinal's large jovial mouth, turned-up pimply nose, bright astute eyes, with some fire lurking in them, and broad bold front, all seemed to correspond well with the outward insignia of the worldly rank he had achieved, and with all the environments—comfortable throne-like arm-chair, champagne chalice, green hock glass and "all other delicacies." He was my-lorded by his flock; I of course gave him only his Italian honour, as 'Your Eminence'—with the distinction. The priests, as they passed his Eminence to take their places at the table, reverentially stooped and kissed his hand. They maintained a *modest* silence during the dinner. I was honoured by a fair share of the Cardinal's discourse, both before, at, and after dinner. . . . He is a very clever man of the world, and knows well the weak points of both Romanism and Anglicanism. I have just returned from greeting and shaking the hand of a very different man, Dr. Livingstone, the African missionary and traveller; he is at this moment with Sir Roderick Murchison and the Secretary of the Geographical Society, at Arrowsmith's, the great map-man, where I left him before a table overspread with the traveller's map, and plans of his route across Central Africa from west to east—the greatest achievement in that field of exploration that has yet been done. Livingstone is looking less aged and worn than I expected. I recognised his bronzed features imme-

diately, although it is now near twenty years since
he took leave of me in the College museum,
where, as a young medical missionary, he called
for instruction as to observing and collecting
natural history. He has not been able, poor
fellow, to do much in that way : his chief zoological experience being the grip of his left arm
by a lion, which he had wounded with his pistol.
The arm was broken and badly set.'

In a letter written not long after he narrates an
incident which happened to Mrs. Livingstone and
himself, which evidently entertained him vastly :—

'After the lecture [by Livingstone at the
Society of Arts], Colonel Sykes asked me if I had
a ticket for the Photographic Soirée at King's
College. I had ; so had he ; and as each ticket
admitted two, *he* took the Doctor, and *I*, Mrs.
Livingstone. It was a dress assembly in the
grand hall. Mrs. L., with a straw-bonnet of 1846,
and attired to match, made a most singular exception to the brilliant costumes. Who can that
odd woman be that Professor O. is taking round
the room and paying so much attention to ? I
caught sight of Will's countenance (he and Carry
had gone with Dr. Farre, before I arrived).
Disgust and alarm most strongly portrayed. He
could not conceive what badly dressed house-
maid I had picked up to bring to such a place !
Carry equally mystified. The extraordinary
scrutinies of many fine ladies as they shrank, at

first, from contact, as far as the crowd permitted !
But when the rumour began to buzz abroad that it
was Dr. and Mrs. Livingstone—then at the acme
of their lion-hood, especially with the Church
party, through Lord Shaftesbury's speech the day
before—what a change came over the scene ! It
was which of the scornful dames could first get
introduced to Professor O., to be introduced to
Mrs. L. ; and the photographs were comparatively
deserted for the dusky strangers.'

Owen had several tales of similar discomfiture,
which he would often relate with the greatest
delight and amusement.

The last lecture which he gave this year was on
' Ivory and Teeth of Commerce,' and was delivered
at the Society of Arts on December 19.

On December 29, 1856, Owen writes to his
friend John Murray on the subject of an article on
' Parthenogenesis ' for the ' Quarterly Review,' in
the course of which letter he remarks : ' The first
question is whether your estimable editor of the
" Quarterly " or yourself would regard the details of
the reproductive economy and apparatus of a *Rose*
and a *Bee* as equally producible in respectable
society. . . . The facts bearing upon this mysterious power of virgin-procreativeness are now so
numerous and varied as to form an important body
of physiological doctrine, of which the " Quarterly "
ought to take cognizance without squeamishness.

For this sensitiveness, truly akin to the Yankee nether-clothing of the pianoforte legs, is shutting out a vast and rapidly increasing store of most interesting and important knowledge relative to those animals which are nearest akin to plants.'

CHAPTER II [1]

1856-81

Soon after his appointment to the Hunterian
Professorship at the Royal College of Surgeons,
Owen's thoughts turned towards the elaboration
of a definite scheme which should allow of the
proper exhibition of the natural history treasures
of the nation. His frequent visits to the British
Museum impressed him more and more with the
conviction that the natural history department
was the most neglected branch of that institution.
This neglect arose from the inadequate space

[1] For the sake of greater clearness, it has been thought advisable to devote a separate chapter to the history of the British Museum of Natural History at South Kensington, instead of dispersing it among the many years of Professor Owen's life through which the discussions were spread. The account is given as nearly as possible in his own words, the substance being taken from his address to the British Association at York in 1881.

allotted to the collections. The convenience of
the arrangements he had been enabled to make
in Lincoln's Inn Fields strongly forced upon his
notice the chaos at the British Museum, and even
as early as the year 1846 he addressed a letter
(vol. i. p. 276) to Lord Francis Egerton. in which
we may see the commencement of the scheme
which began to near completion in 1881.

Others besides Owen had fully recognised the
gravity of the situation at the British Museum,
for in 1854 John Edward Gray. the keeper of
Zoology, had reported on the unfitness of damp
vaults for the storage of zoological material, and
prayed for additional accommodation. The appeal
was referred by the Trustees to the architect, and
on receiving the latter's report, they 'declined to
adopt Dr. Gray's suggestion,' and recommended
'that steps should be taken to obviate the deteriora-
tion of the specimens ' by treatment of the vaults
in which they were stored. In the renewed
appeals of Dr. Gray, the Trustees apparently set
aside the architect as specialist on natural history,
and recommended the erection of 'an additional
gallery to the eastern Zoological Gallery, and the
substitution of skylights for the side windows,
with a view to a further gallery at an elevation
above the floor of the one in use.'

Professor Owen entered the service of the
Trustees of the British Museum on May 26, 1856.
As already stated, he had been offered and

refused five years before a post vacant by the
death of Charles König, the salary of which was
reduced, but on this occasion a special office was
created, and Owen became 'Superintendent of
the Departments of Natural History.' This office
gave place, on his retirement in 1884, to that of
'Director of the British Museum' (Natural History), under which name he was succeeded by
Professor Flower.

On taking up the work of the departments
placed under his charge, Professor Owen became
better acquainted with the melancholy condition of
affairs, and determined to submit to the Trustees
a statement embodying estimates of space required
for exhibition of all the collections, adding to it
considerations on the ratio of increase during the
previous ten years, and the probable future increase by annual additions.

In dealing with the British Museum, however,
Owen had a vastly different task from that which
he had previously undertaken. When at the
College of Surgeons, he was dealing with a Board
of Governors, who, whatever their personal idiosyn-
crasies, were all impressed with the importance
of improving the collections placed under their
charge. With the British Museum and its
Trustees the matter was entirely different. Here
there were several 'departments,' each under the
charge of an energetic if not ambitious head, and
each anxious for a large share of the spoils ; while

the spoils were then, as now, not in the keeping of the Museum Trustees, but of a clerk in the Treasury.

Accordingly, on February 10, 1859, Owen submitted a strong report to the Trustees, setting forth his views as to a National Museum of Natural History, accompanied with a plan, and this was forwarded to the Treasury. The document was remarkable for the complete grasp of the problem and the author's intimate knowledge of the facts concerned ; it was too weighty to be overlooked, and on March 11, 1859, the ' Report with Plan ' was ' ordered by the House of Commons to be printed.'[2] A fac-simile of the original pen-and-ink sketch plan drawn by Professor Owen himself is given on the next page.

This ' Report with Plan ' included estimates of space for the then acquired specimens of the several departments of natural history, together with space for the reception of the additional specimens which might accrue in the course of a generation. It further recommended that ' such a building, besides giving accommodation to the several classes of natural history objects . . . should also include a hall for a distinct department, adapted to convey an elementary knowledge of all divisions of natural history, the large proportion of public visitors not being specially conversant with any particular subject.'

[2] Parl. Papers (126 i.), fo. 1859.

'One of the most popular and instructive features in a public collection of natural history would be a portion devoted to specimens selected to show type-characters of the principal groups of organised and crystallised forms. This would constitute an epitome of natural history, and should convey to the eye in the easiest way an elementary knowledge of the science. An estimate of the space required for such an exhibition was given, and I ventured also on another topic in connection with the more immediate object of my report. Moreover, such a museum of natural history should have wider influences ; and collections of rarities and specimens so restricted as that in Lincoln's Inn Fields (Royal College of Surgeons) had impressed me with the conviction that explanatory lectures had great influence on their growth and applications. I concluded my report, therefore, by referring to the lecture-theatre shown in my plan, and expressed my belief that administrators will consider it due to the public that the gentlemen in charge of the several departments of the National Collection of Natural History should have assigned to them the duty of explaining the principles and relations, by elementary and free lectures, of such departments as, for example, Ornithology, Botany, Geology, Palæontology, Mineralogy, &c.'

'After the lapse of twenty years,' Owen said in 1881, 'I have lived to see the fulfilment of all

the recommendations, save the final one (lecture-
theatre) of my report of 1859. The theatre
was erased from my plan, and the elementary
courses of lecturing remain for the future.'

In communicating this report to Parliament.
Professor Owen felt that he was addressing
representatives of the greatest commercial and
colonising nation on the globe, and that such a
nation and empire might well be expected by
the rest of the civilised world to offer to students
and lovers of natural history the best and noblest
museum for the illustration of this great division
of general science.

But for such a museum a site of not less than
eight acres was required. The effect of restrict-
ing the site to the space, for example, on which
the Museum at Bloomsbury stands was signifi-
cantly demonstrative of difficulties to come, and
Owen pointed to the wisdom which would be
manifested by securing, in a rapidly growing
metropolis, adequate space for future additions
to the building which might be in the first place
erected upon it.

One or two of his intimate and confidential
friends dissuaded him from sending in his report.
They urged that it might be misconstrued, or
' interpreted as exemplifying a character prone to
inconsiderate and extravagant views,' and might
even lead to disagreeable personal consequences.
They further argued that the extended space for

which he asked inevitably involved change of
locality, and that no other plan for gathering
together the whole of the national natural history collections had previously been submitted
to authority. The legislative mind was therefore unprepared for calm and due consideration
of the subject. Still, Owen considered that if the
details and aims and grounds of his report were
known and comprehended, no strong opposition
on the part of Parliament could be expected.
In this he was disappointed. An Irish member [3]
made his ' Report and Plan ' the ground of a
motion for a committee of inquiry, which was
carried.

This committee, after taking the evidence
published in the Blue Book (ordered to be printed
August 10, 1860),[4] reported against the removal
of the natural history collections from the British
Museum. Indeed, as the report states, with one
' eminent exception, the whole of the scientific
naturalists, including the keepers of all the departments of natural history in the British Museum,
are of an opinion that an exhibition on so large
a scale [as that proposed by Owen] tends alike to
the needless bewilderment and fatigue of the
public and the impediment of the studies of the
scientific visitor.' The committee also recommended a more limited form of exhibition, their

[3] Mr. Gregory, M.P. for co.   July 22, 1861).
Galway Hansard, Debate of   [4] Pp. 238, with ten plans.

recommendation being supported by Professors
Huxley and Maskelyne, Drs. Gray and Sclater,
Messrs. Waterhouse, Thomas Bell, Gould, Sir
Roderick Murchison, and Sir Benjamin Brodie.

' Lest, however, the House might attach undue
weight to this exceptional testimony, the chairman
of the committee deemed it his duty, in bringing
up the report, to warn the House of the character
of such testimony, and his speech left, as I was
told, a very unfavourable impression as regards
myself. I was chiefly concerned to know what
might be put upon record in " Hansard." In
that valuable work hon. members revise their reported utterances before the sheets go to press.
I was somewhat relieved to find Mr. Gregory
merely regretting that " a man whose name stood
so high should connect himself with so foolish,
crazy, and extravagant a scheme, and should per-
severe in it after the folly had been pointed out
by most unexceptionable witnesses.

' " They had on one side, and standing alone,
Professor Owen and his ten-acre scheme, and on
the other side all the other scientific gentlemen,
who were perfectly unanimous in condemning
the plan of Professor Owen as being utterly
useless and bewildering." '

One point in particular was especially ridiculed
by Mr. Gregory in the course of the debate in
the House of Commons, and that was 'galleries
850 feet in length for the exhibition of whales.'

It is interesting to note that even this 'extravagant scheme' of Owen's will shortly be realized,
for the construction of an adequate gallery for
the skeletons of these huge cetacea is actually
in contemplation at South Kensington.

The proposal to remove the collections from
Bloomsbury to another site formed a considerable stumbling-block to Owen's plans ; but this
removal was inevitable, for the Government had
neglected to purchase the property surrounding
the British Museum, and thus secure an entire
block.⁵ The value of property in that area tended
in 1860 to increase rather than decrease, and further extensions of any magnitude to the British
Museum seemed then to be impracticable.   Had
the Government thoughtfully considered the
probable needs of a growing collection of books,
antiquities, and zoological specimens, and provided for it by judicious purchase of the surrounding property, no such anomaly as the
housing of the national collections in two buildings three miles apart would have been necessary, and the opposition to Owen's scheme
would have been considerably lessened.   Moreover, the gradual passage of the later geological
periods into those of the historic, with the
accompanying development of the arts, might
have been seen under one roof.   At present the

⁵ The Government purchased   from the Duke of Bedford for
this property in March 1894   200,000l.

history of man is broken off at South Kensington,
and taken up at Bloomsbury, at about the period
of the cave-dwellers ; though it is only fair to
mention that this is due more to the ' department '
system than to the fact of there being two separate institutions.

Professor Owen's evidence before ' Mr. Gregory's Committee' occupies some thirty pages in
the Blue Book. In it he disposes of the suggestion as to risk during removal by pointing out
that two such removals had been made, under his
care, at the College of Surgeons. The collections
of the British Museum were, he said, mainly dried,
and, therefore, would run considerably less risk in
transit than the innumerable delicate preparations
preserved in the collections of the College of Surgeons.

In the course of his evidence Owen made some
interesting remarks concerning Darwin's work on
the ' Origin of Species,' just published, which helps
to strengthen the impression that he was at first
much taken with the new views, and felt the same
friendliness toward them as he had previously
shown to the views expressed in the ' Vestiges of
Creation.' Speaking as to the desirability of
exhibiting every species, or only a proportion of
the species of a group in the proposed new
museum, Owen said before the committee : ' We
are obliged not to have a Procrustean Law for
all classes, but to be guided, as to the proportion

of each class, according to the nature and significance of the differences that exist. With regard
to birds, I must say that not only would I exhibit
every species, but I see clearly, in the present
phase of natural history philosophy, that we shall
be compelled to exhibit varieties also. The whole
intellectual world this year has been excited by a
book on the origin of species; and what is the
consequence ? Visitors come to the British
Museum, and they say, " Let us see all these
varieties of pigeons : where is the tumbler, where
is the pouter ?" and I am obliged with shame to
say, " I can show you none of them ;" [6] and yet
there we give what, we consider, some may think
an extravagant space to the pigeons ; but they
are the pigeons of the whole world. As to showing you the varieties of those species, or any of
those phenomena that would aid one in getting at
that mystery of mysteries, the origin of species,
our space does not permit ; but surely there ought
to be space somewhere, and, if not in the British
Museum, where is it to be obtained ?' The chairman of the committee said to Owen : ' I presume
that the persons who make these inquiries are, to
a certain extent, scientific persons ?' to which he
replied : ' I must say that the number of intellectual
individuals interested in the great question which

---

[6] The reader will remember
that this detail of Owen's great
scheme has been elaborated by
Professor Sir William Flower,
and is exhibited in the Central
Hall of the Natural History
Museum.

is mooted in Mr. Darwin's book is far beyond the
small class expressly concerned in scientific research.'

Among many other interesting suggestions
made by Owen before this committee we find that
he considered that those in charge of national
museums should be occasionally sent on a visit of
inspection to similar institutions abroad, and intimated that these visits should be made at the individual's own expense and in his own time.

The rejection of his scheme by the Government, which considered that a supplementary
exhibition gallery to the British Museum was all
that was reasonably required, caused Owen considerable grief and mortification. But he says : ' I
now feel grateful that the sole responsibility of
the author of the " Report and Plan " is attested in
the pages of a work [7] which will last as long as,
and may possibly outlast, the great legislative
organisation whose debates and determinations
are therein authoritatively recorded.

' I was not, however, cast down, nor did I lose
either heart or hope. I was confident in the
validity of the grounds of my appeal, and foresaw
in the inevitable accumulations year by year the
evidence which would attest its soundness and
make plain the emergency of the proposed remedy.'
Moreover, there was one who, though not a
naturalist, had devoted more time, pains, and

[7] *Hansard.*

thought to the subject than had been bestowed by
any of those, whether naturalist or administrator,
who testified adversely thereon—the Right Hon.
William Ewart Gladstone, an elected Trustee of
the British Museum. From Mr. Gladstone Owen
received the following letter :—

Penmaenmawr, Conway : August 24, 1861.

'Dear Professor Owen,—I do not know whether
it is to you that I am indebted for a copy of your
lecture on a Museum of Natural History contained in some numbers of the " Athenæum ;" but
I have read it with great interest, and I shall be
very happy to enter upon the subject with you in
the course of the autumn. Indeed, the main
purpose of this note is to intimate to you that, so
far at least as my opinion goes, the time has
arrived when the question of space, for this and
other cognate purposes, together with that of
union or severance of the collections at the
Museum, should be not only seriously but definitely considered by the Government.

'I remain, my dear Sir,
'With much respect,
'Very faithfully yours,
'W. E. GLADSTONE.'

Accordingly, on October 21, 1861, Mr. Gladstone made an appointment with Owen to inspect
the Museum. On Mr. Gladstone's arrival at the

British Museum, 'he explored with me,' the Professor continues, 'every vault and dark recess which had been, or could be, allotted to the non-exhibited specimens of the natural history, those, viz., which it was my aim to utilise and bring to light. He gave the same attention to the series selected for exhibition in the public galleries, and appreciated the inadequacy of the arrangements to that end. He listened to my statements of facts, to the grounds of provision of annual ratios of increase, to the reasons for providing space therefor, to my views of the aims of such exhibitions, and to the proposed extended applications and elucidations of the collections. Mr. Gladstone tested every averment, and elicited the grounds of every suggestion, with a tact and insight that contrasted strongly with the questionings in the committee-room, where too often vague interrogations met with answers to match.

'Conformably with Mr. Gladstone's convictions, he, as Chancellor of the Exchequer, moved, May 12, 1862, for "leave to bring in a bill for removal of portions of the Trustees' Collections in the British Museum."

'On May 19, when the bill was to be read a second time, a new, unexpected, and formidable antagonist arose. Mr. Disraeli early got the attention of the House to a speech, warning hon. members of the "progressive increase of expendi-

ture on civil estimates," and laying stress on the
fact that the " estimates of the actual year showed
no surplus." [8]   The influence of this advocacy of
economy is exemplified in the debate which en-
sued.[9]   For repetitions of the nature and terms of
objections to the Report and Plan, as already
denounced by Mr. Gregory, Mr. Bernal Osborne,
and others, reference may be made to the volume
of " Hansard," cited below.   An estimable hon.
member, whose words had always and deservedly
carried weight with the country party, lent his
influence to the same result.   Mr. Henley, representative of Oxfordshire, said : " All the House
knew was that a building was to be put up somewhere.   He considered this a bad way of doing
business, particularly at a time when nobody could
be sanguine that the finances of the country were
in a flourishing state.   Let the stone once be set
rolling, and then all gentlemen of science and
taste would have a kick at it, and it would be
knocked from one to the other, and none of them
probably would ever live to see an end of the
expense." [1]

    ' Permit me to give one more example of the
baneful influence of the opening speech on our
great instrument of scientific progress.   Mr.
Henry Seymour, member for Poole, said : " If a
foreigner had been listening to the debates of that

[8] *Hansard*, 1862, p. 1927.   [9] *Ib.*
                    [1] *Ib.* p. 1932.

evening it must have struck him that it was, to
say the least, a rather curious coincidence that a
proposal to vote 600,000*l.* for a new collection of
birds, beasts, and fishes at South Kensington
should have been brought forward on the very
evening when the leader of the Opposition had
made a speech denouncing that exorbitant ex-
penditure—a speech, he might add, which was
re-echoed by many Liberal members of the
House." [2]

' It was, however, not a "curious," but a "designed coincidence." Mr. Disraeli, knowing the
temper of the House on the subject, and that the
estimates for the required Museum of Natural
History were to be submitted by Mr. Gladstone,
chose the opportunity to initiate the business by
an advocacy of economy which left its intended
effect upon the House. In vain Lord Palmerston,
in reply to the Irish denunciators, proposed as a
compromise to " exclude whales altogether from
disporting themselves in Kensington Gardens." [3]
The Government was defeated by a majority of
ninety-two, and the erection of a National or
British Museum of Natural History was post-
poned, to all appearance indefinitely, and in reality
for ten years.

' Nevertheless, neither averments nor arguments in the House on May 19, 1862, nor testi-
monies in the hostile committee of 1860, 1861,

---

[2] *Hansard,* 1862, p. 1918.　　　[3] *Ib.* p. 1931.

had shaken my faith in the grounds on which my Report and Plan of 1859 had been based. The facts bearing thereupon, which it was my duty to submit in my " Annual Reports on the Natural History Departments of the British Museum," would, I still hoped, have some influence with hon. members of the legislature to whom those reports are transmitted.

' The annual additions of specimens continued to increase in number and in value year by year. I embraced every opportunity to excite the interest of lovers of natural history travelling abroad, and of intelligent settlers in our several colonies, to this end, among the results of which I may cite the reception of the aye-aye, the gorilla, the dodo, the notornis, the maximised and elephant-footed species of dinornis, the representatives of the various orders and genera of extinct Reptilia from the Cape of Good Hope, and the equally rich and numerous evidences of the extinct Marsupialia from Australia, besides such smaller rarities as the animals of the nautilus and spirula.

' Wherever room could be found in the exhibition galleries at Bloomsbury for these specimens, stuffed or as articulated skeletons, or as detached fossils, they were squeezed in, so to speak, to manifest mutely to all visitors, more especially administrative ones, the state of cram to which we were driven at Bloomsbury.

'Another element of my "Annual Reports" was the deteriorating influence on valuable specimens of the storage vaults, and the danger of such accumulations to the entire Museum and its priceless contents. And here, perhaps, you may deem some explanation needful of the grounds of the latter consideration addressed to economical granters of the national funds.

'The number of specimens preserved in spirits of wine amounted to thousands. Any accidental breakage, with conflagration, in the subterraneous localities contiguous with the heating apparatus of the entire British Museum would have been as destructive to the building as the gunpowder was meant to be when stored in the vaults beneath King James's Houses of Parliament.

'At this crisis the "Times," after the stormy debate of May 19, 1862, made the following appeal to me : "Let Mr. Owen describe exactly the kind of building that will answer his purpose, that will give space for his whales and light for his humming-birds and butterflies. The House of Commons will hardly, for very shame, give a well-digested scheme so rude a reception as it did on Monday night." [4]

'My answer to this appeal was little more than some amplification, with additional examples, of the several topics embodied in the original report, and my little book "On the Extent and Aims of

[4] *The Times*, May 21, in a leader on the Museum Debate.

a National Museum of Natural History," with reduced copies of the plans, went through two
editions.

'Another element of reviving hope,' Professor
Owen quaintly remarks, 'was the acceptance by
Mr. Gregory of the governorship of a tropical
island. Mr. Gladstone accurately gauged the
modified feeling—the subsiding animosity—of
Parliament on the subject, and submitted (June
15, 1863) a motion "for leave to purchase five
acres for the required Natural History building."
The choice of locality he left to honourable members.   Lord Palmerston pointed out that the requisite extent of site could be obtained at Bloomsbury for 50,000l. per acre, and that it could be got
at South Kensington for 10,000l. per acre ; and
his lordship distinctly stated that the space, in
either locality, would be bought for the purpose of
a Museum of Natural History.   The purchase of
the land at South Kensington was accordingly
voted by 267 against 135, and thus the Government proposition was carried by a majority of 132.
By this vote the decision of Mr. Gregory's committee was virtually annulled.

'In a conversation with which I was favoured
by Lord Palmerston, I interposed a warning
against restriction of space, and eventually eight
acres of ground were obtained, including the site
of the Exhibition building of 1862, opposite Cromwell Gardens, and that extent of space is now se-

cured for actual and prospective requirements of our National Museum of Natural History.

'Mr. Gladstone, adhering to the convictions which led him to submit his financial proposition of May 1862, honoured me, at the close of that session of Parliament, with an invitation to Hawarden to discuss my plans for the museum building ; and, after consideration of every detail, he requested that they might be left with him. He placed them, with my written expositions of details, in the hands of Sir Henry A. Hunt, C.B., responsible adviser on buildings, &c., at the Office of Works, with instructions that they should be put into working form, so as to support reliable estimates of cost. I was favoured with interviews with Sir Henry, resulting in the completion of such working plans of a museum, including a central hall, an architectural front of two stories, and the series of single-storied galleries extending at right angles to the front, as shown in my original Plan. I was assured that such plan of building, affording the space I had reported on, would be the basis to be submitted to the professional architect whenever the time might arrive for Parliamentary sanction to the cost of such building.

'Here I may remark that experiments which preceded the substitution, in 1835, of the actual Museum of the Hunterian Physiology at the Royal College of Surgeons, for the costly, cum-

brous, and ill-lit building, with its three-domed
skylights, which preceded it, had led to the conclusion that the light best fitted for a museum was
that in which most would be reflected from the
objects and least directly strike upon the eye ;
and this was found to be effected by admittance
of the light at the angle between the wall and roof.
But this plan of illumination is possible only in
galleries of one storey, or the topmost in a many-
storied edifice.

'Sir Henry A. Hunt then wrote me a letter
conveying his conclusions respecting the plan of
building discussed with him :—

"4 Parliament Street : September 25, 1862.

'" My dear Sir,—I return you the drawings of
the proposed Museum of Natural History at South
Kensington. In May last I told Mr. Gladstone
that the probable cost of covering five acres with
suitable buildings would be about 500,000*l*., or
100,000*l*. per acre.

'" The plan proposed by you will occupy about
four acres, and will cost about 350,000*l*., or nearly
90,000*l*. per acre.

'" Having prepared sketches showing the
scheme suggested by you, I have been able to
arrive more nearly at the probable cost than I had
the means of doing in May last. But, after all
the difference is not great ; although the present
estimate is a more reliable one than the other. It

is right, however, to state that the disposition
of the building as proposed by you will give a
greater amount of accommodation, and admit of
a cheaper mode of construction, than I had cal-
culated upon in May (relatively with the space
intended to be covered), and therefore I think
your plan far better adapted for the museum than
the plan I took the liberty to suggest to Mr.
Gladstone.

' " Believe me, &c.,
' " HENRY A. HUNT."

'Sir H. A. Hunt had previously formed an
estimate of cost for the Chancellor of the Exchequer on inspection of the Report and Plan in
the Parliamentary paper of March 1859. The
letter to which I refer I regard as an antidote to
some previous quotations from adverse members
of Parliament.

'The working plans of Sir Henry A. Hunt
were subsequently submitted for competition, and
the designs of the accomplished and lamented
Captain Fowke, R.E., obtained the award in
1864. His untimely death arrested further
progress or practical application of the prize
designs.

'Mr. Alfred Waterhouse was then selected
as architect, and prepared fresh designs;[5] and I

[5] A fac-simile of a tracing of
the plan accepted by the Trustees is here inserted, and will
enable the reader to contrast

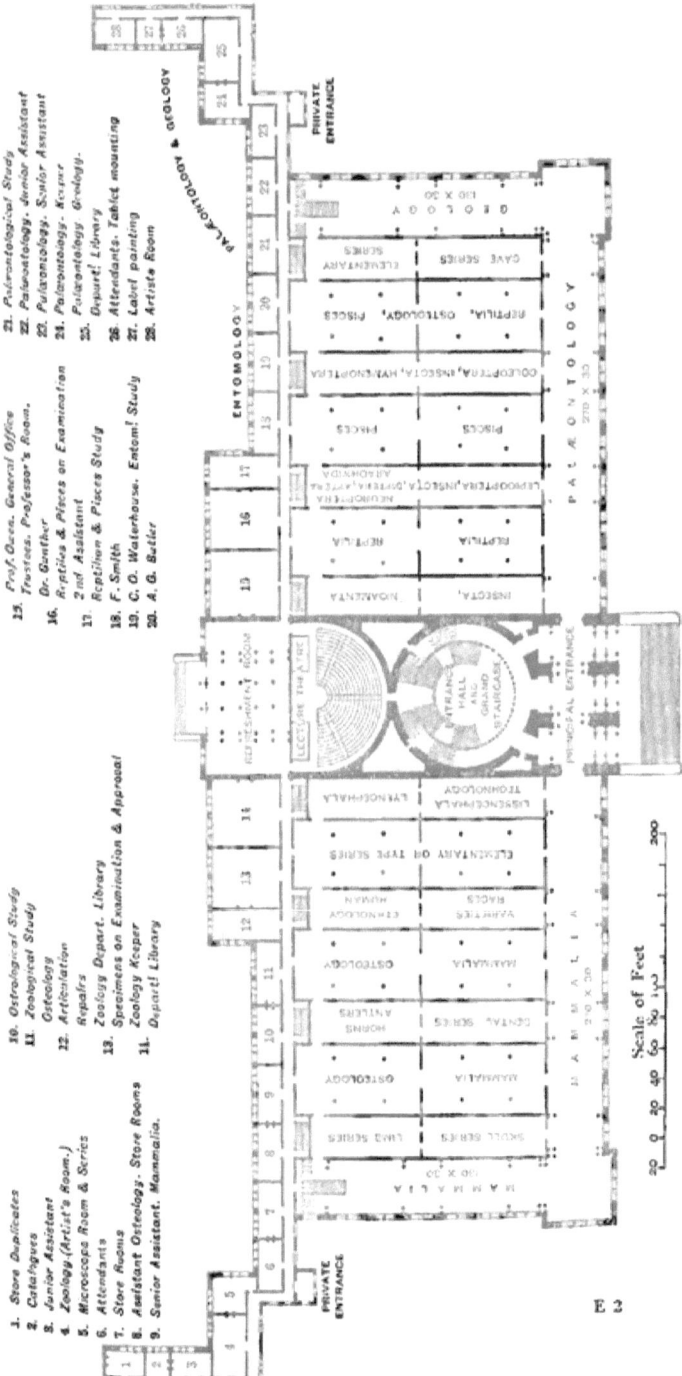

THE ACCEPTED PLAN FOR THE MUSEUM OF NATURAL HISTORY

1. Store Duplicates
2. Catalogues
3. Junior Assistant
4. Zoology (Artist's Room.)
5. Microscope Room & Series
6. Attendants
7. Store Rooms
8. Assistant Osteology. Store Rooms
9. Senior Assistant. Mammalia.

10. Osteological Study
11. Zoological Study
   Osteology
12. Articulation
   Repairs
13. Zoology Depart. Library
   Specimens on Examination & Approval
14. Zoology Keeper
   Depart! Library

15. Prof. Own. General Office
   Trustees. Professor's Room.
   Dr. Günther
16. Reptiles & Pisces on Examination
17. 2nd Assistant
   Reptilian & Pisces Study
18. F. Smith
19. C. O. Waterhouse. Entom! Study
20. A. G. Butler

21. Palæontological Study
22. Palæontology. Junior Assistant
23. Palæontology. Senior Assistant
24. Palæontology. Keeper
25. Palæontology. Geology.
   Depart! Library
26. Attendants. Tablet mounting
27. Label painting
28. Artists Room

Scale of Feet

E 2

took the liberty to suggest that many objects of natural history might afford subjects for architectural ornament ; and at Mr. Waterhouse's request I transmitted numerous figures of such as seemed suitable for that purpose.

'I must mention that in 1867 Lord Elcho pressed upon the House of Commons, through the Hungerford Bridge Committee, the Thames Embankment as a site for the new Museum of Natural History, but unsuccessfully. The debates thereon, nevertheless, caused some further delay.

'In 1871, a vote of 40,000*l.* for beginning the museum buildings at South Kensington was carried without discussion. In 1872 a vote of 29,000*l.* for the same building was opposed by Lord Elcho, but was carried by a majority of 40 (85 against 45).

'At last the necessary building was commenced after conflicts stretching over a score or so of years.

'Mr. Alfred Waterhouse, R.A., for the realisation of the plans and requirements of our Museum of Natural History, chose an adaptation of the Round-arched Gothic, Romanesque, or Romaic of the twelfth century. No style could better lend itself to the introduction, for legitimate ornamentation, of the endless beautiful varieties

the excellent arrangements conveniences of the finished
agreed upon with the in- structure.

of form and surface-sculpture exemplified in the animal and vegetable kingdoms.

' I need only ask the visitor to pause at the grand entrance, before he passes into the impres· sive and rather gloomy vestibule which leads to the great hall, and prepares him for the flood of light displaying the richly-ornamented columns, arcades, and galleries of the Index Museum.

' In the construction of a building for the reception and preservation of natural history objects, the material should be of a nature that will least lend itself to the absorption and retention of moisture. This material is that artificial stone called terra-cotta. The compactness of texture which fulfils the purpose in relation to dryness is also especially favourable for a public edifice in a metropolitan locality. The microscopic receptacles of soot-particles on the polished surface of the terra-cotta slabs are reduced to a minimum ; the influence of every shower in displacing those particles is maximised. I am sanguine in the expectation that the test of exposure to the London atmosphere during a period equal to that which has elapsed since the completion of Barry's richly ornamented palace at Westminster, now so sadly blackened by soot, will speak loudly in favour of Mr. Waterhouse's adoption of the material for the construction of the National Museum of Natural History. A collateral advantage is

the facility with which the moulded blocks of terra-
cotta lend themselves to the kind of ornamentation to which I have already referred.

' In concluding the above sketch of the development of our actual Museum of Natural History,
I may finally refer, in the terms of our modern
phylogenists, to the traceable evidences of " an-
cestral structures."   In the architectural details
of the new Natural History Museum you will find
but one character of the primitive and now extinct museum retained—viz. the central hall.   In
Montague House[6] there were no galleries, but
side-lit saloons or rooms of varying dimensions
and on different storeys.

' In its successor (the Museum developed on
its site at a later period), we find galleries added ;
that, for example, which was appropriated to the
birds and shells being 300 feet in length.   This
architectural organisation still exists at Bloomsbury.

' The Museum, which may be said to have
budded off, has risen to a still higher grade of
structure after settling down at South Kensington.   In its anatomy we find, it is true, the
central hall and long side-lit galleries ; but in
addition to these inherited structures we discern a
series of one-storied galleries, manifesting a developmental advance in the better admission of

[6] The original building occupied the site of the British Museum
Bloomsbury.

light and a consequent adaptation of the walls as well as the floor to the needs of exhibition.'

In concluding this sketch of Owen's great scheme, it will be interesting to quote some of the letters he received while awaiting its realisation.

Thomas Carlyle writes from Chelsea :—

'Dear Owen,—I hope you will get your Museum. I am, for my own share, no great judge of such matters, and have never myself been able to do much good in museums ; but it seems to me that a nation ready to spend any amount of millions on any foolery that turns up, really might as well take counsel of its chief naturalist, and build such a museum as will satisfy him, while its hand is in !

' I read from your little book, with intelligence more or less complete, and always with pleasure in proportion to my clearness. But what interested me more than the museum question was certain characteristics, brief, incidental, which started up here and there—characteristics of the now pleader for such a museum. For instance, that of the winged gentlewoman [1] (in New Holland, I think), who gathers rotten leaves and fermenting substances to do her hatching for her, and how she fared in the Zoological Gardens here. Or still better, that of the cane-billed Passeres, who have "a marriage-bower" (better luck to them), and how the British jackdaw is still a Passer of that

[1] Megapodius.

kind, retaining his old propensities, but checked in a crowded country and in the meanwhile stealing bright objects to right and left, in hope times may mend in that respect! These and the like of these seem to me eminently beautiful indications.

' And in short my opinion is, if the said pleading Professor would gather himself steadily about such a thing, and devote his whole soul to it for a few years, he might write, to be read by the like of me who am exoteric altogether—say in two vols. with portraits (for it ought to be very brief, and distilled to the utmost)—such a book of Natural History as was never written before! which would far outshine the biggest *museum* even the British nation could build, and might a long time outlive such—done by one's own right hand and head, independent of committees! I am quite serious; more so than you think.

' Yours always,

' T. CARLYLE.'

September 15, 1862.

Lovell Reeve, the conchologist, says, June 1863 :—

'. . . I hope we may yet live to see your grand scheme, of what a national museum ought to be, carried out. I quite dread the ultimate destination of Mr. Cumming's collection [of shells], unless more space and supervision are provided for its reception. Mr. Cumming has, unfortunately, no printed record of the vast amount of undigested information still remaining unpublished in his drawers, written only on loose tickets, by thousands, of which a puff of wind or a shake of the drawer would involve an irretrievable confusion.'

In his book on the Natural History Museum, Owen quoted, and commented upon, a defence of the existing state of things which had been seriously put forward. The following extract gives the quotation and the comment :—

'It seems incredible that such an assertion could have been hazarded as the following, by an advocate of the existing state of things. "Students and scientific men greatly prefer to have the specimens for examination in cases occupying but small space in comparison, which admit of their being much more easily handled, compared, and measured." '

The ridiculous aspect of this defence was not likely to escape the keen eye of Dickens, who wrote the following letter to Owen on the subject :—

August 7, 1862.

'My dear Owen,—I have been reading with unspeakable interest and pleasure your charming little book " On the Extent and Aims of a National Museum of Natural History." Pray tell me who is the adventurous creature who made that astounding statement referred to in the footnote (p. 35) regarding what "students and scientific men greatly prefer." A malignant desire is upon me to ticket that specimen of an infernal genus.

'Ever cordially yours,

'CHARLES DICKENS.'

CHAPTER III

1857-59

Lecturer on Palæontology—The 'Prix Cuvier,' 1857—Suspected of the Authorship of 'Scenes from Clerical Life'—Fullerian Professor of Physiology, 1857—Address as President of the British Association, 1858 Discovery of the Remains of John Hunter, 1859—Foreign Member of the Institute of France—Hon. LL.D. of Cambridge, and Rede Lecturer, 1859—The British Association at Aberdeen—Succeeded as President by the Prince Consort—Literary Work and Lectures—Correspondence on Darwin's 'Origin of Species.'

Now that the development of the Natural History Museum at South Kensington has been traced from the early schemes which Owen formed up to their practical realisation, it will be necessary to go back to the year 1857, in order to pick up the thread of his life and work at that date.

This year was marked by his appointment as Lecturer on Palæontology at the Royal School of Mines, Jermyn Street. His first lecture was given on February 26, at the Museum of Practical Geology, and amongst the audience, as an entry in the diary shows, ' were many old friends : Dr. Livingstone, Frank Buckland, the Duke of Argyll with his sons, Sir Charles Lyell, and Sir Roderick Murchison.'

Nor was this attendance a compliment paid by his friends at the commencement of the course. Many of the most distinguished men in London set aside their work at the busiest time of the day in order to be present there. Of subsequent lectures Mrs. Owen wrote in the diary : ' A good proof of the worth of these lectures is afforded by the number of busy men attending them at the inconvenient hour of 2 P.M.'

The interest of the lectures was maintained to the end. ' At Lecture VIII.,' writes Mrs. Owen in the diary, ' I heard the remark that these lectures, as well as their scientific interest, had all the fascination of an Arabian Nights' story, with the picturesque descriptions of the monstrous bears, lions, and elephants. After lecture we called at 57 Sloane Street to see Dr. and Mrs. Livingstone. An artist was painting a three-quarter length portrait of Livingstone, while the latter was writing his book, as he cannot afford time for a regular sitting. Then after dinner to the Princess's Theatre to see Kean as Richard III.'

The last lecture was given on April 2 : ' Theatre crowded. I cannot describe the feelings which this last lecture produced on the audience. R. evidently felt the importance of the address which concluded the course. His design has been clear throughout—to show the power of God in His creation.'

With regard to these lectures Owen himself

writes : ' Their success had exceeded my utmost
expectations.   Milman, Lord Lansdowne, and the
Duke of Argyll hardly missed one.   I am arrang-
ing with John Murray to publish them.   Sir R.
Murchison made a grand party for Carry and me.
Poor Lady Franklin was there, also General
Sabine and Dr. Livingstone.'

, In a letter dated February 27, 1857, Sir
Roderick thus refers to Owen's first lecture and
to his work at the Museum :—

' I never heard so thoroughly eloquent a
lecture as that of yesterday ; and I can assure you
that I have not in the course of my life been more
gratified than by the proofs which Owen gave of
his admirable qualifications for carrying out those
higher behests which, as a Trustee of the British
Museum, it has been my pride to have warmly
assisted in promoting.   It is the first time I have
had the pleasure of seeing our British Cuvier in
his true place, and not the less delighted to listen
to his fervid and convincing defence of the
principle laid down by his great precursor.
Every one was charmed, and he will have done
more (as I felt convinced) to render our institution
favourably known than by any other possible
event.'

At this time Owen saw much of Dr. Livingstone, who was preparing for publication an account
of his African experiences.   The great traveller
presented Owen with a large elephant's tusk,

twisted like a corkscrew and bearing the inscription on a silver plate which is fixed into the
ivory, 'From David Livingstone to Richard Owen.'
This tusk, which is of considerable weight, the
Professor could hold out firmly at arm's length,
even in old age.   There are frequent references
in the diary to visits which Livingstone paid to
Sheen Lodge.   On one occasion, in the early
spring, Mrs. Owen writes : ' I asked the Doctor
at dinner the feelings he had when the lion seized
and crunched his arm, especially whether the
physical pain was great when the lion bit it again
and again.   He said : " No, not very great.   A
feeling of faintness was most observable."   I
asked him whether the suffering was greatest
afterwards.   He said : " By far."   The left arm is
the injured one : the tendons act well, but the
bone has not joined properly.   It seems, from
what R. told me afterwards, that there is little
chance that an operation will succeed.   Livingstone
is going to take advice from Sir Benjamin Brodie
as to a fresh division of the broken pieces of bones,
so as to join them again.   Dr. Livingstone told me
he would like to be back in Africa in June at the
latest, and he is anxious to complete his book before
that time.'

Owen gave as much help as he could to Livingstone in looking over his MS., &c. ; but the book
took him longer than he anticipated.   ' Poor
Livingstone,' Owen writes as late as July 1857, 'he

little thought what it was to write a book when he began!' In the autumn, after the book was published, he notes: 'Livingstone's book has already gone through seven editions, and I am glad to hear that he has cleared something by it.'

Early this year the French Academy awarded to Owen the 'Prix Cuvier,' an honour to which he attached the greatest importance.

About this time he again suffered much from overworking his eyes. Mrs. Owen notes: 'Mr. White Cooper came over without delay, and was much concerned at the appearance of the right eye. He told me that if it had been neglected much longer it might have been too late to save it.' However, by avoiding night-work and sparing his eyes as much as possible, it was not long before Owen could revert to the accustomed use of them.

Strangely enough, the authorship of 'Scenes from Clerical Life' (which was at first published anonymously), was at this time attributed to him. On April 4 there is this entry in the journal: 'An interesting note from Mr. John Blackwood to R. He says that, while he was lodging in Jermyn Street, he happened to be out one day when R. called. His brother was in, but, as R. was in rather a hurry, he left his card, after a short conversation, and went away. When Mr. Blackwood came back his brother said: "I am sorry you were not in. Professor Owen has been

here. He is a deuced clever-looking fellow, with
a pair of eyes in his head! I should not wonder
if he is the author of 'Scenes from Clerical Life'
and had come to unbosom himself."'

Mr. Blackwood's conjecture was not a mere
surmise founded on Owen's appearance. The
idea that he was the author seems to have grown
out of a certain similarity which existed between
Owen's handwriting and that of George Eliot. In
a work by George Willis Cooke called 'A Critical
Study of George Eliot,' he says, à propos of 'Scenes
from Clerical Life:' 'The editor's (Blackwood)
suspicions had all been directed towards Professor
Owen by a similarity of handwriting.'

There must also have been a certain similarity
of thought and feeling, for Professor Owen often
used to remark that no works of fiction appealed
to him like George Eliot's, and that his favourite
novel was 'The Mill on the Floss,' of which she
sent him a copy soon after its publication.

Concerning his work this year at the British
Museum, there are brief entries in his own diary,
to which he has added : 'See Carry's diary for
1857.' From her journal we find that he went
over to Caen in the middle of June to look at a
collection of marine fossils which had been offered
for sale to the British Museum, and that, after
spending a week there, the purchase of these
fossils was concluded. There is also a record of
a meeting of the Trustees of the Museum on

July 17, at which Macaulay, Murchison. the
Speaker of the House of Commons (Denison),
and Sir P. Egerton were present. On the 22nd
the Queen of Holland visited the Museum, and
Owen showed her the chief things of interest in
his own department.

His August holiday was spent with his wife
in the Isle of Wight, and at a visit to Carisbrook
Castle he notes with indignation 'the bronze
armour carefully rubbed bright!' He spent his
time 'walking about antiquity-hunting' and 'getting very wet in rides about the island on the top
of stage-coaches.'

Shortly after their return to Sheen Lodge,
Charles Dickens wrote Mrs. Owen a characteristic
letter, in which he mentions the efforts he had
been making in order to raise a fund for the
widow of Douglas Jerrold :—

> Gad's Hill Place, Higham by Rochester :
> Wednesday, September 2, 1857.

'My dear Mrs. Owen,—Your pleasantest of
letters finds me here, stopping to breathe after
the fatigues of the last two months, which have
been on the whole as great as I have ever under-
gone, and which have left me, for the moment,
just a little dashed. However, we have happily
gained the limit I presented to myself in setting
out—we have raised two thousand pounds—and
our success has been enormous.

'On Monday I am going away for a run to certain out-of-the-way places in opposite corners of the map of England, with an eye to " Household Words." It is probable that I shall not be back here until September is far advanced. I shall then have to give myself up for a week or two to some friends who are coming, and then the dreary leaves will begin to fall and my wintry plans will gather about me.

' So I am afraid I shall not see the old house [1] *this* summer. But you describe it so wonderfully well, that I seem to have seen it already and to be perfectly acquainted with it. That—and your and Owen's remembrance of me—are my consolation.

'With kindest regards to him, and to your son, in which all here join, believe me,

'Always most faithfully yours,

'CHARLES DICKENS.'

In this month there was an interesting discovery made by some engineers at Newcastle, which Owen was called upon to inspect. We have in the diary an account of his report and explanation of the same :—

'*September* 11.—R. going to Newcastle to examine into a discovery which has been made there of the fossil stump of an old forest-tree,

---

[1] An old house in Mortlake which Charles Dickens had said he would like to see.

found in the bed of the Tyne thirty feet deep
whilst the Tyne Dock was being made. This
was considered a testimony to the antiquity of man,
as the fossil tree was certainly cut by man's hand,
and there were fossil chips lying around in the mud,
and the stump, which bore marks of chopping,
was covered with silt to a great depth. R., with
his usual caution, listened to the various accounts,
and then inquired if any workmen had ever been
employed there before. At last he ascertained that
a Northumberland workman called "Darby Joe"
and his gang had been employed about a year ago
to make a horizontal cutting before draining the
whole area. This excavation had then been filled
up. R. insisted on having the man brought from a
distance, where he and his gang were employed,
and, when he arrived, asked him if he remembered
anything about cutting down a hard or stony tree.
Darby Joe considered a moment, and then said he
remembered perfectly coming across a tree which
was in his way—"the hardest bit of wood he ever
see"—and hacking at it with his adze. "And
where did this take place?" "Oh, hereabouts," said
Darby Joe. R. showed him the stump of the tree ;
and the man exclaimed on looking carefully at it,
"Them's my marks, sir." "About how much of
the tree did you cut from the stump?" "About
four feet, sir." R. then instituted a search for the
cut-off piece, and after a bit they found it, and
fitted it on to the old stump! So much for the

antediluvian hewer of wood.   R. made a pleasant stay at Mr. Armstrong's and returned home on the 16th.'

In this year appeared an interesting paper by Owen ' On the Affinities of Stereognathus Ooliti-cus,'[2] a mammal from the Stonesfield slate of Stonesfield, belonging to the horizon of the Lower Great Oolite.   The remains submitted to Owen consisted of two to three inches of a jaw, containing three molar teeth.   In his paper Owen gives a clear statement of the province and application of physiology in the determination of fossil remains, and in the singularly cautious manner peculiar to him compared the stereognathus' jaw with that of a hoofed mammal.   In the light of more modern science, however, it is thought to belong to a peculiar group intermediate between the marsupials and the monotremes.[3]   The paper attracted some attention at the time, for the bare suggestion of a hoofed mammal or ungulate so low down in the series of rocks and so remote in age would throw a new and unexpected light upon the whole of palæozoology, the known remains being exclusively those of marsupials at that time.

Towards the end of 1857 Owen was offered and accepted an appointment which some years previously, while at the College of Surgeons, he was obliged to decline : it was the Fullerian Profes-

[2] *Quarterly Journal Geol. Soc.* 1857.   [3] Animals like the Echidna and Ornithorhynchus.

sorship of Physiology at the Royal Institution of
Great Britain. As the course of lectures was to
begin in January 1858, the latter part of 1857 was
spent in preparing materials for these lectures,
the subject of which was ' Fossil Mammals.'
The course lasted from January 25 to April 12,
1858. As lecturer to the Royal School of Mines,
Jermyn Street, he gave a course on Fossil Birds,
the first lecture being delivered on March 8.

Besides these two courses in the spring of
this year, he also lectured at the South Kensington Museum on the 'Animal Kingdom and its
Economic Use.'

One of Owen's chief discoveries was made this
year—the identification of the fossil skull known
as *Cyamodus* (*Placodus*) *laticeps* as a reptile instead of a fish. Figures of the skull are here
given, and show the great crushing teeth on the
palate.

In a letter to one of his sisters he refers to this
year's course of lectures at Jermyn Street. ' When
they are over,' he says, ' I shall have to buckle-to
with my "Address to the British Association."
I look forward confidently to that being the last
public post or position the duties of which I cannot well decline, and I hope some years of comparative ease may be spared to me. The pencil-
sketches on this page are by Admiral Moorsom,
to whom I have been expounding the action of
fishes' tails in reference to improvements in the

screw propeller. . . . The other day I walked
over to Lord John's (Russell). They were going in

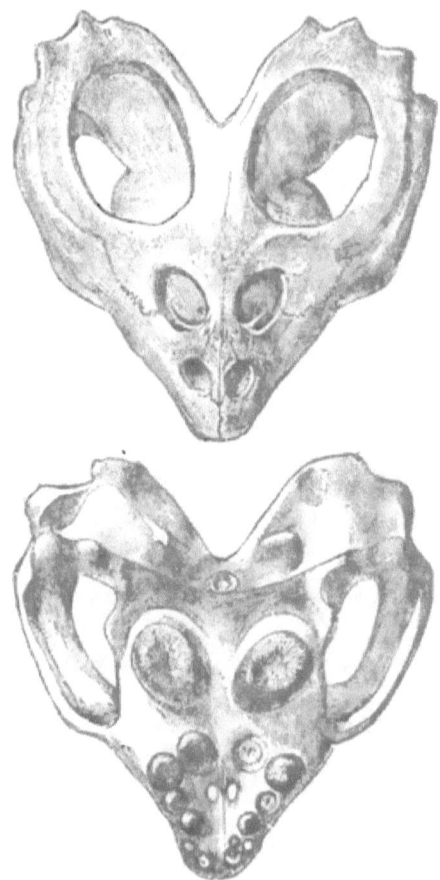

Cyamodus laticeps

Upper and lower aspects of the skull of one of the Placodont reptiles from the
Muschelkalk of Bayreuth. Originally referred to fishes by Agassiz, and first
correctly determined as reptilian by Owen. ⅛ natural size.

to dinner (at 3 P.M.), and made me go in and sit

with them. I had a plate of soup and a pleasant chat, and Lord Dufferin, who was of the party, walked back with me home. Lord John looking wonderfully well. Says he will walk over to see us, now we are come back. No politics, only a little bit of British Museum matters, to prime him, as he has to move the Estimates in the House.'

In February 1858, both Professor Owen and his wife attended the public dinner given to Dr. Livingstone, and Mrs. Owen gives the following account of it in her diary :—

'I found Mrs. Livingstone in the ladies' gallery, and we sat together. Miss Burdett-Coutts came in and sat on the other side of her, and then Lady Franklin next to her. There were between three and four hundred at the dinner. Poor Mrs. Livingstone was in a stout linsey dress, and thick bonnet, and, as the heat was overpowering, even the rest of us (who were in evening dress) suffered considerably from it. I persuaded her to take off as much as she could. She bore the scene wonderfully well, but I saw she kept her eyes intently fixed on her husband the whole time. The honours, paid with three times three, to one woman by such an assembly would have been almost too much to bear for most people, but no Hottentot could have betrayed less emotion under the trying circumstances than she did ; there is doubtless much activity of mind hidden under her extreme quietness. She betrayed, by a slight

twinkle in her dark eyes, that she was gratified
at the Duke of Wellington's speech about her,
as the true helpmate of her honoured husband,
and also at his drinking to her in a glass of wine.
After the whole room had risen to salute her, and
when the cheering and waving of handkerchiefs
had subsided, I told her she ought to acknow-
ledge the attention in some way, and she did it
at once with a calm curtsey. Miss Burdett-
Coutts has been a good friend to her.

 ' After the speeches were over and we had gone
to the tea-room, I had to introduce many people to
her, and was glad to shake hands for the last time
with her husband before his renewed labours and
dangers. Sir R. Murchison's speech was good ;
the Bishop of St. David's was tremendously heavy
and long. R.'s speech came first after. Mrs.
Livingstone seemed pleased at having the different people pointed out to her, and also at my explaining the names of the Scotch airs the band
was playing in honour of their Scotch birth. She
did not recognise any of them, for I suppose
that music was never heard in her father's house.
She, however, expressed her liking to me much
as she might speak of some new and rather extraordinary thing. After the band had ceased playing she whispered, " I think I like music." '

Owen still used to seek his favourite relaxation
at the theatre. On February 24 he went to the
Princess's to see Charles Kean as Louis XI., and

was afterwards introduced to the actor. 'Kean appeared gratified at R.'s appreciation of his Louis XI., and said he would like him to see his Hamlet.' Accordingly, on March 8 Kean sent them a ticket for a box at the Princess's, where he was playing Hamlet that night. Owen remarks, in a letter to his sister Eliza, on the pleasure that this performance afforded him. In another letter to his sister, dated May 1, 1858, he says :—

'I have dined at the last two meetings of "The Club." One of these included Lord Lansdowne, Duke of Argyll, Lord Macaulay, Dean Milman, Whewell, Colonel Leake, Gladstone, Dr. (Sir H.) Holland, Lord John Russell, Dr. Hawtrey, and it was a very brilliant intellectual evening. Gladstone favoured me with an invitation to his Thursday morning breakfasts. At the last meeting poor Hallam was borne in by two men : his meat cut for him. His last stroke leaves but the use of one hand, and his speech is affected, but his intellect is bright, and he expressed himself much pleased at once more meeting his old friends. Lord Enniskillen and Mr. Liddell dined with us yesterday ; we had a merry chatty evening. I have just been lunching in the " Medal Room " on prawns, roll and butter, and soda-water, introduced by my Lord in defiance of " orders of the Trustees " . . . . I go to the " Academy dinner " to-day, afterwards pick up Will at Dr. Farre's concert.'

On June 8 Owen writes in a short note to

his sisters : 'Whewell called on us on Sunday
afternoon and confided to Carry his matrimonial
intentions, . . . and when Mrs. R. heard who the
intended was, she merely observed, " He'll get a
'temper.'"   But I dare say they will be very
well matched, and that there will still be a Master
as well as a Mistress of Trinity.'

In this month Professor Owen ' was honoured
with an invitation from the Prince of Wales to
dine at the White Lodge on ' Saturday,' for so he
writes to his sister Catherine. The Prince was
then in his eighteenth year, and on this occasion had
gathered round him a small party of five. There
was 'much agreeable conversation,' Owen says,
' the form of waiting for a remark or question from
the royal host not being observed. I told the
Prince the latest news of Dr. and Mrs. Livingstone,
and of Madame Pfeiffer, just returned from Madagascar. The history of Richmond Park coming
up, General Bowater remarked that Charles I.'s
enlargement of it was one of the causes of his un-
popularity. " Why should that have made him unpopular?" asked His Royal Highness. " Because,"
replied Mr. Gibbs, " he took other people's land
arbitrarily, or not quite according to law." I
noted the use of such an opportunity of imparting
constitutional principles.'

The frequent memoranda of sums of money
in the corners of letters sent to Professor Owen,
in which a request was made for help, form a

pleasant memory of one who cannot be said to
have been wealthy during his working life. And
that he was ever ready to assist those who applied
to him, in spite of the fact that he had himself
suffered from the usual gratitude of borrowers, is
evident from the following observation in a letter
to his sister Eliza, July 21, 1858 : ‘A friend to
whom last year I lent 50*l.* (a most culpable procedure in a worldly point of view, and of which
sum, from experiences of less amount, I mentally
took leave for ever, expecting also to lose my
friend at the same time agreeably to rule) called
on me on the morning of the 20th, and honour-
ably repaid me, with expressions that showed that
the loan had been of important service ; so, the
sun being very bright, all things concurred to
make the day so [his wedding day].’

Owen's Presidential address to the British
Association this year, of which he made mention
in an early letter to his sister as weighing on his
mind, was delivered in the autumn at Leeds.
This address contains a prodigious collection of
facts, and embraces a large area of scientific
knowledge. A part of it he devoted to his
views on a Natural History Museum, and he
concluded with the following remarks : ‘ The
simplest coral and the meanest insect may have
something in its history worth knowing, and
in some way profitable. Every organism is a
character in which Divine wisdom is written, and

which ought to be expounded. Our present
system of opening the book of Nature to the
masses, as in the galleries of the British Museum,
without any provision for expounding her language, is akin to that which would keep the
book of God sealed to the multitude in a dead
tongue.'

In the course of his address he also touched
upon the progress made in the investigation of
magnetism and electricity, and the attempts 'to
explain the change in the variation of the magnetic needle.' This subject was evidently one of
interest to Prince Albert, for later on in the year
Owen received a letter from Lord Grey enclosing
'a letter which the Prince has signed himself,
and which you can quote in your communications
with the Government expressive of the interest
which he takes in the success of your endeavours
to ascertain, as certainly as you can, the causes of
the deviation of the magnetic needle in different
parts of the world.'

On November 5 Owen was again a guest
at the Prince of Wales's table at the White
Lodge; Lord John Russell also being invited.
'It was a farewell dinner to Richmond Park,' as
the Prince was leaving for Windsor a few days
later, to go to Potsdam. 'We were received,' says
Owen in a letter to his sister Catherine, 'in the
great drawing-room, where we used to play the
"round game" with the good old Duchess [of

Gloucester]. . . . A most pleasant, varied chat all
the dinner time ; no sort of formality.'

' A card of a foot square from the Lord Mayor-
elect, who this year invites the representatives of
British science to the annual banquet.' So Owen
tells his sister, to whom on November 29 he sends
particulars of the Mansion House meeting :—

' The assembled citizens in the room signify
their opinion of the guests named—if worth any
—somewhat in the fashion of the undergradu-
ates in the Senate House. After the dinner,
poor Samuel Warren came up to me. " Why,
Professor, you were received like the Prime
Minister !" I made my best Court bow to the
Lord Mayor, said a few words to my Lord of my
pleasure at seeing Science recognised on this
great occasion, and sailed off to one side to
witness other receptions. Lord D. cross and
fidgety ; old Malakoff very *débonnaire* and jolly,
the Lord Chancellor with his most benevolent
smile. Disraeli with his unmeaning, impassive
aspect. I had a good place assigned me near the
" Court-end " of one of the long tables in full view
of the magnates. Next me a young bride with
widely-developed skirt. Her husband and I had
to lift her, first upon the " form " (which was
fixed close to the table), then to fold her nether
half tightly up and glide her in like a mummy !
Same operation needed with everybody, and *ib.*
to get them out.'

In January 1859 Frank Buckland was struck with the idea of rescuing the remains of John Hunter from the vaults of St. Martin-in-the-Fields, and re-interring them in Westminster Abbey. An account of his proceedings is given in his 'Curiosities of Natural History.'[4] There he narrates how he found in the queer-looking old register of burials in St. Martin's Church the following mysterious entry :—

'Oct. 22, 1793.   Leisester Squar.

'M. John Hunter, Esq., $\frac{1}{4}$ past 4 o'clock, 6*l*. 10*s*. 2*d*. No candles. N.-3-V. Duty, 3*d*. C.4.ij. y^n.

'A perplexy.'

He examined literally hundreds of coffins until there were only two left. But finally, on the brass plate of the last, to his great joy he read the inscription :—

'JOHN HUNTER, ESQ.

Died 16 Octr.

1793.

Aged 64 years.'

The Hunters' arms—viz. a hand with an arrow on it—also the three horns of the hunter, were engraved upon the plate.

[4] Vol. ii. p. 159.

Professor Owen was greatly interested in this discovery, and Mr. Bompas, in his 'Life of Frank Buckland,' gives the following extract from Buckland's diary, February 23 :—

'Down into the vaults . . . again with Professor Owen, who expressed himself much pleased. I wish I could have made a sketch of him, with his hand on the coffin, looking thoughtfully at it. It would have made an excellent subject.'

Owen himself, who had just attended a Levee on that day, thus alludes to the incident :—

'After resuming ordinary costume, I went with Frank Buckland to the vaults beneath St. Martin's Church, which are now being emptied, to see the coffin of John Hunter, which was found in a corner of one of them. It was in good preservation, and I have written to Dean Milman about getting it into St. Paul's. But such a scene! A score of Irish labourers hauling along the coffins, higgledy-piggledy, from one dark recess to the other. The sexton, to show the conscience of undertakers, pointed to one large coffin, supposed to have included a leaden one, but never had. Putting his foot upon it, he pressed it down and drew back the top and one side, exposing to view the black shrivelled remains of the " Hon. Lady ——." A mask of the features had been taken by a mass of the chrysalises of the *Dermestes*, or darkling-beetles, an inch thick. Faugh! I quitted the scene, thinking that *it* and the Levee had been two of the greatest contrasts which London could have exhibited in the same afternoon.'

In reply to Owen's letter asking permission to move the coffin to St. Paul's, Dean Milman wrote the following letter :—

Deanery, St. Paul's : February 25.

' My dear Professor,—Are you quite sure that it is the genuine John Hunter ? I had some correspondence a few weeks ago with my friend Dr. Sutherland, and conversation with Professor Bell on the subject. Since that a rumour reached us that it was the *wrong John.* Remember that your credit is at stake. If you impose upon us the bones of a worthy grocer or warehouseman instead of the immortal surgeon, we shall never trust you again. We shall believe not a word of all your science ; nothing you advance about the ornithorynchus paradoxus, the dodo, or that *refined* chimpanzee which you are making out to be our first cousin—only once removed.

' However, if he be the real John (and it is not necessary for that to anatomise the anatomist), I should be the last person not to wish to do him proper honour. The only difficulty is the anomaly of the case. It must be done *quietly.* The body cannot be removed without a faculty in the Bishop's Court ; of that I presume you can at once ascertain the cost. Nor can there be much obstacle in the way as to any demands of the Dean and Chapter. *All should be done very quietly*, for reasons not less of respect for the dead than lest any excitement should be made among the living.

'I shall be at the Museum at the Committee on Saturday, and will most readily talk over the subject with you.

'Ever, my dear Professor,
'Very sincerely yours,
'H. H. MILMAN.'

The coffin and remains were afterwards removed to Westminster Abbey.

In the early months of 1859 Owen received the news of his friend Broderip's death. Sir Roderick Murchison, in writing to him on the subject on March 7, says :—

'You will see in my Anniversary Geographical [Address] of 1857 how I spoke of Broderip when speaking of Buckland, for the Dean was really and truly turned to geology by our deceased friend.'

Honours were still accumulating on Owen. In April he had the distinction of being elected one of the eight foreign members of the Institute of France.

He had now resumed his lectures at the Royal School of Mines and also as Fullerian Professor at the Royal Institution. 'I have capital

audiences,' he writes to his sister, 'at both
Albemarle Street and Jermyn Street. Thackeray told me the other day that "two young ladies
(I suppose his daughters) were among my great
admirers." '

He also delivered in 1859 the ' Rede ' lecture
at Cambridge. He gave this lecture, which
was on 'The Classification of Mammalia,' on
May 10. and afterwards received the degree of
LL.D., the first honorary degree given by that
University.

' I went to Cambridge last Monday,' he writes
to his sister Catherine, 'to fulfil my duties as
" Sir Robert Rede's Lecturer " in that University. . . . Next day I gave my lecture at
2 P.M. in the Senate House, before the Vice-
Chancellor and University. . . . Wednesday I
had a long morning's work in the Anatomical and
Woodwardian Museums, with Professor Clark
and others. . . . As the new constitution and
statutes of Cambridge now give the Senate the
power of conferring honorary degrees, a special
grace was passed for meeting on Thursday to
confer the first they have given on me ; and mine
is the first name in the book prepared for the
record of those so honoured. . . . I was arrayed
in a scarlet robe and cap, led by the public orator
to the middle of the hall, addressed by him in a
Latin oration, then conducted to the Vice-
Chancellor's throne ; knelt down, placing my

hands within his, and receiving the admission in the name of the Holy Trinity.'

In the summer of this year Owen received an interesting letter from David Livingstone, which is dated May 30, 1859, at Shupanga :—

'My dear Friend,— . . . We went down to the mouth of the river called Kongone in expectation of meeting a man-of-war with salt provisions for our crew, but my letter to the Admiral must have been detained somewhere—no ship appeared on 24th, the day appointed. We are now going up the Tette to embark my brother and to make some magnetical observations for General Sabine at [Lake] Shirwa. We go back to it, and will, of course, make a push for [Lake] Nyinyesi ;⁵ but say nothing about it lest we fail. It is more pleasant to speak after than before. You will get the [elephant] jaws some time or other : probably we may meet a vessel in July. We make our appointment in a bottle buried in an island in Kongone Harbour. We could have had more frequent calls, as the Admiral is very friendly, but some men were lost, and I forbade sending in boats for our letters. A slight difference this—a year without letters, and the penny-post nuisance with which I was deluged ! My wife is at Kuruman, I believe, with her parents, but I hope

⁵ A lake then only known from reports of natives.

to meet her after her confinement, possibly about the end of this year.

' Ever yours,
' DAVID LIVINGSTONE.'

In September Owen paid one of many delightful visits to his friend Mr. (afterwards Sir John) Fowler at Glen Mazeran, near Inverness. His letters are full of the pleasure which he derived from his visits there, and the enjoyment with which he entered into the fishing and shooting expeditions. On this occasion he went from Glen Mazeran to the British Association Meeting at Aberdeen, which, under the presidency of Prince Albert, to whom Professor Owen resigned the chair, was a great success.

On September 18 he writes to his wife :—

'The rush for admission cards (1*l.* Associates) to see and hear the President was such that, at twelve, it was reported to me that 1,900 had been issued. Now, there were at least 500 regular members of the Association ; so, knowing the spirit of a Scotch mob (pardon me, Jessie ![6]), who might have paid for their tickets, and can't find seats or standing-room, I signed and issued an order that no more Associate tickets were to be issued after the No. 2,000 had been reached. . . . Well, at half-past seven we rose from table, were marshalled to our carriages, and returned to

---

[6] Daughter of Dr. Farre, who was staying with Mrs. Owen.

Aberdeen. Bell-ringing, population cheering. Convener, Provost, and I waited in the Hall to receive the Prince and conduct him to the platform. When he had sat down on my right hand, I took the chair, and, silence being restored, rose and spoke for a few minutes ; motioned H.R.H. into the President's chair, and took his. . . . I send with this a copy of H.R.H.'s address. He read it with good effect. We then re-conducted him to his carriage, and all went off perfectly well and quite to my satisfaction.'

The Prince Consort, in the address referred to, spoke of Owen in the following terms :—

' If it were possible for anything to make me still more aware how much I stand in need of your indulgence, it is the recollection of the Person whom I have to succeed as your President —a man of whom this country is justly proud, and whose name stands among the foremost of the naturalists in Europe for his patience in investigation, conscientiousness of observation, boldness of imagination, and acuteness in reasoning. You have no doubt listened with pleasure to his parting address, and I beg to thank him for the flattering manner in which he has alluded to me in it.'

On the 20th Owen writes again to his wife :— ' To-morrow (Wednesday) I go to Sir James Clark's to dine and sleep, and next day to Balmoral, where Her Majesty gives a *déjeuner* to the

chief members of the Association. By this kind
arrangement of Sir James I avoid a forty-miles'
journey in crowded vehicles on Thursday, for most
of the party will have to go and return the same
day from Balmoral, there being no sleeping accommodation. From Balmoral I return to sleep
Thursday night at Sir J. C.'s, and then proceed
on Sunday to Lancaster, and have a couple of
quiet days there to recruit before going on to my
lectures at Manchester and Liverpool, . . . and
have given up visits to the Earl of Aberdeen, Earl
of Caithness, Lord Ashburton, Grant Duff, &c.'

Owen's plans, however, were altered, for in
another letter, September 21, he says: 'Soon
after I despatched my last, I received a kind
invitation from Lady John Russell to spend a few
days with them at Abergeldie (where the Prince of
Wales was staying) after visiting Balmoral, and it
is arranged that I am to sleep there after visiting
Her Majesty to-morrow.'

Owen states in his diary that he lectured at
Manchester on September 26, 29, 30, October 3,
7, 10, and at Liverpool on September 27 and
October 4 and 6.

His position at the British Museum brought
him into contact with many interesting questions
not primarily connected with his own line of work.
He had always been a careful student of Shakespeare, and had this year the opportunity of making
an examination of a copy of the second folio

annotated and 'corrected' throughout in a hand
of about the middle of the seventeenth century.
The facts of the case were these :—Early in 1852,
Mr. Collier, a well-known Shakespearian scholar,
came into possession of this volume, which he
presented to the Duke of Devonshire. On the
death of the Duke in 1859, the volume was de-
posited for examination at the British Museum,
at the request of Sir Frederick Madden and others.
The result of the scrutiny, made with the microscope by Professors Maskelyne and Owen, went
to prove that the pretended old corrections were
nothing but modern forgeries in a pseudo-antique
script, traced first in lead pencil and afterwards
inked over.

Amongst the reviews and articles written for
various magazines by Owen in 1859 may be men
tioned an article on David Livingstone's travels
in the 'Quarterly,' and a review of the 'History
of Ceylon,' by Emerson Tennent, who wrote the
following letter of thanks, dated from the Board
of Trade, October 15, 1859 :—

'My dear Sir,—I have just laid down the
"Edinburgh Review" after reading your article on
my book : and with as much composure as I can
assume after the ecstasy of so much praise I
hasten to offer you my earliest acknowledgments
and my most grateful thanks. You have most
successfully condensed in one attractive chapter

what I had spread over many ; and I am fully conscious of this service rendered to me and my work
by your invaluable review.

' Faithfully yours,

' J. Emerson Tennent.'

On reaching London, Owen writes to his
sister Maria, October 10, 1859, noting his safe
arrival. He had passed the last few days of his
holiday with Mr. James Bateman at Congleton,
'whose grounds and gardens form our friend
Cooke's *beau-idéal.*' He says : 'I spent a day
and night at Leasowe Castle, and was compelled
to bring away two live turkeys of Lady Cust's
pure white breed, which are now ornamenting
our front lawn, as beautiful as silver pheasants.
I had a narrow escape of another kitten ! Then
I spent a Saturday and Sunday at Biddulph
Grange, near Congleton, Mr. Bateman's, who has
a fine show-garden and good estate, bringing
away a large hamper of rare and pretty outdoor
shrubs and plants. So you may imagine my
luggage had grown to a large and miscellaneous
collection, including a folding-seat, worked for
Carry by Miss Gregson, a sage-cheese, and a
sloth in spirits, fossils, &c., &c. Got all of them
safe to the Cottage.'

On November 17, 1859, Owen writes to his
sister Catherine : 'Frank Buckland called here

---

[1] E. W. Cooke, R.A.

this morning to ask me to write the epitaph for his father's monument in Westminster Abbey. I shall try, to-night. . . . We have had severe winter weather—thermometer at 20°—and have been lighting coke fires in the sunk-pits, where the most delicate flower plants are wintered.'

On December 3, 1859, he sends a letter to his sister Eliza, announcing the death of John Brown, of Stanway, and stating that he has been bequeathed some books, instruments, and collections, and a legacy of 50l., and that he is going down with the executor, Professor Henslow, to make arrangements for the funeral. He continues : ' I send Kate a " Times," in which a " leading article " may amuse her. The " Thunderer " proclaims to the universe that he believes in your affectionate brother, R. O.'

Mr. John Brown's collection, amounting to some 8,000 specimens, was bequeathed to Professor Owen, who immediately transferred it to the British Museum, ' with the view that a selection might be made of all such objects as were found to be desiderata to the geological department.' The National Collection was thus enriched by a large number of interesting specimens relating to the Pleistocene geology of Essex.

In the latter part of 1859 Charles Darwin published his ' Origin of Species,' and we gather the value he set upon Owen's opinion from the

following note written to Lyell, which is included
by Francis Darwin in his ' Life ' of his father :—

' How curious I shall be to know what line
Owen will take!   Dead against us, I fear ; but he
wrote me a most liberal note on the reception of
my book, and said he was quite prepared to
answer fairly, and without prejudice, my line of
argument.'

After a meeting with Owen, Darwin writes
him the following interesting letter respecting the
' Origin :'—

Down, Bromley, Kent : December 13 (1859).

' Dear Owen,— . . . You made a remark in
our conversation something to the effect that my
book could not probably be true as it attempted
to explain so much.   I can only answer that this
might be objected to any view embracing two or
three classes of facts.   Yet I assure you that its
truth has often and often weighed heavily on me;
and I have thought that perhaps my book might
be a case like Macleay's quinary system.[8]   So
strongly did I feel this that I resolved to give
it all up, as far as I could, if I did not convince
at least two or three competent judges.   You
smiled at me for sticking myself up as a martyr ;
but I assure you if you had heard the unmerciful
and, I think, unjust things said of my book and to

[8] 'An artificial attempt at a
natural system of classification
which soon became a byword
among naturalists.'—Dict. Nat.
Biogr.

me in a letter by an old and very distinguished friend you would not wonder at me being sensitive, perhaps ridiculously sensitive. Forgive these remarks. I should be a dolt not to value your scientific opinion very highly. If my views are *in the main* correct, whatever value they may possess in pushing on science will now depend very little on me, but on the verdict pronounced by men eminent in science.

> ' Believe me,
> ' Yours very truly,
> ' C. DARWIN.'

In the early part of this letter Darwin says he is not able to hunt up some information for which Owen has asked, as his 'notes for the latter chapters are a chaos.' The 'old and very distinguished friend' Dr. Francis Darwin considers to be Adam Sedgwick.

If not 'dead against' the theory of Natural Selection, Owen at first looked askance at it, preferring the idea of the great scheme of Nature which he had himself advanced. He was of opinion that the operation of external influences and the resulting 'contest of existence' lead to certain species becoming extinct. Thus it came about, he supposed, that, like the dodo in recent times, the dinornis and other gigantic birds had disappeared. But he never, so far as can be ascertained, expressed a definite opinion on Darwinism, and

in the 'Historical Sketch' which prefaces the
sixth edition (1882) of 'The Origin of Species,'
Darwin traces Owen's ideas so far as he could
comprehend them. The singular impartiality of
Darwin and his increasing endeavours to arrive at
,the truth, whether it turned against or supported
him, permit the quotation of his own words in explanation of the question.

Darwin writes : ' When the first edition of this
work[9] was published, I was so completely de-
ceived, as were many others, by such expressions
as " the continuous operation of creative power,"
that I included Professor Owen with other palæ-
ontologists as being firmly convinced of the im-
mutability of species; but it appears[1] that this
was on my part a preposterous error. In the
last edition of this work[2] I inferred, and the
inference still seems to me perfectly just, from
a passage beginning with the words ' no doubt the
type-form,' &c.,[3] that Professor Owen admitted
that natural selection may have done something
in the formation of new species; but this, it appears,[1] is inaccurate and without evidence. I
also gave some extracts from a correspondence
between Professor Owen and the editor of the
" London Review," from which it appeared mani-

[9] *Nature of Limbs*, 1849.
Address to British Association,
1858.

[1] *Anat. of Vertebrates*, vol.
iii. p. 176.

[2] *Origin of Species*.

[3] *Anat. of Vert.*, vol. i. p.
xxxv.

[4] *Ibid.*, vol. iii. p. 798.

fest to the editor, as well as to myself, that Professor Owen claimed to have promulgated the theory of natural selection before I had done so ; and I expressed my surprise and satisfaction at this announcement ; but as far as it is possible to understand certain recently published passages,[5] I have either partially or wholly again fallen into error. It is consolatory to me that others find Professor Owen's controversial writings as difficult to understand and to reconcile with each other as I do. As far as the mere enunciation of the principle of natural selection is concerned, it is quite immaterial whether or not Professor Owen preceded me, for both of us, as shown in this historical sketch, were long ago preceded by Dr. Wells and Mr. Matthews.'

'Owen could never be induced to follow,' writes Mr. Smith Woodward, in ' Natural Science' (February 1893), 'the new school of anatomy and zoology that arose with the epoch-making researches of Von Baer and Rathke in embryology. . . .

' This marked disregard of embryology as the essential adjunct, even if not the key, of comparative anatomy, is all the more surprising, since so large a proportion of Owen's researches on vertebrate animals were devoted to the fossil remains of past ages. If any phase of biological research can benefit by embryology, that is assuredly

[5] *Anat. of Vert.*, vol. iii. p. 798.

palæontology. . . . His statements on the succession of genera and species, and their possible
derivation one from another, were always vague,
and capable of more than one interpretation; and
though there is not much doubt he leaned towards the views of Geoffrey St.-Hilaire, and
those who believed in the evolution of life, his
work, for the most part, is eminently Cuvierian—
a laborious description of the facts, with a detailed
discussion that rarely extends beyond strict comparative anatomy and the phenomena of geographical or geological distribution. Only on two
occasions [6] does he appear to have attempted any
broad philosophical deductions, and, even in those
cases, it is not quite clear how much he admits.
He was perfectly well aware that the facts of progression noticed by the anti-evolutionist Agassiz
among fishes were equally conspicuous among the
higher vertebrates; [7] but he contented himself
with the bare statement that "the inductive demonstration of the nature and mode of operation"
of the laws governing life would "henceforth be
the great aim of the philosophical naturalist." '

Professor St. George Mivart speaks of Owen's
position in these terms. Writing in the same
journal (January 1893), he says: ' Owen . . ·

---

[6] References to horse in
Anat. and Physiol. Vert., vol. iii.
p. 791 (1868), and to crocodiles
in *Quart. Joun. Geol. Soc.*, vol.
xl. p. 157 (1884).

[7] *Palæontology*, ed. 2, p. 444
(1861).

spread abroad in England the perception that
a deep significance underlies the structure of
animals—a significance for which no stress or
strain and no influence of heredity, and certainly
no mere practical utility, can account. The temporary overclouding of this perception through
the retrograde influence of Darwin's hypothesis
of " Natural Selection" is now slowly but surely
beginning to pass away, for which no small thanks
are due to the efforts of his zealous disciples,
Professors Weismann and Romanes. It would be
out of place to trouble readers with a re-statement
of simple facts.[8] . . . We will confine ourselves to
once more repeating that homologies for which
neither heredity nor utility will account reveal
themselves in the limbs of chelonians, birds, beasts,
and most notably in those of man.'

On the subject of the origin of species, Owen
received the following letter from Sedgwick
dated ' Cambridge, Friday morning : '—

' My dear Owen,— . . . There are many
things I want to talk to you about—about
Darwin's book, &c., &c. Though the published
letter contains an outline of my objection to the
theory, yet 'tis a mere sketch written without a
shadow of a thought that the editor would send
it to the Press ; but on seeing it in print I liked
it far better than I expected, and there is not now

---

[8] Readers interested in such questions may be referred to *Proc.
Zool. Soc.*, 1884, p. 462.

a word I would wish to keep back. The second
publication was in consequence of a complaint to
the editor of some glaring misprints—*e.g.* your
name being put for that of Oken, &c., &c. I never
asserted that *creation* (or the appearance of a new
or modified fauna) was not by law. But by what
law? Not, I may say, of natural transmutation—
not by turning fishes into reptiles, whales into
pachyderms, or monkeys into men, in the way
of natural generation, but by a higher law, of
which we may reach the conception hereafter,
as you have reached the conception of an
archetypal form. But that conception does not
mutilate (it rather magnifies and consolidates) our
conceptions of final causes and of a Creator. Our
conception of law is, in most cases, only a conception of a certain definite succession of phenomena;
but in every case there lurks behind the word
law a conception of a higher kind—of an ordinary
and sustaining power exterior to the phenomena
themselves. But I have no time, or head, now
for such discussion. Do you know who was the
author of the article in the " Edinburgh " on the
subject of Darwin's theory? On the whole, I
think it very good. I once suspected that you
must have had a hand in it, and I then abandoned
that thought. I have not read it with any care. I
must conclude or miss the post.

' Yours ever,

' A. SEDGWICK.'

CHAPTER IV

1860-61

Natural History Lectures at Buckingham Palace—Ascent of the
Cime de Jazi—Edition of Hunter's MSS., 1861—Lord J.
Russell—M. Du Chaillu—Popular Lecturing—Death of his
sister Catherine—Death of the Prince Consort.

'I BEGAN my Fullerian course to a crowded audience at the Royal Institution last Tuesday,' Owen
writes to his sister (January 14, 1860); 'but,
as my voice was still a little affected by cold,
I gave them only three-quarters of a lecture, and
stayed at home all the next day.'

Owen had some years previously made the
acquaintance of Jenny Lind (Mme. Goldschmidt),
who was at that time residing at Wimbledon. On
January 14 Owen and his wife met M. and Mme.
Goldschmidt at Sheen House, then occupied by
Mr. Joshua Bates. Thackeray was also one of
the party, and 'an American who must have been
the model of Dickens's Jefferson Brick—a little
red-haired, self-sufficient youth in spectacles.
During dinner there was a sharp exchange of
shots all round on the subject of the abolition of
the slave trade, or of at least ameliorating the con-

dition of the slaves. Our host got a little riled,
for Jenny unexpectedly spoke out vehemently.
"Jefferson Brick" declared that it was out of the
question to think of treating the niggers as human
beings. R. would not allow for a minute that the
admitted inferiority of the negroes was any argument in favour of the slave trade. It then appeared that our host was possessed of two estates
worked by slaves which fell to him through a
mortgage, so the discussion dropped. After dinner Jenny was much pleased to sit and talk
with R.'

On April 23, 1860, Owen gave, by request
of the Prince Consort, some lectures to the royal
children at Buckingham Palace.

'I think you may like to know,' he writes
to his sister, 'the arrangements made for these
lectures. After consulting with me, Sir James
[Clark] had a drawing-room at Buckingham Palace
fitted up at one end with a large green-baize cur-
tain, on which I have the selected illustrations
fastened. Sofas and arm-chairs are arranged in
a semicircle at a little distance from that end, on
which sit the Prince Consort and the children ;
behind them are seats for the lords and ladies
and gentlemen of the Court. They muster about
30 to 40. These enter first, and then the Prince
with the children ; one day I had the Prince of
Wales, on the other days all that remain at home ;
the young sailor Duke of Edinburgh is amongst

them, and I make as much of my discourse suitable
to him as I can, and generally introduce two or
three anecdotes for the younger children.   They
are all attentive, and seem often to be deeply
interested ; and much of what I have had to say
is evidently new to all.

'My first lecture was on Mammalia, the second
on Birds, the third on Reptiles, and the fourth on
Fishes and other marine animals and insects. My
continuous discourse is about three-quarters of an
hour, and the rest is occupied by question and
answer, in which the Prince Consort takes a good
share in explaining to the youngest children any
matter that seems difficult to them.   I have given
little Prince Arthur a coloured illustrated book on
Natural History, and to Prince Alfred a Manual
for observing Natural History phenomena at sea.
They took leave of me to-day very affectionately,
and the youngest Prince waylaid me in the cor-
ridor and played me a tune on his large musical
box, and begged Major Elphinstone, his tutor, to
let him come to the British Museum to see my
animals there.   The three young Princesses are
very sweet and unaffected in their manner, and
I think they have all been rather struck by hearing
so much in an uninterrupted extempore discourse.
· · · The Prince wishes me to publish my discourses, and, if I can find time for an elementary
work, on the plan I have adopted, I would gladly
endeavour to carry out His Royal Highness's

desire. A good elementary work is indeed much needed. But I have no notes of my lectures and had no time for it.'

Soon after the course of lectures at Buckingham Palace was finished, the Prince Consort sent the following autograph letter to Professor Owen, accompanied by the portraits of the royal children who had listened to the lectures :—

'My dear Professor,—Might I ask you to accept the accompanying prints? The faces, I hope, will recall to your recollection the attentive little audience, to whom you devoted part of your valuable time in the delivery of your late interesting lectures.

'Ever yours truly,
'ALBERT.

'B. P. ☿ '60.'

That his hearers did not forget these lectures is shown by the following letter from Prince Alfred, who sent to Owen the head of a dicynodon and other fossil remains which he had obtained in his travels in South Africa :—

November 12, 1860.

'Dear Professor Owen,—In the course of my journey in South Africa I met with two very interesting fossil remains, one, the larger, being the head of a dicynodon.[1] I hope you will accept

---

[1] See Bibliography, 1862.

them from me as being the best specimens I obtained, upon the Prince Consort's suggestion on the occasion of your last lecture, of which series I shall always retain the most agreeable recollection.

'Yours truly,
'ALFRED.'

Amongst Professor Owen's correspondence there remains, unfortunately, but little record of his intimacy with Charles Kingsley, beyond letters from the latter asking for appointments to go round the Museum. The following letter, received in the April of this year, is perhaps the most characteristic :—

Eversley : April 30, 1860.

'My dear Professor Owen,—I have got a wonder for you, which has opened my eyes so wide that I cannot shut them again—an adder with two hind legs. They are one-half to three-quarters of an inch long, just behind the vent (like a tortoise's in form, but with irregular fangs or prickles, instead of nails). I only describe it roughly, because I don't like to cut it or finger it, but leave that for you. I suppose you would wish to have him and trace his " morphology." I have put him in spirits, and will send him up. His slayers say he stood bolt upright on the said legs and his tail " like a Christian," and sprang at them, which he may well have done. I can hardly believe my own eyes ; but here he is in flesh and blood.

> ‘ Yours ever faithfully,
>
> ‘ C. KINGSLEY.’

Although Owen was constantly the recipient of similar curiosities, ‘ I have never permitted myself,’ he writes to his sister Maria, ‘ to begin a private collection, and, of the thousands of objects that have been sent to me, I have always presented them in the name of the senders to the British Museum, or that of the College of Surgeons. . . .

‘ Yesterday evening I played (and won) a game of chess with Mr. Liddell, and his wife played some charming music of Beethoven ; but my greatest treat yesterday was an admission to a private view of Holman Hunt's painting of Christ in the Temple with the Doctors. . . . You may remember that Hunt went to Jerusalem five years ago to make the requisite studies on the spot, and he has devoted all those years, at which his powers were greatest, to this marvellous work. The painter's devotion to his subject is most exemplary.’

July 20, 1860, was Professor and Mrs. Owen's silver wedding day. ‘ We spent this happy day,’ Mrs. Owen writes, ‘ quietly and gratefully. Silver dishes, cruets, spoons and forks, &c., arrived to celebrate our “ Silberhochzeit,” and my dear husband's fifty-sixth birthday.’

In the following August Owen visited Switzer-
land, and he has left an account of his first visit
to a glacier and his first mountain climb in a letter
to his son, dated Riffelburg, August 24, 1860 :—

'On Wednesday evening, August 22, the
party was made for the ascent of the Cime de Jazi,
a mountain of the Monte Rosa range, and the
next to it eastwards, the summit of which, 13,200
feet above sea, commands a view of the lakes, hills,
and plains of Italy, including Milan and part of
Tyrol—Mr. Hinchliff, secretary of the Alpine
Club ; Mr. Hardman, a stout friend of H.'s ; Mr.
Clerk, son of Sir George ; Mr. and Mrs. H. Cole,[2]
myself, and a young German botanist. We had
five guides ; two were to leave us on gaining the
summit, and to go on to their native place in a
valley on the Italian side. Mr. Clerk had his own
guide, and our two were to return with us.

'We were to start at daybreak, weather being
favourable. But at 4 A.M. appearances led the guides
to think that it would not do ; at 5 things looked
better, and we breakfasted all round, and were off
with due supplies, ropes, &c., by 6.15. The mists
were rising from the valleys, and we were soon
in them, but the sun had risen too, and we were
often amused by the mist rainbows. Our main
route to the Görner glacier was along a narrow
rough footpath along the steep sides and often
above precipices of the Görnergratz. Fortunately

[2] Sir Henry Cole.

for my head, the mists surrounded everything, save a few yards of the path before us, and I was surprised and rather bored by the *empressement* with which the guides helped me over several parts which offered no particular difficulty. I knew the reason better when we returned !

'At 8 A.M. we passed up the glacier, the first I had stepped on. The ice rose with a bold convexity, was rough, and my nailed shoes clung pretty well to it. With the alpenstock, soon got to the level, much crevassed ; but most of them we could step or easily jump across : the blue shining sides of their ice-walls extending down to depths indicated by the rushing of the hidden river. The surface of the glacier ice was like sugar candy in masses, sparkling in the sun, and crunching under our feet. After an hour's scrambling walk, leaping the awful fissures, crossing them by ice-bridges, and dodging round the treacherous snow-bridges, we left the glacier for some rocks, which we gained at 9 A.M. Here we rested and took some refreshment, preparatory to the main part of the ascent. This was over snow-covered ice, of mostly a gentle rise, and the snow at this hour still hard enough to yield, but only foot- or ankle-deep, guides carefully probing suspicious parts as we advanced. The mists were dispersed, the bright and hot sun lit up the enormous plain of dazzling snow and the grand mountains bounding it—Monte Rosa, M. Cervin, &c.—which towered

higher as we ascended.   A group of chamois was
discerned by the guides, and seen by some of
the party, but I had my green-glass goggles and
had adjusted my veil, and would not disturb the
essential arrangement against snow-blindness for
the chance of detecting the little antelopes on a
distant rock.   Some of the party had white cloth
masks, with holes for the green spectacles, for the
nose and mouth, and presented most grotesque
figures.   We got to more frozen but finely
granular snow on a steeper rise, sinking in it
often knee-deep or more.   I followed as closely
as I could the footsteps of the guide before me.

'Every now and then was a halt, and we gazed
upon the wonderful and ever-varying environment ;
new snow-capped mountains, with their dark
rocky precipices, coming into view, but, as yet,
not the summit we were bound for.   We passed
some grand crevasses, the openings of yawning
chasms of more than 2,000 feet sheer ; we must
occasionally have traversed snow-bridges over
such.   On one occasion my left leg sank suddenly
up to the hip, and as the guide lifted me out I felt
certain that the foot had no resting-place, but had
projected into a subnival space.   On surmounting
the ascending part of our snowy route we saw the
base of the summit of the Cima, distant by a vast
tract of the glacier, along which we went for a
mile or so by a slight descent or undulating plain.
At length we reached the base of the consummate

cone. There a long halt was made ; the wind
had increased as we rose ; here it was cutting,
and driving fine particles of frozen snow against
faces and hands ; the veil became less manageable.
I resumed my coat, which I had stript on entering
the glacier. Every step of the steep ascent sunk
knee-deep in the powdery frozen snow. Our stout
party was long before obliged to progress, each
hand upon an alpenstock, carried horizontally between two guides ; here his friend Hinchliff lent
additional help, and we left them bearing him
up, like Sisyphus his stone. Only once I felt the
nausea described by many who toil up declivities
in much rarefied air. I stopped, held down my
head, and then proceeded by slow steps, directing
volition strongly into the leg-muscles, and it soon
went off. I kept the same position, and only
became aware of the near termination of the
climb by hearing a " Hurrah ! Bravo Professor !
Here's a macintosh ready for you ! " Upon which I
gladly threw myself at full length and breathed
more freely.

'I then looked round and saw nothing
higher, save the now distant summit of Monte
Rosa, which had seemed nearer until its true
magnitude with that of the base of the Cima
could be appreciated. A keen and strong current
of biting air from the north-west. All on that
side, to windward, in bright and cloudless sunshine ; all on the opposite Italian side in closer

and driving mist. An eagle soared above us,
with lordly mastery over the gale : made a circular
sweep, scrutinising the figures who had dared to
invade his region, and then sailed off with the
breeze into the clouds overshadowing fair Italy,
to seek its prey there. Whether it were Austrian
or French I could not make out. Cole reached
the summit after me ; Mrs. Cole, with Clerk and
two guides, had preceded us ; then came the
young German, much exhausted, and with hæ-
morrhage from his nose. Lastly appeared poor
Hardman, the stout gentleman, his head drooping,
as he was dragged along by a guide at each arm
and pushed behind by his friend. It suggested
to me a new series of illustrations in " Punch "
—" Mr. Briggs on the Alps!" We were soon
all in high spirits. Brandy flasks, sherry and
light red wine and lemonade ; bread and cold
mutton, for which my appetite was quite prepared ;
a few could not manage solids.

'We were soon ready to move again, urged
by the biting cold. My feet felt frozen, and the
tips of my fingers. We descended the steep
summit in a wild scamper, the light disintegrated
snow permitting you to draw out the leg in
time to prevent a summersault, and were soon
at the bottom, when the guides called halt ; then
began the more careful retracing our steps over
the snow-covered glacier ; and now the sun had
softened the snow, and we swayed to and fro like

a drunken man, sinking deeply and often ob-
liquely in the snow.   We had gained the top at a
quarter to one, and left it at quarter-past 1 ; at
3 P.M. we had gained the rocks, whence we
passed on, the unsnowed glacier revealing its
crevasses.   At 5 we commenced the precipitous
mountain path, all its sheer descents too clearly
revealed.   At 6.15 we were greeted by cheers
from the visitors at the chalet, who had spent the
day on a neighbouring height, watching with tele-
scopes our progress.   I changed, had a glass of
milk with a teaspoonful of rum, and lay down till
summoned to the *table d'hôte*, to which I did
ample justice.   Mr. Hinchliff has descended this
morning (23rd) with much inflamed eyes.   Mr.
and Mrs. Cole next appeared, only showing the
effects on the skin of the face.   We rest and
lounge about to-day, and cross into Italy by the
St. Théodule Pass, crossing the great Görner
glacier to-morrow (Friday), the 24th, when we
shall be in Italy, and see Monte Rosa from the
Val d'Aosta.'

Early in September 1860 Owen returned
home, and during the following month, while on a
visit to his friend Mr. White Cooper, at Fulmer, he
took the opportunity of going over Fulmer Place,
the old residence of his family.   He gives the
following account of his visit in a letter to his sister
Catherine : 'On the rising ground, near its [the
village's] upper end, stands " Fulmer Place."

The old brick wall, rounding in on each side the entry gate, is original ; and the noble " Balm of Gilead Fir Tree" within the entrance was doubtless planted by Richard Eskrigge. The two fishponds where he fed the carp are exactly as our poor father saw them when a very little boy. I fancied the old great-grandfather and the child descending the gentle slope of the lawn from the front door to the margin of the ponds. The views from the house are beautifully undulated and wooded, as charming a retreat as a philosopher could desire. Cooper and I had walked down a pathway by the side of the house to the ponds, where one of them extends beyond the garden, when we saw Mr. Wanklyn coming down the opposite slope. He welcomed me most kindly, as the great-grandson of the founder of the house, which he has almost rebuilt and largely added to. He fully enjoys his place and property. . . . He is a man of taste, and has laid out the gardens and grounds so as to effect a very beautiful residence. . . . To-morrow I shall worship in the old church. The leaves enclosed I plucked from an old apple-tree in the orchard.'

During the latter part of 1860 Owen was busily occupied in bringing to a conclusion his task of editing two octavo volumes of Hunter's MSS. He himself attached considerable importance to this work, ' the preparation of which,' as he says in his dedication of the book, ' terminates the

editor's labours in making known the thoughts and
works of the founder of philosophical surgery.'
The work itself was received with no little interest, partly perhaps because there was a special
history attached to it.

When John Hunter died in 1793, he left a considerable quantity of MSS. behind him. These
MSS., which were in the custody of his executor,
Sir Everard Home, soon afterwards mysteriously
disappeared, and on investigation it was discovered that the baronet had ruthlessly committed them to the flames. This strange
proceeding gave rise to considerable suspicion
against Sir Everard. It was well known that
he himself was given to natural history pursuits,
and, although not a man of eminent ability,
was the author of scientific papers announcing
certain small but not uninteresting discoveries.
It was, therefore, surmised that he was indebted to
Hunter's MSS. for his discoveries, and had burnt
the original papers in order to avoid detection.[3]
Unfortunately for Home's reputation, but fortunately for the literary and scientific world, William
Clift, Hunter's favourite pupil and assistant, had
made a practice of copying out these MSS., and
having for about half a century carefully kept his
work, handed it over in his later days to Owen to
use it as he thought best.

Apart from this story, the two volumes of

[3] See *Charlesworth's Geological Journal*, 1846.

'John Hunter's Essays and MSS.,' which Owen
edited, are certainly full of interest.   Charac-
terized as they are by a strange diversity of
thought, they give the impression that the writer
either did not live long enough to complete his
own account of himself, or else that, though
possessing endless industry and immense powers
of observation, he had neither time nor inclination for concentration of thought.   His essays on
natural history contain remarks on the classes of
animals, on the distinctions between animals and
vegetables, the origin of natural production and of
species and varieties, and the properties of matter,
and so forth. In treating of the origin of species,
while he fails to take the extreme Darwinian view,
he nevertheless asks : ' Does not the natural gradation of animals from one to another lead to the
original species ? For example : Are we not led
on to the wolf,' he says, ' by the gradual affinities
of the different varieties in the dog, and is it not
possible to trace out the gradation in the same
way in the horse, sheep, or cat ?' Beyond this
Hunter does not advance.   In his 'Observations
on Psychology' the illustrations that he gives are
exceedingly quaint.   He tells us, for instance, that
' the mind is often in opposition to itself : the state
of the mind if strong shall get the better of another
state which is weak, or the stronger state shall
not allow the weaker to rise ; although the mind
is so circumstanced at the time as to have one

state raised, if the other state which is stronger had not already taken possession of the mind, or driven the other out ;' and, having delivered this proposition, he illustrates it by something which once took place within himself when he went to see Mrs. Siddons act. He entered the theatre with the strong conviction that he should be very much affected and weep copiously ; but he found to his dismay that he had forgotten to bring a handkerchief, and the misery and anxiety that he was in, when he found he was without that requisite for drying up the eyes, and the feeling of horror lest he should cry under those circumstances, so stopped up every tear that he not only did not cry, but actually could not do so.

On December 12 Owen writes to his sister : ' I have just finished my edition of Hunter's MSS. ; it will come out, January, in two vols. 8vo. I shall also then bring out my " Memoir on the Megatherium," in 4to, with 27 large plates ! Messrs. Black write to say that they have only 100 left of " Palæontology," and I am at work on a new edition. I enclose a syllabus of my next and *last* course of Fullerian Lectures. The matter of the Jermyn Street lectures is not yet settled, but I have spoken to Sir R. Murchison of my wish to give them up.'

On December 30 he writes again : ' On Christmas Day I lunched with Lord John Russell, and chatted awhile with him in his study at Pem-

broke Lodge. The floor was literally strewed
with despatch boxes! and he looked like the
hardest-worked man in the realm. Lady John
told me an amusing anecdote of the younger
children. Their pet jackdaw had died, so they
hoisted a black flag on a little castle in the garden,
and the youngest confided to Mamma " that they
had determined not to play at ' railroads' for a
whole week!"—a beautiful kind of Court-mourn-
ing devised by the little dears. The " Times "
has given my " Palæontology " a review.'

At the end of this year David Livingstone
wrote a long letter to Owen, from which some
extracts are given here :—

Senna : December 29, 1860.

' My dear Friend,—. . . By the way, Mr.
Darwin's book upsets my ideas somewhat. There
does not seem to be any great struggle for existence going on in this wide continent. There is
room enough and to spare for both man and
beast. The latter seem to live quite jovially, and
often attain old age. They are subject to various
diseases—whole herds are sometimes swept off by
epidemics, and we meet with diseased animals
constantly. Disease does not select or elect to
leave the strongest, for it cuts off the ox and horse,
and leaves the goat and sheep. . . . My thoughts,
however, may only show my ignorance ; for the
book itself has not yet come this length. I speak

only from what I see in reviews. . . . The flesh
of a fat eland has upset the whole party of about
seventy persons ; this may have given rise to the
feeling that they may be better after domestication.   It is an old complaint against the meat,
however.   A she-giraffe is very much better, but
good English roast beef beats them all. . . .

' Ever affectionately yours,
' DAVID LIVINGSTONE.'

On January 21, 1861, Professor Owen began
his course of Fullerian Lectures for the season,
and on the 8th of the following month he resumed
his lectures at the School of Mines, Jermyn
Street, on ' Reptilia.'

His edition of Hunter's papers had now been
published.   'On the 28th,' he writes to his
sister Eliza, ' I had a very pleasant dinner at Sheen
House, meeting the American Minister and his
family, who seem rather low at the thoughts of
returning to private life in 160th Street, Philadelphia. . . .   To-morrow, after lecture, I dine and
sleep at Henry Cole's, who " wets " his " silk " with
a few friends.   I had much conversation with the
young Comte de Paris on Monday at the Geographical dinner. . . .   I called on Van Voorst
the other day, and received 200l. for my edition
of Hunter's posthumous papers, just out.'

One of the first people to whom Owen sent a
copy was Thomas Bell, who wrote him the fol-

lowing acknowledgment, dated New Broad Street,
March 1 :—

'What thanks do I not owe you for so kindly
sending me that marvellous book? If anything
were wanting to place Hunter in the highest position of human intellect, and as the rarest com-
bination of genius and practical observation, this
would do it. I never read so *full* a book. I sat
an hour with Sir Benjamin Brodie the other day,
and when I went in I found his secretary reading
this book to him. He asked if I had seen this new
book of Hunter's, and said with great emphasis,
" It is a marvellous book." He seems more struck
with it than I ever saw him with anything before.
Your arranging and publishing it has conferred
a great benefit on the scientific public, whilst it
has done justice at last to that great man.'

There appeared an amusing cartoon in ' Punch '
the last week in January, in which Owen is threat-
ened with being skinned by the South American
States for giving it as his opinion that Adam and
Eve were coloured people.

In February he met the African traveller
M. Du Chaillu for the first time, and on the 25th
attended his lecture on gorillas at the Great Room
of the Royal Society, at which lecture Owen
made some prefatory remarks on the structure of
these creatures. Amongst those present was
Mr. Gladstone, and 'when the lecture was over,'
the Professor writes, 'and Mr. Gladstone had

made a short speech, I took the opportunity of saying a word on the subject of such valuable acquisitions to science not having proper accommodation, &c., at the Museum.'

'On March 18,' Mrs. Owen writes in her diary, ' R. and I drove to the Royal Institution, to hear another of M. Du Chaillu's lectures. A tremendous crowd filled the theatre, Sir Roderick Murchison in the chair. M. Du Chaillu gave a very quaint, clear, and interesting account of his travels in Africa, and his meeting with the gorillas, a row of which hideous creatures was overhead : some skulls were before the lecturer, who traced his progress on a large map as the lecture proceeded.'

A few days after this lecture Owen received the following letter from M. Du Chaillu :—

129 Mount Street ; March 22, 1861.

' My dear Sir,—Allow me to present you with a gorilla skin. . . . When I prepared it in Africa it was with the intention that I should present it to you myself, and on this account I did not send it to you from America.

' I think that it is quite time that you should put your foot on the skin of an animal the anatomical character of which you have so thoroughly described in several of the memoirs you have published, and the reading of which has delighted me so much.

' Yours very truly,

' P. B. Du Chaillu.'

Another African traveller whom Professor
Owen met at this time was Mr. Petherick. In a
letter to his sister Maria, March 19, 1861, he
says :—

'Last Thursday I took Consul Petherick to
the Palace at five minutes before eleven, and Lord
Caithness looked into the waiting-room to have a
chat before we were called into the Prince Consort's Library. H.R.H. ordered his last map of
Africa down, and we drew out much curious and
minute information from the traveller. H.R.H.
said, that when he saw a chain of mountains
stretching along a desert part of a map he always suspected them to be put in for the appearance, and it is curious what masses of mountains
do get destroyed, especially in Africa, as soon as
travellers reach their whereabouts. The Prince
then sent for his album of photographs. They
include people of all countries. One was of a Thug,
100 years old, who had committed thrice as many
murders, and the most extraordinary example of
living-skeleton humanity I ever beheld. Sir C.
B. Phipps and Dr. Ruland, the new librarian, were
of the party, which lasted an hour. The problem
of the source of the Nile, and the cause of its
annual overflow, has been almost solved by Mr.
Petherick, and if he is spared he will discover the
remaining facts in his ensuing expedition. I had a
rare audience on Friday—Jermyn Street blocked
up with carriages. Jenny Lind laughed when I

told her ; and commended my intention to bid them a lasting farewell! I really believe I shall be able to manage it. How odd that, besides an acquaintance with a Bonaparte, spending a week at his Palazzo at Rome, with the old Emperor's Longwood furniture in my bedroom, I should come to have a letter from a son of Napoleon's *beau sabreur*, as he used to call the fiery Murat. Some of my scientific relations have brought me into such cognizance with one of the family as to have procured me this sheet from the would-be King of Naples.'

In May 1861 Professor Owen delivered a series of four lectures at Norwich on ' Recent and Fossil Mammalia.' These were of a somewhat elementary description, as may be seen from the following extracts from his introductory lecture ; but they may serve as an example of his style of 'popular' lecturing. He began by remarking that all animals were divided into two great groups—one in which there was no backbone, and no internal hard framework or skeleton, the other in which these characteristics existed. The latter, which was the higher division, was called the vertebrate division. This was divided into other divisions ; one-half being of about the same temperature as the atmosphere in which they lived, while the other half were enabled, by the more perfect and complex character of their organisation, to preserve a more fixed and definite temperature, which was usually higher than the temperature around them. These were the cold-blooded and warm-blooded vertebrates. One class produced eggs, the other produced living young. Some moved on four limbs, others on two ; some had no lower limbs, properly so called. Aristotle had divided the group into bipeds, quad-rupeds, and impeds. The quadrupeds formed the great bulk. The impeds living in the sea, as fishes, were warm blooded and breathed air ; the bipeds were ourselves.

The quadrupeds were so large a proportion that it was necessary to subdivide them ; and Aristotle had said of them that one-half had their limbs terminating with digits ending in claws or nails, while the others had the ends of the digits enclosed in a horny thimble or hoof. Conse-quently, he divided them into the hoofed and clawed quadrupeds. The hoofed quadrupeds he divided according to the number of the divisions of the hoofs, and the others he divided according to their dentition, as carnivorous, graminivorous, and so on. Linnæus was the first who definitely and properly divided the mammalian groups, and it was he who gave them the name Mammalia. The Mammalia also were characterised not only by having living young, but by nourishing their young in a peculiar way. Another characteristic was that of having hair upon their bodies, for those that were not covered with hair were

partially adorned with it, and it was a curious
fact that even very young whales had mustachios
and whiskers. Again, all Mammalia had a complex heart, with ventricles and auricles, which
received and circulated the blood. No other
animals but those belonging to the class Mammalia had a diaphragm. Cuvier had pointed
out some other characteristics; but there were
in his system some apparent anomalies, such as
ranking the mole higher than the lynx, the bat
above the dog, and even the duck mole of
Australia he placed above the elephant.

He (Owen) himself, from the examination he
had made, arrived at the conviction that there
were two or three, or perhaps four, well-marked
steps in the development of the brain, and that
the brain was the organ on the modifications and
differences in the structure of which the Mammalia should be divided. There were in all Mammalia the little brain, or cerebellum, the optic
lobes, in which the nerves going to the eye were
chiefly rooted, the cerebral hemisphere, and
the olfactory lobes, with which the nerves of
smell were connected. In all the cold-blooded
vertebrates, in reptiles, fishes, and birds, the cerebral hemispheres were almost quite detached,
there being nothing between them except a little
cord, and this was the case with a certain portion of the Mammalia, which were called loose-
brained, or, as Professor Sedgwick had quaintly

suggested, scatter-brained. Then there was the brain in which there was a curious apparatus of cross fibres that brought every part of one hemisphere in contact with the other. The next step was where the cerebral hemispheres began to increase in size, and there would not be room in the skull to contain them if they were not folded and packed as we should pack a napkin in a box. This type of brain, which characterised a certain class of Mammalia, was called the wave-brain. Then there came a sudden and marked step in the increase of the relative size and complexity, number and depth of the convolutions of the brain, which was called chiefbrain, and marked a fourth well-defined group. The loose brain was peculiar to two kinds of quadrupeds that belonged almost exclusively to Australia, and the duck mole and the kangaroo might be taken as types of these orders.

Owen then described the construction of various mammals characterised by the different types of brain, proceeding from the lowest to the most perfect in regular order. The gorilla he characterised as the nearest approach to man. It was an animal that had been known, from more or less perfect specimens, for the last eight or ten years, and from the enterprising traveller, M. Du Chaillu, to whom we owed the most perfect of these specimens, he had obtained the skeleton of a fullgrown gorilla, which was placed in the British

Museum. There was in this animal a marked characteristic in the organisation of the innermost digit—the thumb—which was found on both feet and hands, and showed it to be a creature of the forest. The trunk of the animal was the trunk of a giant. The chest was girt with thirteen pairs of ribs—one pair more than ours—and the lungs were well developed, a development that was always in accordance with the physical powers, and which was nowhere greater than in this singular animal. The arms were very long in proportion to the height of the animal ; but, with regard to the brain, it was not one-fourth the bulk of the brain of the lowest form of the human species. The brain, like the eye, was an organ that very rapidly attained its full size in all creatures. In the gorilla, as he had said, it was small compared with that of the human race. The animal had formidable teeth, corresponding with the character of the skull, but the development of the canine teeth was almost peculiar to the males. With the immense strength he possessed, the gorilla could combat the lion, and it was certain that the lion never went near the forest where the gorilla dwelt. He could strangle the leopard, and he was able to defend himself and family from all enemies except man and his rifle. The gorillas had acquired a certain range of rich country on the equator of Africa, and they held their possessions as long as their strength endured. In compensation for the absence of intellectual power, the inability to put two ideas together, to construct a weapon of defence, or to articulate a word, the gorilla had allotted to him the maximum of physical power.

Compared to the gorilla, man was physically but a weak and feeble creature, but man possessed the highest type of brain, his whole structure was beautifully balanced, the lower limbs were equal to the upper, the trunk was not disproportioned to the rest, and the structure of the spine, which bore, well poised, that wonderful bony globe which contained the cerebral region, was beautifully arranged. Man was more independent than any other animal; the backs of the gorilla's hands gave evidence that when he walked on land he was obliged to use his arms as well as his legs for locomotive purposes; but man, and man alone, could walk erect, and use the upper limbs free and independent of the rest of the body.

In the summer of this year M. Du Chaillu was a frequent visitor at Sheen Lodge, and Professor Owen remarks on the pleasure which the purchase of the Gorilla Collection by the British Museum had afforded him. 'Those selected for the Museum,' he says, ' are the best.'

To his wife, who had gone for a holiday to Boulogne, Owen writes, on August 6, 1861, a long letter, full of particulars of his engagements.

He mentions a dinner at Mr. Huntley's, where
' he had out some good maps of the (dis-) United
States before dinner, and interested us by the
comments of General Sir De Lacy Evans on
the great battle, which has been attended with
such disastrous consequences to the Northern
party. . . . Will and I retire to a *tête-à-tête*
dinner to-day. When we left you on Thursday
evening we went to Evans's, and the worthy
proprietor, recognising me, begged me to order
any kind of music I liked, and at Will's
suggestion we had a succession of their best
part-songs and choruses. I think I shall
persuade you and Jessie to accompany us to a
private box to hear the music and see the scene!
The old German imitator performed, and a good
acrobat party. So, you see, we have done our
best to assuage our sorrows under the bereave-
ment, but we shall truly rejoice to see you both
safe back again.'

In September Owen writes to his wife, giving
a few details of the British Association Meeting
at Sheffield, where he gave a course of lectures,
lecturing afterwards at Manchester. This letter
is chiefly occupied with meetings with old friends,
but he does not forget his garden. He says :
'You will think the Chief Baron [Pollock]
in a conspiracy with me to invade your lawn!
But I don't know what he may have sent, except
one *Cryptomeria*—a little one.'

Before returning to London Owen paid a visit to his friend Bateman at Congleton, with Dr. Daubeny, Du Chaillu, E. W. Cooke, and Dr. Garner,[1] and, after staying a few days there, left for Lancaster, Glamorganshire, the Wrekin and Shrewsbury, and so back to London. At Shrewsbury he went to the Museum, which 'contains some old fossil friends, including my *Rhynchosaurus*, and the best of the Roman antiquities of Uriconium.'

He had scarcely returned home when he was summoned to Lancaster to the death-bed of his sister Catherine. On hearing of her illness he wrote at once to say he was coming, and enclosed a letter to his dying sister (October 22) written in large text hand, so that she might be able to read it. 'Believe me, dearest Catherine,' he says, 'I shall ever think of you with the warmest affection and love, forgetting none of the instances of your kind, warm heart and true affection.' 'Her death,' he writes in his diary, 'has come more suddenly than I expected.' He returned home after spending a week at Lancaster with his two surviving sisters.

A few days later (November 6), he gave the inaugural address of the Brighton and Sussex Museum. 'The collection of the beautiful works of Nature,' he remarked, 'is a work in which all of us ought to feel some pleasure. Everywhere, if

[1] Robert Garner, author of *History of Staffordshire*

we had but the inclination to examine the operations of Nature, are we placed in a museum. Look at Gilbert White, who, while living in the little village of Selborne, devoted his intellect to the common objects of the country around him, and who has given us. from the results he then achieved, a book which will probably remain so long as the English tongue is spoken.

'There was also Gideon Mantell, who, when practising in a small obscure town in the provinces, found leisure time to look into the marvels of the country around him, and, as the result of that labour, had enriched scientific literature with descriptions of some of the most extraordinary extinct animals with which his name was linked to science.'

After mentioning the new forms, particularly in fishes, which the rich fossiliferous deposits of that neighbourhood had brought to light, Owen insisted on the importance of local museums, especially as preserving the objects of extinct natural history found in their immediate locality. He closed his discourse by saying that he was brought to the same conclusion at which Newton himself arrived—that there is a great First Cause which, he was convinced, is not mechanical.

In December 1861 the fatal illness of Prince Albert caused a deep feeling of sorrow throughout the country. To Owen the Prince's death was a personal loss. 'You may imagine with

what grief,' he writes to his sister Eliza on the
16th, 'after returning home on Saturday with
hopes of the Prince Consort's recovery, I learnt
the sad news of his death yesterday morning.
His Royal Highness had been a constant and
valuable friend to me, and I was one of the few
who, having access to his private life, were able
to appreciate his kindly and truly natural unassum-
ing disposition.   His loss is a great and unlooked-
for shock to all his friends; still greater to the
Queen and his children.'

In another letter to his sisters, written on the
24th, he returns to the same subject: 'Every now
and then the boom of the minute gun came heavily
over from the Park or Tower.   Collins went
down to take his turn at the long peal of muffled
bells in the old church-tower.   To-day I am at
my post here [British Museum]; to-morrow will
be another holiday; yesterday was a sad one.'

.

CHAPTER V

1862 64

Jenny Lind—Ruskin—Dickens—Made Chevalier of the Italian
Order of S. Maurice and S. Lazare—Inauguration of the Leeds
Institution, 1862—Memoirs on the 'Aye-Aye,' and other
Literary Work, 1863—Lectures before the Queen at Windsor,
1864.

ON January 10, 1862, Owen writes to his sister
Eliza from Dr. Arthur Farre's, Mayfair, where he
was staying :—

'We are now in comfortable London quarters
here. Yesterday we all drove over with the
doctor's pair of horses to dine with Mr. and Mrs.
Goldschmidt. Jenny was in good voice and
kindly sang us a song from Handel's old opera of
"Susannah"—such a beauty ! besides other songs ;
and Mr. G. played charming selections from
Beethoven, &c. Her youngest boy is now a year
old, her golden-haired lassie, about six, very like
herself; there is every sign of a happy, well-
ordered household.'

In February Owen was the guest of Sir
William (afterwards Lord) Armstrong, during a
lecturing tour in the North, spending some days
with Lord Ravensworth during his stay there.

He sends a special note with a message for Mr. Liddell, to say that he won a game of chess from Lord Ravensworth, and read 'Guinevere' to the ladies. His letters are full of the interest he found in the Elswick Works and his astonishment at the methods of manufacture of the guns.

While in the North of England Owen notes in his diary that he gave four lectures at Newcastle and one at Shields. Mrs. Owen writes that her husband, on his return home, showed her an interesting letter sent him, after one of his Newcastle lectures, by a 'clever and evidently deep-thinking, though uneducated, working man,' in which he thanks Professor Owen for his lectures, and expresses his admiration of his powers of mind. 'It was an uncommon letter,' Owen remarks, 'and was very agreeable to receive.'

The following record of one of Dickens's readings at St. James's Hall, to which he invited Professor and Mrs. Owen, occurs in the diary :—

'*April* 10.—Yesterday evening there came a note from Charles Dickens, asking us if we would like to come to St. James's Hall to hear one of his readings. I met R. at the Athenæum, and then we drove together to St. James's Hall, where we were welcomed by Miss Dickens and Miss Hogarth, who sat with us just in front of Charles Dickens, whose reading, or rather acting, was wonderful, and the immense audience seemed to feel it to be so. They applauded at parts which showed that every point told. I was informed afterwards that Dickens was heard at the farthest end of the hall, and, if so, it is extraordinary that one voice should fill such a large space. Both R. and I will long remember the treat. I asked Dickens to come over one June day to see the garden.'

On May 2 Owen writes to his sister Eliza, telling her that his Fullerian Lectures at the Royal Institution began on April 7 and were ' on Birds.' After speaking again of the beauty of his garden, he says : ' May-day was such as the poets sing of : a bright sunny summer day. I passed it pleasantly in my garden, only wishing you had been here to enjoy it. I was reading " Philip," in the last " Cornhill," under my cedar, listening to the trill of the nightingale, about the time of the opening procession amid the crowds at the International Exhibition. I felt my happier position.'

The charm of Owen's country home was felt by others besides himself. Among his visitors was Mr. Ruskin.

' *Sunday, April* 27.—Mr. Ruskin came as expected, and had a walk with R. At dinner we had much pleasant conversation on art and literature. Afterwards R. read part of one of the " Idylls." '

Other interesting visitors appear in the diary.

' *Sunday, June* 1.—We had Charles Dickens,

Miss Dickens, Miss Hogarth, and Mr. and Mrs.
John Forster over here to spend the day.

'C. D. is not improved in appearance by the
scanty beard he has now grown. I think his face
is spoiled by it. He greatly admired the picture,
the "Monastery Interior" in our dining-room, and
he and Mr. Forster were much interested at the
story of it. Mr. F. is as cheerful as ever, and we
were all very lively at dinner. Dickens told us
some funny anecdotes about Frenchmen he had met
abroad, and I told him an adventure which befell
me when dining with M. and Madame Leverrier
in Paris years ago—how M. Leverrier spilt a
glass of champagne over my new dress just after
having taken me in to dinner, and how I, having
recovered from the first shock, was astonished by
his suddenly dropping down on his knees, and
frantically catching me round the petticoats till he
had ascertained, breadth by breadth, that there
was no stain. The conclusion of this affecting
narrative brought us to the end of dinner, and we
retired into the garden, where we wandered about
till it was time for Dickens to go.'

'*July* 17.—A visit from Mr. Waterhouse,
just returned from Pappenheim, where he has
been in treaty for the collection of fossils, in which
is the curious fossil with the alleged feathered
vertebrate tail.[1] The old German doctor is ob-
stinate about his price, and Mr. W. has come

[1] The *Archæopteryx macrura*, a feather-winged vertebrate.

away empty-handed. We ought not to lose the fossil.'

The following extract from Mrs. Owen's diary gives striking evidence of the widespread popularity of Owen's labours :—

'*July* 28.—A letter to-day from the Principal of the College at Amherst, Massachusetts, U.S.A., who encloses a printed sheet with extracts from R.'s Rede Lecture, delivered at Cambridge in 1859. He says this printed sheet is hung up in every public room and every sleeping room in the gymnasium at Amherst.'

The extracts referred to consist of the concluding words of Professor Owen's Rede Lecture. After a description of the human body, the lecturer concludes : ' Such are the dominating powers with which we, and we alone are gifted ! I say *gifted*, for the surpassing organisation was no work of ours. " It is He that hath made us, and not we ourselves." This frame is a temporary trust, for the uses of which we are responsible to the Maker. O you who possess it in all the supple vigour of lusty youth, think well what it is that He has committed to your keeping ! Waste not its energies ; dull them not by sloth ; spoil them not by pleasures ! The supreme work of creation has been accomplished that you might possess a body, the sole erect, of all animal bodies the most free, and for what ? For the service of the soul. Strive to realise the conditions of the possession

of this wondrous structure.   Think what it may become—the Temple of the Holy Spirit!   Defile
it not.   Seek rather to adorn it with all meet and
becoming gifts, and with fair furniture, moral and
intellectual. . . . .'

Owen never let an opportunity pass of seeing
with his own eyes any curious or abnormal development of the human frame.   He once remarked,
à propos of violin-playing, how much struck he
had been in examining Ernst's long, bony, and
muscular fingers, which the great violinist had
obligingly offered for the Professor's inspection.
On one occasion (August 8), ' Frank Buckland
came to the British Museum for R. and took him
to see the French giant, Joseph Brice, now being
exhibited in London. They found him in bed with
a cold.   He looked, R. said, quite a Goliath as he
lay his full length, with his great hands spread
out on the bed, but he is not quite so tall as he is
represented to be.   He is really 7 ft. 6 in.   He is
a great favourite of Frank's, and is certainly amiable and pleasant.'

On September 22. Professor Owen received
a document from the Italian Legation, creating
him a Chevalier of the Order of St. Maurice and
St. Lazare, in the name of the King, Victor
Emanuel.

Owen was the guest of Mr. Gladstone at
Hawarden in September 1862, and wrote to his
sister from that place on the 27th.   He gives little

information about his stay, beyond mentioning
that Mr. Gladstone sang two songs, and that he
had had some conversation with Sir Stephen
Glynn and Miss Burdett-Coutts, and that they had
'a pleasant chatty dinner and evening.'

His lectures at Buckingham Palace were still
bearing fruit. He was now called upon to describe the Dicynodont reptiles and the fossil
remains collected in South Africa by H.R.H.

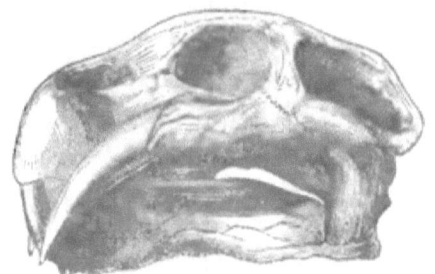

Dicynodon lacerticeps (Owen).

Skull of a primitive reptile from the Karoo formation of Cape
Colony. The first evidence of a new order of animals determined and described by Owen. ⅓ natural size.

Prince Alfred.[2] Sir C. B. Phipps wrote the following letter by command of the Queen in acknowledgment of the paper :—

Windsor Castle : October 8, 1862.

'My dear Professor Owen,—The Queen has
commanded me to return you Her Majesty's best
thanks for your paper upon the fossils collected in
South Africa by Prince Alfred, which you have

[2] This description was pub- *Transactions* of the Royal
lished in the *Philosophical* Society.

sent to her. The Queen knows with what interest this paper would have been read by the lamented Prince, and she will attach particular value to it as coming from one for whom he had a very high respect and regard.

'There is not one of the royal family who does not look back with pleasure to the lectures which you were good enough to deliver to them, and at which I had the high privilege of being allowed to attend.

'Sincerely yours,

'C. B. Phipps.'

In December 1862, Owen inaugurated the Leeds Institution, and he writes to his sister Eliza on the 18th : 'The secretary of the " Institution " was in waiting, and we drove first there, where I inspected the new museum, &c., &c., and then Mr. James Marshall called and drove me to Headingly. On Tuesday the inauguration came off, very successfully. Yesterday Mr. Marshall drove me to a country seat of a gentleman, Mr. Fawkes,[3] who has a wonderful collection of Turner's finest paintings and drawings, and it happened to be a bright sunny day for seeing them. This morning I bade adieu to Headingly, and took my quarters with an old medical friend in the town, for the better convenience of my lectures, of which I gave the first this evening.'

[3] Owen makes a note in his letter to the effect that this gentleman was a 'descendant of Guy F.'

On February 26, 1863, Owen writes to his sister Eliza a long account of the first Levee held by the Prince of Wales, and says : 'His Royal Highness had a severe taste of that part of his future duties : 1,000 presentations ! . . . It was the most crowded ever known, and I was lucky to escape with no other loss than a shoe-buckle. . . . I met the American Minister and Mrs. and Miss Adams, Mr. Bates and M. and Madame Goldschmidt at Mr. Stuart-Wortley's at Sheen last Saturday. The etiquette is not to *ask* Jenny to sing ; but she kindly proposed it after dinner : began with " My mother bids me bind my hair," and ended with a glorious solo from the " Messiah," singing four pieces to perfection, her husband accompanying.'

Another entry in the diary refers to the great singer. When Jenny Lind was coming out of church on a cold day in the very early spring, she expressed her annoyance at the way in which people stared at her, whenever she opened her mouth, and said : ' I think I will never sing again in church.' ' I told her,' writes Mrs. Owen, ' that it was only natural, and that I had a friend staying with me to whom it was a great disappointment that she was too ill to come and see her to-day. Jenny, who evidently felt that the cold had given a tinge to her nose, said : " My dear Mrs. Owen, tell her of my *nose*, and that will be quite enough. Tell her, if you like, that I am a very ugly woman !"

But she is never that, and I have seen her look quite beautiful when singing.'

As the summer of 1863 advanced, the beauties of Owen's garden again fill his letters. On June 5, 1863, he writes to his sister Maria a long account of its glories, and concludes : 'Will's holiday began yesterday, and I accompanied him and a young friend of his to Ascot, my first appearance on that stage. We went by train, and at the Twickenham Station I was recognised by the young Comte de Paris and the Duc d'Aumale, who rallied me on my gay propensities. Of course I found many who knew me, whom I did not know, and had divers civilities proffered, but declined all save one cigar. Enjoyed the races much—a glorious day. The young Prince of Wales drove, in state, to the ground.'

In this year Professor Owen published his interesting ' Memoir on the Aye-Aye' (*Chiromys madagascariensis*). In the course of this memoir he points out in the case of this little Madagascar quadruped the striking instances of the special adaptation of parts to certain uses.

' The aye-aye is stated,' he remarks, ' to sleep during the heat and glare of the tropical day, and to move about chiefly by night in quest of wood-boring larvæ. The wide openings of the eyelids, the large cornea, and expansile iris, with other structures of the eye, are express arrangements for admitting to the retina and absorbing the

utmost amount of light which may pervade the
forests at sunset, dawn, or moonlight. Thus the
aye-aye is able to guide itself among the branches
in quest of its hidden food. To discern this,
however, another sense had need to be developed
to great perfection. The large ears are directed
to catch and concentrate, and the large acoustic
nerve and other structures of the organ seem
designed to appreciate any feeble vibration that
might reach the tympanum from the recess in the
hard timber, through which the wood-boring larva
may be tunnelling its way, by repeated scoopings
and scrapings of its hard mandible. How safe
might seem such a grub in its teak or ebony-cased
burrow! Here, however, is a quadrumanous
quadruped in which the front teeth, by their great
size, strong shape, chisel structure, deep implanta-
tion and provision for perpetual renovation of
substance, are especially fitted to enable their
possessor to gnaw down with gouge-like scoops to
the very spot where the ear indicates the grub to
be at work. The instincts of the insect, however,
warn it to withdraw from the part of the burrow
that may be thus exposed. Had the aye-aye
possessed no other instrument—were no other
part of its frame specially modified to meet this
exigency—it must have proceeded to apply the
incisive scoops in order to lay bare the whole of
the larval tunnel, to the extent at least which
would leave no further room for the retracted grub's

retreat. Such labour would, however, be too much
for the reproductive power of even its strong-built,
wide-based, deep-planted, pulp-retaining incisors ; in
most instances we may well conceive such labour
of exposure to be disproportionate to the morsel
to be so obtained. Another part of the frame of the
aye-aye is, accordingly, modified in a singular and,
as it seems, anomalous way to meet this exigency.
We may suppose that the larva retracts its head
so far from the opening gnawed in its burrow as
to be out of reach of the lips or tongue of the aye-
aye. One finger, however, on each hand of that
animal has been ordained to grow in length, but
not in thickness, with the other digits ; it remains
slender, as a probe, and is provided at the end with
a hook-like claw. By the doubtless rapid inser-
tion and delicate application of this digit, the grub
is seized and drawn out. For this delicate man-
œuvre the aye-aye needs a free command of its
upper or fore-limbs ; and, to give it that power,
one of the digits of the hind foot is so modified
and directed that it can be applied thumb-wise to
the other toes, and the foot is made a prehensile
hand. Hereby the body is steadied by the firm
grasp of these hinder hands during all the operations of the head, jaws, teeth, and fore-paws
required for the discovery and capture of the
common and favourite food of the nocturnal
animal.'

The living aye-aye, it may be added, was visited

in 1864, as the following entry in Mrs. Owen's diary records :—

'*August* 6.—To the Zoological Gardens with R. to see the living aye-aye and the new monkey house. We were glad to see the faithful and good-natured keeper Hunt, the old friend of our early days at the College of Surgeons. He made the hippopotamus come out of the water and show himself.'

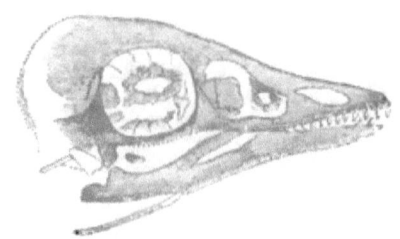

Archæopteryx macrura (Owen).

Head, as seen in the second known specimen, now preserved in the Berlin Museum of Natural History. Natural size.

Amongst Professor Owen's writings which appeared in 1863 may be mentioned his memoir 'On the Archæopteryx' ('Trans. Roy. Soc.'); 'On Dinornis,' Parts VII. and VIII. ('Trans. Zool. Soc.'); 'Osteology of Troglodytes and Pithecus,' Nos. IV. and V. ; and 'Osteology of Anthropoid Apes,' Nos. VII. and VIII.

In September 1863, Owen, accompanied by John Gould, was the guest of the Duke of Northumberland at Alnwick Castle. Afterwards they went to Lord Tankerville's, where, among other things, they inspected the Chillingham cattle.

Archæopteryx macrura (Owen).

A fossil from the Lithographic Stone of Solenhofen, Bavaria, determined by Owen to be a primitive bird, showing certain reptilian characters. In the Natural History Museum. ½ natural size.

'I arrived here [at Alnwick] to dinner on Wednesday,' he writes to his wife (September 5), 'and found Professor Tyndall and Lord and Lady Tankerville, &c. On Thursday there was a grand flower and fruit show in the grounds; since then have arrived, among others, Sir R. Murchison, Captain Grant of Nile celebrity, Sir William Armstrong, and a dark native of Ceylon in gorgeous costume.

'Alnwick Castle is a wilderness of corridors, staircases, and rooms; as Lord Ravensworth remarked last night as we were going to bed, it was hard on gentlemen past sixty to have to mount 170 steps to get to rest!

'Breakfast bell will soon ring, and I have to get ready to start with Lord Tankerville, and so good-bye.'

Chillingham Castle, Alnwick.

• 'Here at Lord Tankerville's am I enjoying a hearty and lively time. I have had a good view of the wild cattle, and have seen a red deer pulled down. This morning am off to Edinburgh.'

In the following month, October 7, 1863, Owen sends in a report to the Trustees of the British Museum about a whale which was stranded on the coast of Caithness, and which he was anxious that the Museum should possess.[1]

[1] It is the skeleton of this whale that now stands in the entrance hall of the Museum of Natural History, South Kensington.

He says : ' Professor Owen has the honour to
report to the Trustees that, having heard of the
stranding of a whale on the coast of Caithness,
upon the estate of Captain Macdonald, near
Thurso, he wrote to that gentleman, who in
reply stated that, if Professor Owen would inspect
the specimen and superintend or give directions
for the preparation of the bones, he might have
them at his own valuation.

' Professor Owen, after conferring on the
subject with the Duke of Northumberland and
Sir Roderick Murchison, proceeded to Thurso,
inspected the whale, which proved to be a fullgrown female cachalot (*Physeter macrocephalus*),
and, after ascertaining the probable cost of cleaning, preparing, and packing the bones, offered the
sum of 30*l.* for them, which was accepted by
Captain Macdonald.   Part of one paddle was lost,
and the jaw was fractured, and some teeth of the
lower jaw were missing, but in other respects the
skeleton was more complete than is usual with
those of full-sized whales.   Its length was sixty
feet.   After forming the nearest estimate of the
specimen which circumstances would permit, Professor Owen engaged the services of an intelligent
carpenter, to assist in the examination and dissection of the whale, and confided to him, with
written instructions, the cleaning, bleaching, and
packing of the bones.   Professor Owen believes
that the bones of the cachalot will be received in

London at a cost not exceeding 80l., covering all expenses. There is no skeleton of this species in the Museum, and he requests the sanction of the Trustees for the steps he has taken to acquire it for the department of Zoology.'

There is added as a postscript :—

'On his return to the Museum, Professor Owen has found a letter from Captain Macdonald, liberally offering to present the bones to the Museum under certain conditions. In acknowledging this letter, Professor Owen has begged leave to omit the reference to himself in the proposed inscription [of the whale], inasmuch as he had simply performed his duty as an officer of the Trustees in regard to the specimen.'

In various quarters of the globe Owen had friends who were working to enrich the natural history collection under his charge. He received, in this and the following year, valuable specimens, which were sent him from Africa. The first collection was sent by Dr. John Kirk, Livingstone's companion and fellow-traveller; the second by M. Du Chaillu.

In December 1863 Dr. Kirk wrote the following letter to Professor Owen with regard to the specimens which he was sending :—

'After our last interview the African fever again returned, and haunted me, coming on at the most awkward times when in company, and forcing me to retire to bed. . . . I have been to-day at

Kew and packed up a case of birds' skins, which
will be sent off to-morrow addressed to you at
the Museum, that you may take whatever is of
interest from among them. . . . Among the birds
you will find, I fear, little new.   The ornithology
seems to differ little from that of the West Coast
and contains very many South African species [a
long list of names follows]; one species of duck
is wanting, the specimens having been destroyed
by insects before leaving the Zambesi while I
was away with Dr. Livingstone on one of the
land journeys.

'The only specimens I have got of a small
agapornis were stolen along with my baggage at
Lake Nyassa, by the treacherous natives of that
part, who nearly had our scalps as specimens to
adorn the trees which constitute their Zoological
Gardens, or to form part of some powerful fetish
to be worn by their headmen.

'Still, the collection will give some idea of what
kinds inhabit these parts.

'There is one bird, a corythaix, which Dr.
L. and I found on our first trip among the
Mangunja Hills, one of the handsomest in the
country, and very local in its distribution.   Even
the common birds will be of interest to me when
determined, as giving the native names some
degree of interest. . . . I shall only be too glad
to go over them and give any details I may know.
Those that are not of any value to the Museum

I shall be glad of as a means of thanking Mr. Young, whose kindness to the expedition throughout has been very great. Among the skins is one of a young crocodile, and it will be followed by two more young ones preserved in spirit. I find many things sadly injured from wet; they lay at Mozambique, having been left to take their chance after they had gone out of my hands. I learn from the owners that the vessel in which I expected the remainder of the specimens of 1862 and 1863 will be here in January or February.'

The other specimens came from M. Du Chaillu. The French hunter, on his first visit to England, was severely if not rancorously attacked by certain persons in London, who refused to believe the story of his travels, and even went so far as to deny that he had ever seen a live gorilla. Though Owen, Murchison, and most of the leading scientific men stood staunchly by him, it was impossible that Du Chaillu, a young man and a foreigner, should not feel their taunts keenly. As the best means of proving his own veracity, he, in 1864, returned to the Gaboon, and in due course sent to England a fresh consignment of dead gorillas and one living one, which only survived a short time.

In October 1864, Sir Roderick Murchison wrote Professor Owen the following letter from Torquay with regard to M. Du Chaillu:—

'. . . I have had a charming letter from Du

Chaillu. It is so good, so superior to his earlier letters, so full of fire, noble, and self-sacrificing resolution, that I shall read it as our opening *morceau* at the Geographical, November 12.

'He tells me he has sent to the British Museum many insects, butterflies, &c., &c., and twenty gorillas, and a live one for the Zoological. You have probably heard too. He was just going off into the vast interior with a stout heart and in good spirits at having been replenished with his scientific instruments.

'Never were we more in the right than when we stood up for this fine little fellow.'

A few weeks later, arrived some African articles from M. Du Chaillu for Owen himself. These consisted of a number of mats, a piece of native cloth, a drum, and a kind of harp, 'a well-made but primitive instrument. The piece of skin which is stretched over the wood-work is an elephant's ear.'

With such incessant work on his hands, Owen would have been more than human if he had altogether escaped illness. At the close of 1863 —on December 28—he writes to Mr. White Cooper : 'For a wonder (and I can't be sufficiently thankful for having been free so many years), I am tied to my house by sciatica in the left limb, which keeps me awake half the night. . . . Poor Thackeray's departure was a sorrowful shock to me ; I had been greeted by him only the Friday previously at the club.'

The sciatica seems, however, to have soon yielded to treatment. Within a few weeks he was again on his travels. Towards the end of January 1864 he paid a visit to the South of France, to the Vicomte de Lastic at Salette, to report upon a collection of human remains associated with flint implements and bones of Mammalia found in the caverns of that district. 'I was met at the station,' he writes to his wife, January 21, 1864, 'at 5 P.M. by the Vicomte, and have had a most kind reception. Found a blazing wood fire in my dressing-room (for all was hard frost this morning when I got out at Périgueux and began my day's journey); the last forty miles through mountain scenery like that we passed through in our Highland trip—very beautiful. At Paris I spent some hours in the Jardin d'Acclimatation, arriving at 7.30 A.M., and quitting the same hour the same evening. . . .'

'*February* 5.—This is a charming family, the representative *débris* of one of the old seignorial lords of the country. . . . an old château, hid in a valley alongside the river Aveyron, with hills and precipices on each side. An old coach, and coachman, and pair of black horses with long manes and tails, just as figured in old books. No neighbours.'

In view of this expedition, Owen only gave three lectures (on Fishes) at the Royal Institution, as Fullerian Professor, before starting for France.

These lectures were delivered on January 4, 11, and 18.

To secure the safe arrival of the collection a second visit to France was necessary. On February 13, 1864, he writes to his sister Eliza : 'The Trustees have bought the whole of the Vicomte de Lastic's collection, and *I must go*, with a professional packer from Paris, to superintend the packing . . . The Emperor sent a commissioner to see and report on the collection the day after I left Salette, but I have been too quick for him.'

'This time,' Owen writes to his wife (February 19), 'we had a frightful passage, being detained for a long time off Calais in a dense fog. I arrived at the Vicomte de Lastic's feeling desperately queer, but nothing could be kinder than my nurses here. I have been able to superintend the packing (February 2?), and all will go off to London to-morrow. . . . My dear old *femme de chambre* seems to have slept by snatches of fifteen minutes during the last few days and nights, for I think she has not left me longer out of her sight day or night, and our colloquies have been of the most comical description.'

In March and April 1864 Owen had the honour of lecturing before the Queen and royal children at Windsor Castle in the White Drawing-room. There being no conveniences for the display of diagrams, the Professor utilised a high-backed chair as an easel and illustrated his lecture

by Wolf's coloured drawings of animals. His
audience on March 29 included the Queen,
the Princesses Helena and Louise, and Princes
Arthur and Leopold; and that of a later lecture,
the King of the Belgians. Of this later lecture,
Owen has left an account in a letter to his sister
Maria, April 5, 1864 :—

'I was much interested in seeing the good old
King of the Belgians walk in ; he bears his height
well.   Both he and the Queen honoured me with
a long conversation after my lecture, asking many
questions. The Queen told me they were plagued
with toads at Osborne, and that they had the
spawn destroyed whenever it could be found near
the house.   Her Majesty wrote to ask me to give
the lecture yesterday at one, instead of three, as
" she should have visitors at that hour."   I
reached the Castle a little after twelve, and got my
diagrams on two large *clothes-horses*, which were
brought into the grand drawing-room assigned for
the purpose.   As the luncheon hour is two, I
made my lecture short, and this left more time
for the conversations and questions, about dogs,
and the gorilla, and M. Du Chaillu, and whether
babes had ever been brought up by wolves, and
if such children could speak, and a very amusing
variety of chat ; old King Leopold asking many
thoughtful questions suggested by the lecture.
The Dean of Windsor (Gerald Wellesley), who
was present with all the Court, and Highnesses,

both Serene and Royal, "had no idea before
that the frog was ever a tadpole!" or that the
tadpole turned into a frog! I had described
the chief part of the metamorphoses. After
their Majesties' departure there is of course much
chat with the lords and ladies in waiting. Her
Majesty sent to ask if I would see "Beatrice"
after luncheon, and accordingly about a quarter to
three I was conducted from the Lords in Waiting's
luncheon table, by an usher, to a long gallery,
with oriel windows and beautiful paintings. The
lady in special charge of little Beatrice led me
some way along the gallery, where a short distance further we came upon Lord Russell, and
I had a very cordial greeting from my neighbour in Richmond Park. Then we went on a
little further, and again stopped, and I could see
the Queen and King Leopold walking arm-
in-arm along the further end of the gallery,
which is in a curve, and coming towards us; we
stopped in the embrasure or oriel till they had
turned back, and then crossed the gallery and
out of a door which led along the passage to
the Princess Beatrice's room. She has beautiful long sandy golden hair, hanging wavy down
her back. She will be eight years old on the
14th of April. We went to the lecture-room,
and I told her stories about the animals in the
diagrams for about half an hour. She is considered too young to come in to the lectures

Lord Russell and I returned by the same train home.'

In June Owen read a paper at the Royal Society ' On the Cavern of Bruniquel and its Human Remains.' Writing to his sisters on the subject of these remains, he says : ' The case contained skulls and other bones of the men who made flint tools, and by means of these made weapons and implements out of the bones and horns of the deer and oxen they killed and ate. The deer were reindeer, the oxen a gigantic extinct kind which we call *Bos primigenius*. Of the flint and bone implements there are thousands, all got out of the cave, which must have been inhabited for generations by this primæval race of men. They even made needles of bone, so perfect you might hem with them.'

Some years previously Professor Owen had delivered a lecture to the Young Men's Christian Association at Exeter Hall ' On some Instances of the Power of God as manifested in His Animal Creation.' Certain statements in this lecture apparently gave offence to the Committee of Publication, for its publication was cancelled. It appeared, however, this year (1864) as ' Instances of the Power of God, &c.,' 12mo.

Professor Owen defended himself in a lecture given at Leeds, in which he says : ' If the letter killeth and the spirit giveth life, . . . how deeply ought we to be concerned in more fully and clearly delivering the religious truths which we accept and reverence as teaching us the things *essential* to eternal life!

'Those who contend that such vital truths rest essentially on the basis of the literal and verbal accuracy and acceptability of every physical proposition in the Pentateuch, hazard much, and incur grave responsibilities.

'When the canonical statement and the scientific demonstration do concur, who rejoices more than the Christian philosopher? When they do not, and the opposing statements are irreconcilable, who is more bound than the Christian philosopher to deliver the truth and declare the error, and fling from him the sophism by which the error is salved or veiled, that it may still be reverently cherished, notwithstanding the admitted demonstration of its erroneous nature? For such demonstrations are not to be confounded, as they have been by those against whose prepossessions they jar, with the speculative philosophies condemned by the Apostle. Nothing can be further from the uniform experience of the temperament and character of great inductive discoverers than to ascribe the results of their patient and laborious research to arrogant and wilful intellect soaring to regions of forbidden mysteries. For the most part the discoverer has been so placed by circumstances as to have his work of investigation allotted to him as his daily duty, in the fulfilment of which he is brought face to face with phenomena into which he must inquire, and the results faithfully impart—acting, in all this, as the servant of his Master, and with the sense of responsibility for the use of the talents allotted to him. " So man," in the noble and eloquent language of the revered and lamented Prince Consort, " is approaching a more complete fulfilment of that great and sacred mission which he has to perform in this world. His reason being created after the image of God, he has to use it to discover the laws by which the Almighty governs His creation, and by making those laws the standard of action to conquer Nature to his use : himself a Divine instrument."'

Owen spent his holiday at Swansea, and took the opportunity of inspecting the museum there. ' It has a fine collection of local fossils,' he says, ' but a ridiculous looking stuffed wild boar leaning against the wall in a most maudlin attitude.'

On October 3 he started for Birmingham, where he gave a short course of lectures, and then proceeded to Leamington. Writing to his sisters on October 26, he says :—-

' I am writing in a bedroom, looking into one of the large squares of this pretty town. I am staying with a friend who was an influential member of the Philosophical Society of Leeds when I opened their new buildings. He now lives at Leamington, and came over to my lectures at Birmingham, of which I delivered the last on

Monday evening. I was then the guest of an old Bartholomew's friend. On Tuesday I left Birmingham to meet by appointment the Council of the Philosophical Society there at the museum. Inspected that, and the beautiful church ; then to the Castle. Much interested in all I saw. To-day I see Kenilworth, to-morrow home.'

On December 1 Owen had two strange visitors at the British Museum—'General' and Mrs. Tom Thumb. They called upon him in great state, and were shown up to the Professor's room by the hall-porter. In going over the Museum, Mrs. Tom Thumb, it seems, hung her head, as if not liking to be looked at by the people there, but the 'General' was quite self-possessed, and looked at the different things in an observant way, beguiling the time with conversation about his visit to the Prince of Wales.

'I had a pleasant gossip,' says Owen to his sister Eliza (December 6, 1864), ' with the Dean of Westminster last evening, who sat next to me at the "Literary Club," about the weddings at Alderley, and the Holy Land, and the extra verse in the Cambridge copy of the Greek MS. of the N. T., and about the Davenport Yankee Brothers and conjurors in general, and the geology of Westminster. My other neighbour, the Under-Secretary of State for India confessed to having paid his guinea and been banged by the guitars, &c.[5]

[5] At one of the spiritualistic *séances* of the Davenport Brothers.

Other members present were—Mr. Walpole (in the chair), Judge Erle, Dr. Travers Twiss, Dr. Southey (interesting to look at such a representative of the poet, now old and drooping), the Editor of the " Edinburgh Review," Richmond the painter, Newton the discoverer of the Mausoleum. The old Bishop of Lichfield sent his resignation : had been a member since 1824. . . . We like our clergyman much ; and his curate, who preached his first sermon at our little iron church, I also like, and am glad we are so well provided in spirituals. The vicar has organised evenings for amusing his poorer parishioners by " Readings," to give which gentlemen volunteer. I have consented for Monday, 19th, and have chosen some quiet chapters from Galt's "Annals of the Parish " to begin with. I may give a bit of Milton or of Tennyson before I have done with them.'

CHAPTER VI

1865-68

ON January 28, 1865, Owen writes to his
sisters :—

'We have now a Siberian landscape from
the Cottage, very bright and beautiful though.
. . . I was tempted by an invitation from a
railway millionaire on Wednesday to Chipstead
Place, a fine old manor house once owned by a
son-in-law of Oliver Cromwell, full of wainscoted
rooms and a very fine library full of choicest
editions—all the 4to plays of Shakespeare, a first
edition of the folio, &c. On Thursday drove to
Penshurst Place, where I saw all the relics of Sir
Philip Sidney : the card table which Queen Elizabeth had worked for him, the pair of glass chan-
deliers which she presented to the ballroom after
her "progress" to Penshurst, and a most quaint

painting of Queen Elizabeth and the Earl of
Leicester dancing a saraband. . . .'

On March 4 he tells his sisters to get their
'migratory plumage into proper order for the end of
April. Large parties,' he continues, 'are already
going on. On Tuesday Mr. Gladstone's rooms were
crowded. I looked in there after dining with " The
Club," and heard a chorus and a tenor solo ; it was
a musical evening. I glanced at my watch to save
the midnight train, and meanwhile had got so
jammed up into a corner of a far sofa that it
required an exertion to drag myself between the
gilt legs of a heavy table and the green velvet
folds of the ample garment of the middle-aged
lady with whom I had been talking. Lady Walde-
grave's " early evenings " similarly crowded.' De
scribing a dinner at the Comte de Paris' he says :
' The bride of the Comte de Paris is beautiful ; the
wife of the Comte d'Eu looks old, with eyes of
a wearied expression. He is handsomer than his
cousin, and will be Emperor of Brazil ; the other
may be King of the French. The portraits of
the Duke and Duchess d'Orléans, of the ex-
Queen and King of the French, are full of inte·
rest ; the furniture in the large drawing-room at
York House is that worked by the ladies of Paris
for the youthful pair—glorious flower-groups on
cream-coloured silk or satin ! I wish I knew the
French dame who sailed me in to dinner ! There
I tasted for the first time " bustard " in a pie, like

a Yorkshire one, which had been sent to them by the Queen of Spain from Madrid ; it was of a snipey flavour, very good.'

On April 13, 1865, he writes to his sister Maria, in anticipation of the coming visit from his sisters : 'We have now a lovely bed of hyacinths out, and the adjoining tulip-bed is beginning to show colour. The horse chestnut leaves are unfolding, but it is unseasonably dry. The orchard-house shows a glorious blaze of blossom, with the bees busily humming, and the warmth giving quite a midsummer character to the interior. The wild hyacinths, arums, &c., I brought last year from Norfolk are all springing up or in flower. I think you will find the garden this year quite up to the mark.'

In a brief scrap of a note to his wife in May 1865 Owen refers to the extraordinary applications which he was constantly receiving from persons who seemed to think that they had merely to apply to him, and he, by some mysterious arts, would immediately obtain for them their request, however wild and extravagant it might be :—

'Among my letters this morning,' he says, ' I have one asking for a royal living (vicarage, &c.), another for a lieutenant-colonelcy ! ! '

In another amusing letter to his wife Owen relates an incident which occurred this year in a certain small town in Suffolk in which he was lecturing. After saying that the inhabitants seemed to derive some occult pleasure out of his lecture 'On Birds generally, and Dinornis specially,' he continues : ' Just before going in, the beadle came with Mr. Mayor's compliments, and he was very sorry he could not take the chair, as his wife had died that afternoon, and would I be so good as to let his daughter have my autograph? Fact !! I gravely wrote it and gave it, with due condolences, and walked on to the platform.'

In 1865 Livingstone was again in England, and from an entry in Mrs. Owen's diary we find him on May 14 one of a large party of friends at Sheen Lodge. 'There came Dr. Livingstone and his daughter, now grown up, and going on with her father to Paris; Charles Hallé and his two eldest daughters, Dr. Becker, &c., &c. Hallé played several times during the evening. Dr. Becker took away with him the long-guarded cast of Shakespeare's face.'

'*July* 4.—R. lunched at the Deanery, Westminster, to meet the Queen of the Netherlands, who talked a good deal on scientific matters, and knows something of the subject. Tennyson and Max Müller were also there.'

'*July* 12.—To Nuneham Park (Mrs. V. Harcourt). Travelled down with Lady Houghton and her daughter, who were also going there. The election prevented many from coming. The next day we made up a party to go to Oxford, consisting of Lord and Lady Houghton and their daughter, aged thirteen, R. and myself, and one or two others. After seeing the College gardens, in full bloom, called on Sir Benjamin Brodie. Returned that evening to Richmond Park, found Mr. John Ella[1] there, who stayed for a day or two. He played all the evening, while we had the large telescope out on the verandah and looked at Jupiter. Next morning Professor Babbage came. He sent in a curious bit of metal, like a cogwheel, with his name in red on it, and the words, " No cards." Believe it is a bit of his calculating machine.'

Owen spent part of his August holiday in Scotland. He writes to his sister, in a letter dated August 5, care of J. Fowler, Esq., Inverbroun Lodge, by Dingwall, Ross-shire, N.B. : ' If you glance at a map of Scotland you will see the west coast, opposite the Isle of Skye, indented with deep inland bays. One of these forms the large lake I look out upon as I raise my eyes from the paper to the window. It is enclosed by mountains, the furthest shutting out the sea, and bathed in the deep pearly blue light that poor Robson knew so well how to render. Yesterday our drive took us to rocky chasms, waterfalls, and mountain " tarns," the road in part like those Swiss roads on the edge of a precipice, but safe enough with the steady horses ; though, by the way, when we got

[1] Of the Musical Union.

to the high ground, the gnats stung them almost
to unmanageableness.'

On August 30 he writes to tell his sisters that
he is back home again and ready for work at the
Museum. But he miscalculated his strength and
powers of endurance during his Highland tour, as
will be seen from a letter written to his friend
White Cooper :—

'You know that my wife and I spent August
among the mountains of Ross and Inverness.
There I stalked with the stalkers, and walked or
scrambled with the grouse and ptarmigan-shooters,
and even waded the salmon streams, rejoicing in
my well-conserved vigour, outlasting younger
men. Foolish philosopher! to think of doing at
sixty the feats of fifty or forty. Since our return
home I have become affected with loss of muscular
power—my arms more feeble than my legs. I've
not long been able to hold a pen, and have made,
I see, a shameful blot by mismanaging the ink-
stand.'

Soon after his Highland holiday he wrote to
Alfred Tennyson to ask the 'quantity' of the word
'embryonic.' He received the following reply
from Faringford :—

'My dear Owen,—I suppose when you say
"quantity," like most English people, you mean
accent. "Embryónic" would be the accent,
though the syllable is a short one—embryŏnic,
not embryōnic. As for "embryonal," I never

heard of such a word, but if there be such, it may
be a moot point whether you laid the accent on
the first syllable or on the one before the last ; for
there is a word " émbryonate " (being in the state
of an embryo), which I find accented on the first.
" Embrýonal " would be certainly wrong ; but except you really want the two words for some
scientific distinction, it would be better to stick to
" embryónic."

   ' I and my wife too are grieved to hear that
you have overtasked your muscular powers in
your Highland holiday. Pray, for your own and
your friends' sake, obey your doctors (you can
scarce have a better or a kindlier than Paget), and
cease to work for awhile that you may work better
hereafter. We cannot afford to lose your brains
—not at least till all our lizards are dug out, and
this stretch of red cliff which I see from my attic
windows no longer needs such an interpreter.

' Believe me,
' Ever truly yours,
' A. TENNYSON.'

On October 18 Owen writes to his sisters :
' My doctors—Paget and Farre—were with us,
dining on Sunday, and considered me convalescent.
I have had no particular ailment, but a general
loss of muscular power, rather more in my arms
than legs, with loss of appetite. This has come
back, and so, I trust, shortly all my old strength.

As for giving up work, poor creatures of habit and circumstances as we are!   Not while I can do it and it comes in my way—at all events, in finishing what I've made good progress in.   Ask Pearson [2] [Langshaw] if he thinks it likely!'

THE DODO. $\frac{1}{9}$ natural size

In October 1865 Owen received a parcel of bones of the dodo, through the Bishop of Mauritius, and in acknowledging these important remains he says :—

'Through your kind offices my eyes have at length been gladdened by the sight of the bones

[2] His Lancaster friend.

of the dodo. Mr. George Clark's second parcel
has been brought to me, and, having completed
the first comparisons and rough determinations
of their nature, I lose no time in acknowledging
and replying to your most acceptable letter.
Mr. Clark's collection includes most of the bones
of the skeleton and all those of importance for
testing the hypotheses of the affinities and place
in nature of this most strange and extinct bird,
the *Didus ineptus* of Linnæus. Besides bones
of the dodo, there are a few referable to a small
beast and a large tortoise.

'The dodo's bones belong to five or six
different individuals; the toe bones are wanting,
. . . and now, having gratified my long-felt
yearnings to know more of *Didus*, I find those
with regard to *Æpyornis* growing stronger.
Madagascar marshes and turbaries may yield
similar evidences of this gigantic extinct bird.
After the aye-aye the *Æpyornis* is the main
desideratum from that island for zoology. . . .
Thank you again for all the kind and valuable
interest you have taken in this matter.'

Respecting this parcel of dodo's bones, Owen
writes to his sister: 'The dodo I owe mainly
to the Bishop of Mauritius: it was found—its
bones to wit—in a morass by one of the diocesan
schoolmasters, for whom I hope to get 100*l*.
I have been working in the day and dreaming at
night about my Xmas bird for a fortnight past.

It proves to be a great ground pigeon, grown too big to fly, and so let its wings go to waste.'

The last fortnight of November was occupied in a course of lectures delivered before the Literary and Philosophical Society of Hull. Here, and elsewhere, Owen experienced the great interest which he was able to excite in the subject of his lectures, and he felt that the opportunity only was wanting to arouse the same intelligent interest among artisans. With this object, and also in the hope of supplying profitable occupation for their idle moments, he desired to organise a course of Sunday lectures for the working classes. In this scheme, which he had deeply at heart, Charles Dickens warmly sympathised.

But apparently the working man first thought he would like them, then thought he would not, and finally was not at all clear as to what he did like or want. The two following letters from Dickens were received on the subject :—

Saturday, November 4, 1865.

'My dear Owen,—Is it quite settled and resolved on that you begin the Sunday lectures for the Sunday League? Because if it be, I will certainly follow so noble a leader, and give them a Sunday reading. One word in answer will be sufficient.

'Ever faithfully yours,
'CHARLES DICKENS.'

After the lapse of a month came the second letter :—

Sunday, December 6, 1865.

' My dear Owen,—I have sent the Secretary of the Sunday League a letter, of which I enclose you a copy. It is clear to me that they are wrong in their facts, and that the time is not ripe for the proposed lectures. They *cannot* get working men together in sufficient force to declare their desire for that Sunday recreation. On the other hand, their opponents can (and do) get working men together in sufficient force to put them down, and declare that they don't want it.

' Ever cordially yours,

' C. D.'

Amongst the papers written by Owen which appeared in 1865 the following may be mentioned : ' On the Homology of the Tooth ' (' Archives of Dentistry,' vol. i. p. 309) ; ' On the Marsupial Pouches, Mammary Glands, and Fœtus of the *Echidna hystrix* ' (' Phil. Trans.') ; ' On Indian Cetacea' (' Zool. Trans.').

In society he found his relaxation, and he enjoyed to the full the pleasures of social life. Mrs. Owen's diary is full of such entries as the following :—

' *January* 5, 1866.—R. and I dined at Pembroke Lodge ; sat next to Lord Russell, with whom I always get on well. After dinner he took

" Punch " off the table, and showed me a caricature of himself with a baby in his arms, and John Bright as clown pulling it away ; but he said he did not think the likeness as good as usual. He was much amused with an anecdote which I told him about R., who was coming down from town one day, and bought " Punch " at the station, with his lordship figuring in it in some ridiculous way. When he got into the train he did not notice the other occupant of the carriage, who had got in just before him, and was beginning to laugh loudly over the picture, when, on lifting his eyes from the page, he was suddenly petrified to see the original of the sketch sitting opposite. He hastily crammed " Punch " into his pocket, but was in another moment relieved, and much amused to see Lord R. produce a copy out of his own pocket, and read it with much apparent enjoyment.'

'*January* 15.—R. went to dine at the Garrick Club. Many old friends there—Mr. John Murray, M. Du Chaillu, Mr. Pentland, &c. Our bust of Shakespeare, which was bought by the Duke of Devonshire, and presented to the Club, looked very well.'

Other references to his wide circle of friends constantly occur in his letters. Thus, in January 1866, he went with Mr. Fowler to the Isle of Wight, where he visited Alfred Tennyson. On the 21st he writes to his wife from St.

Lawrence : ' Mr. F[owler] and I return to London to-morrow. Mrs. Tennyson sends her best love to you. . . . My host and hostess were charmed with their reception at Faringford ; we were there from 1 to 3 P.M. The poet is very well ; we had fair weather for our drive, and I had half an hour to look over the Rev. Mr. Fox's fossils [3] at Brixton *en route*.'

Writing to his sister Eliza on February 14, 1866, he says : ' I have just returned from The Club. . . . I sat next the Premier and opposite the Lord Chancellor. The Duke of Argyll was in the chair, supported by the Duc d'Aumale and the Dean of Westminster ; then Lord Stanley, Earl Stanhope, Lord Kingsdown, Sir H. Holland, Froude, Dean Milman, Mr. Stirling, Sir Edward Head, Spencer Walpole, and the Editor of the " Edinburgh Review " (Reeve) completed the party. . . . There are two vacancies, and Sir Hugh Cairns and a Mr. Twiselton—a wonderful Hebrew scholar—are proposed. Wonderful French *bons mots* were passed across our end of the table between the Duc d'Aumale and Lord Stanhope ; Lord Russell and I talked about our gardens, primroses, male aucubas, and new things from Japan. We all had pancakes ! according to custom. I've a whole holiday to-morrow.'

[3] Mr. Fox discovered the *Poikilopleuron* and other interesting fossil Dinosaurs.

The last two sentences of this letter read more like those of a boy at school than of a busy man of sixty-two, and serve to illustrate the wonderful spirits which Owen enjoyed throughout his life.

'Poor Whewell,' he writes to his sister Maria on February 27, 1866, 'is reported rather more favourably of in this morning's "Times;" but it is not a very hopeful case. I think it not unlikely that he had a kind of stroke while on his horse, and so startled the animal before he fell. There will be expectancies now raised that were kept in abeyance through belief in the long-aged constitution of the strong-looking man.' A few days afterwards Whewell passed away, and by his death Owen lost a school-fellow and an old and lifelong friend.

Owen thus writes to a correspondent in Germany who is desirous of translating his 'Palæontology' into German (March 16, 1866):—

'I have communicated your request to Messrs. Black, who have the copyright of my "Palæontology," and have this morning heard from them. They have no objections to the translation of the work into German, and I shall have pleasure in its being undertaken by so devoted a zoologist and palæontologist as yourself. Whatever additions you may think fit to make will receive my best attention in relation to a third edition of the English issue, which may shortly be called for. The organic character of Eozoön[1] is still contested by some of our experienced names ; but not conclusively, to my mind.

Now and again a touch of pardonable pride at the verification of his discoveries crops out in his letters. Writing to his sisters in April 1866, he says :—

'To-night I preside at the Royal Academy of Arts, when a paper is read on Cattle Disease, including that singular form occasioned by my wee worm *Trichina spiralis*, which some of my friends are at length obliged to own that I did discover.'

With his friend Mr. (now Sir John) Fowler, who was President of the Institution, he dined with the Civil Engineers. To his sister Maria he sends, on May 16, 1866, an account of the banquet : 'After the great dinner H.R.H. Prince of Wales sent to ask me to come to him in the smoking-room, where a select party were gathered for more social chat than the formal banquet and its speech-making

---

[1] 'Eozoön' is a singular structure discovered by Logan and Dawson in the Laurentian Rocks of Canada, which was said to be Protozoan, and supposed to represent the earliest form of life preserved on this planet. The history of this structure may be found in King and Rowney, *An Old Chapter* of the *Geological Record*, 1881. The mineral nature of 'Eozoön' was, however, strongly insisted upon by King, Rowney, Moebius, and others, and the recent researches of Gregory and Johnston-Lavis upon the lavas of Vesuvius have practically demonstrated its inorganic nature.

allowed. His Royal Highness, after alluding to
the pleasure he had in my lectures at Buckingham
Palace, and to the cosy little dinner-parties at the
White Lodge, chiefly chatted about the interest
of his sport in Germany, stalking and shooting
bustards, and whether they could be got back into
Norfolk, &c. At the dinner I sat opposite Prince
Alfred, and had some conversation with His Royal
Highness there, as well as after in the smoking-
room. There were gathered the Duke of Buc-
cleuch, Lord Caithness, Lord Stanley, Hon. Mr.
Cowper, &c.

'The Prince of Wales's Equerry, Colonel
Teesdale, gave me a very interesting account of
his Crimean adventures, and the siege of Kars.
I walked home with Fowler, sincerely congratu-
lating him on the success of his great day. I
also had the honour of a conversation with Prince
Teck. . . . Mr. Cooper writes that "Fulmer
Place" is in the market. The owner has had
losses. I think if I had thirty or forty thousand
pounds to spare I should be tempted ; it will
bring now a good figure, being so easily reached
by the Great Western Railway.'

On August 26, 1866, he writes to his wife, who is
away from home on a holiday : ' On Monday Lord
Russell rode over here before I had returned from
the British Museum, so yesterday I went over
to Pembroke Lodge. Lord R. was out riding,
but was expected shortly, so Lady R. pressed

me to stay, and showed me her garden and pet
flowers. . . . Then the Earl arrived and we had
much talk, and he listened to all I earnestly urged
about the British Museum, and promised to do
his best next year : in the middle of which, bang!
went a gun, close to the drawing-room window.
Lord R. rushed to the window, past which
the smoke was drifting. It was Willie (Lord
Russell's son) who had shot a rabbit. He brought
it to the window to show his father in triumph.
" Take it to the cook, boy, take it to the cook,"
said the noble Earl testily. I walked home after
a cup of tea.'

Part of his own holiday was this year spent
at Lord Stratford de Redcliffe's. There he met,
as he tells his sister in September, Sir Henry
Storks, ' and I heard much curious and interesting
talk on Jamaica and the negroes at first hand.
Also much on the Turkish Empire and Russian
policy.'

In the autumn he resumed his work as a
lecturer. His diary records that he gave two
lectures at Bradford in October, as he had pur-
posed to do in the early part of the year. On his
return journey, he writes to his sister : ' I found
Sir J. Kay-Shuttleworth and his son in the carriage I got into, and we had some vigorous talk
en route, so much so that a gentleman seated in
the corner begged to ask to whom he was listening.
We duly enlightened him, and he told us his

name ; he was a lecturer to factory and other wage people.'

This year appeared Owen's account of the packet of bones sent him in 1865 by the Bishop of Mauritius : ' Memoirs on the Dodo,' 4to ; ' Evidence of a large Parrot contemporary of the Dodo (*Psittacus mauritianus*)' (' Trans. Zool. Soc.') ; ' The Anatomy of the Aye-Aye ' (' Trans. Zool. Soc.,' vol. v. p. 33) ; and last, but not least, Parts IX., X., XI., and XII. ' On Dinornis,' which appeared in ' Trans. Zool. Soc.,' vols. v. and vi.

In January 1867 Professor Owen wrote and received many letters on the subject of the marriage of his only son, which took place on the 5th. To his friend Mr. White Cooper he says : ' You may be sure we bore off in triumph what I think the most tasteful of all the gifts that were contributed to what we called the " International Exhibition." For a thorough winter's morning nothing could be brighter : the whole park was frosted like a gigantic bride-cake, the sun shone at its best between eleven and twelve, and our little church, with its Xmas ornaments and painted windows, looked decked for a wedding. A charming sister of the bride, æt. sixteen, was bridesmaid. I returned to a rich and tasteful wedding breakfast at Percy Lodge, and the happy pair rode off in a shower of old shoes.'

Among those who wrote to congratulate him

on the event was Charles Dickens. 'I must write,' says the novelist, 'the word of congratulation to you all on the interesting intelligence you give me. Your delight in it has delighted me, and I cannot too cordially assure you of my heartfelt sympathy. . . .'

To a correspondent who asked for information regarding the Siamese twins, Professor Owen replied in a letter dated March 27, 1867 : 'I made, at the request of the late Sir Astley Cooper, a minute examination of the connecting band of the Siamese twins in 1835, in relation to a possible and safe severance, but . . . it was evident that the operation would have been attended with imminent danger of peritonitis and death of probably both, unless, as suggested, a long continual compression of the under part of the band had obliterated the part of the peritoneal cavity there situated. To this the youths and their guardian objected. The firm elastic part of the connecting band was formed by a continuation, not of the sternum (breast-bone), but of the xiphoid cartilage below it from one individual to that of the other.'

Writing to his sister on April 12, 1867, Professor Owen says :—

'Yesterday I went to a big dinner at Fishmongers' Hall, where Mr. Fowler, as President of Institute of Civil Engineers, had been invited. And lo! the toastmaster came to charge me with the duty of proposing the health of the " Prime Warden "

in the chair!   I can generally manage a "return"
for the Royal Society and Science, &c., but this
was a new departure. . . . Not long ago I met at
a dinner at Lord Leven's, Dhuleep Singh and his
wife, who was in grand Oriental costume.   The
Maharajah is intelligent, and talked much to me
on the subject of fossils.   The Maharanee is deci-
dedly pretty.'

In the early spring of this year Owen gave
the inaugural lecture of a literary and scientific
society at Hampstead, 'Wayside Gatherings and
their Teachings.' This lecture was afterwards
printed in the July number of the 'Gentleman's
Magazine,' 1867.   Extracts from it are subjoined,
as they may serve to show Owen's power of
extempore lecturing and of investing the commonest objects with interest and attraction.   'I
looked forward,' he begins, 'to leisure for some
preparation (for this lecture), but one pressing call
for work followed another until, being immersed
in the additional labours which this season entails
of annual summaries, stock-taking, and reports on
the year's increase to our vast and ever-growing
national Departments of Natural History, I found
myself suddenly driven so closely to the appointed
evening that I had no other resource but to
throw myself on your indulgence for such unpre-
meditated remarks as might be suggested by a
few common objects of natural history which I
hastily gathered together on my way, and have

brought for the occasion. And now that I am here launched into my course with this unpromising cargo, it strikes me—and I am encouraged by the thought—that it will be an advantage to younger members of a local association for the mind's improvement to see how independent they may be of rare, strange, or exotic products of Nature for subjects of thought and means of expanding their knowledge of her laws and operations.

'I proceed, therefore, to empty my bag of the specimens I put into it that lay nearest at hand when I left home on my present mission. They are, in fact, such common objects as lie about my dwelling, or may be picked up on the roadside along which I pass daily in Richmond Park to my work in London.

'First I set before you these handfuls of dead leaves. These withered glories of the summer, their fall in the sere and yellow state of autumn, are symbolic. There are vivid and noisy pleasures ; there are those also of the quiet kind, and not the less pleasing, even perhaps more cherished in memory, when tinctured with some sadness : and in such a mood have I watched, on a still, calm day in latter autumn, when no breath of wind was stirring, the leaves settling straight down in silent tremulous fall, "one after one," suggesting and recalling the friends and loved ones that had successively and peacefully passed away out of my life. . . .'

The Professor then proceeds to discuss the question, ' Do Leaves fall in Autumn because they Die ? ' and when that question is concluded he dips again into his bag and brings out a series of deers' horns. ' In Richmond Park,' he continues, ' we have a great quantity of deer, both red and fallow but chiefly the latter kind ; and I go out in May, when the antlers are shed, and pick up such varieties as I can find. The horns of the deer consist of pieces of bone, which grow out as processes of the skull. They are not like the horns of sheep or our ordinary cattle : they have no true horny matter about them, but are wholly bone, and are not retained or " persistent." I have selected from my gatherings of the horns of deer, which fall every year like the leaves of trees, the series I now exhibit, varying in size and character and shape. These horns, or " antlers," as they are properly called, are renewed, grow, and develop year by year as they are shed. They begin to be formed in the latter part of the month of May. At the end of August they are complete, and remain from August till May, more or less perfect. About the middle of that month they are shed. Such are the phenomena that take place annually with the fallow-deer in Richmond Park.'

Specimens of horns in their various stages of growth were then exhibited and their development explained : ' and so we discern the provision for the growth of a stronger, or better, or longer antler, year after year, till the antler acquires its perfection as a weapon of combat.

' The last series of objects,' the Professor proceeds, 'which for the present purpose I have picked up by the wayside are a number of pebbles—common wayside stones. They abound in many parts of Richmond Park, in accumulations of gravel resting upon hollows of the clay —the " London Clay " of geologists—which there forms the general substratum.

' In some of these deposits we find that the pebbles for the most part are broken, with the edges slightly rounded. In other heaps we find the pebbles are completely or smoothly rounded. Such at once suggest a resemblance to those pebbles which you may have seen on a tidal shore, worn to the same state by the incessant operation of the ebb and flow with the more violent washing of breakers and surf-waves. Are we required to believe that the rounded pebble was so created, and placed as such, where we happen to pick it up ? If not, what a series of thoughts and conjectures such a stone conjures up ! We know the cause in operation adequate to its rounding. We have seen and heard the ceaseless roll of the sea-bed moved by the surging tide. On what shore did this take place ? How was the rounded pebble transported, with its gravel bed, to its present position ? In the

N 2

first place, I have to remark that all these pebbles are composed of flint—of the same mineral substance as the dark masses which at some parts of our white coast-cliffs you may see studding, in parallel but distant rows, the face of the chalk in which they are imbedded. Our pebbles are fragments of such flints that have been more or less rolled and rounded by the action of the sea. In the gravel-heaps they are dispersed through siliceous sand—*i.e.* flint in a more comminuted state, with a small proportion of clay or loam, stained yellow or reddish by oxides of iron, as is the surface of the pebbles also for some depth. Are we to suppose that the pebble was created so stained, or that it acquired the stain by being subjected long enough to the colouring cause? I assume the latter.'

The Professor then gives an account of the 'London Clay' and some of its deposits, and concludes: 'Wherever you contemplate Nature you see renewal prepared for wearing out and passing away.

'How narrow, how selfish, how akin to Egyptian darkness of thought, seemed it then to repine that life must end—to deem of death only as an evil! Whereas, therein is the necessary stipulation for that succession which involves the purest pleasures of life—the reverential love of parents, the sweet affection for children, the closest union of hearts, as of husband and wife.

Furthermore, add the assurance that all ends not here, that powers of work are entrusted gifts, with the glorious hope of a higher sphere of action, if they have been used as intended by our beneficent Creator.'

Owen was occupied with his daily work at the British Museum until September, when he writes an account of his holiday to his wife :—

Westbrook Hey, Hemel Hempstead : September 5.

'After the British Museum on Thursday, I took the train to Boxmoor, and arrived here about five, had a cup of tea and a turn in the garden with Lord S. de Redcliffe and Mr. Motley (author of "History of Dutch Republic"), then to dress for dinner. After dinner a rubber of whist, with Lady Stanhope for partner, against Lady Sophia Macnamara and Mr. Motley ; won 1s. 6d. Next morning a long ramble and much interesting and instructive discussion with Mr. Motley. Next day a drive to Ashridge ; looked over house, pictures, and gardens, and so back to the same party at dinner. Afterwards I was positively ashamed of my winnings at *vingt-et-un !* To-day Lord Lyons comes, prior to his going as Ambassador to Paris.'

The question of the building of the Natural History Museum was at this date very far from being settled, as will be seen from the account given in the chapter devoted to the subject.

Sir Roderick Murchison wrote the following letter to Owen on the subject of an article which appeared in the ' Pall Mall Gazette : '—

Sir R. Murchison to R. Owen

November 3, 1867.

' My dear Owen,—I see by the second article signed " C." [or " O." ?] (Saturday's paper) in the " Pall Mall" that the writer is taking a line which, *if it succeeded*, would quite suit my book—viz. that the colossal Greek and Egyptian statues should be united with the old pictures of the best masters in the National Exhibition. This is just the moment to show that Nature's products can well fill the whole of the British Museum around the Great Library.

' This arrangement would be peculiarly gratifying to *Cockneydom*, provided it be decided that the Parliament will not pay for the grand extension *in situ Bloomsberiano* which would be required.

' You will best know how to deal with the suggestion of exhibiting types only.

' But whoever he is, the author seems to have his line distinctly marked out.

' When he has done his best, I hope you will try your hand.

' Yours sincerely,

' RODERICK I. MURCHISON.'

But to this letter Owen apparently never replied.

The holiday was short. In November, Professor Owen gave two lectures at Bradford, and afterwards two at Newcastle. From Bradford he wrote a long descriptive letter to his wife (November 16, 1867), extracts of which are given below :—

'. . . On Tuesday and Thursday we drove to the Lecture Hall at 8.30 each day, and got back soon after 10 ; I slept well after holding forth to large and apparently gratified audiences. To-day the members of the Philosophical Society give me a dinner. Yesterday I was driven over to see the wonderful establishment for woollen and alpaca at Saltaire. . . . I was most struck, I think, with the spectacle of the men, women, and children leaving for dinner at 12 o'clock.

' Returned to Bradford in time to dress for another public banquet, in which I had to respond to Science and Literature. From the dinner we adjourned to the great music-hall, crammed in the centre with four thousand operatives : the *haut ton* of Bradford (I was obligingly informed), male and female, were in the side boxes. Addresses were delivered by various political notabilities. I was much interested, having a good seat on the platform, near the chairman, and came in, on entering, for a round of applause. . . . On Wednesday morning I had a seat on the bench to see the Mayor administer justice in the Town Hall, for the first time. There were some civil cases, and among other indictments, school boys "had up" for stealing pigeons. The whole scene strangely recalled Sancho Panza's administration of justice in Barataria. . . . After a quiet day's rest to-morrow, I proceed to Sir William Armstrong's at Newcastle, and give at that town the same two lectures as here. . . .'

On hearing of the illness of his sister Eliza, Owen writes, December 26 :—

'Nothing could have been kinder or more prompt than (Dr.) Pearson Langshaw's reports of your symptoms. Any wish of his or yours I will fulfil at once, for I have escaped cold hitherto, though at the Museum almost daily.

'On Wednesday I made a pilgrimage to St. Gabriel's, Warwick Square, in my new and proud capacity as grandfather and godfather.'

The following letter illustrates Owen's readiness, even in the busiest moments of his life, to interest himself in those who had to make their own way in the world. It was written to a young working man who had endeavoured to educate himself in geology and was anxious for a position in the British Museum :—

'I have received your letter of January 1868, and have read with interest the essay accompanying it. The evidence of worth in both made me feel, what I have often felt before on like occasions, sorry for my inability to offer you a position in

the Geological Department of the British Museum.
Every appointment is made by the principal
Trustees, and depends as a rule upon vacancy.
It is perhaps natural that you should suppose me to
have a power or influence in such appointments
which I do not possess. . . . With regard to the
position of Science and certain statements in Holy
Writ proved by God's instruments to be incorrect,
we must remember that in those writings, truly
called sacred, there are higher truths than those of
Science, sufficing for all guidance and every need.
. . . Next as to calling names. It is well to avoid
lending the least countenance to it, even through
repeating such remarks as " They say So-and-so'
is a scoundrel." Now those who call Lyell "in-
fidel" mean by that something much worse than
scoundrel. Do the work that lies before you.
Some might add : " In whatsoever position you
have been placed, therewith be content." I don't
altogether think so. At your age the ambition to
rise above it is legitimate, indeed a duty, if you
feel your powers to rise by their legitimate exercise. . . .'

On February 3, 1868, Owen received a letter
from the Emperor of Brazil, accompanying the
official notice making him a Knight of the Order
of the Rose. Some years later the Emperor, when
in England, paid Professor Owen a visit at Sheen
Lodge.

A large part of this year was spent by Owen

in working at his papers on the great extinct birds
of New Zealand. There appeared in the ' Transactions of the Zoological Society : ' ' On Dinornis,' Parts XIII., XIV., XV. (*Aptornis* and
Notornis), XVI. (*Apteryx*, brain), and XVII.
These gigantic fossil birds had occupied Owen's
attentions since 1833, and collections of their
bones were often sent to him by his corre-
spondents. For some years it was believed that all
the bones were from different species of the same
genus, but it soon became apparent that many
different genera were represented by the imperfect
remains. Now the family of the Dinornithidæ,
as they are called, contains, according to modern
authors, many genera and numerous species.

Part II. of his researches on the dodo was
also issued this year.

To his sister Maria, writing on March 2, 1868,
Owen says : ' I lecture at Hampstead to-night.
It may be my last, but people seem very fond of
them. I, however, begin to feel sixty-four years.
I have finally settled with the Government architect on the plans for the new museum. There
remains the " passing of the bill," if it be brought
in, then the erection of the building, so that
one may look for two years before anything to
the purpose can be done.'

On April 8, 1868 : ' . . . I presided last
evening at " The Club "—Duc d'Aumale on my
right, and Lord Clarendon on the left, and a very

pleasant chatty dinner. Lord Dufferin, Sir H. Holland, Froude, &c.'

And again, May 20, 1868 : ' Last evening we had a visit which was interpreted in the village as a royal one—barouche and pair, two outriders on fine grey horses ; second barouche and pair. They brought Beresford Hope, my Lady Mildred, and four daughters. Arriving at five, they stayed till half-past seven, had tea and cake, perry and muscat wine ; and I believe thoroughly enjoyed themselves in the garden and park and over all the cottage. . . . I dined with the remnant of my old Bart.'s contemporaries—nine of us—our thirty-seventh anniversary ! on Tuesday last.'

In September 1868 Owen paid another visit to Mr. Fowler at Braemore, Ross-shire, and, writing to his wife on the 7th of the month, he says : ' Mrs. Fowler has received a few guests since I last wrote, but Sir Edwin Landseer alone now remains.' He goes on to say, in reference to his wife's feeble health, that, having received a hundred pounds from his publishers, ' if we should be moved to make a winter in milder climes, I can well devote the needful to easy journeyings to Cannes, Naples, Rome, Florence, Venice, &c., for January, February, and March. I have not been permitted to take one " stalk," or do more than agreeable walks. Always wishing you could be with us by means of a " wishing carpet " to waft you over the 400 odd miles.'

After his return home, his sister becomes again his correspondent. In November he describes an interview with the Queen of Holland :—

'Last Monday was a fine bright day, so I walked across the park to Pembroke Lodge, and at 1.30 the Queen of Holland arrived, attended by a young lady and a Dutchman with a riband in his button-hole. I was the only guest invited to meet Her Majesty, who had intended to have proceeded to Bushey to visit the Duc de Nemours, but had received a call to Windsor, so we had a long talk on divers subjects, for Her Majesty knows much both as to things and persons.'

On December 5 Owen was subpœnaed to appear on the 9th at the Court of Common Pleas, Guildhall, in the case of a vessel which claimed damages from the underwriters on account of a hole, some three inches in length, which had been bored in the side. The question was, whether the leak was made purposely or whether it was the work of a swordfish. Owen's opinion was asked as to the power of the fish to withdraw the sword after piercing the ship, which seldom happens. His evidence persuaded the jury that the leak was not an intentional act of dishonesty, as had been supposed. The hole was made by a young swordfish, and as it had only entered three inches, its sword could have been withdrawn. This would not have been the case had it entered much deeper. Frank Buckland also gave evidence to the same effect.

On December 16, 1868, Owen writes to his sister Maria : '. . . I lately attended one of our Club meetings, Marquis of Exeter in the chair. . . . It must have been a relief to Gladstone to have a quiet literary gossip without a bit of politics.'

There were present on this occasion, according to a plan of the table appended to the letter : Duke of Argyll, Lord Romilly, Grote, Holland, Walpole, Murchison, Twiselton, Reeve, Smith, Lord Stanley, Lord Dufferin, Sir David Dundas, the Lord Chancellor, and Earl Stanhope.

CHAPTER VII

1869-71

First Visit to Egypt, 1869—Lecture on the 'Scientific and Literary Results of the last Nile Expedition,' 1870—Second Visit to Egypt, 1870 71—Braemore and Carlyle, 1871—Refusal of Presidency of Geological Society—Snake-charming.

In 1869 Owen paid his first visit to Egypt. He could scarcely have made such an expedition under circumstances more favourable to sight-seeing, for, at the instance of the late Duke of Sutherland, he was invited to join the Prince of Wales's party. In communicating his plans to his sister Maria, January 3, 1869, he says : ' My medical friends have strongly urged me to pass January and February in a milder climate, and, this coming to the ears of the Duke of Sutherland, he communicated to me a gracious intimation that I should join the Prince and Princess of Wales's party to Egypt. The expedition is under the direction of Sir Samuel Baker (Nile discoverer) and Mr. Fowler, who is to inspect the Suez Canal and explain the works, and who is ordered with me to embark along with Sir Samuel in the steamer from Marseilles to

Alexandria on the 9th. . . . The Prince of
Wales, Duke of Sutherland, and their suite join
us at Cairo. . . . It is impossible to imagine
more favourable conditions for enjoying what I
have long cherished—a desire to see that wonderful old historical country.'

Owen kept an interesting record of all his
experiences during his Egyptian tour. These
notes, despatched at intervals to his wife on this
and his subsequent visits to Egypt, would of
themselves easily fill a volume ; but only a few
extracts of general interest are given here.

'On board the " Nyanza,"' he writes (January 11), ' were the Bishop of Bombay (Dr. Douglas) and His Excellency Nubar Pacha, who
promised me a practised fisherman for the Nile
and salt lakes. . . . The steamer lay to about
forty miles from Alexandria, waiting till daylight
to be piloted through the intricate passages. . . . .
Then we saw that all the Egyptian ships were
dressed out in holiday colours, and as we came
among them to the anchorage a salute was fired
from the fort and answered by the men-o'-war.
It was a most unexpected gala. Some said it
was for the arrival of Nubar Pacha, some for the
Bishop, others for the Professor. One rationalist
of the party suggested that with the new moon
the feast of Rhamadan ended this year and the
feast of Beiram began. And so it was.

'After landing, Nubar invited Mr. Fowler, Sir

S. Baker, and myself into his carriage, and off we went. Everything that now met my eye was new. White storks in the fields, great plovers, large kingfishers, and the Fellah ploughing with an ox and a dromedary, the kites and hawks hovering above, and all with explanations from the amiable Pacha of any objects of interest. While the old stave from " Bluebeard " *would* run in my head, " 'Tis a very fine thing to be father-in-law to a very magnificent, &c., &c." '

'*January* 15.—Took counsel how to see the Pyramids. Hear that the Viceroy will give us a special audience at his Levee to-morrow morning at eleven o'clock. Evening dress ! white tie !! gloves !!! (haven't any). . . .'

' 16*th*.—Received the following invitation : " Le Maître des Cérémonies, par ordre du Khédive, a l'honneur de prier M. le Professeur Owen de vouloir bien assister au bal qui sera donné au Palais de Gizereh le 18 janvier, 1869, à neuf heures du soir."

' Arrived at the Palace at 9.45 (the Viceroy had intimated that when he invited guests for nine he did not expect them at eleven). Amongst the guests, pachas, beys, civil and military officers, blazing with orders, turbaned sheiks, red-capped Turks, &c. The supper-rooms were opened soon after twelve. Now when I say everything was perfect, you will imagine the style in which it was all conducted. . . . We left about 1.30 and so got our carriage. Those who stayed later did not get home till six or seven, through difficulties with their various conveyances. Estimates of the cost of this ball, bridge included, with the illuminations in the gardens, its kiosque, grottos, &c., ranged from 20,000*l.* to 100,000*l.* !'

'21*st.*—Made an expedition, consisting of a carriage with four horses, also six donkeys and nine men, to the Desert in order to inspect the petrified forest. Drove along, escorted by donkey boys, through a very finely wooded suburb and came upon the Desert, where the Tombs of the Caliphs—mosque-like structures of the colour of the ground—rise in great number and various proportions ; then on and on over the roughest ground under difficulties—not from sand but mud, the Desert being saturated by the extraordinary rainfall and presenting exactly the appearance of the sands at Morecambe Bay. The nature of this boundless tract as an upraised sea-bed was vividly impressed upon me. Owing to the rain the scattered clumps of Desert shrubs were at their greenest, and snails of new forms to me were feeding on them. . . . As we approached the scene and object of our journey, detached bits of petrified palms were to be picked up, with odd fossil oysters and murex shells. I suppose the palms must have been floated down on some branch of the Nile when the Desert was a delta, their own natural silex attracting

that of the sea water during the long ages before
the uplifting. Acres and acres were strewed
with petrified fragments of palms of all sizes. At
the centre of the bed the trunks, many feet in
length, lay imbedded. We had two large fragments
broken off and gathered divers small specimens '

' 22nd.—This morning inspected Miss Whateley's school for native girls and the Viceroy's
school for the boys to be taught English. Some
of these repeated their lessons to us. . . .
After luncheon drove to the Viceroy's stables
and saw his stud and museum (it may be called) of
carriages. The Duke of Sutherland arrives to-
morrow.'

Amongst his other amusements, Owen describes a visit to a celebrated wizard and an examination of the 'magic crystal.'

' Time, 11 P.M. Scene, grand drawing-room
of Nubar Pacha's palace. *Dramatis personæ*, the
Duke of Sutherland, Sir Samuel Baker, Lord Staf-
ford, myself, a Nubian, a young boy and the old
Arab conjuror with his brazier sending up ever
and anon bright perfumed flames as he dropped
in pinches of incense. The charm on paper laid
upon the boy's head, beneath the turban, the
end of the half sheet overshadowing his brow
and eyes, he bends over, intently gazing upon the
magic glass. The old wizard mutters his charm.
Such a group for Phillips!—the obscure smoky
atmosphere of the room, ill-lighted by wax

candles, and fitfully illuminated by the incense-
burning brazier.

Each put his question. Being appealed to,
I said there were three people I should like to ask
about, but would take one of them, Archbishop
Manning. "What was Manning doing?" What
do you suppose was the answer? "*Nursing his
baby*"!! (quite seriously given by the boy, who
saw it, he said, in the magic glass, and gravely
translated by the beneficent Bey, who in Nubar's
absence acted as host.)

'The only good shot was a question about
the Prince of Wales, but I could see the old
impostor, muttering so that the boy might hear,
" He was neither short nor tall, was on the
sea, and had a lady with him."

' After a few very bad guesses the conjurors
were dismissed with a couple of sovereigns.'

The next day Owen visited the Suez Canal in
a small screw steamer with a little cabin.

'. . . The canal is not as broad as the
Thames at Hampton, usually with high banks
made of the stuff dredged or dug out. Occasionally we had views of the Desert on each
side. . . .'

He then gives an amusing account of the way
in which M. de Lesseps played a little trick upon
him : ' The steamer had taken us to sea, so
that we might view the piers of huge artificial
blocks of stone intended to keep open the entry

of the harbour. We then returned to inspect the artificial stone-work. M. de Lesseps with an innocent air brought me a piece of stone with some shells embedded in it and asked me what formation I thought it belonged to. I said it was the most recent I had seen, and from the fossils evidently new to geology. On the whole, I should describe it as *la formation Lessepsienne*, which pleased the old gentleman amazingly; he would have it repeated several times over before we got to our quarters. . . . Fowler and I are installed in a neat ground-floor bedroom, still as guests of the Viceroy; and I have scribbled this while waiting for my friend to go to dinner, having dressed quicker than he.'

The Professor makes notes of the fossils, &c.. which he finds, and describes all that he sees of interest until he arrives at Cairo. ' At the hotel,' he says, ' no bells, no nothing, a black Nubian boy stays all day and all night (seemingly) in one corner, and obeys the clapping of your hands to light your candles or call the waiter.'

' *February* 1.—After a dawdling breakfast the Duke drove up to our hotel, and we were driven to the Musée d'Antiquités. Here we were joined by Mariette Bey (the Director) and Hekekiah Bey, from both of whom I got a clearer notion of the dynasties and ethnology of this country than I have ever yet had.'

Owen then minutely describes the entry of

the Prince and Princess of Wales into Cairo,
with the attendant festivities, and on February 4
gives an account of the entry of the pilgrims into
the city, with rough sketches. 'Good old Hekekiah
Bey,' he adds, 'gave me two jars of fine baccy,
and also lent me a book and some maps of the
voyage.'

After the arrival of the Prince and Princess,
the voyage up the Nile was almost immediately
begun. The entry in Owen's diary for February
7 begins with ' On the Nile :'—

'After sunset and the afterglow—for here
night follows quickly and the stars seem to
assemble above in a hurry—we came to moor-
ings under a high black bank, on which we saw
many indistinct dark figures and a few pale ones
—the muffled faces of the "women in white,"
and a wonderful picture they presented. . . .
A plank was shoved off from the bank, across
which came the Duke to tempt us on shore to
see the village . . . We climbed the bank, not
until after crossing the plank, at which at first
I own to have jibbed. It crossed a deep, dark
gulf, along which the rush of the river was
heard. The Duke went first, then Fowler, and
then I put one foot on and hesitated, but with the
help of the firm hand of my friend I crossed, and
was not sorry to step on to the Nile deposit and
clamber up the bank . . . I had been wandering
by myself about the strange characteristic scene

on the banks of the Nile, which beats any
allegory, when the Duke came up and said,
"The Prince wants you to dine with them; there's
no dress, so you can 'clean yourself' in my cabin."
I dipped into a basin with about a pint of soup-
coloured water in it, and off we were again to the
bank, requiring hands and feet to climb up, and
then on to the plank leading to the royal yacht.
I had on a light summer suit, Sir S. Baker one of
whitey-brown canvas, and all the party were in
shooting or yachting costume. The Prince
talked a good deal about the White Lodge in
Richmond Park, and the Princess about the
scenes in Cairo. I asked her if she had read
Tennyson's "Haroun-al-Raschid" and she said
she had. Before leaving, I took the opportunity
of putting in a word for Miss Whateley's school
at Cairo for native girls, hoping the school might
be a germ, growing in time to put an end to the
cruel superstition which prevents the mothers
from driving away the flies from the poor babies'
eyes, and from ever washing them till they are
able to wash themselves, of which sad absurdities
H.R.H. had never heard. The Princess soon
afterwards said good-night, and retired. Then a
chat on deck for a short time, a few refreshments,
and the Prince accompanied us back to the plank.
I was the last to cross the plank, and was about
half way over, when out of the darkness one of
the party rushed back, and, grasping both of my

hands, landed me across. I was protesting with
dignity that such assistance was unnecessary, as
I was now quite used to the plank, when by the
flare of the torches I saw it was the Prince who
had come to the rescue. The Duke of Sutherland
had told him of my first hesitation with the plank,
and the Prince had hurried on for this bit of fun.'

After visiting Siout, some impromptu lectures
were got up.

'The Prince showed me all his bird-skins (I
forgot to say he had an excellent taxidermist with
him), and he had just shot a fine wild drake.
Fowler had with him his Report and Plans of the
Suez Canal, and I had some fossils illustrative of its
geology. It being announced that the Princess was
ready, we proceeded to the dining saloon, at the
door of which Lord Carrington posted himself with
" Tickets, gentlemen." I produced the smallest
of Egyptian coins (value $\frac{1}{20}$th of a farthing), and
went in to find the chairs already arranged. A
large plan of the isthmus hung in front of the
piano ; on one side of it stood Fowler to give his
discourse, and on the other side I sat with the
Princess's parasol to point out the localities referred to. Fowler gave an excellent clear account
of the wonderful undertaking. I followed with a
brief reference to the geology of the isthmus,
showing a very large shark's tooth—one of the
fossils. The Prince then gave me his seat to
tell the ladies how the geological changes had

taken place—with the Sahara dry desert and its
salt, &c. &c., and an hour and a half was spent in
a very entertaining way. Before leaving the
saloon the Prince put on my broad-brimmed
wide-awake hat. People don't know the size of
my head, till they try on my hat!'

On February 16, Owen visited Thebes with
the Royal party, made a few pen-and-ink sketches,
and wrote a long description. They then proceeded to Karnac and luncheon. 'During luncheon
I took off my wide-awake for coolness, when
H.R.H. remarked: " Professor, I see you have
reserved your visit to this palace in order to
assume the purple." Some one else chimed in:
" The Professor has not lost the grace of blushing,
but it is at the top of his head." The Princess
pointed out the crimson silk lining in the crown
of my hat. The heat of the ride and the clamber
among the glories of Karnac had transferred
that rosy tint to the top of my pate! Before
we parted the Prince remarked that he had a
special "physiological curiosity" to show me to-
morrow. . . .

'" For symmetry of architecture and elegance of
sculpture, the Memnonium may vie with any other
Egyptian monument." Truly so, Sir Gardner,
and much obliged for the rest of your account,
for I am getting rather tired, and have had enough
sight-seeing for to-day. . . . After returning to
our vessels, I made what *toilette* I could (morn-

ing clothes with dust shaken out), and then on
to the Prince's boat to dinner. The Princess
had a curiosity for me—a mummy foot. After
dinner and chibouks, we proceeded to Mustapha's
house in the Luxor Temple, and there beheld the
" physiological curiosity " (tell it not in Gath !)—
the dancing girls. One of these ladies, in richly-
coloured gown, with old ornaments and coins,
seemed like one of the old frescoes which had
stepped out of the wall of her tomb for an hour
or so ; the attitudes were exactly those which are
often reproduced on the walls.

'I was hard pressed to accompany the royal
party to the Cataracts, but had to explain reasons
for returning to the Museum and work, as soon
in March as might be.

'Next day the party went through " the Valley
of the Shadow." We were nearing a bank where a
practicable road was narrowing, when Fowler said :
" More to the left, Professor." Turning round,
I saw the Princess on her white donkey and the
rest of the party which had overtaken us. Her
Royal Highness said : "Where were you last night,
Professor ? Oh, I know," lifting up a finger.
" Then I shall write to Mrs. Owen and tell her of
your doings." Lunch was laid out in the shade of
the corridors and massive columns of the Memnonium. . . . After lunch the Admiral got to fencing
with Abdul Kader Bey with palm sticks, to our
great amusement. I took the Princess and Mrs.

Grey to show them the very beautiful face of one
of the large coloured *basso-relievos* on the wall.
Then we looked at the figures of Rameses re-
viewing the tale of hands cut off the victims of
war, very similar to the Assyrian sculptures where
heads are counted.   Then the ride back to the
river. . . .

'After visiting the " Leaning Pillar " by torch-
light, I bade farewell to the Prince and Princess
and to the rest of the party, for they start at daybreak to-morrow on the upward voyage to the Cataracts.   You may imagine, amid the manifold con-
course of the royal party and all its attendants, the
pachas and Theban authorities, with sundry extraneous visitors, the difficulty of recovering in
so extensive a wilderness your own particular
donkey.   I held up my stick more in fun than
expectation of any result, when from behind
the gloom of a mighty pillar glided forth that
marvellous donkey-boy and his beast (the "good
donkey ").   He had never lost sight of me. . . .
At the Palm Avenue I dismounted, and made
my donkey-boy happy with well-merited " back-
sheesh." '

Returning to Siout, Owen 'landed there, and
Fowler, with me as assistant measurer, went off
to inspect the neighbouring canal wall.'   The
journey home had now begun, Brindisi, Mont
Cenis, and Milan being visited on the way.   'At
Paris,' says Owen, 'I occupied my seat at the

" Institut" as one of the eight foreign members.
read a paper there "On the Geology of Egypt,"
and so home on March 18.

On the occasion of the Royal Geographical
Society dinner, which was given on May 25, 1869,
Owen, in answering the toast 'The Scientific and
Literary Results of the last Nile Expedition,' gave
some account of his observations during his recent
tour.   He said: 'In the grand and praiseworthy
labours of the accomplished engineers of the Suez
Canal I had opportunities of seeing sections of the
Desert—deposits of unusual depth and extent.
In parts of these were alternations of strata, thin
beds of argillaceous deposit between thicker ones
of silico-calcareous and gypseous materials, which
suggested that the old ocean of that locality—for
all the Desert is an upraised seabed—had begun
to receive, about the close of the Miocene period,
alluviums, or the wear by fresh water of an adja-
cent land, and these at regularly repeated intervals.
The phenomena and fossils suggested to me that
the surface contour of the African continent
might about that time have gained so much of its
present form as to cause a watershed in the direction indicated by the course of the present Nile.   In
the Desert deposits of the nummulitic and cretaceous periods there is no trace of this fresh water
alternating admixture.   So far as my limited
opportunities of observation extended, I found
no evidence of those repeated disturbances or

changes of condition of which the various marine
and fresh-water strata of the Pliocene and Post-
Pliocene periods in Britain and Europe are results.
In that part of the Lybian Desert remarkable for
the quantity of silicified wood and tree trunks
superficially distributed, there is evidence of vol-
canic action, probably submarine. But in the
main the origin of the dry land resulting in
fertile Egypt seems to be due to slow elevation
and annual alluviums, which for long ages were
spread out beneath estuary seas, but finally adding
to and superficially forming upraised dry land.

' Of fertile and habitable land Egypt is the most
recent or last formed, and it is that which yields
the most ancient evidences of social and civilised
man. Of these marvellous evidences —marvellous
for their magnitude, number, and variety—I shall
only say that they transcend all previous conception. With regard to the Egyptian fauna, how
interesting was it to the naturalists to witness, as
they steamed along, so many kinds of birds,
previously studied as stuffed specimens in our
cabinets or as captives in our Zoological Gardens !
to witness and compare the flight of flocks of
flamingoes, spoonbills, pelicans, the varied forms
of waders, the graceful undulatory course of the
crested hoopoes, the darting of the kingfishers,
the manœuvres of the birds of prey, from the
vultures and eagles to the kites and sparrowhawks !
Of the rarest of all these Egyptian birds, I had

the opportunity, so much valued by ornithologists,
of handling the recently killed specimens which
were shot by the Prince.   The addition to the
staff of a skilled taxidermist, equal to the prompt
preparation of any rare bird, bat, beast, or fish,
was no suggestion of mine, but of the Prince, as
was likewise the provision of a seine net, the use
of which enabled me to observe, fresh or living,
the curious forms of siluroids, snouted mormyri,
and other Nilotic scaled rarities, which previously
I had known only in a dried state or preserved
in spirits.   Of crocodiles I saw none : steam
and improved rifles have driven them to the
Cataracts.   The consequence is that between
Cairo and Thebes the fishes have marvellously
multiplied, and, correlatively, the pelicans, flamingoes, spoonbills, and all the varied forms of
heron, ibis, and curlew that feed upon the spawn
or fry of fishes.   This is interesting evidence of the
effects of disturbing a natural balance in the
contest for existence.   So much for zoology.

'Nor was I less indebted to His Royal Highness for occasions of adding to my physiological
knowledge.   Through the Prince's kindness, I
for the first time had the opportunity of observing,
in the living state, that remarkable species, the
Lacerta agilis, seldom to be seen save in Oriental
and sub-tropical countries.   They are highly
organised, though belonging to a low class.'

On June 27, 1869, Owen received at the Col-

lege of Surgeons the ' Baly medal, the first given
since its foundation.

The summer holiday was spent mainly in
Ireland. On September 20 Owen writes to his
sister from Florence Court : ' I have been passing
a very pleasant holiday with my old friend Lord
Enniskillen. I leave to-morrow, sleep at Dublin,
see my scientific friends and their museums there,
and then sail for Holyhead, go on to Barmouth,
spend a few days there, and then home.' ' Your
rival as regards my pen, ' Owen writes to his
sister, December 6, ' has been a monster kangaroo, which I have been hunting for more than
thirty years, and at length have caught, all but
his feet. However, I cannot wait any longer for
them, and so shall introduce him to the Royal
Society next week, and prop him up as well as I
can. His head is a yard long, his bones and teeth
(fossil) have been gathered from divers localities
in Australia.'

Meanwhile, the struggle in Parliament over
the new museum was gradually coming to an
end. If Owen had not obtained all that he
wished, he was more than satisfied with the result.
The passing of the Bill gave an additional charm
to the summer holiday of 1870. Writing to his
wife on August 4, from Pendell Court, Owen
says : ' You would perhaps see that the Museum
Bill has passed the House. They gave me four
acres for the building, and 3,500*l.* We ask this

year only enough to clear the ground, but the
main matter is now safe and much better than I
expected.'

In November 1870 Owen made his second
journey to Egypt. On this occasion he accompanied Mr. McClean, M.P., and his family. It
was hoped that the dryness and warmth of the
climate would benefit his health. The expedition
at least enabled him to escape two of the most
trying months in England. 'December and
January,' he tells his sister on the eve of starting
for the East, 'passed in the climate of the Nile will
strengthen my lungs for the rest of the winter.'

He kept a journal as heretofore, but, as he
travelled over much the same ground as in 1869,
a few brief notices only need be given. On December 10 the party arrived at Alexandria.
From Cairo, on the 17th, Owen writes to his wife :
' To-day I took the opportunity of renewing my
acquaintance with worthy old Hekekiah Bey, and
had a chat with him and his wife—a nice old lady.
Nothing in Cairo has changed. I feel like an
old inhabitant. Indeed, the number of greetings
that met me at the station was more like a return
home than getting out upon so far-away a rail-
road station.'

Christmas Day was spent at Thebes. ' Much
sand has again accumulated round the base of
our obelisk, which the Prince had cleared out in
March 1869.'

' *Esneh* (*Latopolis*), *December* 29.—On the walls, among other subjects, are many sculptured fishes—the old name of the place indicating the special worship of the Lates (a Nile fish), combined with the giant deities, made me suggest the possible origin of the exclamation, " O ye gods and little fishes ! " '

' 30*th*.—Reached our furthest point, the Isle of Philo, and returned to Assouan, below the First Cataract, and there saw the new year in.'

On the voyage from Alexandria to Brindisi he encountered rough weather. ' I tumbled out,' he says, 'and got on deck, where I danced a sort of impromptu and irregular hornpipe until I finally settled down to my sea legs.'

' *Naples, January* 19, 1871.—At Foggia the main part of the train runs northward, and our part was closely packed with passengers. I was the only man who ventured into one of the few first-class carriages, which was already occupied by a young couple and their three months' old baby, and as one after another of the males (the ladies being safely stowed) put their heads in at the window, the cries of " Bambino" put them to a precipitate flight. As a grandfather, I stuck to my seat, and no sooner was the train in motion than the infant went to sleep, and I, having the whole of the opposite side, slept blissfully till daybreak. In the intervals I studied the whole process of swathing, and a very artful piece of

broad bandaging it is ; when done, " Bambino "
was propped upright in a corner and seemed to
like it, crowing loudly, and its two fore-paws like
a little Punch, sticking out of the top of its
mummy case. After the process of wrapping,
the little mummy smiled and shook its little hands
in a very pretty way to my advances to intimacy.
. . . Reached Naples at 9.30 and found the other
men of our party had been packed like herrings
and got no sleep !'

Early in February 1871 Owen returned to
England and to his work at the British Museum.
In this year he contributed to the Palæontographical Society a 'Monograph of the Fossil Mammalia
of the Mesozoic Formations.' This publication
was chiefly devoted to a detailed account of the
remarkable discoveries made since 1854 by Mr.
Beckles in the Purbeck Rocks near Swanage.
It established the existence of a large fauna of
small marsupial mammals, 'insignificant in size
and power, adapted for insect food, for preying
upon small lizards, or on the smaller and weaker
members of their own low Mammalian grade.'

In August 1871 Owen visited Mr. Fowler
at Braemore, Ross-shire, whence, on August 13,
1871, he writes to his wife : 'I am now the only
guest. Lady Ashburton and T. Carlyle drove
over and took tea with us on Friday (11th), and
strolled along the easier walks. He is much
emaciated, can digest but little, and hardly gets

any sleep. He was most friendly and, I thought, took his last leave of me at parting. They drive twenty-six miles, and the same in returning. Lady A. intimated it was mainly his wish to see me that brought them so far. He painfully, with a pencil, put his name in the Visitors' Book.'

'*From Braemore, August* 20.—On the 19th Prince Hassan and his tutor arrived at Braemore. He has quite fallen into English ways and speaks English perfectly. On Monday he made his first stalk on the mountains, and was so excited by the thought of it that he threw all the cushions about in the drawing-room! I ascended Ben Derig yesterday—the highest mountain in these parts. I saw the rare "parsley-fern" peep out from under the flat stones which protect its long roots. To-morrow we are to have a yachting day.'

'*September* 24.—At the British Museum. I am shaking hands, literally, with the Iguanodon, having *got both his fore paws*, each with a bayonet-like weapon of great power.' Of his other papers this year may be mentioned 'Extinct Leonine Marsupial (*Thylacoleo carnifex*) ;' 'On the Fossil Mammals of Australia, genus *Phascolomys*;' 'Fossil Reptilia of Cretaceous Formations,' 4to, 37 plates.

On October 4, 1871, he writes again to his wife: 'I went to lunch with "Rob Roy," who inquired most kindly after you. His chambers in the Temple are a quaint museum—an epi-

tome of his various journeys. I went mainly to
see the human skull he brought from Holland.'

In 1871 Owen was again offered the Presidency
of the Geological Society. This he refused, giving
as his reasons the increased duties and responsibilities of his official position, his advanced age,
and declining health. With reference to this
event, it is interesting to read the following remarks from his old friend Sir Philip Egerton,
which occur in a letter dated December 22, 1871.

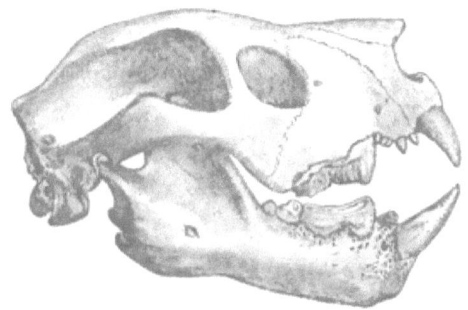

SKULL OF THYLACOLEO, AN EXTINCT AUSTRALIAN MARSUPIAL
DESCRIBED BY OWEN AS A 'POUCHED LION.' ½ Natural size.

Sir Philip says : ' I am exceedingly glad for your
sake that you have declined the G. S. chair. It
would be a great clog round your leg for two
years ; ' and, with the characteristic spirit of an
old member, he adds : ' The social aspect of the
Society is very different nowadays from what it
was in the halcyon days of yore.'

Owen contributed an interesting article this
year to ' Blackwood's Magazine,' descriptive of

some serpent-charming he had witnessed in Cairo. He was convinced that the 'charmers' were frauds after an examination of their methods :—

'The charmer came to appointment, accompanied by a boy with a bag, said to be for the snakes that were to be captured.

'The houses were of the low tumble-down character common in those suburbs ; most of them detached, in patches of slovenly-cultivated ground.

'I suggested that the charmer should have his garments searched before entering ; but he refused, and even resisted the temptation of half a sovereign extra—a large sum in piastres—which I thought suspicious. The outer garment of the villainous-looking old sheik was the long, loose frock of a coarse blue-cotton stuff, called "galabieh," with large baggy sleeves, or what looked like sleeves from the mode of its adjustment. A conjuror could have concealed the major part of his property in its ample folds.

'He entered a house, followed by his boy and ourselves. The sheik, on entering, stepped forward, mysteriously glancing to the right and left, muttering and occasionally whistling, and passing from room to room, closely followed and watched by us ; he, however, left that house, intimating that it was free from snakes.

'In the next house—and whenever any inhabitant was visible, the charmer was reverently wel-

comed—on entering the second room I noticed
that a doorway led from it to a darkened apartment without other entry or exit. The charmer
stood at this doorway, his legs apart, his arms on
the lintel, his turbaned visage poked forward, and
the incantation and whistling becoming more
emphatic. I tried to get into the place, but there
was no passing without shoving the fellow aside,
and the boy loudly protested against my proximity
and disturbance. The charmer next stretched
forward the hand carrying his stick and tapped
the wall of the darkened room ; then, suddenly
turning round to us, exclaimed, according to my
interpreter, " The snake, my cousin, there he is ! "
and stepped down into the room. We followed,
and a small specimen of the common harmless
house-snake of Egypt (*Coluber atrovirens*), half
coiled in seemingly a semi-torpid or sluggish
state, lay on the floor. On the supposition that
it had been coaxed out of a chink in the wall, I
should have expected to see some movement of
the reptile or endeavour to escape ; but we were
given to understand that it was charmed. The
boy seized it behind the head, and, after I had
inspected it, popped it into his bag, which I observed to contain others, apparently of the same
kind.

· We visited four or five other houses, in two
of which a serpent on the floor was the result of
the incantations and movements exhibited by the

charmer at the entry to the alleged infested apartment.

‘ I noted that he never “charmed” save when he came upon a room to which there was no other entry than a doorway from the apartment we happened to be in.

‘ To my strongly-urged desire to first enter such *cul-de-sac*, in order to see the issue of the mesmerised serpent from its lurking-place, I was told that the charmer objected, on account of the evil influence of the presence of an “uncomplimentarily-specified individual ” upon the operation of the magic process.

‘ It reminded me of the objections of our own spiritualists to the presence of a sceptic, and to too much light in the room.

‘ I thereupon watched the sheik the more closely, and distinctly detected a slight but rapid and energetic quivering movement of the left arm and sleeve, immediately preceding his announcement of the success of his incantation. The poor snake, which had been jerked out, lay, like the first, in a half-coiled, sluggish state on the floor.

‘ I charged the impostor with the fact, and was happily unacquainted with the meaning of the loud and voluble remonstrances of the dervish and his gathering of dusky believers, to which my friendly conductor put a stop by threatening to thrash the saint.

‘ I returned to the hotel with the conviction

that "serpent-charming" was not conducted under circumstances favourable to a rational or scientific explanation of the process ; that, on the contrary, it was attended, like other marvels which dread the light, with purposive obstructions to fair and accurate observations ; and, finally, that it was a rude mode of conjuring, in which the snake, professed to be charmed out of a hole in the wall, was concealed upon the person of the conjuror, and transferred by sleight of arm and hand to the floor of the room alleged to have been infested.'

At the close of 1871 Owen received the following letter from one of his oldest friends. Thomas Bell :—

From Thomas Bell to Richard Owen

December 27, 1871.

' I find as I get on further and further towards the close of life that I feel more and more drawn to those whom I have most and longest esteemed, and, as there are few whom I have known longer and none whom I have more esteemed than yourself, I feel impelled to offer you my best and most cordial wishes for a happy and peaceful new year.   Amidst the jarring and discordant elements of which the present scientific atmosphere is almost exclusively composed, it is a relief to bring oneself into contact with such men as yourself, dear old Sedgwick, and a few others who have not been led astray from the simple pursuit of Truth for her own sake, unbiassed by personal vanity and love of notoriety on the one hand, and the opposition of self-seekers on the other. May you and I yet be spared to see the downfall of scientific quackery, and the triumph of simple philosophical truth.

　　　　　　' Ever, my dear Owen,
　　　　　　　　' Your affectionate old friend,
　　　　　　　　　　　' THOMAS BELL.'

CHAPTER VIII

Third Visit to Egypt, 1873—Death of Mrs. Owen, May 1873—Com-
panion of the Bath—Robert Lowe—Earl Russell—Fourth Visit
to Egypt, 1874—George Eliot and G. H. Lewes, 1876—The
Emperor of Brazil, 1877—Oliver Wendell Holmes, 1878—
'Specimens of my Correspondence'—Opening of the New
Museum, 1881—Mr. Ruskin—Lord Tennyson.

In January 1872 Owen received a letter from Dr.
Julius von Haast, announcing the discovery of
the remains of *Aptornis owenii* in the swamp
at Glenmark, New Zealand. This letter he communicated to the Zoological Society, January 16.

There appeared this year also Part XIX.
'On Dinornis,' containing descriptions of a new
genus of large wingless bird, *Dromornis australis*
(Owen), from a post-tertiary deposit in Queensland, Australia.[1]

Owen spent the August of 1872 at Braemore
(Mr. Fowler's). Writing to his wife, he says :—

'*August* 5.—Got up at 5 A.M., and drove to
the head of the loch, and there we got on board a
screw steamer. The colour of the lake and sky
was like that of the Bay of Naples. Medusæ

[1] *Trans. Zool. Soc.,* viii. pt. vi.

were swimming with their rhythmical movements
in the clear blue, and there were many varieties
of Northern sea-birds to be seen.   Fished, but
the sky and water too bright for much sport. . . .
As we steamed out of the loch I saw a pair of
grand sea-eagles soaring above the rocky precipices.'

This letter occupies many pages, describing
the local scenery and the great Druidical circle at
Callernish.

On August 28 he writes to inform his sister
of his safe arrival home, and of the renewal of his
work at the British Museum.

Writing to his wife on Wednesday, September
4, he says : ' This day last week Albert Günther
accompanied me from the Museum.   We sat down
to chess before dinner, when the Bishop of London
was announced ; as he rode over with one of his
pretty daughters, Albert held his lordship's horse
and chatted with the young lady while I took the
Bishop round the garden. . . . I went to Fulham
on Friday ; rambled through the gardens, discussed the trees, was shown the additions to the
palace, and so home to a quiet seven o'clock
dinner.'

An amusing incident occurred on October 9,
when Owen was engaged to dine with Mr. John
Murray at Wimbledon.[2]   He arrived half an hour
late, and pleaded as an excuse for his unpunc-

---

[2] Kindly communicated by Mr. Murray.

tuality the fact that just as he was getting into
his carriage a groom rode up to the gate, presented a note, and requested an immediate answer.
The note ran as follows :—

October 9, 1872.

' My dear Sir,—I should feel greatly obliged
to you if you would be so kind as to inform me
whether this is or is not the tooth of a dog.   It
was found in a sausage, and I should like to feel
sure about it before saying anything about it
to the tradesman.   Will you kindly return the
enclosed with your reply ?

' I am, dear Sir, &c., &c.'

Owen returned to his study, and in reply to his
correspondent, who evidently suspected the introduction of unlawful meats into the sausage skin,
wrote that the tooth was merely that of a sucking-
pig.

On another occasion a footman came over
from Pembroke Lodge with a large bone wrapped
up in paper, and a note from Lord John Russell
requesting Owen to let him know to what animal
the bone belonged.   The Professor looked at it,
and at a glance perceived that it was a ham bone
of an ordinary pig.   The description was transferred to paper, and the footman returned to
Pembroke Lodge, leaving Owen at a loss to
understand why a *ham bone* should have been
sent to him.

Some days passed, and, hearing nothing further from Lord John, he walked over on a Sunday afternoon to ask for an explanation.

'The fact is,' Lord John Russell said, ' President Grant made me a present of what purported to be a bear's ham (which is considered a great delicacy), but as I had my doubts about it I sent you the bone.'

Early in 1873 Owen made his third journey to Egypt, this time in the company of his friend Mr. Fowler and his family.

From Cairo he wrote to his wife :—

'*February* 15.—Oddly enough, I heard of Emerson's arrival in Cairo yesterday, and of his having expressed his pleasure that I was here, mentioning some civilities we showed him when he was in London twenty years ago.   He wrote to me yesterday : " I am not without hope that I may find or make an opportunity to thank you for your old kindness to me in London, and to be able to say to Mr. Agassiz at home that I have seen you."

'Yesterday also (John Hunter's anniversary) I enjoyed the hospitality of young Prince Hassan, whom I had lately met in England.   I had the Khedive's carriage and servants all to myself on the way to the Abbasieh Palace.   The guard turned out as we drove through the gateway into the brilliantly-lighted courtyard.   Two large reception-rooms were filled with uniforms, stars,

and decorations.   I was the only person without
any, and did not explain to His Highness that
Mrs. O. kept my museum of such specimens at
home carefully locked up.   I was placed at dinner
considerately near a Minister of the Khedive, who
had accompanied him two years ago to London,
whom I had met at the Athenæum, and who spoke
English. . . . After dinner the guests went to
billiards, coffee, and cigars, and then there was
the most splendid display of fireworks I ever saw.'

Then there follows a long account of the procession of Prince Hassan's bride, which Owen
witnessed on the 13th.   'A lady friend,' he says,
'gave me an account of her presentation at the
Harem.   The bride, in white, about fourteen or
fifteen, was led, looking much abashed, and
attended by six bridesmaids in green, to a chair
of state between those occupied by her grand-
mother-in-law and her mother-in-law.   After refreshments had been handed round, the two old
ladies showered handfuls of small gold coins upon
their guests.   The grandmamma-in-law threw a
large handful over my friend, who said she shook
forty or fifty out of her dress when she got home.
A valuable shawl was presented to each guest. . . . .

'I have had two days in the Desert, doing my
twenty miles on donkey-back at each.   One to
the Petrified Forest (of which I have sent an
account to the "Garden"), and the next to the
Southern Necropolis of Memphis.'

On his return journey Owen visited Naples and Malta.

'The Ambassador's yacht was put at our disposal to take us on to Naples from Malta, as the steamer for Syracuse and Naples could not wait. It is wonderfully swift, and beautifully fitted up. The ground for this favour was the opportunity of having the sanitary condition and water-supply of the forts, barracks, and island generally surveyed and reported on by my fellow-traveller, Mr. Fowler, assisted by the old "Commissioner for the Health of Towns." While at Malta I inspected the Museum, and was kindly received by the keeper, who had some fossils to show me, and then went on to see St. John's Church, which is a museum in itself of marbles and mosaics. On Sunday we went, by Admiral Sir Hastings Yelverton's invitation (he is the late Lady Hastings' husband), to morning service on board the flagship. The boat was in waiting for us, and we were rowed to the ship at ten. The service was held 'tween decks, and was exceedingly well sung. After service went over the "Lord Warden," and after luncheon Mr. Emerson had provided carriages for a drive to that part of the coast where St. Paul was wrecked. He read to us on the spot the account of the shipwreck in the Acts, which brought the whole scene plainly and vividly before our eyes. A quiet dinner with Emerson closed the day.'

On his arrival in England (March 15), he found his wife seriously ill, and throughout that month and those following he records in his diary the various stages of her illness. She made no improvement, but on May 7 passed away, and Owen lost one who had been his fitting helpmate for nearly forty years, and who had, in her younger days especially, assisted his work in no small degree both by her acute powers of observation and by her artistic skill. After the severe blow of her death, Owen's letters became far less numerous.

On May 10 he wrote to his sister: 'We have just returned from my dear Caroline's last resting-place on earth, in the quiet, peaceful churchyard of Ham; a sweet summer's day. Should I be called away here, I should desire to rest by her side.'

On May 15, 1873, he received a letter from the Prime Minister, Mr. Gladstone, saying that he remembered 'with dissatisfaction that a name so distinguished in the history of research remains without a note of honour from the State,' and so offering him a choice of distinctions. In reply to this letter, Professor Owen intimated that he would prefer the C.B., and on June 17 of the same year he received the official announcement from the College of Arms.

Considerations for the completeness of the new Museum were always present in Owen's mind, and it is interesting to note from the following letter that Mr. Robert Lowe (Lord Sherbrooke), when Chancellor of the Exchequer, was one of the earliest to see the importance of properly organised lectures on natural history subjects at the Museum. Even now there is no lecture theatre :—

11 Downing Street, Whitehall : July 14, 1873.

'Dear Sir,—With reference to the memorandum you sent to the Chancellor of the Exchequer, I am desired to say that he would be much obliged if you would be good enough to tell him if the plan of the Natural History Museum, now in course of building, comprises a theatre for a lecture-room. It has been represented to Mr. Lowe that no provision of the kind has been made, and he is desirous of ascertaining for certain whether or not what appears to him to be a serious omission has been made. He would also be glad to be favoured with any observations you may have to make in reference to this matter. . . .

'Yours very faithfully,
'E. W. HAMILTON.'

In a letter to his friend Pearson Langshaw, November 2, Owen mentions that his sister has come to live with him and keep house at Sheen Lodge. He says she 'has now settled down very comfortably in her new home, and has made it less lonely for me. . . . I dined yesterday with good old Lord Russell. He sat down to dinner in a comfortable cloak and black cap, like a lively, keen-eyed mummy : as full of bright mind and anecdote and fun as ever.'

Owen had not yet heard the last of 'frogs in stones' and other wonders. In November he writes to a lady, who affirms that she saw 'with the utmost surprise,' a frog come out of a bit of rock which was taken out of a pit, and asks how long it had been there. 'My dear madam,' the Professor replies, 'the time during which the frog was in the pit will depend a good deal upon whether it came out of a cleft in the stone, into which it could have crept before being disturbed by the men, or whether it had been imbedded in the substance of that stone. If the latter, it must have got in before the stone was stone—when, e.g., it was sand.

'The living state of the frog tells against that hypothesis. The astonishment and "utmost surprise" of the spectators are unfavourable states of mind to clear insight and cool consideration of the circumstances of the case. . . . No coal or stone exists in any museum bearing the impress of a toad or frog therein embedded. *Verb. sap. !*

Madam, yours faithfully and obliged,

'RICHARD OWEN.'

In 1873 Owen described in the Journal of the Geological Society the skull of a toothed bird from the London Clay of Sheppey, which he named *Odontopteryx toliapicus*. This was one of four birds which he had from time to time made known from this geological period.

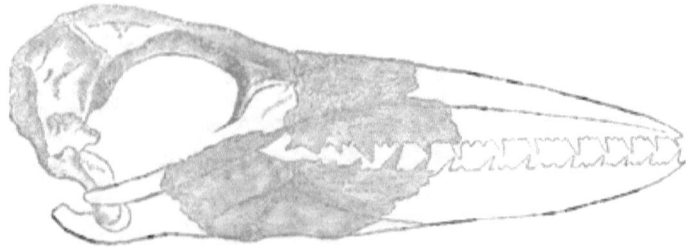

ODONTOPTERYX. ¾ natural size

In January 1874 we find Owen for the fourth time wintering in Egypt.

Writing from Cairo to his sister, he says : 'I often thought of you at your quiet fireside on my journey, wondering how I could have been beguiled into undertaking some thousand miles of land and sea at my time of life. Well, it will be the last, and it must be a strong lever which will again dislodge me from home. Yet, now that the journey's over, I feel it to be well worth being here. E. W. Cooke, R.A., is one of our fellow-travellers, and we joined Carl Haag, Frank Dillon, and other artists here.'

Owen saw a good deal of Carl Haag at Cairo. After the voyage the artist presented him with a water-colour that he had painted there of a Nubian standing with a pitcher, in an Egyptian landscape, with the inscription :—

'To Professor Richard Owen.

In grateful remembrance of happy hours spent with him at Cairo.—Carl Haag. 1874.'

The following notes are taken from letters to his sister, written from Egypt :—

'*February* 22.—At the breakfast table I was greeted by Colonel Gordon (Chinese Gordon), on his way to the scene of Sir S. Baker's adventures. . . . Captain Stuart kindly agreed to take us through the canal to Timsah, but we were to go on board that night.

'23*rd*.—We were flattering ourselves that we should have got into Lake Timsah in time for the train to Cairo ; or at least in time for M. de Lesseps' dinner, to which he had telegraphed an invitation to Suez. But, alas ! at 3 P.M. we stopped. The captain pointed to a distant semaphore, in which two balls indicated a " stop " till a vessel in the canal had emerged into the Bitter Lakes. The " Simla " was in charge of a Suez Canal Company's pilot and nothing could be done. At 4.30 we saw the masts of the opposing vessel. At 5.15 she emerged from the canal, a large French screw with the mail-bags. We then moved on nearer to the entry and stopped for the night.'

Owen returned home by Brindisi, Bologna, Turin, and arrived in London on April 3. On May 12 he writes to Dr. Pearson Langshaw :—

' Last Friday I dined with the Junior Contem-

porary—Bartholomew men.   It was odd, with my
recollections of many of them as they looked in
1835, to find them grey and bald ; and there was
I, with Burrows and Frederick Farre—the *débris*
of an older set.'

The Professor notes in his diary that on
September 14 he delivered an address to the
' Ethnological Section' of the Congress of Ori-
entalists, and on October 1 he presided at the
dinner of the St. George's Hospital Medical
School. In this year he wrote 'A Sketch of
Hunter's Scientific Character and Works,' which
appeared in Tom Taylor's ' Leicester Square.'

On July 10, 1874, his old friend Sir Henry
Parkes wrote informing him that the Government
of New South Wales had voted him a sum of
150*l.*, to enable him to issue in a separate form
his papers on the ' Fossil Mammals of Australia.'
The two volumes devoted to this subject appeared
in 1877, and consisted of collections of separate
copies of papers which had appeared in the publications of various societies, bound up, indexed,
and issued with a new title-page.

At the close of this year Owen was made
' Associé Étranger' of the Academy of Medicine,
Paris.

Richard Owen to Mr. White Cooper

British Museum : September 7, 1875.

'I cannot keep away from my work-room : some singular new sauria from South Africa absorb my thoughts.

'Your news of Fulmer[3] interests me much. If I could, with a small mortgage, have raised the amount, what could I do with it ? Willy, also, has his lot and work in life made for him in Downing Street.

'If any of his lads should take to money-getting lines of work, they may care to bring the property into the old line. But the world fades as one ages, like a receding landscape, and one feels more and more that it is no abiding place.'

On November 24, 1875, Professor Owen writes to Mr. Townsend-Mayer from the British Museum :—

'I am still able to come here—well muffled—to daily task-work. When brain gives signs of weariness I toddle homewards, and, after dining, rest the tired organ with a " St. James's," or " Mrs. Burton," or a novel till bed-time. I am loth to "put on the spur"—as dear old Walter did—till the machine gave way. For an old friend—Froude—I did so, in behalf of his young suc-

---

[3] Mr. William White Cooper at that time had a house near Fulmer Place, and he had informed Professor Owen that the old property of Fulmer Place was for sale.

cessor—as Editor of "Fraser"—a poet whose
acquaintance I made at Tennyson's. But it was
a work of groans, lazy groans perhaps. Quarter-
lies, also, besiege me, mostly in vain. A life-
long friendship with Livingstone led me to do his
"Last Journals" in "The Quarterly."[4] Murray
told me Miss Livingstone that was—she, I
think, is now wedded—asked for the secret of the
authorship, and I felt well repaid by being told
that the family liked it better than any other
notice. Poor dear Livingstone! He brought
me the tusk of an elephant, twisted like a corkscrew, from his first great journey. My best
remembrances to your good and kind wife. I
hope we may meet next summer. I am not yet
bad enough to take flight to Brindisi; but the
irritation and extra secretion of the "bronchials"
won't go at my age.

'Believe me, a sympathising but poor
"broken reed,"

'RICHARD OWEN.

'P.S.—Our good friend "Orion's"[5] reve-
lations of Mrs. B. make me afraid of putting pen
to paper.'

In 1876 Owen brought out a 'Descriptive and
Illustrated Catalogue of the Fossil Reptilia of

---

[4] Review of H. Waller's *The Last Journals of David Living-stone in Central Africa, from* 1865 *to his Death.*

[5] T. H. Horne.

South Africa' in the collection of the British
Museum. He varied his more serious work by
contributing an article on 'Petroleum and Oil
Wells' to 'Fraser's Magazine.'

A frequent correspondent of Owen's was G.
H. Lewes. The following letter, dated Christmas Eve, 1876, is interesting, as it gives a few
particulars about George Eliot's 'Daniel Deronda,'
and will also serve to show the strong feeling of
friendship which existed between both of them
and Owen.

G. H. Lewes to Richard Owen

The Priory, 21 North Bank, Regent's Park :
Christmas Eve, '76.

'My dear Owen,—It was a most pleasant
reminder of the bygone happy days when we
used to see much of each other, greatly to my
profit, that letter of yours, with its accompanying
paper !

'It is cheering also to contemplate the work
you are still doing, though I am forced to admire
it at an ignorant distance, feeling how much I
need to approach and appreciate it. I don't find
my own powers of work at all what they were—
very far from it—but I go on "doggedly," as
Johnson said, with the uncomfortable sense that
the more I study the nervous system the feebler
my grasp of it gets, and the profounder my conviction that most of what is taught in the text-

books is a " false persuasion of knowledge "
which needs uprooting.

'The kiss you pressed upon the last page of
" Deronda " was at once transferred to its proper
place on the lips, which gratefully accepted it.

'The English public seem to have been
amazingly dead to the attempt to enlighten it
about the Jewish race ; but the Jews themselves
—from Germany, France, and America, as well
as England—have been deeply moved, and have
touchingly expressed their gratitude.   Learned
Rabbis, who can alone appreciate its learning,
are most enthusiastic.

'Is it not psychologically a fact of singular
interest that she was never in her life in a Jewish
family, at least never in one where Judaism was
still a living faith and Jewish customs kept up ?.
Yet the Jews all fancy she must have been
brought up among them ; and in America it is
positively asserted that *I* am of Jewish origin !

'With the best wishes of the season, believe
me, dear Owen, ever yours truly,

                              'G. H. LEWES.'

The opening paragraph of this letter probably
refers to the pleasant rambles in Richmond Park,
often enjoyed by the three friends, and often
referred to by Owen.

On July 12, 1877, the Emperor of Brazil
arrived in London, between five and six o'clock

PROFESSOR OWEN AND THE SKELETON OF *DINORNIS MAXIMUS*.
Taken about 1877.

in the morning, and came down to Sheen Lodge about an hour later in order to breakfast with Professor Owen. The Emperor, who was much interested in scientific questions, stayed some time looking at the Professor's collections of different curiosities, greatly admiring the garden and the beautiful trees in it. Some years previously when the Emperor came over to England he had paid Owen a similar visit.

It was rarely that Owen omitted to date his letters ; but about this time he wrote an undated letter to Dr. Milroy, in which he says : 'You have done good work in the thorough investigation of leprosy, and I trust you may be spared to receive evidence of the predicted results of the more rational treatment of the afflicted ones.

'In my less practical or applicable labours, I have to report that the " Researches on the Fossil Mammalia of Australia," 2 vols. 4to, are now in the binder's hands.

'This being issued, I push on to completion a similar series of researches on the " Fossil Birds of New Zealand " (this with 150 plates, the other 130). But then there remains the completion of a greater work (already partially issued), " On the Fossil Reptiles of Great Britain." Will my old cephalo-thoracic mucous tract outlast that labour ?' [6]

[6] The two volumes relating to the fossil birds of New Zea- land to which Owen refers in this letter consisted of separate

Owen relates an amusing interview which he once had with the Income Tax Commissioners on the subject of the supposed profit arising from the sale of his works.[7] ' I was once very much amazed,' he said, ' by receiving notice that the return I had made to the Income Tax Commissioners was to be surcharged. I had made a perfectly honest return, and felt indignant that my figures should be disputed. I was told that I might appeal on a certain day and hour at the Board Room. I arrived at the time stated, at some inconvenience to myself—for I was very busy—and found that it would be at least an hour before I could be heard. I spent the time in an untidy old churchyard, just under the Board Room windows, and occupied myself in reading inscriptions, &c. When my turn came I expressed my surprise at the notice I had received. The chairman said, with much suavity : " Oh, Professor Owen, we know that you have published some important works, and we thought perhaps you might have forgotten to mention the proceeds in your return !" I assured him I had forgotten nothing, produced what evidence I

copies of papers published in the *Transactions of the Zoological Society* between 1844 and 1877, with the addition of a paper on the ' Anatomy of the *Apteryx australis*,' a plate (life-size) of the *Notornis*, and a geological map of New Zealand, showing the localities from whence these fossils were obtained.

[7] In a letter to Dr. Pearson Langshaw.

could, and added : " If any of you gentlemen will
pay me the cost of publication, you are quite
welcome to the proceeds." The Board was satisfied, and bowed me out. I was not quite so
satisfied, especially when I thought of my wasted
morning, so, turning to the Commissioners, I
proceeded to describe the unhealthy state of the
churchyard, and observed : " Gentlemen, are you
aware of the fact that this room must be full of
the most deadly germs ? I may add that I should
be sorry to answer for the health of any of you,
especially as you have been sitting here all the
morning with those windows open." With that
Parthian shot I retired, and as I left the
room I heard one of the Commissioners shout,
" Shut them windows ! " I think I paid them
out.'

On April 25, 1878, Professor Owen wrote to
Mr. C. T. Newton with reference to a letter from
the Duke of Somerset, suggesting the opening of
the galleries of the British Museum on all days of
the week. Owen intimates that, as the removal
of the natural history portions of the collection is
taking place, the reduction rather than the increase of hours of admission for the public is to
be desired. But he adds : ' His Grace will be
gratified to learn that arrangements in the
Museum of Natural History were suggested in
the original plan (February 10, 1859), and have
been carried out in the building, to allow of daily

admission of the public, and also of nightly admission and admission on Sundays, to portions of the building, with exhibited objects of interest and extent sufficient to gratify any reasonable expectation, and requiring a minimum of supervision.'

The removal from Egypt to England of Cleopatra's Needle greatly interested Owen, who was anxious that the Government should have the obelisk placed in the great forecourt of the Museum at Bloomsbury, where it would form a fitting supplement to the antiquities within. He accordingly wrote letters on the subject, and interviewed officials at the Board of Works.[8] H.R.H. the Prince of Wales, in 1869, was at the cost of removing the dust and displaying England's obelisk in its whole noble length.

This obelisk, however, was eventually placed on the Thames Embankment, not without protest on the part of Owen and other Egyptologists, who objected to its incongruous position.

A long letter from Oliver Wendell Holmes written to Owen, and dated Boston, December 18, 1878, is characteristic and interesting. Some extracts from it are given below.

'My palæontological accomplishments are but

---

[8] The obelisk in question is the fellow of that now in America, for it is one of a pair. It was given to England by Mohammed Ali in commemoration of the victories in Egypt in 1801, but remained, half buried in the sand, till Erasmus Wilson paid for its removal to London in 1877.

slight, my museum in that department consisting of a single trilobite given me by Professor Gray the botanist, and which I keep before my eyes (mounted in the form of a paper-weight) to make the *aeternitas a parte ante* in some measure palpable to my apprehension, and to cool my egoism when it gets too warm with exercise and needs to be reminded that its subject is one in a long procession. But I have been a lecturer on human anatomy for more than thirty years, and so can understand your paper[9] and see its interest, for, without having made an express study of comparative anatomy, I have necessarily rubbed against it so much and from so many points of view that I find myself in possession of a certain amount of knowledge, hardly knowing how I came by it. . . . I have a reminiscence which will call up a name well known to you. In the year 1834, I think it was, that I visited London and carried a letter to your father-in-law, Mr. Clift, from an old fellow-student. He received me very kindly, and I have a distinct recollection of passing an evening most agreeably at his house. I was for many years—that is, during his whole residence in America—on intimate terms of friendship with Louis Agassiz, being one of the four whom he had as associates under the name

---

[9] 'On the Occurrence in North America of Rare Extinct Vertebrates found fragmentarily in England' (*Annals and Magazine of Natural History*).

of " Faculty of the Museum," holding the purse-
strings of his expenditures, which was not a sine-
cure.   I suppose you know all about his son Alex.
and his monograph on the "Acheenodaarms,"[1]
as his father used to call them ; also how he went
up to Lake Superior and got hold of some copper
mines, which made him and his friends so rich
that some of them do not know what to do with
their money. . . .   I beg your pardon for gossip-
ping as I have done.'

On December 17, at a meeting of the Royal
Colonial Institute, Owen made a speech on 'New
Guinea,' which was printed in 'The Colonies,'
December 21.

In May 1879 Owen again delivered a lecture
at the Colonial Institute on 'The Extinct Animals
of the British Colonies.'   As is well known, he
always made a point of asking colonial officials
and travellers to collect and forward to him as
many remains as they could procure of the extinct
animals to be found in the localities which they
visited.   Bishops, governors, missionaries, and
medical men from all parts of the globe worked
for him in that way.   His appeals 'to be borne in
mind when the opportunity of collecting such
fossils might occur' (as he writes to a Governor of
Queensland who had contributed part of the
materials of his 'Fossil Mammals of Australia') were

---

[1] Echinoderms.

generally liberally responded to, and a large variety of specimens was frequently sent to him. These miscellaneous contributions he kept in memory, and as occasions offered, pieced together. Sometimes years elapsed before he had received sufficient material to afford him conclusive proof of the facts at which he had perhaps long ago arrived by induction. Threads had often to be dropped which he had no opportunity of picking up again for long intervals of time. But when some missing link arrived, it was at once utilised in the construction of the extinct animals on which he was patiently engaged.

In this lecture at the Royal Colonial Institute he spoke of the 'absorbing pleasures of the chase,' which these pursuits afforded him, and declared that 'in the sporting world there was no hunt that was so exciting, so full of interest, and so satisfactory, when events prove one to have been on the right scent, as that of a huge beast which no eye will ever see alive, and which, perhaps, no mortal eye ever did behold. Such a chase is not ended in a day, in a week, nor in a season. One's interest is revived and roused year by year, as bit by bit of the petrified portions of the skeleton comes to hand. Thirty such years elapsed before I was able to outline a restoration of *Diprotodon australis.*'

Sometimes, however, other materials than extinct fossil remains were submitted to Owen for examination. 'In March,' he writes in his diary, 'I spent some time at the Home Office comparing microscopically the surface-characters of the bullet from the body of the policeman murdered by Peace, with those of a bullet fired for that purpose, from the burglar's revolver, and of bullets from other revolvers. I was able to testify that the bullet which slew the policeman agreed so closely with one subsequently fired from Peace's revolver, as to impress me with its identity ; there were unexpected and marked differences in bullets fired from revolvers of another make. Sir Richard Cross and Sir Adolphus Liddell were glad to have this result and testimony as far as it went.'

In November 1879 the Professor received the freedom of the Leathersellers' Company. It was enclosed in a casket beautifully engraved, mounted in silver, bearing a suitable inscription engraved and the note : 'This box is made of hippopotamus leather which required nearly four years to tan.'

Owen's chief desire was to live long enough to see the removal of the British Museum specimens to South Kensington. Writing to a friend in September of 1879, he says :—

'As my strength fails, and I feel the term of my labours drawing nigh, how I long to see the conclusion of their main aim!—the exposition of our national treasures of natural history in a manner worthy of the greatest commercial and colonial empire of the world.'

Writing on the same subject to Dr. Pearson Langshaw, December 21, 1879, he says :—

'I nurse my old chronic "bronchitis" by the fireside, *whenever I can*, hoping still to survive the arrangement in systematic order of the national treasures of natural history in their noble new building. But the halter of an Affghan is a costly affair ; so is a bullet in the body of a Zulu. Mr. Robert Lowe let the "tail of the cat" out of the bag, when he told the public that the sum for the purchase of books for the National Library had been cut down. If he had let out the "whole animal," he would have dealt a better blow. "We cannot afford the furniture," &c., &c.! and the prospect of getting in, even in 1881, is poor, unless we have a Chancellor of the Exchequer who will lay on a 1s. or 1s. 6d. in the pound income tax, and pay the debts of the year within the year like decent, honest people.'

In 1879 a fitting tribute was paid to a man who had been an active member of the Commission for the first Great Exhibition. Nearly thirty years had elapsed between that appointment and Owen's nomination to be a Member of the Royal Commission for the British Section of the International Exhibition of Melbourne, 1880.

A man who held for so many years so prominent a position as Owen inevitably becomes the
victim of strange requests. As years passed,
he formed a small collection of letters, which
he labelled ' Specimens of my Correspondence.'
One of these he received on January 23, 1880.
It was a twelve-page letter, closely written, from
a gentleman who forwarded at the same time a
large packet of poems of his own composition,
which he desired the Professor to read through
with comments and return. The letter contained
a biography of the writer, with a minute account
of his poetic instincts and aspirations. Owen
answered the letter politely, but at the same
time begged to be excused from perusing the
poems on account of their length, and concluded his letter with the following words : ' In
my seventy-sixth year, with rare materials
awaiting examination and the impending labour
of the transfer of our Natural History Museum
hence to South Kensington, you will condone a
request to spare both our brief allotted time for
work—yours in writing, mine in reading and
replying.'

Another specimen may be quoted, which the
Professor has endorsed 'A characteristic request !
from a perfect stranger ! !' It runs thus :—

' Dear Professor Owen,—A few months hence,
all being well, I leave England to return to the
United States. My wife and I are gathering

" memories " of literary favourites, friends, and acquaintances, to carry with us to our home across the Atlantic. By parcels post I have ventured to send you a page of my wife's album, and we shall feel grateful if you will enrich it with a brief autographic contribution. We shall hail the veriest trifle with very great pleasure.

'I remain,

'Yours most truly,

'_____'

'Since the old Park mole-catcher went to earth,' the Professor wrote,[2] March 1, 1880, 'my plague of moles has returned, and my front lawn is seldom free from one or more evidences, cumulative, of the wonderful little tunneller's operations. In our village there is a belief that "the 'Fessor keeps a mole," and I have seen children, when they come to play about the Pond, peer through the light fence to see the "'Fessor's mole." Well! I have lately benefited by an unexpected ally. A fine young cat, reared by the cook, has taken to catching moles. She steals out in the gray of the morning, listens, and sits where she hears the little grubber coming near the surface, and, when he pushes his head above the earth-mound, Puss pounces upon him and hales him out.'

The mole-catcher in question, from whom the

[2] To Dr. Pearson Langshaw.

R 2

Professor used to extract a good deal of amusement, was a disreputable old person, long since deceased, whose nefarious proceedings were described in an article contributed by Owen to ' Blackwood's Magazine' in 1871.

From 1880 to 1884 Owen was engaged in superintending the removal of the specimens from the British to the Natural History Museum at South Kensington, which was now prepared to receive them. He thus lived to enjoy the realisation of his life-long wish. Before his retirement he had the gratification of seeing the collections—many of which had been crowded in the dark vaults of the old Bloomsbury Museum, where it was impossible that they could be properly exhibited—now safely transferred and displayed to their best advantage in the new museum.

The new museum was not a source of unmixed delight to everybody. Mr. Ruskin wrote the following letter to Owen about this time in answer to an invitation to go over the building :—

John Ruskin to R. Owen

November 6.

' Dear Professor Owen,—I am entirely grateful for your most kind letter and memory of me ; but I can't come to-day (for cold in teeth and throat). Alas! My dear old musty Museum was as much a hobby to me as your new one to you, and it would be mere misery to me to see your new

abode   I wished yesterday Guy were himself
again, and would blow up both Houses of Parliament, and all the West End with them ; then
there might be a chance for the east, and for the
Sun and Aurora again.

      ' Ever yours affectionately,

                   ' J. RUSKIN.

   ' I *can* write steadily still when I am not in a
rage—but that's not often.'

   ' I dine with Paget,' Owen writes[3] (March 23,
1881), ' the day after to-morrow to meet Tennyson.
I fear the poet will miss his pet pipe.' In another
letter (March 27) he gives a description of some
of the conversation, and continues : ' When the
ladies retired our host benevolently sent for *the
Pipe*; we accompanied, with mild cigarettes,
the Poet, who then began to unroll (a hedgehog
simile). But in the drawing-room he was " very
good," and read to us his " Maud "—-I think his
favourite.'

   In the Grosvenor Gallery of 1881 Professor
Owen's portrait appeared, painted by Mr. Holman
Hunt. The ' Times,' in speaking of this portrait,
says (May 2): ' Perhaps the finest portrait in the
gallery among so many that are very fine is the
" Professor Owen " of Mr. Holman Hunt. This
is a work which is full of Mr. Hunt's peculiarities
of colour. The flesh of the face is that curious

        [3] To Dr. Pearson Langshaw.

reddish yellow with purple shadows in which the artist delights, and it is painted with all the sculptured accuracy that is familiar to us in Mr. Hunt's religious subjects. None the less is it a fine portrait and also a fine likeness.'

In the same year Mr. Hamo Thornycroft exhibited a bust of Owen. In a letter to the writer he mentions how exemplary a sitter the Professor was. 'He was good enough,' he writes, 'to give me about a dozen sittings for the portrait bust. His very charming and genial manner, as he sat and told me anecdotes of men long past—Turner and Chantrey—made these occasions very delightful and interesting to me. I modelled the bust in 1880, but the marble was not exhibited in the Academy until 1881.'

On April 6 Owen went to Folkestone in order to unveil a statue of William Harvey. In memory of this occasion the Mayor and Corporation of that borough presented him with a copy of Harvey's works. Under the title of 'Experimental Physiology' (1884), we have, in an amplified form, and with various additions, the substance of the address which Owen delivered there.

Until 1883 the Professor was almost daily at the new Museum, where there was still much to be done. With regard to the skeleton of the whale which now stands in the entrance hall, he writes to Mr. A. Waterhouse, July 31, 1882 :—

'After much consideration, . . . I concluded
that the skeleton of a fine cachalot whale would
least interfere with the *ensemble* unglazed.   It is
low, like all Cetacea, though long, leaving ample
room on each side, and not obstructing the view
of the staircase.   My scientific object was to give
the public an idea of the bulk that might be
attained by an animal of the existing kinds.   No
extinct monster equals it.'

CHAPTER IX

In 1883 Owen received from Frédéric Cuvier the present of a seal which had belonged to Georges Cuvier. The high value that he placed upon this important relic is shown by his reply to his 'dear and truly esteemed friend :'—

'For such is the relation in which I have ever held yourself, bearing the honoured name of the great teacher from whom I received my final instructions, as pupil at the Jardin des Plantes, in the sciences I have since cultivated. Whatever success may have attended my labours is due to the principles there inculcated, and to the example there manifested. I was favoured by admission at 6 A.M. to the laboratory, where the master examined and noted the characters of the subjects of his last great work, "Sur les Poissons."

'Of the many recognitions, by my Sovereign, by her Prime Minister, by my late masters the Trustees of the British Museum of Natural History, and by my fellow-officers, not any has yielded me more heartfelt gratification than the precious relic you have been pleased, with most estimable and characteristic forethought, to enrich me with.   It will be worn by me whilst I live, and I believe it will be cherished by my son and his sons as evidence of their regard of the representative of the name they have so often heard me mention with grateful reverence.

'There are fashions of thought as well as of dress.   A somewhat prevailing one, to which you allude, I have occasionally referred to as the *Biologie conjecturale* ; but the science of living things which will endure is based on the foundation of the *faits positifs* made known, with the true methods of their discovery, in the immortal works of Georges Cuvier.'

In his declining years it was one of Owen's favourite amusements to observe the habits of the birds which frequented his garden.   The notes which he made upon his feathered visitors were, as he writes in his diary, 'communicated to my friend Robinson's weekly paper "The Garden" in successive numbers.'   A few extracts from these 'Notes on Birds in my Garden,' which were published in 1883, throw light on Owen's interests and occupations.   The number of birds

which the Professor noted in his garden at Sheen
Lodge is surprising :—

'I have entered in my garden book,' he
writes, 'the name of every kind of bird which I
have noted there, distinguishing the permanent
dwellers from the occasional residents, and the
latter according to the periods of their temporary
sojourn, whether to breed or to feed—in other
words, the summer and winter visitors.

'The list, however, would have been incom-
plete without the aid of my lamented friend,
John Gould. It was ever with him a favourite
summer afternoon's holiday, after a ramble in
the park, to pass an hour in the garden. On
one of these occasions, in early June, we rested
on a seat overshadowed by a weeping ash, but
allowing a view of the lawn. Happening to
show him my ornithological list at that date,
Gould said, "You have got more birds in the
garden than I see here, I expect." Now he
possessed in a remarkable degree the faculty
of imitating the various notes of all our vocal
species. He bade us sit still and be silent ;
then began. After emitting a particular
"motivo" for a few minutes, he would quietly
point to a little bird which had flown from an
adjoining bush upon the lawn, and was there
hopping inquisitively to and fro, gradually
nearing the locality of its specific song. We
could then recognise the species to which Gould

gave the name. This attraction and its result
was repeated ; and we enjoyed the same instructive amusement in subsequent summer
vacations, to which I am indebted for additions
that would otherwise probably have escaped
my observation.'

There then follows a list of birds, with
characteristic remarks and observations. Concerning the tits he writes :—

' These lively little birds—the greater tit
(*Parus major*), blue tit (*Parus cærulcus*), with
the rarer long-tailed tit (*Parus caudatus*)—I
tempt into view at the time of hardest frosts.
Then to the leafless branch of a creeper[1] which
crosses my bed-room window I suspend by a
wire, with a fishing swivel, a small wire cage,
about the size of a nutmeg. This is filled at
night with a lump of suet. At early dawn I
note from my pillow the swift flight of a little
bird to a branch of the Gleditschia, also in view,
on which it turns or jerks about as if moved by a
spring. Then mustering courage it darts upon
the suet cage, clinging like a parrot to the wire,
and whirling about to show all its plumage. It
is the blue tit ; but hardly has he enjoyed a few
pecks when he suddenly lets go and is off again
to his post on the great tree. What has startled
him in this calm dawn of prevailing frost ? The
handsome greater tit takes his place, and not

[1] *Pyrus japonica.*

until he is satisfied does the smaller one resume
his breakfast.   But the pugnacious robin is not
to be so scared.   It is true he cannot cling
while fighting like the tits; but he takes his
stand on the window-sill, ruffles his plumage out
to make the most of his size, and attacks *Parus
major* by successive flights, assaulting him from
below.   The tit gives way, and the redbreast
then makes a series of flying pecks at the suet.'

Of the throstle he says :—

'There are a few old cherry trees in the
garden; one of them a Bigarreau.   This I
netted in my first summer's possession to preserve the tempting fruit.   When the dish came
to table, I thought of the frequent pleasures
which the morn and evening warblings of the
little robbers had given me, and felt ashamed at
fencing off what I could cheaply get, as fresh
and better, from neighbouring market gardens.
I never repeated the practice, but left Bigarreaus
with the other cherries as " salary of the orchestra."

'*Sparrow* (*Passer domesticus*).—Our colony
remains pretty stationary as to numbers; they
are never molested, and are fed in winter.
Being formerly accustomed to coax these town
birds at that season to the windows of my
official residence in Lincoln's Inn Fields, I was
hardly prepared to do justice to the well-marked,
agreeable, un-sooted attire which both sexes, and

especially the males, present in the clear atmosphere of my present abode.

'From the rook (*Corvus frugilegus*) I have
received nothing but favours. They take their
share in diminishing lawn pests and other insect
plagues ; their ways and instincts afford endless
interest. When I took up my abode at Sheen
Lodge there was in the elm wood leading there
from Sheen Gate a small rookery at our end. I
am bound to say that at the nesting season
complaints of being awoke and kept awake, from
3 A.M., were frequent and well founded ; but this
is the only exception to the pleasure which the
cawings at evening and other seasonable times
have given to one whose busy life, in great proportion, is spent in London.

'Broderip, the author of "Recreations in
Natural History," especially enjoyed his visits
at the rooks' breeding season, and the worthy
magistrate declared that he should unquestion-
ably commit certain members of the cawing
community for theft and burglary if they had
been other than feathered bipeds. The case
was this. A young married couple could always
be discriminated by the unusual activity displayed in preparing the abode for the incubator
and her coming brood, yet, by reason of the
unconscionable practice of their elders, and
possibly parents, they spent twice the time
and trouble in completing the nest than did

the more experienced birds or than was fairly
needful.

'The old couple, perched near the framework of their former nest on a higher branch,
instead of flying forth to collect their own lining
materials, awaited the return of the younger
pair, each with a beakful of moss or wool, which
they then busied themselves in properly dis-
posing in their unlined nest. This being done,
forthwith off they flew again to gather more
material, whereupon the stationary old rooks, who
had generally monopolised the topmost localities,
would hop down from twig to twig and delibe-
rately transfer the lining material of the young
pair's nest to their own; nor, until the old birds
had thus provided for themselves, were the young
couple permitted to finish theirs.

'We sometimes fancied we saw movements
of the plundered ones, after fruitless flights,
indicative of suspicions of foul play. But, in
the long run, all went on well; the coming generation was duly hatched out and provided for.
Food could not be larcenously fetched from the
beaks of the new-wedded one's brood so easily as
the wool from their nests.

'I can well understand the condition of our
latitude and environment, which tempts the night-
ingales to our groves and gardens for their breeding ground.

'And here I may remark how rarely I have

succeeded in finding a nightingale's nest, though more than one pair annually rear their brood in the garden. On one of these occasions the nest was hidden near the base of a holly ; the soft, warm, nursing chamber was walled round by a ring of dead and shed holly leaves stuck upright with their margins overlapping each other.

' *Night-Jar*, *or Churn Owl* (*Caprimulgus europæus*).—I owe an occasional sight and more frequent hearing of this strange bird to the advantageous location of my garden and abode. Close to it begins a preserve, which extends along the eastern boundary of the park to near Roehampton Gate. On one side of the preserve is the park with old oaks ; on the other side is the quietest and least frequented of commons, hight " Pale-well," from the spring of pure water rising therein. No cultivation is carried on outside the garden wall. Such are the conditions suitable to the night-jar's singular habit of oviposition and hatching of the eggs, usually a pair, on the bare ground ; of nest-building the bird seems ignorant. She selects some bare spot with which her own colours so closely match that she is hard to recognise even when you are near, and she is so hardy that you may stand and contemplate her for some time, and may have to move a step or two nearer before she takes to flight. Since my first acquaintance I have never disturbed mother or eggs, but always quietly retired when I have come in view of them. And, so retiring, I have marvelled at the seeming knowledge possessed by the bird of her own tints, and have pondered upon the instinct which has guided her choice of the limited patch of ground best according with them. If a night-jar possessed the strange faculty of the chameleon, the trout, or the cuttle-fish, and was able to change its colour to that of the spot on which it rests and nidificates, the explanation of the baffling correspondence would be easy ; but the mystery of the colorific movements in the skin and of the volition, conscious or unconscious, which the chameleons obey, remains. I have generally recognised the advent in May of this migratory bird by its singular jarring note. But when its favourite food, the large moths and chaffers, abounds, its active wheeling flight about the old oaks is remarkable.'

The mention of the night-birds suggests a characteristic story of Owen which is told by Dr. A. S. Murray, of the British Museum :—

'One day when Professor Owen was passing through the room of Greek and Roman bronzes, as he often did in his Bloomsbury days, I happened to be at work there. He stopped to speak, and while speaking observed close beside him the well-known bronze head of Hypnos with the wing still springing from one of its temples. The form of the wing caught Professor Owen's eye, and he asked, "Have you observed that this is the wing

BRONZE HEAD OF HYPNOS IN THE BRITISH MUSEUM.

of a night-bird which flies noiselessly?" and then
added: " It was a beautiful idea of the Greeks to
give the God of Sleep wings which would enable
him to visit his patients without a murmur of
sound."[2]   He knew the passage in the " Iliad"
where Hypnos takes the form of the bird which
" men call Chalkis but the gods Kumindis." I was
greatly struck by the observation, not so much
because of the identification of the wing of the
night-bird—that must have been easy for a
naturalist, and had indeed been once remarked
before, as I learned afterwards—but because of
what appeared to me the singularly poetic insight
which had led Professor Owen to note the noise-
lessness of the night-bird's wing and its beautiful
appropriateness to the God of Sleep.   These were
two points which no archæologist had dreamt of,
and yet this particular head of Hypnos had been
made the subject of an elaborate investigation by
the most practically minded of German critics,
Heinrich Braun.   But surely the true beauty of
the conception was lost until we recognised what
Professor Owen was the first to point out.'

Nor is this an isolated instance of the imagina-
tive faculty which is essential to any great exponent
of science.   Owen was always a reader of poetry,
and drew from the stores of his retentive memory

[2] It is curious to contrast
with this the practice of modern
painters to represent angels
with the wings of a swan, one
of the most noisy of birds.

an abundance of apt quotations and illustrations. It was his habit to write such quotations on the fly-leaf of his different works. From his own interleaved copies the following examples are taken at haphazard :—

In his ' British Fossil Mammals and Birds,' for example, there is the appropriate quotation, ' Bones bear witness.'[3]

In his work descriptive of the extinct gigantic sloth, the Mylodon, he has written : ' Framed in the prodigality of nature.'

In his earliest volume of Hunterian Lectures, when he was just starting on his scientific career, he has written : ' If the Lord will, we shall live, and do this or that ' (James iv. 15). And in a later volume of lectures :

> ' Ut primum inspexi, me non vigilare putavi,
> Luminibusque meis visa neganda fides.'

And as another example (' On the Nature of Limbs '): οἷον πέπονθεν ὄνυξ πρὸς ὁπλὴν καὶ χεὶρ πρὸς χηλήν (Aristotle).

> ' Each part may call the farthest brother,
> And hand with foot hath secret amity.'

The autumn of 1883 found Owen still hard at work completing the arrangement of the Natural History collections in their new home. On September 22 he wrote to Pearson Langshaw regretting that he could not attend the

[3] *Comedy of Errors*, iv., 4.

Southport Meeting of the British Association, and thus continued : 'To the usual inquiry from our masters the Trustees, I replied that " I had no intention to take any vacation this year." So, at present, I am almost the only officer on duty at the New Museum. But my work there is, as you may imagine, one of love. . . . . The birds have been received into their gallery, and the beasts into theirs ; and both are steadily getting into their proper places. We are also receiving, without interruption, the other classes of the existing creation, to which the west wing of the New Museum is devoted.

'What a contrast the two gatherings which give food to columns in the daily papers present ! Philosophers in sober garments ; emperors, kings, princes and princesses in gorgeous uniforms and brilliant orders, watching the evolutions of thousands of well-drilled soldiers ! . . . .

'I derived a wholesome lesson from the inaugural address of my old friend the Cambridge Professor of Mathematics. *I could not comprehend a word of it !* My brain was a blank ! Palæontology may be as strange to him !'

'With this year (1883),' Owen has written in his diary, ' end my official relations with the national collections of natural history, the several departments—Zoology, Geology, Fossils, Minerals, Plants—being arranged and displayed in their respective galleries. I felt that I could now "depart

in peace," for mine eyes had seen *their* sal-
vation.'

On January 5, 1884, Professor Owen was
gazetted K.C.B. on his retirement from the
Museum ; on Mr. Gladstone's initiative, his pen-
sion was supplemented by 100*l.* annually.

A few words will suffice to tell the story of
the remaining years of his life.

After the death of his only son in 1886, shortly
followed by that of his sole remaining sister, his
eldest grandson lived with him at Sheen Lodge
until 1889, when his daughter-in-law and the
rest of her children came also to reside there.
The Professor occupied his time chiefly with his
correspondence and in reading. He would read
anything that came to hand, from the latest
scientific work that was sent him to the ' Queen '
newspaper, which journal was a source of unfailing amusement to him, owing to the numerous
advertisements of hair-dyes, washes for the
complexion, and the 'anatomical impossibilities,'
as he called the ladies of the fashion-plates.

Two red-letter days in the year were Christmas Day and his birthday, July 20. On these
occasions a few old friends, up to the last, came
to keep the feast. Prominent amongst these
was Mr. R. D. Blackmore, whose novels, one of
which is dedicated to the Professor, occupied an
honoured place in his well-filled library.

A keen chess-player himself, Sir Richard was

always ready for a game in the evenings, and until very recent years played exceedingly well. His chief relaxation, however, was music, of which he had always been passionately fond. He was never tired of listening to his favourite compositions, although as he grew older his taste in music became much narrower, and he could only listen with pleasure to the music admitted to be ' classical ' in his younger days. Wagner, Grieg, and more modern composers were to his mind ' tolerable and not to be endured.' The keys of his little old-fashioned piano had been touched by many of his musical friends—Moscheles, John Ella, and Hallé, and had served many a time to accompany Jenny Lind and his own famous 'cello by Forster.

The love of his home and of his beautiful garden only grew stronger with his declining years. Every day he would go round his garden —no small distance—supported by his favourite curiously-carved stick ; then he would generally make his way to an extraordinary specimen of a garden-seat, made out of the vertebra of a whale, which he himself had put up. There are many such curiosities to be seen in that picturesque piece of ground. The skull of a huge crocodile, most of whose teeth are missing, owing to dental experiments made with champagne-nippers by certain small grandchildren, grins out of a rockery. The plaster cast of a seated Egyptian figure rests on a pedestal at the end of the ' west walk,' and a

few great bones repose gracefully against a tree
in that wooded part of the garden which has
always been left entirely to Nature. These little
woods are still full of the wild flowers which the
Professor gathered in his travels on the Continent
or his rambles in the country, the roots of which
he brought home with him and planted himself.

Thus his latter days peacefully glided away.
His old friends were gradually leaving him, and
of his scientific contemporaries hardly any remained, so many changes of scientific thought
had he lived to see, and so long a period had his
life embraced. The last letter which he received
from perhaps the oldest of them, Lord Enniskillen,
is dated August 19, 1885 : 'Neither of us,' he
writes, 'my dear old friend, are so young as we
were, nor nearly so active as when we used to
clamber over the cliffs with Mary Anning.[4] By-
the-by, I have just bought from a nephew of
Mary's a number of drawings and manuscripts,
many of them by De la Beche and Conybeare,
but I have not examined them yet.'

In proportion as Sir Richard's memory
became more failing with regard to present-
day matters, it became all the clearer as to the
time of his schooldays and early youth.

He often used to tell stories of his school-
fellows, and still oftener of his mother, of her
goodness to him, of her love of music. He

[4] The collector at Lyme Regis.

never forgot those friends with whom his
younger days were intimately associated, and in
this connection a letter from Mr. William White
Cooper is interesting :—

May 28, 1886.

'My very dear Friend,—I think it due to you
as my oldest and most valued friend to com-
municate direct to you the information that I
have this day received from Mr. Gladstone—the
announcement that the Queen intends to confer
upon me the honour of knighthood. . . . When
I look back upon the incidents of my life I am
struck with the part played by you in them :
How you went down to Derby to my wedding
and gave away my dear wife ; how I owe to
you the delightful tour we had together in
Germany, of which memory recalls so many
little incidents ; how we "faced" one another in
the ranks of the H.A.C. at the Coronation ; how
we went to the Grand Review at Woolwich and
saw the great people, including old Soult, and
saw the big gun fired, the report of which gave
me a kick in the stomach ! But I must stop. It
has been my proud lot to see *you* receive the
honours so justly your due, and at a very humble
distance I follow ! . . . .

'I am ever most sincerely yours,
'W. WHITE COOPER.'[5]

[5] Mr. White Cooper's death took place very shortly after- wards ; before, indeed, the knighthood could be actually conferred upon him.

Another of his oldest friends was Pearson Langshaw, of Lancaster. The following anecdote, gleaned from his experiences as a commissioner to inquire into the water-supply of his native town, is extracted from a letter written to his fellow-townsman by Owen in March 1889. It at least illustrates the way in which his mind reverted to the home and familiar accents of his childhood. ' I knew,' he writes, ' the wretched character of its water-supply from household wells and pumps, which yielded very hard water. I also knew that a hill of primitive rock, a few miles from the town, going from a level higher than the church steeple, carried off the purest rainfall to the neighbouring sea. That fine water was brought to the town, and has proved an unfailing supply to every class of dwelling. There were two elderly widows, inhabiting neighbouring abodes, who had adopted the economical habit of taking tea with each other alternately. On the first occasion of using the purer water, the visitor exclaimed, " Eh ! Betty, thou's put a power o' tea into pot to-neet !" " Nay, Jennie," replied the hostess, " it's nobbut t' new watter." '

As the circle of his old friends contracted it was hardly to be expected that their places would be taken by new. Sir Richard lived out of London, almost in country retirement. Unable, except at rare intervals, to travel to town, and especially incapable of night journeys, he was

obliged to give up his attendance at 'The Club.'
Of this body he had been since 1879[6] the senior
member in point of priority of election, and he
was also the first honorary member who was
elected. On April 16, 1886, he received the
following letter from Mr. Henry Reeve, Treasurer
of 'The Club : '—

'My dear Sir Richard,—The Club having
unanimously agreed to the proposal for electing
honorary members, who are precluded from habi-
tual attendance, their first act was to confer that
distinction upon you, and you were so elected.

'As an honorary member you retain all the
privileges of membership, and I am particularly
desired to say to you that it will give The Club
very great pleasure if you can occasionally join
its meetings.

' Believe me,

'With the greatest regard,

' Yours very faithfully,

' H. REEVE.'

While his grandson was at Cambridge, Sir
Richard wrote him letters nearly every week.
Their cheerful tone is surprising in a man over
eighty. In spirit they were still young, and, to
the last, the writer took the keenest interest in
everything that went on at the University.

A few extracts from these letters from Sir

[6] He became a member of that society in May 1845.

Richard Owen to his grandson Richard Owen are given below :—

'I read with pleasure your sketch of Dr. Harvey Goodwin's [7] visit to Cambridge and of his University sermon. . . . We were always on friendly terms, and Mrs. Harvey Goodwin keeps up an occasional correspondence with me.

'Your account of the Musical Society concert makes me think of the old days when I had my seat at St. James's Hall. I seldom missed a " Pop," and did not give up my stall till I was too deaf to hear the first violin. I have been a fellow-guest of Madame Patti's more than once at my hospitable friend Hume Dick's house at Thames Ditton. I found her very agreeable and quite disposed to have a chat with me. . . .'

'. . . . I enjoyed a charming dinner at White Lodge since you left for Cambridge, but time passes very quietly and peacefully with me at home ; a brief sunshine occasionally tempts me round the garden. I can hardly conceive a more thankworthy condition, at the close of a busy life, than that which I am now enjoying. . . .'

'. . . . Chadwick drove me to London on the 24th for the anniversary of the Linnean Society.

[7] Late Bishop of Carlisle. He was an old friend of Owen's, and one of the few photographs which the Professor kept on his library mantel-piece was a framed portrait of this bishop.

My part in the proceedings was comparatively easy, being confined to the reception of the Gold Medal. This concluded the Linnean meeting, which was fully attended, with a gallery of fair ladies. I was kindly led to an arm-chair near the President, but the meeting was longer than Chadwick could wait for, so I got a train to Mortlake, and found a spare cab which set me down at my gate. . . . Quartos and other forms of publications arrive almost daily from divers parts of the world. I enclose a cheque, so I trust you will not think " there is *nothing* in this letter." '

March 8, 1889.

' I was glad to know the interval between this date and your arrival here is so brief. The ice is now off the pond and my white ducks on it.

' I find eighty-five years a heavy weight to carry, but I shall endeavour shortly to get up to town and look in at the Athenæum again.'

Sept. 27, 1890.

' I look forward to lasting to greet you here at your Christmas holidays. You deserve a longer letter than my late severe illness has left me the power to write. Should you finally determine to take Holy Orders, I please myself in believing that you will do well in the Church ; but, however this may happen, I pray God that He will guide you to a satisfactory career.'

Sir Richard still received occasional commu-

nications from his scientific *confrères* abroad.
On August 7, 1889, the following telegram was
despatched to him from the Zoological Congress
which met at Paris on that day: 'Congrès
Zoologique exprime son admiration pour vos
beaux travaux et ses vœux pour la continuation
d'une santé si utile à la science.— Le Président,
MILNE EDWARDS.'

To this telegram Owen replied to Professor
Milne Edwards: ' Be pleased to convey to the
Congrès Zoologique the expression of my deep
sense of the honour conferred upon me by the
distinguished members of that scientific body over
which you so worthily preside, and my deep
interest in the success of that association for the
advancement of our common science.—Your faithful friend and fellow-labourer, RICHARD OWEN.'

Other proofs were not wanting that Sir
Richard's lifelong labours were not forgotten.
The gracious permission of Her Majesty the
Queen that his family should, after his death, con-
tinue to reside at Sheen Lodge was a recognition
of his services which afforded him the keenest
satisfaction. But he was now growing daily more
feeble in body. Except at his own home, he
rarely saw his friends. There his Royal neighbours
in Richmond Park not unfrequently paid him a
visit, and he often spoke of their constant kindness to him in terms of much affection. Beyond the

gates of his garden he so seldom ventured that
an occasional dinner at White Lodge or a rare
visit to the Athenæum and the Bank were almost
the only exceptions to what had become the habit
of his life.   Almost the last of his expeditions to
London was made in the autumn of 1889.   He
was driven to town by Sir Edwin Chadwick,
accompanied by Dr. (now Sir) B. W. Richardson,
and the party took the opportunity of being photo-
graphed together.

Early in the following year Sir Richard was
seized with an attack of illness very like a paralytic
stroke, from which he never entirely recovered.
By sheer force of will he rallied from it in a way
which was little short of marvellous.   When he
was considered to be almost at death's door, he
left his bed without assistance, dressed himself,
and was found sitting in his library as if he had
never been ill at all.   But this attack enfeebled
his memory, and to a great extent deprived him of
the use of his limbs, though it did but little to
impair his handwriting, which remained almost as
neat and clear as ever.

After his illness he scarcely ever moved out
of his two rooms, the library and bedroom, which
open out of each other.   The library is an old-
fashioned room, with a low ceiling, and with
windows looking on to the park at one side and
into the garden at the other.   On the wall-spaces
of this room not filled with book-shelves hang

medallions and miniatures of various men—
Newton, Cuvier, John Hunter, William Clift,
Joseph Banks, and others—as well as oil-paintings
of John Hunter and Oliver Cromwell.

In this room he would sometimes sit for hours,
looking out wistfully at the park view, the little
piece of water with the two old oaks by its side,
the wide expanse of green, and the dark back-
ground of trees.

His favourite library companion was a little
black and white Persian cat.　He was always fond
of cats, and his last intelligible words were spoken
to this animal, which was with him to the hour of
his death.

In the early morning of his last birthday (July
20, 1892), the tree which he admired more than
any in the garden—the Gleditschia—fell down with
a crash, leaving only part of the trunk and a few
branches, although there was little or no wind at
the time.

By a curious coincidence, on that day Sir
Richard showed marked symptoms of failing
strength.　But as he did not feel positively ill,
and was in very good spirits, no particular alarm
was felt.　It was not till the end of August that
any anxiety was felt at his symptoms, and Dr.
Palmer, of East Sheen, who visited him con-
tinuously with unfailing kindness and consideration to the end, was called in.

On August 25, Dr. Palmer writes : ' I found

him in bed, suffering from a severe form of stoma-
titis. His temperature was normal, pulse good
though irregular, but his articulation and deglutition very difficult.'

His throat at this time was so much blocked
up by exudation that conversation had to be carried
on by signs or in writing, and for some days he
lay in this serious condition. On August 30 his
old friend Sir James Paget paid him a visit, and
tried to converse with him ; but Sir Richard,
owing to his prostration and difficulty in articulation, was unable to sustain the effort long.

These symptoms, however, cleared up entirely
in September. His throat resumed its natural
appearance, and he was able to take solid food
again, but, although he made satisfactory progress
towards recovery, he never made any attempt to
leave his bed.

'In reply to my repeated inquiries,' Dr.
Palmer continues, ' Sir Richard invariably answered : " I feel no pain at all, but I have no desire
to rise from this bed." In direct proportion to
the improvement in his symptoms, his intelligence
returned and his faculties recovered. His deafness became less marked, and he was able to converse for a short time without fatigue. He would
even occasionally discuss some of the questions of
the day in his usual kind and courteous manner.
While in this condition Sir Richard received a
visit from the Prince of Wales, who called to see

him with Princess May and the Duke of Teck,
and stayed for some time and talked at his bed-
side.   This visit Sir Richard greatly appreciated,
and when he was told that His Royal Highness
was downstairs and wished to see him, he put
his black velvet skull-cap straight, smoothed
his hair, and said : ' Then I must try and pull
myself together.'

Although his deafness made conversation very
difficult on this occasion, he was still able to converse for a short time with his royal visitors.

During the whole of his illness the Duke
and Duchess of Teck and Princess May frequently came to Sheen Lodge, and were often
good enough to stay and talk with him.

Towards the end of November he seemed to
be not so well again, and complained of coldness
in the extremities.   Any attempts at conversation
now exhausted him exceedingly ; he began to
take less and less nourishment, and from the first
week of December he never exhibited the smallest
disposition to rally.   On December 16 he ceased
to recognise those that were standing round him,
and became very restless.   Soon after his breath-
ing became stertorous, and it was plain that the
end could not be far off.   A little before three
o'clock on Sunday morning, December 18, 1892,
he passed peacefully away, without a struggle,
leaving the world poorer by the loss of an untiring
worker and of a most genial and kind-hearted man.

OWEN'S POSITION IN THE HISTORY OF ANATOMICAL SCIENCE

THE RIGHT HON. THOMAS H. HUXLEY, F.R.S.

——•◦•——

THE attempt to form a just conception of the value of work done in any department of human knowledge, and of its significance as an indication of the intellectual and moral qualities of which it was the product, is an undertaking which must always be beset with difficulties, and may easily end in making the limitations of the appraiser more obvious than the true worth of that which he appraises. For the judgment of a contemporary is liable to be obscured by intellectual incompatibilities and warped by personal antagonisms ; while the critic of a later generation, though he may escape the influence of these sources of error, is often ignorant, or forgetful of, the conditions under which the labours of his predecessors have been carried on. He is prone to lose sight of the fact that without their clearing

VOL. II.   T

of the ground and rough-hewing of the foundation-stones, the stately edifice of later builders could not have been erected.

In view of these considerations, it was not altogether with a light heart that I assented to the proposal Sir Richard Owen's biographer did me the honour to make, that I should furnish him with a critical estimate of the extensive and varied labours in the field of natural science carried on, for some sixty years, with singular energy, by that eminent man. For I have to reckon, more than most, with those causes of imperfect or distorted vision to which, as I have said, the eyes of con-temporaries are obnoxious ; and, however con-fident of the will to correct their effects, I can hardly hope to be entirely successful, without more good fortune than I have a right to look for.

It is an enhancement of the difficulties of the task set me, that what I have to say must be addressed not to experts, but to the general public, to the great majority of whom anatomy is as much a sealed book as the higher mathe-matics. Even if some few have penetrated a little way, their progress has probably been arrested by the discovery that discussions about anatomical topics are, as a rule, pre-eminently dry and tech-nical. It must be admitted that there is some justification for the popular distaste for anatomical science. The associations of the subject are not wholly pleasing ; and, undoubtedly, a long and weary process of initiation is indispensable to the neophyte, who aspires to become an adept and to feel at home in the arcana of the higher anatomy. But I think it ought to be possible to lead any one, who will give a reasonable amount of attention, to a point, from which he may obtain a sufficiently accurate general view of the scope of anatomical science, by a shorter and easier road. In any case, it is laid upon me to attempt to show the way there, inasmuch as the purport of much of Sir Richard Owen's work cannot be understood, nor can his position in science be properly appreciated, unless such a point of view is attained. And in proffering such guide's service it may be well to remind those who accept the offer, that in this, as in so many other cases, ' the longest way round is the shortest way home ;' there is nothing for it but to follow the path of history and eschew short cuts, however tempting they may be.

Etymologically, the word ' Anatomy ' signifies no more than ' cutting up,' or ' dissection ;' but, in course of time, the idea of the chief means by which the structure of animals and of plants was ascertained merged with that of the results it yielded. And since structure, or inward form, is practically inseparable from shape, or outward form, the latter also fell within the range of the anatomist. Further, it was natural enough that the ' function ' or use of the parts, the inward and

outward form of which they described, should
also be treated of by the early and mediæval
anatomists ; but, as the subject grew, division of
labour not only became practically necessary, but
was theoretically indicated by the diverse characters of its moieties.   Form can be considered
without any reference to function ; and function
can be studied with very little reference to form.
One need know nothing of the structure of the
eye, for example, to make sure that it is the organ
of vision ; and a minimum of anatomical lore
suffices to establish the familiar truths that the
stomach is largely concerned in digestion, and
the lungs in respiration.   Moreover, the preliminary training required for the effectual prose-
cution and advancement of the several studies of
form and of function is so different, that, in
modern times, the two have steadily tended to
fall into different hands.   The doctrine of form,
whether in the shape of anatomy, histology, embryology, taxonomy (that is, systematic arrangement),
or distribution, has become the business of the
'morphologist,' to whom it is a matter of no
essential importance whether the subjects of his
inquiries are alive or have been dead for millions of
years.   On the other hand, since functions are the
modes of manifestation of the activities of living
matter, in ultimate resort they must be studied
in living beings.   The exact forms which the me-
chanisms of the functions may assume is a matter

of subordinate interest. By a curious and somewhat unfortunate chance, the name of 'physiologist,' originally applied to those primal philosophers of ancient Greece who took all Nature for their province, has been inherited by the investigators of function, to whom it has no more special application than to any other students of Nature.

Arrived at the parting of the ways,[1] the one of which leads to the province of physiology, the other to that of morphology, we must take the latter. It is no disparagement to Owen to say that he was not a physiologist in the modern sense of the term. In fact, he had done a large part of his work before modern physiology, in which no progress can be made without clear mechanical, physical, and chemical conceptions, came into existence ; and I think it may be doubted whether he ever became fully aware of the vastness of the interval which separates the physiology of John Hunter from the physiology of Johannes Müller and his successors.

Morphology has grown out of anatomy ; and anatomy, like most branches of science, if not begotten and born amongst the ancient Greeks, was nurtured and brought up in the way it should

[1] It will be understood that the separation between Morphology and Physiology can be maintained only so long as the view is confined to the phenomena of form or to those of function. Both are equally important to the aetiologist, who seeks for the causes of biological phenomena.

go by them.   Aristotle, with his immediate predecessors and successors, took the broadest
possible view of the subject ; the structure of
cuttlefishes and crayfishes interested them as
much as that of the higher animals.   And inasmuch as the taint of impurity which, in ancient
times, attached to contact with the dead human
body, hindered them from obtaining a knowledge
of the structure of man directly, they were compelled to divine it, by way of analogy, from their
observations on apes.   In fact, their over-con-
fidence in the extent to which the likeness extended led them into serious errors. .At the revival
of learning, things took another turn.   Anatomy
sank to the level of a mere handmaid to practical
and theoretical medicine.   It was only very much
later, as the anatomical, like other pure sciences,
progressed backwards to their original dignity
and independence, that the position of Democritus
and of Aristotle was once more reached ; and,
the study of the living world being taken up for
the sake of knowledge alone, man assumed his
place as neither more nor less scientifically interesting than his fellows.   In the sixteenth and
seventeenth centuries, however, the great anatomists of the Low Countries and of Italy had pushed
their investigations so far, that more was known
of the structure of man than of that of any other
animal.   It was therefore natural, and indeed
unavoidable, that the structure of man should

become the standard of comparison, or, in other words, the 'type' to which all other kinds of animal structure were to be referred. The organs of animals were interpreted by the analogy of those of man; the terminology of human structure was extended to the structure of animals in general.

Thus the anatomy of the whole of the rest of the animal world came to be regarded as a sort of annexe of human anatomy; it acquired the name of 'comparative anatomy,' and the conception of the relations of man to the rest of the living world was completely falsified. Man, regarded merely as an animal, was held to be the most perfect of all the works of Nature, below which all the rest could be arranged in a graduated series of forms to the lowest animals; from thence, the descending steps were traced through the vegetable world to the lowest plants; and through the definitely formed to the apparently indefinite mineral constituents of the globe. Hence arose the conception of *une échelle des êtres*, a ladder between stones and men, the rungs of which are the species or kinds of living things.

But gradation implies a certain community between the grades. Degrees of colour are shades of the same colour, or mixtures in which the same colours exist in varying proportions; gradations of form imply similarities of form between the successive steps of the gradation.

Thus the idea of a scale of organised beings fore-shadows the conception of a more or less widely prevailing unity of organisation among them, and we may regard the promulgation and wide accept-ances of Bonnet's doctrine of the ' scale of beings ' as the dawn of the higher morphology of modern times.

Though but an imperfect apprehension of a great truth, this doctrine exerted a highly bene-ficial influence upon the progress of comparative anatomy. The gradations in structure of the parts and organs of animals were carefully studied. Immense pains were bestowed on the formation of collections of preparations illustrative of grada-tion ; and there is no more remarkable example of such a collection than that formed by the skill and industry of John Hunter, which was the origin, and still constitutes the nucleus, of the present admirably complete museum of the Royal College of Surgeons of England. A full descrip-tive catalogue of such a collection must needs be, in itself, an encyclopædia of comparative anatomy. Daubenton, the collaborator of Buffon in France, went to work upon a different, but quite as important, principle. As Buffon opposed the ex-treme systematizers, who seemed to think it the end of science, not so much to know about an object as to be able to name it and fit it into their system, so Daubenton insisted on the study of each animal as an individual whole.

Zoologists who knew and could properly apply every technical term of the *systema naturæ* without the least real acquaintance with animal structure in general, or with that of any single animal in particular, were not to his mind. He occupied himself, therefore, with the production of the series of admirable monographs appended to the descriptions of Buffon in the 'Histoire Naturelle.'[2]

The effect of the co-operation of many zealous workers, along the first of these lines, culminated in the 'Anatomie Comparée' of Cuvier; while, to the followers of the second method, we owe a host of monographs upon species, or groups of species, belonging to all the divisions of the animal kingdom. In virtue of these labours it came about that, by the year 1830, the province of anatomy had been systematically and, in many regions, minutely surveyed. An adequate, though far from complete, knowledge of all the higher forms had been attained ; and, with the improvement of the microscope, the structural characters of the very lowest forms were beginning to be elucidated.

Thus, the foundations of anatomical science in accurately recorded observations of structure

[2] It is very much to be regretted that his example has not been more largely followed for the commoner animals. We do not possess, at this moment, a history of even the little group of British Mammals up to the level of the work of Buffon and Daubenton, now nearly a century and a half old.

were solidly and securely laid sixty years ago. In
fact, the importance of the work done by that
time cannot be over-estimated; for, as Cuvier
has somewhere said, whatever may become of
hypotheses, the man who has made a permanent
addition to our knowledge of facts, has rendered
an imperishable service to science. Nevertheless,
it is an equally profound truth, of which no one was
more conscious than Cuvier himself, that the
ascertainment of facts, in the narrowest sense of
the word, and the methodical recording of such
facts, though it is the beginning of scientific
righteousness, is only the beginning. To reach
the end, that which is common to groups of details must be carefully sifted out and expressed in
general propositions; and these, again, must be
tentatively colligated by the guarded and re-
strained play of the imagination, in the invention
of hypotheses, susceptible of verification or nega-
tion by further observation.

The vulgar antithesis of fact and theory is
founded on a misconception of the nature of
scientific theory, which is, or ought to be, no more
than the expression of fact in a general form.
Whatever goes beyond such expression is hypothesis; and hypotheses are not ends, but means.
They should be regarded as instruments by
which new lines of inquiry are indicated; or by
the aid of which a provisional coherency and
intelligibility may be given to seemingly discon-

nected groups of phenomena. The most useful of servants to the man of science, they are the worst of masters. And when the establishment of the hypothesis becomes the end, and fact is alluded to only so far as it suits the ' Idee,' science has no longer anything to do with the business.

The nature of plants and animals, on the one hand, and of the human mind on the other, is such that the process of generalisation and that of classification, which is the correlate of generalisation, take place instinctively and find expression in common language. The terms 'beasts,' ' birds,' ' fishes,' are the names of certain groups of animals in the popular classification ; and, though the user of them may not be able to put his thoughts into words, they imply that he has perceived that the things he calls by these several names have certain common and distinctive characters. And that perception, when it is put into words, is a generalisation, which, in so far as it is accurate, also expresses an empirical ' law of Nature.'

The classifications of the scientific taxonomist are of two kinds. Those of the one sort are merely handy reference catalogues. Such are the ' artificial ' systems, useful in their day and for their particular purpose, but of no other value. The others, known as ' natural ' classifications, are arrangements of objects according to the sum of their likenesses and unlikenesses, in respect of certain characters ; in morphology, therefore. such classifications must have regard only to matters of form, external and internal. And natural classification is of perennial importance, because the construction of it is the same thing as the accurate generalisation of the facts of form, or the establishment of the empirical laws of the correlation of structure.

To say that deer, oxen, sheep. goats, antelopes, and so on, form a natural group, definable by the co-existence in them of certain forms of bones, teeth, stomach, and the like, which are not co-existent in any other group, is one way of stating certain facts. It is merely another, if we say that it is an empirical law of existing Nature that such and such structures are always found together ; and that when we meet with one, there is a *primâ facie* ground for suspecting that the others are associated with it. The finder of a recent skull, provided with a pair of horn-cores, in which the front part of the upper jaw is toothless. may thus safely predict that the animal to which it belonged possessed paired hoofs and a complex stomach, though no amount of merely physiological lore would enable him so much as to guess why the one set of characters is thus constantly associated with the other. The key of the enigma, in fact, does not lie in the hand of the physiologist, bu in that of the historian of animal life throughout the ages of its existence.

In the middle of the eighteenth century, the value of the artificial systems invented by Linnæus, as a part of his method of introducing order into the chaos of ' Natural History,' was so much felt, that his clear recognition of their essentially provisional character was ignored by the host of disciples ; who, as usual, appreciated most highly, and were most sedulous to imitate, the weakest parts of their master's teachings. The genius of Buffon strove against this tendency to substitute empty schematisms for science almost in vain. Botany became a cataloguing of ' hay ;' and zoology, of skins and shells ; indeed, of straw, if I may revive a jest of my old friend Edward Forbes —not without serious application even in his time —to the effect that the pure systematic zoologist was unaware that the stuffed skins he named and arranged ever had contained anything but straw.

Before long, however, better days began to dawn ; and the light came partly from the purely scientific anatomists, partly from men of more or less anatomical knowledge, in whom the artistic habit of visualising ideas was superadded to that capacity for exact observation which is the foundation of both art and science.

Scientific observation tells us that living birds form a group or class of animals, through which a certain form of skeleton runs ; and that this kind of skeleton differs in certain well-defined characters from that of mammals. On the other hand, if any one utterly ignorant of osteology, but endowed with the artistic sense of form, were set before a bird skeleton and a mammalian skeleton, he would at once see that the two were similar and yet different. Very likely he would be unable to give clear expression to his just sense of the differences and resemblances ; perhaps he would make great mistakes in detail if he tried. Nevertheless, he would be able to draw from memory a couple of sketches, in which all the salient points of likeness and unlikeness would be reproduced with sufficient accuracy. The mere osteologist, however accurately he might put the resemblances and differences into words, if he lacked the artistic visualising faculty, might be hopelessly incompetent to perform any such feat ; lost in details, it might not even occur to him that it was possible ; or, still more probably, the habit of looking for differences might impair the perception of resemblances.

Under these circumstances, the artist might be led to higher and broader views, and thus be more useful to the progress of science than the osteological expert. Not that the former attains the higher truth by a different method ; for the way of reaching truth is one and indivisible. Whether he knows it or not, the artist has made a generalisation from two sets of facts, which is perfectly scientific in form ; and, trustworthy, so far as it rests upon the direct perception of similarities and dissimilarities. The only peculiarity of the artistic application of scientific method lies in the artist's power of visualising the result of his mental processes, of embodying the facts of resemblance in a visible 'type,' and of showing the manner in which the differences may be represented as modifications of that type ; he does, in fact, instinctively, what an architect, who desires to demonstrate the community of general plan in certain ancient temples, does by the methodical construction of plans, sections and elevations, the comparison of which will furnish him with the 'type' of such temples.

Thus, what I may term the artistic fashion of dealing with anatomy is not only perfectly legitimate, but has been of great utility. The harm of it does not begin until the attempt is made to get more out of this visual projection of thought than it contains; until the origin of the notion of 'type' is forgotten and the speculative philosopher deludes himself with the supposition that the generalisation suggested by fact is an 'Idea' of the Pure Reason, with which fact must, somehow or other, be made to agree.

The old French naturalist Belon, who must have been a good deal of an artist, and illustrated his book, 'L'Histoire de la Nature des Oyseaux,' with many 'naifs portraicts,' initiated this way of dealing with anatomy. The skeleton of a bird is set beside that of a man, and the reader is left to draw

the obvious conclusion as to their 'unity of organisation.' A child may see that skull 'answers' to
skull ; spinal column to spinal column ; ribs to
ribs ; breast bone to breast bone ; wings to arms ;
and legs to legs, in the two. Later on, Peter
Camper, a capital artist as well as an accomplished anatomist, was in the habit of amusing,
while he instructed, his class by showing what
slight strokes of his chalk sufficed to turn the
outline skeleton of a man into that of a dog or of
an ox ; and how these could be metamorphosed
into reptilian or fish forms, without disturbance of
their fundamental features.

The cultivator of botany, who went beyond
the classification of 'hay,' became familiar with
facts of the same order. Indeed, flowering plants
fairly thrust morphological ideas upon the observer. Flowers are the primers of the morphologist ; those who run may read in them uniformity
of type amidst endless diversity, singleness of
plan with complex multiplicity of detail. As a
musician might say, every natural group of
flowering plants is a sort of visible fugue, wandering about a central theme which is never
forsaken, however it may, momentarily, cease to
be apparent.

Vicq d'Azyr, following the line of strict anatomical observation and critical comparison, set
forth the correspondences of plan observable in
the limbs of the higher vertebrates, and may be

considered the founder of the purely scientific higher anatomy.

A few years later, art again took the lead in the person of Goethe. Like all the really great men of literature, Goethe added some of the qualities of the man of science to those of the artist, especially the habit of careful and patient observation of Nature. The great poet was no mere book-learned speculator. His acquaintance with mineralogy, geology, botany, and osteology, the fruit of long and wide studies, would have sufficed to satisfy the requirements of a professoriate in those days, if only he could have pleaded ignorance of everything else. Unfortunately for Goethe's credit with his scientific contemporaries; and, consequently, for the attention attracted by his work, he did not come forward as a man of science until the public had ranged him among the men of literature. And when the little men have thus classified a big man, they consider that the last word has been said about him; it appears to be thought hardly decent on his part, if he venture to stray beyond the speciality they have assigned to him. It does not seem to occur to them that a clear intellect is an engine capable of supplying power to all sorts of mental factories; nor to admit that, as Goethe somewhere pathetically remarks, a man may have a right to live for himself as well as for the public; to follow the line of work that happens to interest him, rather than that which interests them.

On the face of the matter, it is not obvious that the brilliant poet had less chance of doing good service in natural science than the dullest of dissectors and nomenclators. Indeed, as I have endeavoured to indicate, there was considerable reason, a hundred years ago, for thinking that an infusion of the artistic way of looking at things might tend to revivify the somewhat mummified body of technical zoology and botany. Great ideas were floating about ; the artistic apprehension was needed to give these airy nothings a local habitation and a name ; to convert vague suppositions into definite hypotheses. And I apprehend that it was just this service which Goethe rendered by writing his essays on the intermaxillary bone, on osteology generally, and on the metamorphoses of plants.[3]

[3] It is an interesting fact that Goethe took up the metamorphosis of plants after he had been led to a conception of the higher vertebrate type ; and, also, that he was led to discover the intermaxillary bone in man by deduction from his type-theory. He tells us that, early in the eighties of last century, before the idea of plant-metamorphosis occurred to him, he worked hard at osteology, for the purpose of finding the general type of skeleton, which he conceived must be discoverable 'because the already long accepted comparative anatomy involves the assumption that it exists.' The doctrine current among anatomists at that time, that men are distinguished from apes by the absence of the intermaxillary bone, stood in the way of Goethe's hypothesis ; and the importance which he attached to his discovery of evidences of its existence is therefore very intelligible. (See Osteologie, 1819, in Goethe's Werke, ed. 1867, Bd. 32, p. 191.)

I do not think that any one who studies these works, in many ways so remarkable, can doubt that, in the last two decades of the eighteenth century, Goethe arrived, by a generally just, though by no means critical, process of induction, at the leading theses of what were subsequently known as *Naturphilosophie* in Germany, and as *Philosophie anatomique* in France; in other words, that he was the first person to enunciate and conceive as parts of a systematic whole, whatever principles of value are to be met with in the works of Oken, Geoffroy, and Lamarck.

Of the idea of 'unity of organisation' which is fundamental for all three, Geoffroy St. Hilaire himself, writing in 1831, says:

' Elle est présentement acquise au domaine de l'esprit humain ; et l'honneur d'un succès aussi mémorable appartient à Goethe.'

Furthermore, the notions of a necessary correlation between excess of development in one direction and diminution in another ; of the natural evolution of the animal and vegetable worlds from a common foundation ; of the direct influence of varying conditions on the process of evolution, are all to be found, indeed are plainly enunciated in Goethe's writings. In addition, he sometimes uses language which may be fairly interpreted as an anticipation of the fundamental teachings of modern histology and embryology ; a fact which is by no means wonderful, when we consider that

Goethe was well acquainted with Caspar F. Wolff and his writings.

All this is mere justice to Goethe ; but, as it is the unpleasant duty of the historian to do justice upon, as well as to, great men, it behoves me to add that the germs, and more than the germs, of the worst faults of later speculative morphologists are no less visible in his writings than their great merits.[4] In the artist-philosopher there was, at best, a good deal more artist than philosopher; and when Goethe ventured into the regions which belong to pure science, this excess of a virtue had all the consequences of a vice. ' Trennen und zählen lag nicht in meiner Natur,'[5] says he ; but the mental operations of which ' analysis and numeration' are partial expressions are indispensable for every step of progress beyond happy glimpses, even in morphology ; while, in physiology and in physics, failure in the most exact performance of these operations involves sheer disaster, as indeed Goethe was afforded abundant opportunity of learning. Yet he never understood the sharp lessons he received, and put down to malice, or prejudice, the ill-reception of his unfortunate attempts to deal with purely physical problems.

Goethe's contributions to the science of

---

[4] See, for example, the essay 'Ueber die Spiraltendenz der Vegetation' in the *Morphologie*.

[5] *Morphologie Geschichte meines botanischen Studiums.*

morphology (the very term 'morphology,' in its technical sense, is his) were by no means so widely known to anatomists, or valued by them, as they ought to have been ; and it was long before their unquestionable merits were properly appreciated. The most brilliant and, at the same time, the soberest representative of the higher or 'philosophical' anatomy, Geoffroy St. Hilaire, seems, at first, to have known nothing of them. Like Goethe, he had studied mineralogy and botany before taking up anatomy and zoology ; an excellent and most industrious observer, he was, at the same time, a man of high intellect and comprehensive views. Intimately associated with young Geoffroy, and only a couple of years older, was Cuvier, one of the most remarkable intelligences of his own or any time. And when these energetic allies turned their attention to vertebrate anatomy, in 1794-5, it was impossible that the facts which had impressed Goethe should fail to lead minds such as theirs towards ideas of the same order. But, the minds of the two having a widely different commixture of qualities, the way in which they dealt with the same objective material presented corresponding differences; and these differences went on widening until, thirty-five years later, these two bosom friends became the antagonists in the most famous of all scientific duels.

However, during the earlier part of his career, I doubt if Cuvier would have categorically denied any of Geoffroy's fundamental theses. And even in his later years, Sir Charles Lyell, many years ago, gave me reasons for the opinion that Cuvier was by no means confident about the fixity of species. There was never any lack of the scientific imagination about the great anatomist ; and the charge of indifference to general ideas, sometimes brought against him, is stupidly unjust. But Cuvier was one of those happily endowed persons in whom genius never parts company with common-sense ; and whose perception of the importance of sound method is so great that they look at even a truth, hit upon by those who pursue an essentially vicious method, with the sort of feeling with which an honest trader regards the winnings of a gambler. They hold it better to remain poor than obtain riches by the road that, as a rule, leads to ruin.

So far as Cuvier was actuated by such feelings, one can but applaud the course he took. For it is plain to anyone, who studies these old controversies by modern lights, that Geoffroy, however good his general ideas may have been, was singularly unfortunate in his attempts to illustrate and enforce them. Even where he was strongest, as upon the topic of the unity of organisation of the Vertebrates, I do not think there is one of his exemplifications of that unity which has withstood criticism ; and, in respect of the primary cause of contention in 1830, the comparison of the vertebrate and the cephalopod types, he was quite hopelessly in the wrong.

To anyone possessed of Cuvier's vast knowledge and dialectic skill, therefore, it was rarely difficult to cut the ground from under his opponents' feet ; to say, in short, whether you are right or wrong, the evidence you adduce in support of your case, where it is not demonstrably contrary to fact, is inadequate. And, in the main, Cuvier has been justified by the larger knowledge of our day. There is no 'unity of organisation' in the sense maintained by Geoffroy, though there is in another sense. Neither Geoffroy, nor Lamarck, adduced any evidence of the modifiability of species sufficient to overcome the strictly scientific arguments adduced on the other side ; and it was not till many years later, that the progress of palæontology justified the hypothesis of progressive modification, which Geoffroy himself, fully admitting the lack of evidence, put forward merely as a suggestion.

In later life, however, Cuvier seems to have become so much disgusted by the vagaries of the *Naturphilosophie* school, and to have been so strongly impressed by the evil which was accruing to science from their example (let those who are disposed to blame him read Oken's 'Physio-philosophy'), that he was provoked into forsaking his former wise and judicious critical attitude ; and, in his turn, he advocated hypotheses, which were

none the better than those of his opponents
because they happened to be in favour with the
multitude, instructed and uninstructed. The doc-
trines of *emboîtement* in embryology ; of periodical
geological catastrophes ; of the fixity of species ;
of physiological deduction as the basis of palæontology ; and the restriction of the scope of biological science to mere observation and classification—which is fairly deducible from some of
Cuvier's dicta, though I do not believe he ever
intended that it should be—are not one whit
more scientifically respectable than the least
sober speculations of Geoffroy.

The irony of history is nowhere more apparent than in science. Here we see the men,
over whose minds the coming events of the world
of biology cast their shadows, doing their best to
spoil their case in stating it ; while the man who
represented sound scientific method is doing his
best to stay the inevitable progress of thought
and bolster up antiquated traditions. The progress of knowledge, during the last seventy years,
enables us to see that neither Geoffroy, nor
Cuvier, was altogether right, nor altogether
wrong ; and that they were meant to hunt in
couples instead of pulling against one another.
Science has need of servants of very various
qualifications ; of artistic constructors no less
than of men of business ; of people to design her
palaces and of others to see that the materials are

sound and well fitted together; of some to spur
investigators and of others to keep their heads
cool. The only would-be servants, who are entirely unprofitable, are those who do not take the
trouble to interrogate Nature, but imagine vain
things about her; and spin, from their inner con-
sciousness, webs, as exquisitely symmetrical as
those of the most geometrical of spiders, but,
alas! as easily torn to pieces by some uncon-
sidered bluebottle of a fact.

Naturally, it is Cuvier, in his capacity of the
man of business, who has been held in almost
exclusive veneration by those (and they are
always the majority) who engage in merely adding to the capital stock of science. For them,
he has done everything and is the highest of
exemplars. And justly, for Cuvier's monographs,
and the osteological treatises interpolated in the
'Ossemens Fossiles,' are of unsurpassed excellence; while, for the sagacious application of the
data of osteology to the interpretation of fossil
remains, he has never had a superior. Again,
Cuvier's clear logical head and marvellously wide
acquaintance with animal forms enabled him to
reform classification; and to set forth, in the
'Règne Animal,' a generalized statement of the facts
of animal structure which was, in itself, a sufficient
refutation of the doctrine of unity of organisation
as it was conceived by Goethe and Geoffroy.
The mere quantity of the palæontological work

alone which Cuvier turned out is amazing, and it
hardly ever falls below the level of the highest
excellence.   Moreover, Cuvier incidentally did as
great service to the cause of sound morphology
as any of the philosophical anatomists.   He
worked out the principles of the latter as far as
they could be safely carried, and showed that
their method must needs, in the end, stop short
for want of a criterion.   The study of the connections of parts, by no means always enables
us to determine whether they 'answer to one
another' or not; and the philosophical anatomists
too largely ignored other means of testing their
hypotheses.

The constructive efforts of Goethe, with
the *Philosophie anatomique* of France and the
Naturphilosophie of Germany on the one hand,
the critical negations of the Cuvierian school on
the other, do not represent all the lines of biological work in the period under consideration.
There is another, which it is the great defect of
Cuvier and his school to have underrated and
neglected; while it is the great misfortune of
Geoffroy that it made its importance fully felt too
late for him.   This is Embryology, or Development; that is, the study of the manner in which
individual living things acquire the structure
which they possess.

The science of development, in the modern

acceptation of the term, came into existence when
Wolff demonstrated the fallacy of the *emboîtement* theory; and also proved that the leaves, the
petals, the stamens, and so forth, of flowering
plants do, as a matter of fact, start from one and
the same primary form in the bud and become
differentiated as they grow.   It was thus that,
thirty years before Goethe saw how the relations of
living forms could be ideally represented, Wolff
proved what they in fact are.   In quite another
sense from that of Goethe's reply to Schiller, the
embryologist showed cause for the belief that
' unity of organisation ' is not an idea, but a fact.
The study of the actual process of individual
evolution, thus put on a firm foundation, steadily
advanced, until Von Baer[6] arrived at the great
generalisation that all such evolution is a progress
from relative simplicity to relative complexity;
in other words, that it is the gradual differentiation
of a relatively homogeneous living substance represented by the egg; that, in so far as all individual living beings start from ova of essentially
similar simplicity of structure, and as the earliest
steps of their development or evolution are
similar, the fundamental unity of their organisation is a fact; on the other hand, that, in so

[6] My translation of ' Fragments relating to Philosophical
Zoology, selected from the
Works of K. E. Von Baer,' was
published in ' Scientific Memoirs' for February and May
1853. Up to that time, I believe, Von Baer's ideas were
hardly known outside Germany.

far as the typical forms of the several groups
to which they belong are soon assumed, and,
thereafter, each pursues the special line of
modification characteristic of its group, 'unity of
organisation' soon ceases to be strictly predicable.
Thus Geoffroy was right about the fundamental
unity of animal organisation, and Cuvier was right
about the existence of different types irreducible to
one another ; while each erred in thinking his own
views incompatible with those of his opponent.

In the course of the discussions about the
corresponding, or answering, parts in different
organisms, or in the same organisms, and about
questions of classification, a very useful terminology had been invented. When the systematists
attempted to construct a scientific classification,
they found themselves obliged to discriminate
between different kinds of resemblances.   Take,
for example, the question whether a whale is a
fish or not, which, I observe, is not yet quite settled
for some people.   As a whale is not a little like a
fish outside, and lives permanently in the sea,
after the manner of a fish, why should it not be
classed with the fishes ? The answer, of course,
is that the moment one compares a whale with any
one of the thousands of ordinary fishes, the two
are seen to differ in almost every particular of
structure ; and, moreover, in all these points in
which the whale differs from the fish, it agrees

with ordinary mammals. Therefore, zoologists
put the whale into the same class as the mammals, not into that of the fishes. But this conclusion implies the assumption that animals should
be arranged according to the totality of their
resemblances. It means that the likenesses in
structure of whales and mammals are greatly
more numerous and more close than the likenesses
between whales and fishes. The same argu-
mentation applies to the likeness between bats
and birds. These are few and superficial, while
the resemblances between bats and ordinary
mammals are innumerable and profound. Therefore bats go into the class Mammalia, not into the
class Aves. In these cases, the estimation of the
relative value of resemblances is easy enough; but,
in respect of the lesser groups, the problem offered
frequently greater difficulties. Even Cuvier,
misled by certain superficial resemblances, could
refer the acorn-shells and the barnacles to the
class of Mollusks.

Thus, in course of time, there arose in the
minds of thoughtful systematists a distinction between 'analogies' and 'affinities;' and, in those
of the philosophical anatomists, a corresponding
discrimination between 'analogous' and 'homologous' structures. Outward resemblances of the
character of those which obtain between a whale
and a fish, a bat and a bird, were said to be mere
analogies, and were properly regarded as of no

classificatory importance.   The deeper structural
likenesses between a whale and a seal, or between
a bat and a shrew mouse, on the other hand, were
affinities : that is to say, the exhibitors of such
resemblances were 'affined' or ' allied' in the sense
of belonging to the same classificatory group.[7]
So, for the anatomists, the shell of a tortoise and
the shell of a crab were merely analogous structures ; while the bones of the arm of a man and
those of the wing of a bird were homologous.

Homology (ὁμολογία) originally signified
agreement either of, or about, things.   The word,
with its derivatives and allies, such as ' homony-
mous,' passed into Latin, French, and German ;
and Anglicised forms of them are to be found in
Nathan Bailey's ' Dictionary,' now a century and
a half old.   Even in its present sense, as an anatomical term, homology was well known as far
back as the early years of this century.   Owen,
writing in 1846, insists upon the fact that, in using
the word, he follows established precedent :—

' But, in thus illustrating the term *homology*,
I have always felt and stated that I was merely
making known the meaning of a term introduced
into comparative anatomy long ago, and habitually
used in the writings of the philosophical anatomists
of Germany aud France.   Geoffroy St. Hilaire

---

[7] It is interesting to observe
how readily the term ' affinity,'
which ordinarily implies blood-
relationship, was adopted by
those who most strongly repu-
diated the doctrine of descent.

also, in defining the term, acknowledges its source :
" Les organes sont *homologues* comme s'expri-
merait la philosophie allemande ; c'est-à-dire, qu'ils
sont analogues dans leur mode de développement,"
&c. (" Annales des Sciences," tome vi., 1825,
p. 341.)[8]

The last words of the citation from Geoffroy St.
Hilaire have a curious significance. Goethe had
pointed out, and neither he, nor Geoffroy, nor
Oken, were blind to the fact, that the study of
development must have a good deal to say about
the problems of philosophical anatomy ; though,
as I have mentioned, that branch of morphology
had not advanced far enough to enable Geoffroy
to appreciate its full importance, before the publication of Von Baer's works, in the course of the
decade 1828 to 1838. But embryology began to
show its capacity for playing the part of a criterion
in morphology pretty early. It has already been
stated that Wolff demonstrated the homology
of leaves, stamens, and carpels, by tracing their
development. Later, it was readily shown that
Vicq d'Azyr's doctrine of the homology of the limbs
had its proof in the observation that they arise from
rudiments of similar character and relations. In
all the higher vertebrate animals, the fore and
hind limbs are, at first, very similar, and they
become differentiated by successive steps. So

[8] 'On the Structural Rela-   (*Philosophical Magazine*, xxvii.
tions of Organised Beings'   p. 526).

the earliest rudiments of the spinal column, and
the manner in which it becomes segmented, are
alike throughout.

On the other hand, a favourite speculation of
the philosophical anatomists, that the lower jaw
is formed by the coalescence of a pair of limbs,
for which comparative anatomy seemed to offer
some support; and Geoffroy's tempting suggestion that the opercular bones of fishes answer to
the ear-bones of mammals, were at once negatived
by the study of the development of the parts.
Again, the hypothesis that the skull consists of
modified vertebræ, advocated by Goethe and
Oken, and the subject of many elaborate works,
was so little reconcilable with the mode of its development that, as early as 1842, Vogt threw well-
founded doubts upon it. 'All efforts to interpret
the skull in this way,' said he, 'are vain.'

The preceding sketch of the history of anatomical science, though drawn only in broad outline, may suffice to indicate the courses which
naturally suggested themselves to anyone taking
up the subject in the beginning of the fourth
decade of the present century.

There was the brilliant example of Cuvier in
the 'Anatomie Comparée,' the 'Mémoires sur les
Mollusques,' and the 'Ossemens Fossiles,' for any
one disposed to devote himself to the increase of
the capital stock of knowledge by museum work, or

by anatomical and palæontological monography; there was the path of philosophical anatomy, opened up by Vicq d'Azyr, Goethe, Geoffroy St. Hilaire, Oken, and followed out in the elaborate works of Spix and Carus on the skeleton, with results acutely checked and criticised by Cuvier; there was the study of individual development in its dawn, but with its great future already clearly indicated by Von Baer ; there was the question of the development of animals and plants in general, or what is now commonly understood by the term evolution, waiting to be rescued from the region of speculation, to which it had been relegated for want of positive evidence one way or the other, and a good deal more damaged by its supporters than by its opponents.

It was at this time, namely in 1830, that Owen turned from practical medicine to natural science ; and threw himself into the first-mentioned of these paths of exploration, with an energy which reminds one of Geoffroy and Cuvier, when, a little younger, they set out on their remarkable careers. Owen's first recorded publication is an account of an aneurism. The second work in which he engaged was a catalogue of specimens in the museum of the Royal College of Surgeons. But, in the next year (1831), no fewer than eight papers on the anatomy of various mammals, birds, and reptiles which had died in the Zoological Gardens

bear his name.   This was a pretty good start for
a young man of twenty-six to make ; but the har-
vest of the year 1832 bettered that of its prede-
cessor.   For, without any other work, Owen's
time might, one would think, have been fully
occupied by the famous 'Memoir on the Pearly
Nautilus,' which was published in 1832 and placed
its author, at a bound, in the front rank of anatomical monographers.   There is nothing better
in the ' Mémoires sur les Mollusques,' I would
even venture to say nothing so good, were it not
that Owen had Cuvier's great work for a model ;
certainly, in the sixty years that have elapsed
since the publication of this remarkable monograph, it has not been excelled ; and that is a
good deal to say with Müller's ' Myxinoid Fishes '
for a competitor.

During more than half a century, Owen's industry remained unabated ; and whether we consider the quantity, or the quality, of the work done,
or the wide range of his labours, I doubt if, in the
long annals of anatomy, more is to be placed to
the credit of any single worker.

The preparation of the five volumes of the descriptive catalogue of the Hunterian Museum
and of the annual courses of lectures demanded
from the Hunterian Professor, took Owen over
the length and breadth of the animal kingdom
and involved the making of special investigations
in almost all its provinces.   The wide knowledge

thus accumulated was eventually summed up and published, first in the lectures on the Invertebrates (1843) and, secondly, in those on the Vertebrates (1860–1868).

As methodically arranged and comprehensive repertories of the anatomy of animals, it may be a question whether these works are equal to the contemporary 'Handbuch' of Siebold and Stannius; but it may quite safely be said of them, that they are based on the results of a greater amount of personal investigation than any work of the kind except, perhaps, Cuvier's 'Leçons;' and I put the exception doubtfully, inasmuch as Cuvier was aided by highly skilled assistants.

Further, I think that Owen's monographic work occupies a unique position, if one considers, not merely its general high standard of excellence, but the way in which so many of these memoirs have opened up new regions of investigation. I mention the following, as some of the most important from this point of view, in addition to that on the Pearly Nautilus, to which I have already referred.

To begin with the higher animals, Owen's early memoirs on the anatomy of the anthropoid Apes contained by far the most complete and adequate account of their structure, and of the resemblances and differences between them and man, then extant; and they formed the foundation of

X 2

all subsequent researches in that field.   The same
may be said of his investigations on the Monotremes and Marsupials, the substance of which is,
for the most part, incorporated in the well-known
articles of the 'Cyclopædia of Anatomy and
Physiology.' These remained, for many years,
indeed are still, in most respects, the best source
of information about these animals.

The researches on the minute structure and
the development of the teeth, summed up in the
'Odontography' (1840-45), and the article
'Odontology,'[9] so far as they deal with the outward form, the microscopic appearances, and the
order of succession of the teeth, and furnish a
foundation for a useful and consistent nomenclature of dental arrangements, have been of very
great service both to the ordinary zoologist and
to the student of fossil remains.

In regard to the class of birds, the memoirs
on the Apteryx, the Great Auk, and the Dodo are
particularly noteworthy ; and the article ' Aves '
in the ' Cyclopædia of Anatomy and Physiology '
very long held its own, as the best summary of
avian structure.

The paper on ' Lepidosiren ' left no doubt of
the piscine affinities of that animal.

Among the Invertebrates we have the article
'Cephalopoda' (1836), the ' Memoir on Limulus '
(1873), the ' Researches on the Brachiopoda '

[9] *Encyclopædia Britannica*, 1858.

(1833), and the description of the terrible parasite of man, *Trichina spiralis.*

In regard to Taxonomy, Owen made a variety of proposals, the consideration of most of which would involve discussions altogether out of place in this sketch. But there is a notable exception in the case of the 'attempt to develop Cuvier's idea of the classification of pachyderms by the number of their toes' appended to the 'description of teeth and portions of jaws of two extinct anthracotherioid quadrupeds (*Hyopotamus vectianus* and *H. bovinus*)' (1848), as to the high value of which I think all zoologists are agreed.

In 1837, Owen, without any pause in the long and important series of anatomical investigations which have been mentioned, began those contributions to palæontology which, in after years, perhaps contributed most to his fame with the public. His first work in this department is a memoir, published in the second volume of the Proceedings of the Geological Society, on an extinct mammal discovered in South America by Darwin in 1833, which Owen named *Toxodon Platensis.* It is worthy of notice that, in the title of this memoir, there follow, after the name of the species, the words ' referable by its dentition to the Rodentia, but with affinities to the Pachydermata and the herbivorous Cetacea ; ' indicating the importance in the mind of the writer of the fact that, like Cuvier's *Anoplotherium* and *Palæotherium,*

Toxodon occupied a position between groups
which, in existing nature, are now widely separated.
The existence of one more extinct 'intercalary'
type was established.

From another point of view, this maiden essay
in palæontology possesses great interest.

It is with reference to Owen's report upon
the remains of Toxodon that Darwin remarks
in his journal, six years later : ' How wonderfully are the different orders, at the present time
so well separated, blended together in different
points of the structure of the Toxodon !' while,
in his pocket-book for 1837, he records : ' In
July opened first note-book on Transmutation of
Species.   Had been greatly struck from about
the month of previous March on character of
South American fossils, and species on Galapagos
Archipelago.   These facts (especially latter) origin
of all my views.' [1]

Unless it be in the ' Ossemens Fossiles,' I do
not know where one is to look for contributions to
palæontology more varied, more numerous, and,
on the whole, more accurate, than those which
Owen poured forth in rapid succession between
1837 and 1888.   Yet there was no lack of strong
contemporaries at work in the same field.   De
Blainville's ' Ostéographie ;'   Louis Agassiz's
monumental work on fossil fishes, achieved under
the pressure of great obstacles and full of brilliant

[1] *Life and Letters*, vol. i. p. 276.

suggestions ; Von Meyer's long series of wonderfully accurate memoirs, with their admirable illustrations executed by his own hands, all belong
to Owen's generation. But, perhaps, the fairest
comparison is with Cuvier ; and I do not think
that those who have had to concern themselves
with these subjects will rank any of Cuvier's
memoirs higher than those of Owen on *Mylodon*,
Megatherium, *Glyptodon*, *Macrauchenia*, and
other extinct South American animals, which
followed up the account of *Toxodon*.

In 1838 appeared the memoir on the Stone-
field Slate mammals, then the oldest known,
pointing out their marsupial affinities, and with
this the later investigations on the Purbeck mammals may be grouped. In 1839–40, we have
the first indication of the wingless birds of New
Zealand, widening out, in after years, into the
long series of memoirs on *Dinornis* and the like.
In 1841, the description of the triassic Laby-
rinthodonts of Central England, which, with
Von Meyer's earlier and later work, was the
commencement of the elucidation of the triassic
fauna in all quarters of the world, made its appearance. In 1844, Owen published the memoir
on Belemnites, which had a distinct value,
though not perhaps quite that assigned to it at
the time. In 1845, followed the first view of
the wonderful extinct faunæ of South Africa and
Australia, so largely extended by Owen himself

in later years. In 1849, the first of the long
series of memoirs on British fossil reptiles appeared ; in 1863, the description of the famous
reptilian bird Archæopteryx.

It is a splendid record ; enough, and more
than enough, to justify the high place in the
scientific world which Owen so long occupied.
If I mistake not, the historian of comparative
anatomy and of palæontology will always assign to
Owen a place next to, and hardly lower than that
of Cuvier, who was practically the creator of those
sciences in their modern shape ; and whose works
must always remain models of excellence in their
kind. It was not uncommon to hear our country-
man called 'the British Cuvier,' and so far, in my
judgment, the collocation was justified, high as
the praise it implies.

But when we consider Owen's contributions to
'philosophical anatomy,' I think the epithet ceases
to be appropriate. For there can be no question
that he was deeply influenced by, and inclined
towards, those speculations of Oken and Géoffroy
St. Hilaire, of which Cuvier was the declared
antagonist and often the bitter critic.

That Owen was strongly attracted by the
Naturphilosophie of Germany is evidenced, not
merely by his attitude towards the problems
of philosophical anatomy, but by his article on
Oken in the 'Encyclopædia Britannica ;' and by

the fact that the translation of Oken's 'Lehrbuch der Naturphilosophie' [2] was undertaken at his instance. Thus, when Owen passes from matters of anatomical fact and their immediate interpretation to morphological speculation, it is not surprising that he also passes from the camp of Cuvier into that of his adversaries.

In the advertisement of the work 'On the Archetype and Homologies of the Vertebrate Skeleton,' published in 1848, Owen says :—

'The subject of the following essay has occupied a portion of my attention from the period when, after having made a certain progress in comparative anatomy, the evidence of a greater conformity to type, especially in the bones of the head of the vertebrate animals, than the immortal Cuvier had been willing to admit began to enforce a reconsideration of his conclusions, to which I had previously yielded implicit assent.'

In fact, what I may call 'Okenism' colours Owen's whole cast of thought on these matters, and his admiration for Oken finds frequent vent in his writings. Thus, in a note at p. 8 of the 'Archetype and Homologies of the Vertebrate Skeleton' (1848), we find :—

'Oken's famous "Programm ueber die Bedeutung der Schädelknochen" was published in the same year (1807) as Geoffroy's memoir on the

[2] *Physiophilosophy*, translated by Tulk. Ray Society, 1847.

Bird's Skull; but it is devoted less to the determination of "special" than of "general homologies;" it has, in fact, a much higher aim than
the contemporary publication of the French anatomist, in which we seek in vain for any glimpse of
those higher relations of the bones of the skull,
the discovery of which has conferred immortality
on the name of Oken.[3]'

And the 'Conclusion' of the same work (pp.
171–172) abounds in the sense of the Okenian
philosophy. The explanation of the facts of morphology is sought in the 'principle of vegetative
repetition;' in the interaction of a 'general and
all-pervading polarising force,' with an 'adaptive
or special organising force,' identified with the
Platonic ἰδέα. Whether they be sound or un-
sound, nothing can be more opposed to the
Cuvierian tradition than speculations of this
order.

The 'Programm' to which these sympathetic
references are made, opens with some sentences
which are worth attention, since they furnish a
typical example of the speculative procedure of
the *Naturphilosophie* school.

'A vesicle ossifies, and it is a vertebra. A
vesicle elongates into a tube, becomes jointed,
ossifies, and it is a vertebral column. The tube

---

[3] There are even stronger
expressions to the same effect
in the French version of the
treatise, *Principes d'Ostéologie
comparée*, published in 1855.

gives off (according to laws) blind lateral canals ; they ossify, and it is a trunk skeleton. This skeleton repeats itself at the two poles, each pole repeats itself in the other, and they are head and pelvis. The skeleton is only a developed, rami- fied, repeated vertebra ; and a vertebra is the pre-formed germ of the skeleton. The entire man is only a vertebra.'

All this may be in accordance with the ' Idee,' and demonstrable à priori ; but the plain, prosaic inquirer into objective truth may be excused if he finds nothing in it but a series of metaphorical mystifications ; for which, so far as they are to be taken seriously, no empirical justification ever existed. There is not, and there never was, any ground for believing that a vertebra is an ossified vesicle ; or that a vertebral column, or a trunk skeleton, is produced in the way asserted ; or that a head is a repeated pelvis, or vice versâ ; while the intelligibility of the final assertion that 'the entire man is only a vertebra,' is not apparent. The spirit which animates these oracular utter- ances pervades all the writings of Oken and his school ; it provided Cuvier with the subject- matter of his severest, as well as of his most justi- fiable sarcasms ; and every one who has the inte- rests of sound science at heart must feel Cuvier's debtor for the pertinacity with which he combated, and finally drove out of the field of science, this pseudo-philosophical word-play.

I do not for a moment suggest, indeed I cannot imagine, that Owen approved of such extra-
vagances as those which I have cited; but that he
was deeply influenced by the philosophy of Oken,
bringing it, apparently, in his own mind into har-
mony with that of the English Platonists, and
especially of Cudworth, is a conclusion which can
hardly be avoided.   The following passages alone
appear to me to be decisive :—

'Now, besides the ἰδέα, organizing principle,
vital property, or force, which produces the diversity of form belonging to living bodies of the same
materials, which diversity cannot be explained by
any known properties of matter, there appears also
to be in counter-operation, during the building-up of
such bodies, the polarizing force pervading all space,
and to the operation of which force, or mode of
force, the similarity of forms, the repetition of
parts, the signs of the unity of organisation may
be mainly ascribed.

'The Platonic ἰδέα, or specific organising principle or force, would seem to be in antagonism
with the general polarizing force, and to subdue
and mould it in subserviency to the exigencies of
the resulting specific form.' [4]

'Now, however, the recognition of an ideal
Exemplar for the Vertebrated animals proves that

[4] *On the Archetype and Homologies of the Vertebrate Skeleton*
(1848), p. 172.

the knowledge of such a being as Man must have existed before Man appeared. For the Divine mind which planned the Archetype also foreknew all its modifications.

'The Archetypal idea was manifested in the flesh, under divers such modifications, upon this planet, long prior to the existence of those animal species that actually exemplify it.

'To what natural laws or secondary causes the orderly succession and progression of such organic phenomena may have been committed we are yet ignorant. But if, without derogation of the Divine power, we may conceive the existence of such ministers, and personify them by the term " Nature," we learn from the past history of our globe that she has advanced with slow and stately steps, guided by the archetypal light, amidst the wreck of worlds, from the first embodiment of the Vertebrate idea under its old Ichthyic vestment, until it became arrayed in the glorious garb of the Human form.' [5]

Those who know Owen's mind only on the side reflected in the exact observations, the clear-headed and sagacious interpretations, of the anatomical and palæontological memoirs, should ponder over these and other passages of like tenor, if they wish to form a just judgment about the position which he took up in morphology ; and, later, in regard to the Darwinian revivification

[5] *On the Nature of Limbs*, pp. 85, 86. 1849.

of the doctrine of evolution. On the speculative
side, the very same mind has a distinct leaning
towards realistic mysticism, while remaining
liberally, perhaps prodigally, eclectic. A subli-
mated Theism, after the manner of Cudworth,
lies at the foundation of Owen's speculations;
while the 'Archetype' takes the position of a
Platonic ἰδέα, indeed, almost that of an Alexan-
drian λόγος. The essentially naturalistic abstrac-
tions—'secondary causes,' 'forces,' and 'polarity'
—are personified and regarded as agents.

If, in the 'Nature of Limbs' (pp. 84, 85), the
argument from Design is momentarily shattered
by the admission that some parts of animals are
'made in vain;' it is immediately redintegrated
by the suggestion that they are illustrations of the
design manifested in the 'Archetype.' The looking to 'natural laws' and 'secondary causes' for
the 'progression' of 'organic phenomena' is the
substantial acceptance of evolution, as set forth
by Goethe, Oken, Lamarck, and Geoffroy; but
the picture of 'Nature,' advancing 'amidst the
wreck of worlds,' fits in, no less admirably, with
the catastrophism of Cuvier.

Owen's morphological labours appear to me to
be completely pervaded by the spirit, and restricted
to the methods, of the philosophical anatomists;
if I may, for the nonce, use that name in a limited
sense, for the scholars of Oken, rather than for
those of Geoffroy. But, from this point of view,

the theory of the vertebrate skeleton had been so elaborately worked out by Spix (1815), Carus (1828), and others, that the vein might well seem to be exhausted. Carus, especially, had visualized his hypotheses in diagrams, to which he gave the names of 'Grundform' and 'Schema;' and which are the equivalents of the 'Archetype' and its derivatives. Thus, when Owen took up the subject, many years after Carus, there really was nothing new in principle to be done, so long as the method of his predecessors was followed. All that could be hoped from renewed investigation, along the same lines, was the rectification of erroneous, and the suggestion of unsuspected, homologies. And this is what we find; new homologies for the cranial bones; original speculations respecting the nature of the bony walls of the inferior cavities of the skull; as to the proper connections and homology of the pectoral arch; and so on.

I believe I am right in saying that hardly any of these speculations and determinations have stood the test of investigation, or, indeed, that any of them were ever widely accepted. I am not sure that any one but the historian of anatomical science is ever likely to recur to them; and considering Owen's great capacity, extensive learning, and tireless industry, that seems a singular result of years of strenuous labour.

But it will cease to be so remarkable to those who reflect that the ablest of us is a child of his

time, profiting by one set of its influences, limited
by another.   It was Owen's limitation that he
occupied himself with speculations about the
'Archetype' some time before the work of the
embryologists began to be appreciated in this
country.   It had not yet come to be understood
that, after the publication of the investigations of
Rathke, Reichert, Remak, Vogt, and others, the
venue of the great cause of the morphology of the
skeleton was removed from the court of comparative anatomy to that of embryology.[6]   When
developmental investigation had proved that
even the segmentation of the vertebrate body is
not its primary condition ; that such segmentation
without founding it largely on embryology cannot
be traced throughout the cranial region ; that a
process of chondrification, or formation of carti-
laginous hard-parts, precedes ossification, and is
not the same in the skull as in the spinal column ;
that bones are not all similar in respect of their
mode of origin ; it was obvious that no satisfactory
theory of the skeleton could be attained without
taking these facts into serious consideration, and,
indeed, without founding it largely on embryology.

It would be a great mistake, however, to con-

---

[6] And even this appeal is not
final. We have still to look to
palæontology for confirmation or
contradiction of our deductions
from the facts of embryology.
Biological evolution is based
on the history of life on our
planet, as evidenced by the facts
of palæontology, however these
facts may be supplemented and
speculatively interpreted.

clude that Owen's labours in the field of morphology were lost, because they have yielded little
fruit of the kind he looked for. On the contrary,
they not only did a great deal of good by awaken-
ing attention to the higher problems of morphology
in this country ; but they were of much service in
clarifying and improving anatomical nomenclature, especially in respect of the vertebral region.

Apart from questions of classification, the only
special work of Owen, which deals directly with
the greater problems of biology, is the discourse on
' Parthenogenesis, or the Successive Production
of Procreating Individuals from a single Ovum,'
originally delivered in the form of the opening
two lectures of the Hunterian Course for 1849.

In these discourses, an attempt is made to correlate, and furnish an explanation of, the phenomena
of sexless proliferation ; that is to say, of the production of offspring by a plant or an animal, without the intervention of sex. In the vegetable
world, such phenomena, as exemplified by the
growth and detachment of buds or bulbs, or
of young plants, like those formed on strawberry
' runners,' have been known from time imme-
morial ; among animals, they were first carefully
elucidated by Trembley and Bonnet in the
middle of the eighteenth century.

One of the commonest and most striking cases
is that of the plant lice, or *Aphides*, which are the
commonest of pests in our gardens. The young,

which these animals produce with such wonderful
fertility in summer, are all fatherless.   So are the
drones in a hive of bees.

Among the aphides, this state of things, as a
rule, persists throughout the summer ; and it is
not until the autumn arrives, that the broods
produced take on the characters of males and
females, which die after their functions are performed and the eggs are laid.   The eggs remain
dormant during the winter ; and when they hatch,
in spring, the aphides produced are sexless,
though in some respects they resemble the true
females.   These sexless forms produce living
broods, having the same characters as their pro-
ducer ; and these give rise to others, in like manner,
through the summer.   It has been proved that this
state of things may be maintained for three years,
by keeping the insects warm and supplied with
food ; indeed, there is no positive evidence that it
need ever come to an end.

The males and females are, in many respects,
different from the sexless proliferators.   Thus,
to superficial observation, it appears as if the
sexed ' generation,' which may be called the form
A, was succeeded by a certain number of sexless
' generations' of the form B ; these by A, these
by B again, and so on.   In other words, the ' generations' A and B alternate.

In the course of the early decades of the nine-
teenth century, the wide extension of exact investi-

gation among the lower groups of the animal kingdom, especially the polypes, worms, star-fishes, ascidians, crustacea, and insects, brought to light a great number of new facts of the same order ; and, in 1842, the Danish zoologist, Steenstrup, collected all of them known at that time, and applied to the phenomena the general formula of the ' Alternation of Generations.' He was met, at the outset, by a difficulty of nomenclature. In the majority of cases, the one term, or the one set of terms, of the alternation is sexless. The germs from which its offspring are produced are not true eggs and are uninfluenced by males. Therefore, it is obviously inexact to call these proliferating forms ' females.' Steenstrup got over the difficulty by terming them ' nurses ;' though, thereby, he un-doubtedly somewhat strained the usually admitted attributes of a nurse. I do not imagine that Steenstrup supposed that he had contributed anything towards the explanation of these re-markable phenomena by the nomenclature he proposed. However this may be, his work was of much use by drawing the attention of biologists to their general nature, no less than by bringing into one view all the various forms of proliferation which are exhibited by living matter, and all the physical and metaphysical difficulties, with which the problem of animal and vegetable individuality bristles. Objections might be raised to the term ' Parthenogenesis,' used by Owen, not merely for

the autonomous proliferation of true females, but
for the production of progeny by organisms which
are not really female, and the vestalship of which
is therefore physically indefeasible. In fact, it is
strictly applicable only to a comparatively few
cases among insects and crustacea. And even
here, the queen-bee, under ordinary circumstances, would have to be excluded. The fatherless drones are, usually, not merely produced by a
true female : but she is already mother, in the
ordinary sense, of thousands of daughters.

But questions of names are of no particular
importance. We know what the processes de-
noted by the term ' Parthenogenesis ' are ; and
the point is to ascertain how far Owen's work
contributed to a better knowledge of them ;
or to that construction of an explanation of
the phenomena which is the end of investigation.

With respect to the first point, the work on
' Parthenogenesis ' contains no addition, that I am
aware of, to the common stock of observed facts.
In truth, the great majority of the subjects of
these processes are either the smaller insects and
crustacea, which lay out of Owen's range of study ;
or the marine invertebrates, which were, in those
days, hardly accessible to any but persons who
lived on, or by, the sea. Moreover, the investigation lay eminently in the province of the histological microscopist, in which Owen was less at
home than elsewhere.

In trying to form a judgment of the value of the explanation offered, it is a necessary preliminary to consider what there was to explain.

Among the animals with which we are familiar, proliferation, or the production of offspring, invariably implies the concurrence of two parents, a father and a mother. We are, therefore, naturally led to regard this method of proliferation as the rule, and any other as an exception. But, as we have seen, if our daily experience had been derived from many of the lower animals and plants, we might just as well have been led to think sexless proliferation the rule, and the other the exception. Whatever the outward form of the process of proliferation, in substance it always comes to the same thing. It is the detachment of a parcel, A, of the living substance of the parent, which either before, or · after, detachment evolves into a complete, physiologically independent, organism. There are innumerable cases in which this process takes place, in virtue of the autonomous activities of the living substance of an organism. The progeny in this case is a detached fragment of A, and nothing else. Why is it that, in equally numerous other cases, a parcel of the same kind may be similarly detached from A, but does not evolve, unless another parcel, B, of living substance, derived from the same, or another, organism, not merely comes into contact with A, but fuses with it ; so that the substance of the progeny is A + B, and not merely A ? What we want to explain is, not only why sexless proliferation takes place in the animals or plants in which it occurs, but why it does not take place in other closely allied forms. It is not legitimate to assume that sexless proliferation is secondary and exceptional, and sexual proliferation primary and normal. On the face of the matter, it is just as likely to be the other way.

In the essay under consideration, however, Owen starts with this assumption. He conceives that B is the agent by which a certain 'spermatic force' is transmitted to A ; and that, when apparently sexless proliferation takes place, the evolution of the germs is really due to the presence in them of this hypothetical ' spermatic force,' transmitted from the first sexual proliferation. Starting from the established truth that, where sex is concerned, the essential step of the production of progeny is the coalescence of substances contained in two cells, one derived from the one parent, and one from the other, and the subsequent division and subdivision (with concomitant growth) of the combined mass into the primary cells of which the embryo is constructed, Owen goes on to say (p. 5) :—

' Not all the progeny of the primary impregnated germ-cell are required for the formation of the body in all animals ; certain of the derivative

germ-cells may remain unchanged, and become
included in that body, which has been composed
of their metamorphosed and diversely combined
or confluent brethren ; so included, any derivative
germ-cell, or the nucleus of such, may commence
and repeat the same processes of growth by imbi-
bition, and of propagation by spontaneous fission,
as those to which itself owed its origin ; followed
by metamorphoses and combinations of the germ
masses so produced which concur to the development of another individual ; and this may be, or
may not be, like that individual in which the
secondary germ-cell or germ-mass was included.'

Again (p. 72) :—

' It would be needless to multiply the illustrations of the essential condition of these phenomena.   That condition is, the retention of certain
of the progeny of the primary impregnated germ-
cell, or, in other words, of the germ-mass, unchanged in the body of the first individual
developed from that germ-mass, with so much of
the spermatic force inherited by the retained
germ-cells from the parent cell or germ-vesicle as
suffices to set on foot and maintain the same
series of formative actions as those which constituted the individual containing them.

' How the retained spermatic force operates
in the formation of a new germ-mass from a
secondary, tertiary, or quaternary derivative germ-
cell or nucleus, I do not profess to explain ;

neither is it known how it operates in developing the primary germ-mass from the impregnated germ-vesicle of the ovum. In both we witness centres of repulsion and attraction antagonising to produce a definite result.'

But the primary assumption that this 'spermatic force' is necessary to the evolution of germs, that, therefore, sexless proliferation is only, as it were, sexual proliferation, one or more degrees removed, begs the whole question, which is exactly whether spermatic influence is, or is not, necessary to proliferation.

The other part of Owen's hypothesis, that proliferation depends upon the presence, in the proliferating region, of unchanged descendants of the primitive spermatized cells of the embryo, could not and cannot be supported by observation ; and is, indeed, contradicted by plain facts. In mosses, for example, there are very few parts of the whole organism which will not, under favourable circumstances, give rise to bud-like germs, whence new mosses proceed. And, in closely allied animals, in which the cells of the respective ovaries are equally near in descent to those of the embryo, the one will regularly proliferate, without male influence, and the other will never do so.

Owen, in fact, got no further towards the solution of this wonderful and difficult problem than Morren and others had done before him. But it is an interesting circumstance that the leading idea of ' Parthenogenesis ; ' namely, that sexless proliferation is, in some way, dependent upon the presence, in the prolifying region, of relatively un-altered descendants of the primary impregnated embryo cell (A + B)—is at the bottom of most of the attempts which have recently been made to deal with the question. The theory of the con-tinuity of germ-plasm of Weismann, for example, is practically the same as Owen's, if we omit from the latter the notion that the endowment with ' spermatic force ' is the indispensable condition of proliferation. The great progress of knowledge, about these matters, since 1849, lies in the demon-stration of the importance of a certain formed material which is met with in the nuclei of cells ; of the fact that this substance, growing and dividing, is distributed from the nucleus of the primary cell to the nuclei of all the cells of the organism ; that, in sexual proliferation, the nuclear substances of A and B pass, bodily, into the nucleus of the resulting embryo cell, without losing their inde-pendence, and are similarly transmitted to all the cells of the adult ; whence it follows, that every histological element of the adult living body thus produced contains associated, but yet materially distinct, descendants of the nuclear elements de-rived from each parent.

This discovery ranks, in my judgment, as the greatest achievement of morphological science

since the establishment of the cell theory.[7]   Its
importance as a factor in every theory of heredity
is obvious ; and it must have an equally important influence upon all theories of proliferation.   But, for the present, I must express the
opinion that it affords very little more help
towards a scientific explanation of the phenomena
of ' Parthenogenesis ' than Owen's theory afforded
in the infancy of histological inquiry.   Except by
the help of assumptions, of which there is no
proof, I do not see that modern speculation, at
present, gives us any better explanation why
the leaves of some plants prolify readily and
regularly, while those of others never do so ; or
why female cockroaches never exhibit sexless proliferation while queen-bees always do so.   The
ingenuity which fits hypotheses to facts by the
help of other hypotheses is always worthy of
admiration ; but, if it is to be useful, its purely
speculative character should never be lost sight
of.   If science is to retain its strength, it must
keep in touch with the solid ground of observation.
In reading some of the biological literature of
the present day, I sometimes rub my eyes and
wonder whether I am not dreaming of the good
old days of the *Naturphilosophie*.

In the preceding pages I have endeavoured to

[7] I refer to the morphological generalisations known
by this name ; not to any hypotheses based upon them.

give the general reader an outline sketch of the scope
and the course of modern biological science ; of the
condition of its several great divisions when Sir
R. Owen commenced his career sixty-four years
ago ; of the influence of his work upon the extra-
ordinarily rapid advance of biology in the course
of that time ; and it may be well that, arrived at
the end of my task, I recall my allusion, at the
outset, to the special difficulties in the way of the
satisfactory performance of it.

It does not appear to me that anything need be
said here about the many scientific controversies
in which Owen was engaged. I should be of this
opinion if I had not been concerned in any of them ;
for I do not see what good is to result from the
revival of the memory of such conflicts. And
whether I am right or wrong in this opinion,
I am well assured that, if anything is to be said
upon this topic, I am not the proper person to
say it.

But notwithstanding my determination to
ignore controversies, and a strong desire to
appreciate rather than to criticise, I am sensible
that the discussion of the 'Archetype' and ot
'Parthenogenesis' not merely allows the wide
differences of opinion, which unhappily obtained
between Sir R. Owen and myself, to appear, but
occupies an amount of space which may be
thought excessive, in relation to that filled by my
endeavour to do justice to the great and solid

achievements in Comparative Anatomy and Palæontology which I have recounted.

But this really lay in the nature of things. Obvious as are the merits of. Owen's anatomical and palæontological work to every expert, it is necessary to be an expert to discern them ; and endless pages of analysis of his memoirs would not have made the general reader any wiser than he was at first. On the other hand, the nature of the broad problems of the 'Archetype' and of 'Parthenogenesis' may easily be stated in such a way as to be generally intelligible ; while from Goethe to Zola, poets and novelists have made them interesting to the public. I have, therefore, permitted myself to dwell upon these topics at some length ; but the reader must bear in mind that, whatever view is taken of Sir Richard Owen's speculations on these subjects, his claims to a high place among those who have made great and permanently valuable contributions to knowledge remain unassailable.

A BIBLIOGRAPHY OF RICHARD OWEN [1]

1830–1889

1830

An Account of the Dissection of the Parts concerned in the Aneurism for the cure of which Dr. Stevens tied the internal iliac artery at Santa Cruz in the year 1812. *Trans. Med. Chir. Soc.* xvi. 219–235, pl.

Catalogue of the Hunterian Collection in the Museum of the Royal College of Surgeons in London. Pt. I. comprehending the Pathological Preparations in Spirit. 4to, *London*, 1830, 98 pp. [Anonymous.]

Ibid. Pt. II. comprehending the Pathological Preparations in a dried state. 4to, *London*, 1830, 56 pp. [Anonymous.]

Ibid. Pt. IV. (1) comprehending the first division of the Preparations of Natural History in Spirit. 4to, *London*, 1830, 144 pp. [Anonymous.]

1831

Catalogue of the Hunterian Collection in the Museum of the Royal College of Surgeons in London. Pt. III. comprehending the Human and Comparative Osteology. 4to, *London*, 1831, 266 pp. [Anonymous.]

Ibid. Pt. V. comprehending the Preparations of Monsters and

---

[1] By the courtesy of Dr. P. L. Sclater, Messrs. Waterhouse & Doubleday made a copy of the entries under Owen in the Royal Society's *Catalogue of Scientific Papers.* These entries have now been verified emended, and included in this Bibliography.—C. DAVIES SHERBORN.

Malformed Parts in Spirit, and in a dried state. 4to, *London*, 1831, 92 pp. [Anonymous.]

Ibid. Pt. VI. comprehending the Vascular and Miscellaneous Preparations in a dried state. 4to, *London*, 1831, 56 pp. [Anonymous.]

[N.B. These Catalogues formed apparently a preliminary list of the Hunterian specimens, and the preparation of these was presumably Owen's first duty after his appointment as Assistant Curator. There is absolutely no doubt that Owen was entirely responsible for Pt. IV. (1), and there is every reason for supposing that he largely assisted Clift in the compilation of the others.]

On the Anatomy of the Orang Outang (*Simia Satyrus*, L.) *Proc. Comm. Sci. Zool. Soc.* i. 1831, pp. 4-5, 9-10, 28 29, 67-72.

On the Anatomy of the Beaver (*Castor fiber*). *Proc. Comm. Sci. Zool. Soc.* i. 1831, pp. 19 20.

On the Anatomy of a Female Suricate (*Ryzæna tetradactyla*, Ill.). *Proc. Comm. Sci. Zool. Soc.* i. 1831, pp. 39-41.

On the Anatomy of a Male Suricate. *Proc. Comm. Sci. Zool. Soc.* i. 1831, pp. 51-52.

On the Anatomy of the Acouchy (*Dasyprocta acuschy*, Ill.). *Proc. Comm. Sci. Zool. Soc.* i. 1831, pp. 75-76.

On the Anatomy of the Thibet Bear (*Ursus thibetanus*, Cuv.). *Proc. Comm. Sci. Zool. Soc.* i. 1831, pp. 76-77.

On the Anatomy of the Gannet (*Sula bassana*). *Proc. Comm. Sci. Zool. Soc.* i. 1831, pp. 90-92.

On the Anatomy of the Nine-banded Armadillo (*Dasypus peba*, Desm.). *Proc. Comm. Sci. Zool. Soc.* i. 1831, pp. 141-144.

1832

Memoir on the Pearly Nautilus (*Nautilus Pompilius*, Linn.), with illustrations of its external form and internal structure. 4to, *London*, 1832. Pp. 68, pls. i-viii. (Royal College of Surgeons.)

Catalogue of Preparations illustrative of Human and Comparative Anatomy, presented by Sir William Blizard to the Royal College of Surgeons. 4to, *London*, 1832, p. 36. [Anonymous.]

On the Anatomy of the Seal (*Phoca vitulina*, Linn.). *Proc. Comm. Sci. Zool. Soc.* i. 1832, pp. 151 154.

On the Anatomy of the Weasel-headed Armadillo (*Dasypus sexcinctus*, Linn.). *Proc. Comm. Sci. Zool. Soc.* i. 1832, pp. 154-157.

On the Organs of Generation of the Female Kangaroo (*Macropus major*, Shaw). *Proc. Comm. Sci. Zool. Soc.* i. 1832, pp. 159-161.

On the Anatomy of the American Tapir (*T. americanus*, Gmel.). *Proc. Comm. Sci. Zool. Soc.* i. 1832, pp. 161–164.

On the Anatomy of the Sharp-nosed Crocodile (*Crocodilus acutus*, Cuv.). *Proc. Comm. Sci. Zool. Soc.* i. 1832, pp. 139–141, 169–170.

Characters of some New Species of Stomapodous Crustacea, collected by Mr. Cuming. *Proc. Comm. Sci. Zool. Soc.* ii. 1832, pp. 5 6.

On the Habits of the *Birgus latro*, Leach. *Proc. Comm. Sci. Zool. Soc.* ii. 1832, p. 17.

On the Morbid Appearances observed on the *post-mortem* examination of the Mandrill, *Cynocephalus Maimon. Proc. Comm. Sci. Zool. Soc.* ii. 1832, p. 17.

On the Anatomy of the *Cercopithecus albogularis*, Sykes. *Proc. Comm. Sci. Zool. Soc.* ii. 1832, pp. 18–20.

On a Malformation of the Beak of *Psittacus erithacus*, L. *Proc. Comm. Sci. Zool. Soc.* ii. 1832, pp. 23–24.

On the Anatomy of the Ariel Toucan (*Ramphastos Ariel*, Vig.). *Proc. Comm. Sci. Zool. Soc.* ii. 1832, pp. 42–46.

On the Anatomy of the Animal of *Stylifer astericola. Proc. Comm. Sci. Zool. Soc.* ii. 1832, pp. 60–61.

On the Anatomy of *Capromys Fournieri*, Desm. *Proc. Comm. Sci. Zool. Soc.* ii. 1832, pp. 68–76.

On the Peculiarities of the Skeleton of *Capromys Fournieri*, Desm., and *Dasyprocta acouchy*, Fr. Cuv. *Proc. Comm. Sci. Zool. Soc.* ii. 1832, pp. 100–104.

On the Anatomy of Two Species of Armadillo (*Dasypus*, L.) *Proc. Comm. Sci. Zool. Soc.* ii. 1832, pp. 130–132.

On the Osteology of the Weasel-headed Armadillo (*Dasypus sexcinctus*, L.) *Proc. Comm. Sci. Zool. Soc.* ii. 1832, pp. 134–138.

On the Anatomy of the Flamingo (*Phœnicopterus ruber*, L.) *Proc. Comm. Sci. Zool. Soc.* ii. 1832, pp. 141–143. [Includes *Tænia lamelligera*.]

On the Mammary Glands of the *Ornithorhynchus paradoxus. Phil. Trans.* 1832, pp. 517–538, pls. xv–xviii.

1833

Descriptive and Illustrated Catalogue of the Physiological Series of the Hunterian Collection in the Museum of the Royal College of Surgeons. 4to, *London*, 1833, vol. i. Including the Organs of Motion and Digestion, p. 272. [Anonymous.]

On the Mammary Gland of the *Echidna hystrix*, Cuv. *Proc. Comm. Sci. Zool. Soc.* ii. 1833, pp. 179–181.

On the Teeth of the Capybara (*Hydrochœrus capybara*, Erxl.). *Proc. Comm. Sci. Zool. Soc.* ii. 1833, pp. 187–188.

On the Anatomy of the Cape Hyrax (*Hyrax capensis*, Schreb.). *Proc. Comm. Sci. Zool. Soc.* ii. 1833, pp. 202–207.

On the Mammary Glands of the *Ornithorhynchus*. *Proc. Zool. Soc.* i. 1833, pp. 30–31, 95–96.

On the Sacculated Form of the Stomach in the Genus *Semnopithecus*, F. Cuv. *Proc. Zool. Soc.* i. 1833, pp. 74–76.

On the Sacculated Form of the Stomach as it exists in the Genus *Semnopithecus*, F. Cuv. *Trans. Zool. Soc.* i. 1833, pp. 65–70, pls. viii, ix.

On the Anatomy of the Brachiopoda of Cuvier, and more especially the Genera *Terebratula* and *Orbicula*. *Proc. Zool. Soc.* 1833, pp. 125–128 ; *Trans. Zool. Soc.* i. 1834, pp. 145–164, pls. xxii, xxiii.

On the Anatomy of the Cheetah (*Felis jubata*, Schr.). *Proc. Zool. Soc.* 1833, p. 108 ; *Trans. Zool. Soc.* i. 1834, pp. 129–136, pl. xx.

Mémoire sur l'Animal du *Nautilus Pompilius*. *Ann. Sci. Nat.* xxviii. 1833, pp. 87–158.

The Zoological Magazine ; or, Journal of Natural History. 8vo, *London*, 1833. [This was a venture of Owen's, but only six numbers appeared.]

1834

Descriptive and Illustrated Catalogue of the Physiological Series of the Hunterian Collection. 4to, *London*, 1834, vol. ii. Including the Absorbent, Circulatory, Respiratory, and Urinary Systems, pp. 164. [Anonymous.]

On the Period of Uterine Gestation, and the Condition of the New-born Fœtus in the Kangaroo (*Macropus major*, Shaw). *Proc. Zool. Soc.* i. 1834, pp. 128–132.

Account of the Anatomy of the young Concave Hornbill (*Buceros cavatus*, Lath.). *Proc. Zool. Soc.* i. 1834, pp. 102–104.

On the Distinguishing Peculiarities of the Crania of the Lion and Tiger. *Proc. Zool. Soc.* ii. 1834, pp. 1–2.

On the Anatomy of the Purple-crested Touraco (*Corythaix porphyreolopha*, Vig.). *Proc. Zool. Soc.* ii. 1834, pp. 3–5.

On the Anatomy of the Capybara (*Hydrochœrus capybara*, Erxl.). *Proc. Zool. Soc.* ii. 1834, p. 9.

On the Structure of the Heart of the Perennibranchiate Amphibia, or *Reptiles douteux* of Cuvier. *Proc. Zool. Soc.* ii. 1834, pp. 31–33.

On the Anatomy of the *Calyptrœidœ*. *Proc. Zool. Soc.* ii. 1834, p. 14 ; *Trans. Zool. Soc.* i. 1835, pp. 207–212, pl. xxx.

On the Young of the *Ornithorhynchus paradoxus*, Blum. *Proc. Zool. Soc.* ii. 1834, pp. 43, 44 ; *Trans. Zool. Soc.* i. 1835, pp. 221–228, pls. xxxii, xxxiii.

On the Anatomy of the Concave Hornbill (*Buceros cavatus*, Lath.). *Trans. Zool. Soc.* i. 1834, pp. 117–122, pl. xviii.

On the Generation of the Marsupial Animals, with a description of the impregnated uterus of the Kangaroo. *Phil. Trans.* 1834, pp. 333–364, pls. vi, vii.

On the Ova of the *Ornithorhynchus paradoxus*. *Phil. Trans.* 1834, pp. 555–566, pl. xxv.

Observations sur les Jeunes de l'Ornithorhynque. *Ann. Sci. Nat.* sér. 2 (Zool.), 1834, ii. pp. 303–308.

1835

Descriptive and Illustrated Catalogue of the Physiological Series of the Hunterian Collection. 4to, *London, 1835*, vol. iii., Pt. I. Nervous System and Organs of Sense. Pp. 1–208. [Anonymous.]

Marine Invertebrate Animals. An Appendix to the Narrative of a Second Voyage in search of a North-West Passage, &c. By Sir John Ross. 4to, *London*, 1835. [Owen contributed to this chapter a description of the genus *Rossia* (pp. xcii–xcix, pls. B and C, dated 1834). This paper has been quoted as 'An Account of Marine Invertebrate Animals inhabiting parts of the Arctic Ocean.' 2 pls., 1834.]

Description of a recent *Clavagella*. *Proc. Zool. Soc.* ii. 1835, pp. 111, 112.

On the Anatomy of *Macropus Parryi*, Benn. *Proc. Zool. Soc.* ii. 1835, p. 152.

Notes of a Dissection of a Long-tailed *Dasyurus* (*Dasyurus macrourus*, Geoffr.). *Proc. Zool. Soc.* iii. 1835, pp. 7–9.

Notes on the Anatomy of the Red-backed Pelican (*Pelecanus rufescens*, Gmel.). *Proc. Zool. Soc.* iii. 1835, pp. 9–12.

Description of a Microscopic Entozoon infesting the Muscles of the Human Body. *Proc. Zool. Soc.* iii. 1835, pp. 23–27 ; *Trans. Zool. Soc.* i. 1835, pp. 315–324, pl. xli, with an appendix, p. 323 *. [*Trichina spiralis*.]

On the Anatomy of *Linguatula tœnioides*, Cuv. *Proc. Zool. Soc.*

VOL. II. Z.

iii. 1835, pp. 27-28 ; *Trans. Zool. Soc.* i. 1835, pp. 325-330, pl. xli.

On the Comparative Osteology of the Orang and Chimpanzee. *Proc. Zool. Soc.* iii. 1835, pp. 30-40.

On the Osteology of the Chimpanzee and Orang Outang. *Trans. Zool. Soc.* i. 1835, pp. 343-380, pl. xlviii lviii.

On the Anatomy of *Distoma clavatum*, Rud. *Proc. Zool. Soc.* iii. 1835, pp. 72-73 ; *Trans. Zool. Soc.* i. 1835, pp. 381-384, pl. xli.

Remarks on the Entozoa, and on the Structural Differences existing among them ; including suggestions for their distribution into other classes. *Proc. Zool. Soc.* iii. 1835, pp. 73-76 ; *Trans. Zool. Soc.* i. 1835, pp. 387-394.

Notes on the Anatomy of the Kinkajou (*Cercoleptes caudivolvulus*, Ill.). *Proc Zool. Soc.* iii. 1835, pp. 119-124.

On the Anatomy of *Clavagella*, Lam. *Trans. Zool Soc.* i. 1835, pp. 269-274, pl. xxx.

On the Structure of the Heart in the Perennibranchiate Batrachia. *Trans. Zool. Soc.* i. 1835, pp. 213-220, pl. xxxj.

Description of a New Species of Tape-worm *Tænia lamelligera*, Owen. *Trans. Zool. Soc.* i. 1835, pp. 385-386 (previously described in Notes on the Anatomy of *Phœnicopterus ruber*, 1832).

1836

Descriptive and Illustrated Catalogue of the Physiological Series of the Hunterian Collection. 4to, *London*, 1836, vol. iii. pt. 2. Connective and Tegumentary System and Peculiarities, pp. 209-314. [Anonymous.]

Articles in Todd's ' Cyclopedia of Anatomy.' [Acrita, 1836 ; Articulata, 1836 ; Aves, 1836 ; Cephalopoda, 1836 ; Entozoa, 1839 ; Mammalia, 1847 ; Marsupialia, 1847 ; Mollusca, 1847 ; Monotremata, 1847 ; Teeth, 1852.]

Descriptions of some New or Rare Cephalopoda, collected by Mr. George Bennett. *Proc. Zool. Soc.* iv. 1836, pp. 19-22.

On the Shell and Animal of *Argonauta hians*, Lam. *Proc. Zool. Soc.* iv. 1836, pp. 22-24.

Remarks on the Secretion in the Lachrymal Sinus of the Indian Antelope (*Antilope cervicapra*, Pall.), with a tabular view of the relations between the habits and habitats of the several species of Antelopes and their suborbital, maxillary, post-auditory, and inguinal glands. *Proc. Zool. Soc.* iv. 1836, pp. 36-38.

On the Morbid Appearances observed in the Dissection of a Chimpanzee (*Simia troglodytes*, Linn.). *Proc. Zool. Soc.* iv. 1836, pp. 41-43.

Notes on the Anatomy of the Wombat (*Phascolomys Wombat*, Pér.). *Proc. Zool. Soc.* iv. 1836, pp. 49-53.

1837

M. J. F. Palmer, ' The Works of John Hunter, F.R.S.' with notes. 4 vols. 8vo. *London.* [Owen contributed notes to vol. iv. (1837) of this work on 'Observations on Certain Parts of the Animal Œconomy, inclusive of several papers from the Philosophical Transactions, &c.']

On a New Orang (*Simia morio*). *Proc. Zool. Soc.* iv. 1837, pp. 91 96.

Anatomical Descriptions of Two Species of Entozoa, from the Stomach of a Tiger (*Felis tigris*, Linn.), one of which forms a new genus, *Gnathostoma*. *Proc. Zool. Soc.* iv. 1837, pp. 123-126.

Dissection of the Head of the Turkey Buzzard and that of the Common Turkey. *Proc. Zool. Soc.* v. 1837, pp. 34-35.

On the Structure of the Shell of the Water Clam (*Spondylus varius*), *Proc. Zool. Soc.* v. 1837, pp. 63-66.

Description of the Cranium of the *Toxodon platensis*, a gigantic extinct mammiferous species, referable by its dentition to the Rodentia, but with affinities to the Pachydermata and the herbivorous Cetacea. *Proc. Geol. Soc.* ii. 1837, pp. 541-542.

On the Structure of the Brain in Marsupial Animals. *Phil. Trans.* 1837, pp. 87-96, pls. v-vii.

Description of the Membranes of the Uterine Fœtus of the Kangaroo. *Mag. Nat. Hist.* i. 1837, pp. 481-484.

1838

On the Cranium of *Simia Wurmbii*, Fischer. *Proc. Zool. Soc.* v. 1838, p. 82.

On the Existence of an Allantois in a Fœtal Kangaroo (*Macropus major*). *Proc. Zool. Soc.* v. 1838, pp. 82-83.

Remarks on the Separation of the Shell of *Argonauta*. *Proc. Zool. Soc.* v. 1838, p. 84.

Notes on the Anatomy of the Nubian Giraffe. *Proc. Zool. Soc.* vi. 1838, pp. 6-15, 20-22.

On the Genus *Menopoma*. *Proc. Zool. Soc.* vi. 1838, p. 25.

On the Anatomy of the Dugong (*Halicore*). *Proc. Zool. Soc.* vi. 1838, pp. 28 45.

Description of the Organs of Deglutition in the Giraffe. *Proc. Zool. Soc.* vi. 1838, pp. 47, 48.

Descriptions of some New and Rare Cephalopoda. *Trans. Zool. Soc.* ii. 1838, pp. 103-130, pl. xxi.

On the Dislocation of the Tail, at a certain Point, observable in the Skeletons of many Ichthyosauri. *Proc. Geol. Soc.* ii. 1838, pp. 660 662.

A Description of Viscount Cole's specimen of *Plesiosaurus macrocephalus* (Conybeare). *Proc. Geol. Soc.* ii. 1838, pp. 663 666.

On some Fossil Remains of Palæotherium, Anoplotherium, and Chæropotamus, from the Freshwater Beds of the Isle of Wight. *Proc. Geol. Soc.* iii. 1838, pp. 1-3.

On the Jaws of the *Thylacotherium Prevostii* (Valenciennes), from Stonesfield. *Proc. Geol. Soc.* iii. 1838, pp. 5-9.

On the *Phascolotherium* [and *Thylacotherium*]. *Proc. Geol. Soc.* iii. 1838, pp. 17-21.

On Marsupiata. *Rep. Brit. Assoc.* 1838, pt. 2, p. 105.

On the Structure of Teeth and the Resemblance of Ivory to Bone, as illustrated by microscopical examination of the teeth of Man and of various existing and extinct animals. *Rep. Brit. Assoc.* 1838, pt. 2, pp. 135-150.

[Remarks on the Physiology of the Marsupialia, being] a reply to the communication addressed by M. Coste to the French Academy of Sciences, entitled 'Mémoire en réponse à la lettre de M. R. Owen.' *Mag. Nat. Hist.* ii. 1838, pp. 94-96, 183 198.

Observations upon the Camerated Structure in the Valves of the Water-Clam (*Spondylus varius*, Sow.). *Mag. Nat. Hist.* ii. 1838, pp. 407 412, 2 figs.

On a New Species of the Genus Lepidosiren of Fitzinger and Natterer (*L. annectens*). *Proc. Linn. Soc.* i. 1838, pp. 27 32.

Description d'une Mâchoire Inférieure et de Dents de *Toxodon* trouvées à Bahia-Blanca, à 39° de latitude sur la côte Est de l'Amérique méridionale. *Ann. Sci. Nat.* sér. 2 (Zool.) ix. 1838, pp. 45-54.

Remarques sur une Communication de M. Coste relative à l'Œuf du Kangourou. *Comptes Rendus*, vi. 1838, 147-149. [See also *Mag. Nat. Hist.* N. S. ii. 1838, pp. 94-96, 183-198.]

1839

The Zoology of Captain Beechey's Voyage ; compiled from the collections and notes made by Captain Beechey, the Officers and Naturalist of the Expedition, during a voyage to the Pacific and Behring's Straits performed in his Majesty's ship ' Blossom' under the command of Captain F. W. Beechey, R.N., in the years 1825-28. 4to, *London*, 1839. [Crustacea. By R. Owen, pp. 77-92.]

[On the Anatomy of the Apteryx.] *Proc. Zool. Soc.* vi. 1839, pp. 48-51, 71, 72, 105-110.

On the Osteology of the Marsupialia. *Proc. Zool. Soc.* vi. 1839, pp. 120-148.

On the Dentition of the Koala (*Lipurus cinereus*, Goldf.). *Proc. Zool. Soc.* vi. 1839, pp. 154-156.

Outlines of a Classification of the Marsupialia. *Proc. Zool. Soc.* vii. 1839, pp. 5-19 ; *Trans. Zool. Soc.* ii. 1840, pp. 315-334.

On the Paper Nautilus (*Argonauta argo*). *Proc. Zool. Soc.* vii. 1839, pp. 35-48.

Notes on the Birth of the Giraffe at the Society's Menagerie. *Proc. Zool. Soc.* vii. 1839, pp. 108-109.

Notes on the Anatomy of the Nubian Giraffe. *Trans. Zool. Soc.* ii. 1839, pp. 217-248, pls. xl-xlv.

Osteological Contributions to the Natural History of the Orang Utangs (*Simia*, Erxleben). *Trans. Zool. Soc.* ii. 1839, pp. 165-172, pls. xxx-xxxiv.

Observations on the Teeth of the Zeuglodon (*Basilosaurus* of Dr. Harlan). *Proc. Geol. Soc.* iii. 1839, pp. 24-28.

Description of a Tooth and Part of the Skeleton of the *Glyptodon*, a large quadruped of the Edentate order, to which belongs the tessellated bony armour figured by Mr. Clift in his memoir on the *Megatherium* brought to England by Sir Woodbine Parish. *Proc. Geol. Soc.* iii. 1839, pp. 108-113.

Report on British Fossil Reptiles. Part I. *Rep. Brit. Assoc.* 1839, pp. 43-126.

On the Relation existing between the Argonaut-shell and its Cephalopodous Inhabitant. *Mag. Nat. Hist.* iii. 1839, pp. 421-431. [Reprint of *Proc. Zool. Soc.* vii. 1839, 35-48.]

Description of the Jaw of the Fossil *Macacus* from Woodbridge. *Mag. Nat. Hist.* iii. 1839, pp. 446-448.

Note sur les différences entre le *Simia morio*, d'Owen, et le *Simia*

Wurmbii dans la période d'adolescence, décrit par M. Dumortier. *Comptes Rendus*, viii. 1839, 231-236 ; *Ann. Sci. Nat.* sér. 2 (Zool.) xi. 1839, pp. 122 125.

Sur la Structure Microscopique et le Développement des Dents des Poissons Gymnodontes. *Ann. Sci. Nat.* sér. 2 (Zool.) xii. 1839, pp. 347 353.

Recherches sur la Structure et la Formation des Dents des Squaloïdes, et application des faits observés à une nouvelle théorie du développement des dents. *Comptes Rendus*, ix. 1839, pp. 784-788 ; *Ann. Sci. Nat.* sér. 2 (Zool.) xii. 1839, pp. 209-229.

1840

Descriptive and Illustrated Catalogue of the Physiological Series of the Hunterian Collection, . . . 4to, *London*, vol. iv. Organs of Generation, p. 208. [Anonymous.] 1840.

Ibid., 4to, *London*, vol. v. Products of Generation, p. 284. [Anonymous.] 1840.

Odontography ; or, a Treatise on the Comparative Anatomy of the Teeth ; their physiological relations, mode of development, and microscopic structure, in the Vertebrate Animals. Text and Atlas. 4to, *London*, 1840-45. Pt. I. : 1840 ; pp. 1 112, pls. i-l. II. : 1841 ; pp. i-xl, 113-288, pls. li-lxxxix A (excl. lxii A). III. : 1845 ; Title-page, pp. xli-lxxiv, 289-655, pls. i, ii, lxii A, xc-cl (some of these plates are dated 1844).

The Zoology of the Voyage of H.M.S. ' Beagle,' under the command of Captain Fitzroy, R.N., during the years 1832 to 1836. Part I. Fossil Mammalia, 1840. By R. Owen. Pp. iv, 112, 32 pls.

Exhibition of a Bone of an Unknown Struthious Bird from New Zealand. *Proc. Zool. Soc.* vii. 1840, pp. 169-171.

On the Anatomy of the Biscacha (*Lagostomus trichodactylus*, Brookes). *Proc. Zool. Soc.* vii. 1840, pp. 175 177.

On the Anatomy of the Southern Apteryx (*Apteryx australis*, Shaw). *Trans. Zool. Soc.* ii. 1840, pp. 257 302, pls. xlvii-lv.

A Description of the Soft Parts and of the Shape of the Hind Fin of the Ichthyosaurus, as when recent. *Proc. Geol. Soc.* iii. 1840, pp. 157, 158.

Description of the Fossil Remains of a Mammal, a Bird, and a Serpent, from the London Clay. *Proc. Geol. Soc.* iii. 1840, pp. 162-165.

Description of the Remains of a Bird, Tortoise, and Lacertian

Saurian, from the Chalk. *Proc. Geol. Soc.* iii. 1840, pp. 298-300.

Note on the Dislocation of the Tail at a certain point observable in the Skeleton of many Ichthyosauri. *Trans. Geol. Soc.* v. 1840, pp. 511–514, pl. xlii.

A Description of a Specimen of the *Plesiosaurus macrocephalus*, Conybeare, in the Collection of Viscount Cole. *Trans. Geol. Soc.* v. 1840, pp. 515–536, pls. xliii–xlv.

Description of the Mammalian Remains found at Kyson, in Suffolk. *Ann. Nat. Hist.* iv. 1840, pp. 191–194.

On the Application of Microscopic Examinations of the Structure of Teeth to the Determination of Fossil Remains. (First paper to Microscopical Society: *Athenæum*, 7 Mar. 1840, p. 194.)

1841

John Hunter's Observations on Animal Development, edited, and his illustrations of that process in the Bird described, by Richard Owen. Fol. *London*, 1841, 64 pp., 12 pls.

On the Skeleton of the *Talegalla Lathami*. *Proc. Zool. Soc.* viii. 1841, pp. 112, 113.

[Read a description of a New Genus and Species of Sponge, which he proposes to call *Euplectella aspergillum*.] *Proc. Zool. Soc.* ix. 1841, pp. 3–5.

On the Osteology of the Marsupialia. *Trans. Zool. Soc.* ii. 1841, pp. 379–408, pls. lxviii–lxxi.

Description of the *Lepidosiren annectens*. *Trans. Linn. Soc.* xviii. 1841, pp. 327–362, pls. 23–27.

On the Teeth of Species of the Genus Labyrinthodon (*Mastodonsaurus salamandroides* and *Phytosaurus* (?) of Jäger), from the German Keuper, and the Sandstone of Warwick and Leamington. *Proc. Geol. Soc.* iii. 1841, pp. 357–360.

Description of Parts of the Skeleton and Teeth of Five Species of the Genus *Labyrinthodon*, from the New Red Sandstone of Coton End and Cubbington Quarries; with remarks on the probable identity of the *Cheirotherium* with that genus of extinct Batrachians. *Proc. Geol. Soc.* iii. 1841, pp. 389–397.

Description of some Remains of a gigantic Crocodilian Saurian, probably marine, from the Lower Greensand at Hythe; and of teeth from the same formation at Maidstone, referable to the genus *Polyptychodon*. *Proc. Geol. Soc.* iii. 1841, pp. 449–452.

Description of a Portion of the Skeleton of the *Cetiosaurus*, a gigantic extinct saurian reptile occurring in the Oolitic Formations of different portions of England. *Proc. Geol. Soc.* iii. 1841, pp. 457-462.

Description of the Remains of Six Species of Marine Turtles (*Chelones*) from the London Clay of Sheppey and Harwich. *Proc. Geol. Soc.* iii. 1841, pp. 570-578.

Description of some Fossil Remains of *Chæropotamus, Palæotherium, Anoplotherium,* and *Dichobunes,* from the Eocene Formation, Isle of Wight. *Trans. Geol. Soc.* vi. 1841, pp. 41-46, pl. iv.

Observations on the Fossils representing the *Thylacotherium Prevostii,* Valenciennes, with reference to the doubts of its mammalian and marsupial nature recently promulgated ; and on the *Phascolotherium Bucklandi. Trans. Geol. Soc.* vi. 1841, pp. 47-67, pls. v, vi.

Observations on the *Basilosaurus* of Dr. Harlan (*Zeuglodon cetoides,* Owen). *Trans. Geol. Soc.* [2] vi. 1841, pp. 69-80, pls. viii, ix.

A Description of some of the Soft Parts, with the Integument, of the Hind Fin of the Ichthyosaurus, indicating the shape of the fin when recent. *Trans. Geol. Soc.* vi. 1841. pp. 199-202, pl. xx.

Description of a Tooth and Part of the Skeleton of the *Glyptodon clavipes,* a large quadruped of the Edentate order, to which belongs the tessellated bony armour described and figured by Mr. Clift in the former volume of the ‘Transactions of the Geological Society ;’ with a consideration of the question whether the *Megatherium* possessed an analogous dermal armour. *Trans. Geol. Soc.* [2] vi. 1841, pp. 81-106, pls. x-xiii.

Description of the Fossil Remains of a Mammal (*Hyracotherium leporinum*) and of a Bird (*Lithornis vulturinus*) from the London Clay. *Trans. Geol. Soc.* [2] vi. 1841, pp. 203-208, pl. xxi.

Description of some Ophidiolites (*Palæophis toliapicus*) from the London Clay at Sheppey, indicative of an extinct species of serpent. *Trans. Geol. Soc.* vi. 1841, pp. 209-210, pl. xxii.

Account of a *Thylacinus,* the great Dog-headed Opossum, one of the rarest and largest of the Marsupiate family of animals. *Rep. Brit. Assoc.* 1841, pt. ii. pp. 70, 71.

Report on British Fossil Reptiles. Part II. *Rep. Brit. Assoc.* 1841, pp. 60-204.

On the Structure of Fossil Teeth from the Central or Cornstone Division of the Old Red Sandstone, indicative of a new genus of Fishes, or fish-like Batrachia, for which is proposed the name of Dendrodus. *Microsc. Journ.* i. 1841, pp. 4-8, 17-20.

On the Anatomy of the *Pholadomya candida*, Sowerby, and *Lithedaphus longirostris*. 4to, pp. 16 (1841-42).

Two sets of proof-sheets, which, according to a MS. note by Lovell Reeve, were intended to form an appendix to his 'Conchologia Systematica.' Abstracts of these two papers were published in *Proc. Zool. Soc.* x. 1842, pp. 147-150; copies of the proof-sheets can be seen in the Brit. Mus. (Nat. Hist.)

1842

Description of the Skeleton of an Extinct Gigantic Sloth (*Mylodon robustus*, Owen), with observations on the osteology, natural affinities, and probable habits of the Megatherioid Quadrupeds in general. 4to, *London*, 1842 (*Royal Coll. Surgeons*). Pp. 176, 24 pls.

Description of the Stomach of the *Colobus ursinus*, Ogilby. *Proc. Zool. Soc.* ix. 1842, pp. 84-85.

[Read the second part of his Monograph on the *Apteryx australis*.] *Proc. Zool. Soc.* x. 1842, pp. 22-41.

Notes on the Birth of the Giraffe at the Zoological Society's Gardens, and description of the fœtal membranes and of some of the natural and morbid appearances observed in the dissection of the young animal. *Trans. Zool. Soc.* iii. 1842, pp. 21-28, pls. i, ii.

Notice of a Fragment of the Femur of a Gigantic Bird of New Zealand. *Trans. Zool. Soc.* iii. 1842, pp. 29-32, pl. iii.

Report on the Missourium now exhibiting at the Egyptian Hall, with inquiry into the claims of the *Tetracaulodon* to generic distinction. *Proc. Geol. Soc.* iii. 1842, pp. 689-695.

Description of the Remains of a Bird, Tortoise, and Lizard from the Chalk of Kent. *Trans. Geol. Soc.* [2] vi. 1842, pp. 411-414, pl. xxxix.

On the Teeth of Species of the Genus *Labyrinthodon* (*Mastodonsaurus* of Jaeger), common to the German Keuper formation and the Lower Sandstone of Warwick and Leamington. *Trans. Geol. Soc.* [2] vi. 1842, pp. 503-514, figs.

Description of Parts of the Skeleton and Teeth of Five Species of the Genus *Labyrinthodon* (*Lab. leptognathus*, *Lab. pachygnathus*, and *Lab. ventricosus*, from the Coton-end and Cubbington Quarries of the Lower Warwick Sandstone; *Lab. Jaegeri*, from Guy's Cliff, Warwick; and *Lab. scutulatus*, from Leamington); with remarks on the probable identity of the *Cheirotherium* with this genus of extinct Batrachians. *Trans. Geol. Soc.* [2] vi. 1842, pp. 515–544, pls. xliii xlvii.

Report on the British Fossil Mammalia. Part I. *Rep. Brit. Assoc.* 1842, pp. 54 74.

Description of an Extinct Lacertian Reptile (*Rhynchosaurus articeps*, Owen), of which the bones and footprints characterise the Upper New Red Sandstone at Grinsill, near Shrewsbury. *Trans. Cambr. Phil. Soc.* vii. 1842, pp. 354–369, pls. v, vi.

On the Blood-discs of *Siren lacertina*. *Microscopic Journ.* for 1842, pp. 73–75, pl. i.

Description of some Molar Teeth from the Eocene Sand at Kyson, in Suffolk, indicative of a new species of *Hyracotherium* (*H. cuniculus*). *Ann. Mag. Nat. Hist.* viii. 1842, pp. 1, 2.

Note to Bellamy's Account of two Peruvian Mummies in the Museum of Devon and Cornwall Nat. Hist. Soc. *Ann. Mag. Nat. Hist.* x. 1842, p. 100.

1843

Lectures on the Comparative Anatomy and Physiology of the Invertebrate Animals, delivered at the Royal College of Surgeons in 1843. (From notes taken by W. W. Cooper.) 8vo, *London*, 1843, 392 pp. (ed. 2, 1855). [Hunterian Lectures, vol. i.]

On a Specimen of *Nautilus pompilius*. *Proc. Zool. Soc.* x. 1843, p. 143.

On the Anatomy of the *Lithedaphus longirostris*, Owen. *Proc. Zool. Soc.* x. 1843, pp. 147–150.

On the Anatomy of the *Pholadomya candida*. *Proc. Zool. Soc.* x. 1843, p. 150.

On *Dinornis Novæ-zealandiæ*. *Proc. Zool. Soc.* xi. 1843, pp. 8–10, 144 146 (1844).

Description of a New Genus and Species of Sponge (*Euplectella aspergillum*, O.) *Trans. Zool. Soc.* iii. 1843, pp. 203 206, pl. xiii.

Appendix to Profesor Henslow's paper, consisting of a description of the fossil tympanic bones referable to four distinct species of *Balæna*. *Proc. Geol. Soc.* iv. 1843, pp. 283–286.

Report on the British Fossil Mammalia. Part II. *Rep. Brit. Assoc.* 1843, pp. 208 241.

On the Generation of the Polygastric Infusoria. *Edinb. New Phil. Journ.* xxxv. 1843, pp. 185 190.

Zoological Summary of the Extinct and Living Animals of the Order Edentata. *Edinb. New Phil. Journ.* xxxv. 1843, pp. 353–361

Letter on R. Harlan's Notice of New Fossil Mammalia. *Amer. Journ. Sci.* xliv. 1843, pp. 341–345.

On the Discovery of the Remains of a Mastodontoid Pachyderm in Australia. *Ann. Mag. Nat. Hist.* xi. 1843, pp. 7 12.

Additional Evidence proving the Australian Pachyderm, described in a former number of the 'Annals,' to be a *Dinotherium*, with remarks on the nature and affinities of that genus. *Ann. Mag. Nat. Hist.* xi. 1843, pp. 329-332.

On the Structure and Homology of the Cephalic Tentacles in the Pearly Nautilus. *Ann. Mag. Nat. Hist.* xii. 1843, pp. 305–311.

Notice of a New Species of Seal (*Stenorhynchus serridens*). *Ann. Mag. Nat. Hist.* xii. 1843. pp. 331 332.

Description d'une Squelette d'un Paresseux Gigantesque Fossile (le *Mylodon robustus*), suivie d'observations sur les quadrupèdes mégathérioïdes en général. *Ann. Sci. Nat.* ser. 2 (Zool.) xix. 1843, pp. 221-263. [Long abstract of Monograph, 1842.]

1844

Notes on the Dissection of a Female Orang-Utang (*Simia satyrus,* Linn.). *Proc. Zool. Soc.* xi. 1844, pp. 123 124.

On the Rudimentary Marsupial Bones in the *Thylacinus*. *Proc. Zool. Soc.* xi. 1844, pp. 148 149.

On Dinornis, an Extinct Genus of tridactyle Struthious Birds, with descriptions of portions of the skeleton of five species which formerly existed in New Zealand. (Part I.) *Trans. Zool. Soc.* iii. 1844, pp. 235–276, pls. xviii xxx.

Description of certain fossil crania, discovered by A. G. Bain, Esq., in sandstone rocks at the south-eastern extremity of Africa, referable to different species of an extinct Genus of Reptilia (*Dicynodon*), and indicative of a new tribe or sub-order of Sauria. *Proc. Geol. Soc.* iv. 1844, pp. 500-504.

A Description of certain Belemnites, preserved with a great proportion of their soft parts in the Oxford Clay, at Christian Malford, Wilts. *Phil. Trans.* 1844, pp. 65 85, pls. i–viii.

Report on the Extinct Mammals of Australia, with descriptions of certain fossils indicative of the former existence in that country of large marsupial representatives of the order *Pachydermata*. *Rep. Brit. Assoc.* 1844, pp. 223 240.

Characters of a New Species of Axolotl. *Ann. Mag. Nat. Hist.* xiv. 1844, p. 23.

Description of a Fossil Molar Tooth of a Mastodon, discovered by

Count Strzlecki [*sic*] in Australia. *Ann. Mag. Nat. Hist.* xiv. 1844, pp. 268-271.

Considérations sur le Plan Organique et la Mode de Développement des Animaux. *Ann. Sci. Nat.* sér. 3, vol. ii. 1844, pp. 162-168.

Recollections and Reflections of Gideon Shaddoe, Esq. No. V. *Hood's Magazine*, vol. ii. 1844, pp. 442-450. [Under the pseudonym of 'Silas Seer,' Owen contributed to these 'Recollections' his ghost story of Lancaster Gaol.]

1845

Descriptive and Illustrated Catalogue of the Fossil Organic Remains of Mammalia and Aves contained in the Museum of the Royal College of Surgeons of England. 4to, *London*, 1845, pp. 392. [Anonymous.]

Report on the State of Lancaster. 8vo. *London* (Health of Towns Commission), 1845, 28 pp.

Observations on the Living Echidna exhibited at the Menagerie of the Society in May 1845. *Proc. Zool. Soc.* xiii. 1845, pp. 80 82.

On the Existence of Two Species of Wombat (*Phascolomys*). *Proc. Zool. Soc.* xiii. 1845, pp. 82-83.

Appendix to Professor Henslow's Paper, consisting of a description of the fossil tympanic bones referable to four distinct species of *Balæna*. *Quart. Journ. Geol. Soc.* i. 1845, pp. 37-40, fig.

Account of Various Portions of the *Glyptodon*, an Extinct Quadruped, allied to the Armadillo, and recently obtained from the tertiary deposits in the neighbourhood of Buenos Ayres. *Quart. Journ. Geol. Soc.* i. 1845, pp. 257-262. [Extracted from Descriptive Catalogue of Museum of Royal College of Surgeons.]

Description of certain Fossil Crania, discovered by A. G. Bain in Sandstone rocks at the south-eastern extremity of Africa, referable to different species of an extinct genus of Reptilia (*Dicynodon*), and indicative of a new tribe or sub-order of Sauria. *Quart. Journ. Geol. Soc.* i. 1845, pp. 318-322 ; *Trans. Geol. Soc.* vii. 1845, pp. 59 84, pls. iii vi.

Reply to some Observations of Professor Wagner on the Genus *Mylodon*. *Ann. Mag. Nat. Hist.* xvi. 1845, pp. 100-102.

Observations sur l'Appareil de la Circulation chez les Mollusques de la classe des Brachiopodes. *Comptes Rendus*, xx. 1845, pp. 965-967.

Notice sur la Découverte, faite en Angleterre, des Restes Fossiles d'un Quadrumane du genre *Macaque*, dans une formation d'eau douce appartenant au nouveau pliocène. *Comptes Rendus*, xxi. 1845, pp. 573 575.

Sur la Classification et les Analogies des Dents Molaires des Carnivores. *Ann. Sci. Nat.* sér. 3 (Zool.) iii. 1845, pp. 116 128.

Lettre sur l'Appareil de la Circulation chez les Mollusques de la classe des Brachiopodes. *Ann. Sci. Nat.* sér. 3 (Zool.) iii. 1845, pp. 315 320.

Memoria sull' Anatomia de' Brachiopodi. *Atti Scienz. Ital.* (Naples) 1845 (1846), pp. 740-746.

[Osservazioni Anatomiche sugli Organi Salivari de' Bruti.] *Atti Scienz. Ital.* (Naples) 1845 (1846), pp. 767, 768.

Recollections and Reflections of Gideon Shaddoe, Esq. *Hood's Magazine*, vol. iii. 1845, pp. 294-303. [Under the pseudonym of 'Silas Seer,' Owen contributed to these ' Recollections ' his ghost story of ' The Negro's Head.']

1846

A History of British Fossil Mammals and Birds. 8vo, *London,* 1846. [Issued in 12 parts between 1844 and 1846.]

Lectures on Comparative Anatomy and Physiology of the Vertebrate Animals, delivered at the Royal College of Surgeons of England in 1844 and 1846. Part I. Fishes. 8vo, *London,* 1846. [Hunterian Lectures, vol. ii.]

Notes on the Dissection of a Female Chimpanzee (*Troglodytes niger*). *Proc. Zool. Soc.* xiv. 1846, pp. 2-3.

On the Dinornis. *Proc. Zool. Soc.* xiv. 1846, pp. 46 49.

Observations on the Skull and on the Osteology of the Foot of the Dodo (*Didus ineptus*). *Proc. Zool. Soc.* xiv. 1846, pp. 51-53.

On the Anatomy of the *Apteryx australis*, Shaw. Part II. (Myology). *Trans. Zool. Soc.* iii. 1846, pp. 277 302, pls. xxxi-xxxvi.

On the Osteology of the Marsupialia (Part II.). Comparison of the Skulls of the Wombats of continental Australia, and of Van Diemen's Land, whereby their specific distinction is established. *Trans. Zool. Soc.* iii. 1846, pp. 303 306, pl. xxxvii.

On Dinornis (Part II.) : containing descriptions of portions of the skull, the sternum, and other parts of the skeleton of the species previously determined, with osteological evidences of three additional species, and of a new genus (*Palapteryx*). *Trans. Zool. Soc.* iii. 1846, pp. 307 330, pls. xxxviii-xlviii.

Observations on the Dodo (*Didus ineptus*, Linn.). *Trans. Zool. Soc.* iii. 1846, pp. 331 338, pls. xlix, l.

On the supposed Fossil Bones of Birds from the Wealden. *Quart. Journ. Geol. Soc.* ii. 1846, pp. 96-102, figs.

Description of an Upper Molar Tooth of *Dichobune cervinum* from the Eocene Marl at Binstead, Isle of Wight. *Quart. Journ. Geol. Soc.* ii. 1846, pp. 420-421, fig.

Notices of some Fossil Mammalia of South America. *Rep. Brit. Assoc.* 1846 (pt. 2), pp. 65 67.

Report on the Archetype and Homologies of the Vertebrate Skeleton. *Rep. Brit. Assoc.* 1846, pp. 169-340.

Notice of Dr. Meiggs's Paper on the Generation of the Opossum (*Didelphis*). *Proc. Amer. Acad.* i. 1846, pp. 178, 179.

Observations on Certain Fossils from the Collection of the Academy. *Proc. Acad. Nat. Sci. Philad.* iii. 1846, pp. 93-96.

On Mr. Strickland's article, ' On the Structural Relations of Organised Beings.' *Phil. Mag.* xxviii. 1846, pp. 525 527.

1847

Notes on the Characters of the Skeleton of a Dugong (*Halicore australis*) from the North Coast of Australia, indicative of its specific distinctness from the *Halicore indicus* and *Halicore tabernaculi.* In J. B. Jukes, Narrative Voyage Fly, vol. ii. 1847, pp. 323-331, figs.

Metropolitan Sanitary Commission. First Report of the Commissioners appointed to enquire whether any and what special means may be required for the improvement of the Health of the Metropolis. Parl. Paper, fo. *London,* 1847, 52 pp., and minutes of Evidence, 190 pp. [With Chadwick, Southwood Smith, and others.]

—— Second Report. *Ibid.* 1848, 36 pp., and minutes of evidence, 44 pp.

—— Third Report. *Ibid.* 1848, 30 pp., with plan. [Brit. Mus. 1847-8, xxxii.]

On the Extinct Fossil Viverrine Fox of Oeningen, showing its specific characters and affinities to the family *Viverridæ. Quart. Journ. Geol. Soc.* iii. 1847, pp. 55-60, figs.

On the Batracholites, indicative of a small species of Frog (*Rana pusilla*, Owen). *Quart. Journ. Geol. Soc.* iii. 1847, pp. 224, 225, figs.

On the Fossils obtained by the Marchioness of Hastings from the Freshwater Eocene Beds of the Hordle Cliffs. *Rep. Brit. Assoc.* 1847, pt. 2, pp. 65, 66.

Observations on Certain Fossil Bones from the Collection of the American Academy of Sciences. *Journ. Acad. Nat. Sci. Philad.* ser. 2, i. 1847, pp. 18-20, pl. vi.

Notice of an Ichthyolite from Sheppey, in the collection of Mr. Tennant. *Ann. Mag. Nat. Hist.* xix. 1847, pp. 25-27.

Description of the Atlas, Axis, and Subvertebral Wedge Bones in the *Plesiosaurus*, with remarks on the homologies of those bones. *Ann. Mag. Nat. Hist.* xx. 1847, pp. 217-225.

Note on Dr. Meiggs's Memoir on the Reproduction of the Opossum. *Ann. Mag. Nat. Hist.* xx. 1847, pp. 324 328.

General Geological Distribution and Probable Food and Climate of the Mammoth. *Amer. Journ. Sci.* ser. 2, iv. 1847, pp. 13-19. [Extract from Brit. Foss. Mamm., 1844-6.]

Review of W. J. Broderip's Zoological Recreations, 1847. *New Monthly Mag.* clxiii. 1847.

Teleology of the Skeleton of Fishes. *Edinb. New Phil. Journ.* xlii. 1847, pp. 216-227. [From Lectures on Comp. Anat. vol. ii.]

1848

On the Archetype and Homologies of the Vertebrate Skeleton. 8vo, *London*, 1848, viii., pp. 172, pls.

On the Remains of the Gigantic and Presumed Extinct Wingless or Terrestrial Birds of New Zealand (*Dinornis* and *Palapteryx*), with indications of two other genera (*Notornis* and *Nestor*). *Proc. Zool. Soc.* xvi. 1848, pp. 1-11.

On a New Species of Chimpanzee (*Troglodytes Savagei*). *Proc. Zool. Soc.* xvi. 1848, pp. 27-35, 53 56.

On Dinornis (pt. iii.), containing a description of the skull and beak of that genus, and some of the same characteristic parts of *Palapteryx*, and of two other genera of birds, *Notornis* and *Nestor*; forming part of an extensive series of ornithic remains discovered by Mr. Walter Mantell at Waingongoro, North Island of New Zealand. *Trans. Zool. Soc.* iii. 1848, pp. 345-378, pls. lii-lvi.

On the Fossil Remains of Mammalia referable to the Genus *Palæotherium*, and to two Genera, *Paloplotherium* and *Dichodon*, hitherto undefined, from the Eocene Sand at Hordle, Hampshire. *Quart. Journ. Geol. Soc.* iv. 1848, pp. 17-42, pls. iii, iv Containing :—Pt. 1. Description of the teeth of a Palæothere, &c. Pt. 2. Description of lower molar teeth from Hordle (*Paloplotherium*). Pt. 3. Description of a lower jaw, &c. (*Palo-*

plotherium). Pt. 4. Description of a portion of a skull and upper teeth of the same species of Paloplotherium (*P. annectens*). Pt. 5. Description of the teeth and the lower jaw of an extinct species of mammal, &c. (*Dichodon*). [Owen had a few copies of these printed on quarto paper, bound up with four quarto plates, and issued by R. and J. E. Taylor as *Contributions to the History of British Fossil Mammals* (First Series), 1848.]

Notice of the Occurrence of Fossil Remains of the *Megaceros hibernicus* and of *Castor europæus* in the Pleistocene deposits forming the brick-fields at Ilford and Grays-Thurrock, Essex. *Quart. Journ. Geol. Soc.* iv. 1848, pp. 42-46, figs.

Description of Teeth and Portions of Jaws of Two Extinct Anthracotherioid Quadrupeds (*Hyopotamus vectianus* and *Hyop. bovinus*), discovered by the Marchioness of Hastings in the Eocene deposits of the N.W. coast of the Isle of Wight; with an attempt to develop Cuvier's idea of the classification of pachyderms by the number of their toes. *Quart. Journ. Geol. Soc.* iv. 1848, pp. 103-141, pls. vii, viii, and figs.

On the Os Humero-capsulare of the *Ornithorhynchus*. *Rep. Brit. Assoc.* 1848, pt. 2, p. 79.

On the Communications between the Tympanum and Palate in the Crocodiles. *Rep. Brit. Assoc.* 1848, pt. 2, pp. 79-80.

On the Homologies and Notation of the Dental System in Mammalia. *Rep. Brit. Assoc.* 1848, pt. 2, pp. 91-93.

On the Value of the Origin of Nerves as a Homological Character. *Rep. Brit. Assoc.* 1848, pt. 2, pp. 93-94.

Remarks on the 'Observations sur l'Ornithorhynque par M. Jules Verreaux.' *Ann. Mag. Nat. Hist.* ser. 2, ii. 1848, pp. 317-322.

The Great Sea-serpent. *Ann. Mag. Nat. Hist.* ser. 2, ii. 1848, pp. 458-463. [Letter to *The Times*.]

1849

A History of British Fossil Reptiles. 4 vols. 4to, *London*, 1849-84. [See 1884.]

On Parthenogenesis, or the successive production of procreating individuals from a single ovum. 8vo, *London*, 1849, 76 pp.

On the Nature of Limbs. A discourse delivered February 9 at an evening Meeting of the Royal Institution of Great Britain. 8vo, *London*, 1849, 120 pp., 2 pls.

Zoology, in 'A Manual of Scientific Enquiry; prepared for the use of Her Majesty's Navy: and adapted for travellers in general.' 16mo. *London*, 1849, pp. 343-399. [Several editions.]

Notes on the Anatomy of the Male Aurochs (*Bison europæus*). *Proc. Zool. Soc.* xvi. 1849, pp. 126-133.

Osteological Contributions to the Natural History of the Chimpanzees (*Troglodytes*, Geoffroy), including the description of the skull of a larger species (*Troglodytes gorilla*, Savage). discovered by Thomas S. Savage in the Gaboon Country, West Africa. *Trans. Zool. Soc.* iii. 1849, pp. 381-422, pls. lviii-lxiii.

Notes on Remains of Fossil Reptiles discovered by Professor Henry Rogers of Pennsylvania, U.S., in Greensand Formations of New Jersey. *Quart. Journ. Geol. Soc.* v. 1849, pp. 380-383, pls. x, xi.

On the Development and Homologies of the Carapace and Plastron of the Chelonian Reptiles. *Phil. Trans.* 1849, pp. 151-171, pl. xiii, figures in text.

On *Lucernaria inauriculata*. *Rep. Brit. Assoc.* 1849, pt. 2, pp. 78-79.

Monograph of the Fossil Reptilia of the London Clay. Part 1. Chelonia, pp. 1-76, pls. i-xxviii, viii. A, x. A, xiii. A, xviii. A, xix*., xix. B, xix. C, xix. D. *Pal. Soc.* ii. 1849. [With Thomas Bell.]

On the Structure of the Teeth of some Fossil Fish of the Carboniferous Period. *Ann. Mag. Nat. Hist.* ser. 2, iii. 1849, pp. 41-42.

Instructions for Collecting and Preserving Invertebrate Animals. *Edinb. New Phil. Journ.* xlvii. 1849, pp. 280-292. [Reprint of 'Zoology' in Manual of Scientific Enquiry.]

1850

Description of Two Mutilated Specimens of *Spirula Peronii*, with some observations on *S. australis* and *reticulata*. In Zool. Voyage Samarang, 4to, *London*, 1850, pp. 6-17, pl. iv.

Report of the Commissioners appointed to make enquiries relating to Smithfield Market, and the Markets in the City of London for the Sale of Meat. Parl. Paper, fo. *London*, 1850, 148 pp., plans. [Brit. Mus. 1850, xxxi.]

On Dinornis (Part IV.): containing the restoration of the feet of that genus and of *Palapteryx*, with a description of the sternum in *Palapteryx* and *Aptornis*. *Trans. Zool. Soc.* iv. 1850, pp. 1-20, pls. i-iv.

On the Development and Homologies of the Molar Teeth of the

VOL. II.   A A

Wart Hogs (*Phacochœrus*), with Illustrations of a System of Notation for the Teeth in the Class Mammalia. *Phil. Trans.* 1850, pp. 481-498, pls. xxxiii, xxxiv.

On the Communications between the Cavity of the Tympanum and the Palate in the Crocodilia (Gavials, Alligators, and Crocodiles). *Phil. Trans.* 1850, pp. 521-528, pls. xl-xlii.

A Memoir of William Clift. *Proc. Roy. Soc.* v. 1850, pp. 876-880. [Anonymous.]

Monograph of the Fossil Reptilia of the London Clay. Part II. Crocodilia, Ophidia, pp. 1-68, pls. i-xvi, xxix, ii. A. *Pal. Soc.* iii. 1850. ['Ophidia' has a separate title-page.]

Observations on Three Skulls of *Naloo africanus*. *Journ. Ethnol. Soc.* ii. 1850, pp. 235-237.

The Hippopotamus at the Zoological Gardens. *Ann. Mag. Nat. Hist.* ser. 2, v. 1850, p. 515-518.

On British Eocene Serpents and the Serpent of the Bible. *Edinb. New Phil. Journ.* xlix. 1850, pp. 239-242. [Extract from Brit. Foss. Rept.]

Review of R. G. Cumming's 'A Hunter's Life in South Africa,' 1850. *Quarterly Review*, lxxxviii. 1850.

1851

Report on Animal and Vegetable Substances, chiefly used in Manufactures, as Implements, or for Ornaments. (In Reports by the Juries. Exhibition of the Works of Industry of All Nations.) *London*, 1851. Vol. i. pp. 163-358. [There were several editions of this Report.]

On a New Species of Pterodactyle (*Pterodactylus compressirostris*, Owen) from the Chalk : with some remarks on the nomenclature of the previously described species. *Proc. Zool. Soc.* 1851, pp. 21-34.

On the Anatomy of the Indian Rhinoceros (*Rh. unicornis*, L.). *Trans. Zool. Soc.* iv. 1851, pp. 31-58, pls. ix-xxii.

On Dinornis (Part V.) : containing a description of the skull and beak of a large species of *Dinornis*, of the cranium of an immature specimen of *Dinornis giganteus* (?), and of crania of species of *Palapteryx*. *Trans. Zool. Soc.* iv. 1851, pp. 59-68, pls. xxiii, xxiv.

Description of the Impressions on the Potsdam Sandstone, discovered by Mr. Logan in Lower Canada. *Quart. Journ. Geol. Soc.* vii. 1851, pp. 250-252.

Letter 'On the Track of a Quadruped imprinted on Lower Silurian Sandstone, from Beauharnois, 20 miles above Montreal (Chelonian).' *Quart. Journ. Geol. Soc.* vii. 1851, p. lxxv.

On Metamorphosis and Metagenesis. *Proc. Roy. Inst.* i. 1851, pp. 9-16.

On New Fossil Mammalia from the Eocene Freshwater Formation at Hordwell, Hants. *Rep. Brit. Assoc.* 1851, pt. 2, p. 67.

On the Megatherium (*Megatherium americanum*, Blumenbach). Part I. Preliminary Observations on the Exogenous Processes of Vertebræ. *Phil. Trans.* 1851, pp. 719 764, pls. xliv-liii.

Monograph on the Fossil Reptilia of the Cretaceous Formations. Pt. I. Chelonia (Lacertilia, &c.), pp. 1 118, pls. i-xxxvii, vii. A, and ix. A. *Pal. Soc.* v. 1851.

Synopsis of the Hunterian Lectures on Comparative Osteology. *Edinb. New Phil. Journ.* l. 1851, pp. 329 334.

Comparison of the Modification of the Osseous Structure in the Megatherium with that in the other known existing and extinct Species of the class Mammalia. *Edinb. New Phil. Journ.* li. 1851, pp. 350 356. [Extract from *Phil. Trans.*]

Review of Lyell's 'Principles of Geology,' 8th ed. ; 'Manual of Elementary Geology,' 3rd ed. ; and 'Anniversary Address to the Geological Society, 1851.' *Quarterly Review*, lxxxix. 1851.

1852

Descriptive and Illustrated Catalogue of the Physiological Series of Comparative Anatomy contained in the Museum of the Royal College of Surgeons. Vol. i. Including the Organs of Motion and Digestion. 2nd ed. 4to, *London*, 1852, 276 pp., 13 pls.

On the Raw Materials from the Animal Kingdom. Lecture on the Results of the Great Exhibition of 1851, delivered before the Society of Arts. No. 3, vol. i. pp. 75-132, 8vo, *London*, 1852.

On the Anatomy of the Wart Hog (*Phacochœrus Pallasii*, Van der Hoeven). *Proc. Zool. Soc.* xix. 1852, pp. 63-69.

Description of the Impressions and Footprints of the Protichnites from the Potsdam Sandstone of Canada. *Quart. Journ. Geol. Soc.* viii. 1852, pp. 214-225, pls. ix-xiv. A.

Note on the Crocodilian Remains accompanying Dr. T. L. Bell's paper on Kotah. *Quart. Journ. Geol. Soc.* viii. 1852, p. 233.

1853

Descriptive Catalogue of the Osteological Series contained in the Museum of the Royal College of Surgeons of England. 2 vols. 4to, *London*, 1853. Vol. i. Pisces, Reptilia, Aves, Marsupialia. Pp. 352. Vol. ii. Mammalia Placentalia. Pp. 353–914.

Notes on the Eggs and Young of the Apteryx, and on the Casts of the Eggs and Certain Bones of *Æpyornis* (Isid. Geoffroy) recently transmitted to the Zoological Society of London. *Proc. Zool. Soc.* xx. 1853, pp. 9–13.

Osteological Contributions to the Natural History of the Chimpanzees (*Troglodytes*) and Orangs (*Pithecus*). No. IV. Description of the Cranium of an adult male Gorilla, from the river Danger, West Coast of Africa, indicative of a variety of the Great Chimpanzee (*Troglodytes gorilla*), with remarks on the capacity of the cranium and other characters shown by sections of the skull in the Orangs (*Pithecus*), Chimpanzees (*Troglodytes*), and in different varieties of the human race. *Trans. Zool. Soc.* iv. 1853, pp. 75–88, pls. xxvi–xxx.

Notes on the above-described fossil remains. *Quart. Journ. Geol. Soc.* ix. 1853, pp. 66, 67, pl. ii. [*Dendrerpeton acadianum.*]

Notice of a Batrachoid Fossil in British Coalshale. *Quart. Journ. Geol. Soc.* ix. 1853, pp. 67–70, pl. ii. [*Parabatrachus Colei.*]

Description of some species of the extinct genus *Nesodon*, with remarks on the primary group (*Toxodontia*) of Hoofed Quadrupeds, to which that genus is referable. *Phil. Trans.* 1853, pp. 291–310, pls. xv–xviii.

On the Anatomy of *Terebratula* (pp. 3–22, pls. i–iii). In T. Davidson's 'British Fossil Brachiopoda,' Introduction to vol. i. *Pal. Soc.* vii. December 1853.

A Monograph of the Fossil Chelonian Reptiles of the Wealden Clays and Purbeck Limestones, pp. 1–12, pls. i–ix. *Pal. Soc.* vii. 1853. [This is the first part, and contains *Chelonia*.]

Note on the Transverse Processes of the Two-toothed Dolphin (*Hyperoodon bidens*). *Ann. Mag. Nat. Hist.* ser. 2, xii. 1853, pp. 435, 436.

Recherches sur l'Archétype et les Homologies du Squelette Vertébré. *Comptes Rendus*, xxxvii. 1853, pp. 389–394.

Nouvelles Observations sur l'Ostéologie du *Troglodytes gorilla*. *Ann. Sci. Nat.* sér. 3 (Zool.) xx. 1853, p. 120.

1854

Descriptive Catalogue of the Fossil Organic Remains of Reptilia and Pisces contained in the Museum of the Royal College of Surgeons of England. 4to, *London*, 1854, pp. 184. [Anonymous.]

The Physiology of Animal and Vegetable Life. 12mo, *Philadelphia*, 1854, 56 pp. (Circle of the Sciences, No. 2). [With Orr.]

Geology and Inhabitants of the Ancient World. 12mo, *London*, 1854, 39 pp., figures. [A guide-book to the Extinct Animals in the grounds of the Crystal Palace.]

On the Anatomy of the Tree Kangaroo (*Dendrolagus inustus*, Gould). *Proc. Zool. Soc.* xx. 1854, pp. 103-107.

On the Anatomy of the Walrus. *Proc. Zool. Soc.* xxi. 1854, pp. 103-106.

On the Anatomy of the Great Anteater (*Myrmecophaga jubata*). *Proc. Zool. Soc.* xxii. 1854, pp. 154-157.

On a Fossil embedded in a Mass of Pictou Coal, from Nova Scotia. *Quart. Journ. Geol. Soc.* x. 1854, pp. 207, 208, pl. ix ; ix, 1855, pp. 9, 10. [*Baphetes planiceps.*]

On some Fossil Reptilian and Mammalian Remains from the Purbecks. *Quart. Journ. Geol. Soc.* x. 1854, pp. 420-433, figs.

Description of the Cranium of a Labyrinthodont Reptile (*Brachyops laticeps*) from Mangali, Central India. *Quart. Journ. Geol. Soc.* x. 1854, pp. 473, 474 ; xi. 1855, pp. 37-39, pl. ii.

On the Structure and Homologies of Teeth. *Proc. Roy. Inst.* i. 1854, pp. 365-374.

On the Anthropoid Apes. *Rep. Brit. Assoc.* 1854, pt. 2, pp. 111-113.

1855

Lectures on the Comparative Anatomy and Physiology of the Invertebrate Animals, delivered at the Royal College of Surgeons. 8vo, *London*, 1855, 690 pp. [This is not a reprint of the 1843 ed.]

Principes d'Ostéologie Comparée, ou Recherches sur l'Archétype et les Homologies du Squelette Vertébré. 8vo, *Paris*, 1855.

Instances of the Power of God as manifested in His Animal Creation. *London*, 1855 (ed. 2, 1864).

On the Bones of the Leg of *Dinornis* (*Palapteryx*) *struthioides* and the *Palaptcryx gracilis*. *Proc. Zool. Soc.* xxii. 1855, pp. 244-248.

Description of the Skull of a Large Species of Dicynodon (*D. tigriceps*, Owen), transmitted from South Africa by A. G. Bain, Esq. *Trans. Geol. Soc.* vii. 1855, pp. 233-248, pls. xxix-xxxii.

Notice of some New Reptilian Fossils from the Purbeck Beds near Swanage. *Quart. Journ. Geol. Soc.* xi. 1855, pp. 123, 124, fig. [*Saurillus.*]

Notice of a New Species of an Extinct Genus of Dibranchiate Cephalopod (*Coccoteuthis latipinnis*) from the Upper Oolitic Shales at Kimmeridge. *Quart. Journ. Geol. Soc.* xi. 1855, pp. 124, 125, pl. viii.

On the Fossil Cranium of *Dicynodon tigriceps*, Owen. from South Africa. *Quart. Journ. Geol. Soc.* xi. 1855, p. 532 (abstract).

On the Remains of *Dicynodon tigriceps*, Owen, from South Africa. *Quart. Journ. Geol. Soc.* xi. 1855, p. 541 (abstract).

On the Fossil Skull of a Mammal (*Prorastomus sirenoides*, Owen), from the Island of Jamaica. *Quart. Journ. Geol. Soc.* xi. 1855, pp. 541-543, pl. xv.

On the Megatherium (*Megatherium americanum*, Cuvier and Blumenbach). Part II. Vertebræ of the Trunk. *Phil. Trans.* 1855, pp. 359-388, pls. xvii-xxvii.

Monograph on the Fossil Reptilia of the Wealden Formations. Pt. II. Dinosauria, pp. 1-54, pls. i-xix, and xvi. A. *Pal. Soc.* viii. 1855.

On the Anthropoid Apes, and their Relations to Man. *Proc. Roy. Inst.* ii. 1855, pp. 26-41.

On some Remains of an Ichthyosaurus discovered by Captain Sir Edward Belcher, C.B., R.N., at Exmouth Island, in lat. 77° 16′ N., long. 96° W. In 'The Last of the Arctic Voyages : being a Narrative of the Expedition in H.M.S. "Assistance," under the Command of Sir Edward Belcher, in search of Sir John Franklin, during the Years 1852-54.' 2 vols. 8vo, *London*, 1855.

1856

Descriptive Catalogue of the Fossil Organic Remains of Invertebrata contained in the Museum of the Royal College of Surgeons of England. 4to, *London*, 1856, p. 260. [Cephalopoda, and Notes to the Gasteropoda by Owen : the bulk of the volume by John Morris.]

Rapports du Jury mixte Internationale. . . . Exposition Universelle de 1855, 8vo, *Paris*, 1856. [As *Robert* Owen in xi⁰ classe, 'Préparation et Conservation des Substances alimentaires,' pp. 613-664 : President of the Jury.]

On Dinornis (Part VII.) : containing a description of the bones of the leg and foot of the *Dinornis elephantopus*, Owen. *Proc. Zool. Soc.* xxiv. 1856, pp. 54 61.

Description of a Fossil Cranium of the Musk-Buffalo [*Bubalus moschatus*, Owen ; *Bos moschatus* (Zimm. and Gmel.), Pallas ; *Bos Pallasii*, De Kay ; *Ovibos Pallasii*, H. Smith and Bl.] from the 'Lower Level Drift,' at Maidenhead, Berkshire. *Quart. Journ. Geol. Soc.* xii. 1856, pp. 124-131, figs.

On the Affinities of the Large Extinct Bird (*Gastornis parisiensis*, Hébert), indicated by a fossil femur and tibia discovered in the lowest Eocene formation near Paris. *Quart. Journ. Geol. Soc.* xii. 1856, pp. 204-217, pl. iii.

Description of some Mammalian Fossils from the Red Crag of Suffolk. *Quart. Journ. Geol. Soc.* xii. 1856, pp. 217-236, 24 figures.

On Parts of the Skeleton of the Trunk of the *Dicynodon tigriceps*. *Trans. Geol. Soc.* vii. 1856, pp. 241-248, pls. xxxiii, xxxiv.

On the Megatherium (*Megatherium americanum*, Cuvier and Blumenbach). Part III. The Skull. *Phil. Trans.* 1856, pp. 571-590, pls. xxi-xxvi.

On the Ruminant Quadrupeds and the Aboriginal Cattle of Britain. *Proc. Roy. Inst.* ii. 1856, pp. 256-261.

On the *Dichodon cuspidatus*, from the Upper Eocene of the Isle of Wight and Hordwell, Hants. *Rep. Brit. Assoc.* 1856, pt. 2, p. 72.

On a New Species of Anoplotherioid Mammal (*Dichobune ovina*, Owen), from the Upper Eocene of Hordwell, Harts, with remarks on the genera *Dichobune*, *Xiphodon*, and *Microtherium*. *Rep. Brit. Assoc.* 1856, pt. 2, pp. 72, 73.

On a Fossil Mammal (*Stereognathus ooliticus*) from the Stonesfield Slate. *Rep. Brit. Assoc.* 1856, pt. 2, p. 73.

On the *Scelidotherium leptocephalum*, a Megatherioid Quadruped from La Plata. *Rep. Brit. Assoc.* 1856, pt. 2, pp. 73, 74.

A Brief Notice of the Aztec Race, followed by a Description of the so-called Aztec Children exhibited in 1853. *Journ. Ethnolog. Soc.* iv. 1856, pp. 120-137. [With Richard Cull.]

A Visit to Selborne. *Blackwood's Edinburgh Mag.* Aug. 1856, pp. 175-183. [Under the pseudonym of 'ΕΝΝΩ.]

1857

On the Anatomy of the Great Anteater (*Myrmecophaga jubata*, Linn.) Part II. *Proc. Zool. Soc.* xxv. 1857, pp. 22-24.

Osteological Contributions to the Natural History of the Chimpanzees (*Troglodytes*) and Orangs (*Pithecus*). No. V. Comparison of the lower jaw and vertebral column of the *Troglodytes gorilla*, *Troglodytes niger*, *Pithecus satyrus*, and different varieties of the human race. *Trans. Zool. Soc.* iv. 1857, pp. 89-116, pls. xxxi-xxxvi.

On the Anatomy of the Great Anteater (*Myrmecophaga jubata*, Linn.). *Trans. Zool. Soc.* iv. 1857, pp. 117-140, pls. xxxvii-xl.

On *Dinornis* (Pt. VI.) : containing a description of the bones of the leg of *Dinornis* (*Palapteryx*) *struthioides*, and of *Dinornis gracilis*, Owen. *Trans. Zool. Soc.* iv. 1857, pp. 141-147, pls. xli, xlii.

On the Affinities of the *Stereognathus ooliticus*, Charlesworth, a mammal from the Oolitic Slate of Stonesfield. *Quart. Journ. Geol. Soc.* xiii. 1857, pp. 1-11, pl. i.

On the *Dichodon cuspidatus*, Owen. *Quart. Journ. Geol. Soc.* xiii. 1857, pp. 190-196, pl. iii.

On the Fossil Vertebræ of a Serpent (*Laophis crotaloïdes*, Owen), discovered by Captain Spratt, R.N., in a Tertiary formation at Salonica. *Quart. Journ. Geol. Soc.* xiii. 1857, pp. 196-199, pl. iv.

Description of the Lower Jaw and Teeth of an Anoplotherioid Quadruped (*Dichobune ovina*, Owen), of the size of the *Xiphodon gracilis*, Cuv., from the Upper Eocene Marl, Isle of Wight. *Quart. Journ. Geol. Soc.* xiii. 1857, pp. 254-260, pl. viii.

On the Scelidothere (*Scelidotherium leptocephalum*, Owen). *Phil. Trans.* 1857, pp. 101-110, pls. viii, ix.

Description of the Fœtal Membranes and Placenta of the Elephant (*E. indicus*, Cuv.), with remarks on the value of placentary characters in the classification of the Mammalia. *Phil. Trans.* 1857, pp. 347-354, pl. xvi.

Description of a New Species of *Euplectella* (*E. cucumer*, Owen). *Trans. Linn. Soc.* xxii. 1857, pp. 117-124.

On the Placenta of the Elephant. *Proc. Roy. Soc.* viii. 1857, pp. 471-473.

Monograph on the Fossil Reptilia of the Wealden Formations. Part III. *Megalosaurus Bucklandi*, pp. 1-26, pls. i-xii. *Pal. Soc.* ix. 1857.

1858

Additional matter in Buckland, 'Geology and Mineralogy.' Third edition. 2 vols. 8vo, *London*, 1858.

Mollusca. From the 'Encyclopædia Britannica.' 8th edition. 4to, *Edinburgh*, 1858. [Mainly written by Samuel Pickworth Woodward.]

Odontology. From the 'Encyclopædia Britannica.' 8th edition. 4to, *Edinburgh*, 1858.

Palæontology. From the 'Encyclopædia Britannica.' 8th edition. 4to, *Edinburgh*, 1858.

Oken. 'Encyclopædia Britannica.' 8th edition. 4to, *Edinburgh*, 1858.

On *Dinornis* (Pt. VII.) : containing a description of the bones of the leg and foot of *Dinornis elephantopus*, Owen. *Trans. Zool. Soc.* iv. 1858, pp. 149-157, pls. xliii-xlv.

On *Dinornis* (Pt. VIII.) : containing a description of the skeleton of the *Dinornis elephantopus*, Owen. *Trans. Zool. Soc.* iv. 1858, pp. 159-164, pls. xlvi, xlvii.

Osteological Contributions to the Natural History of the Chimpanzees and Orangs. No. VI. Characters of the skull of the male *Pithecus morio*, with remarks on the varieties of the male *Pithecus satyrus*. *Trans. Zool. Soc.* iv. 1858, pp. 165-178, pls. xlviii-l.

On the Anatomy of the Great Anteater (*Myrmecophaga jubata*, Linn.) Pt. II. *Trans. Zool. Soc.* iv. 1858, pp. 179-181, pls. li-liii.

Description of a Small Lophiodont Mammal (*Pliolophus vulpiceps*), from the London Clay, near Harwich. *Quart. Journ. Geol. Soc.* xiv. 1858, pp. 54-71, pls. ii, iii, iv.

Note on the Bones of the Hind Foot of the Iguanodon, discovered by S. H. Beckles. *Quart. Journ. Geol. Soc.* xiv. 1858, pp. 174-175.

On some Outline Drawings and Photographs of the Skull of *Zygomaturus trilobus*, Macleay, from Australia. *Quart. Journ. Geol. Soc.* xiv. 1858, pp. 541-542; xv. 1859, pp. 168-176, pls. vii, viii.

On the Characters, Principles of Division, and Primary Groups of the Class Mammalia. *Journ. Linn. Soc.* ii. (Zool.) 1858, pp. 1-37.

Description of the Skull and Teeth of the *Placodus laticeps*, Owen ;

with indications of other new species of *Placodus*, and evidence
of the Saurian nature of that genus. *Phil. Trans.* 1858, pp.
169-184, pls. x, xi.

On the Megatherium (*Megatherium americanum*, Cuvier and
Blumenbach). Part IV. Bones of the Anterior Extremities.
Phil. Trans. 1858, pp. 261-278, pls. xviii-xxii.

On a New Genus (*Dimorphodon*) of Pterodactyle, with Remarks on
the Geological Distribution of Flying Reptiles. *Rep. Brit.
Assoc.* 1858, pt. 2, pp. 97-98.

On Remains of New and Gigantic Species of Pterodactyle (*P.
Fittoni* and *P. Sedgwickii*) from the Upper Greensand near
Cambridge. *Rep. Brit. Assoc.* 1858, pt. 2, pp. 98-103.

Monograph on the Fossil Reptilia of the Wealden Formation.
Part IV. *Hylæosaurus*, pp. 8-26, pls. iv-xi. *Pal. Soc.* x.
1858.

Monograph of the Fossil Reptilia of the London Clay. Part I.
(Suppl. I.), Chelonia (*Emys*), pp. 77-79, pls. xxviii. A, B. *Pal.
Soc.* x. 1858.

Monograph on the Fossil Reptilia of the Wealden and Purbeck
Formations. Suppl. I. Dinosauria (*Iguanodon*), pp. 1-7, pls.
i-iii. *Pal. Soc.* x. 1858.

[On the *Ichthyosaurus.*] *Ann. Mag. Nat. Hist.* ser. 3, i. 1858,
pp. 388-397. [Report of a lecture at Museum of Practical
Geology.]

1859

[Observations and Reflections on Geology by John Hunter, F.R.S.
4to, *London* (Coll. of Surgeons), 1859. Pp. i-lviii.] [Anony-
mous.]

Report, with Plan, on a Museum of Natural History, ordered by
the House of Commons to be printed. This is to be found in
—British Museum, a 'Copy of all Communications made by
the officers and architect of the British Museum to the Trustees,
respecting the want of space for exhibiting the Collections in that
Institution, as well as respecting the enlargement of its Buildings,' 'and, of all minutes of the Trustees. . . .' Parl. Paper,
fo. *London*, 1859, 26 pp., with a plan. [*Brit. Mus.* 1859, xiv.]

On the Classification and Geographical Distribution of the Mammalia, being the Lecture on Sir Robert Rede's Foundation,
delivered before the University of Cambridge, in the Senate
House, May 10, 1859. To which is added an Appendix 'On

the Gorilla,' and 'On the Extinction and Transmutation of Species.' 8vo, *London*, 1859, 104 pp. [The Appendix is divided into 'A, On the Extinction of Species. Being the Conclusion of the Fullerian Course of Lectures on Physiology for 1859.' 'B, On the Orang, Chimpanzee, and Gorilla. With reference to the Transmutation of Species.'

Manual of Zoology. 12mo, *London*, 1859. [From Admiralty Manual of Scientific Enquiry. Third edition. See 1849.]

On the Gorilla (*Troglodytes gorilla*, Sav.). *Proc. Zool. Soc.* 1859, pp. 1–23.

On a Collection of Australian Fossils in the Museum of the Natural History Society at Worcester ; with descriptions of the lower jaw and teeth of the *Nototherium inerme* and *N. Mitchelli*, Owen ; demonstrating the identity of the latter species with the *Zygomaturus*, Macleay. *Quart. Journ. Geol. Soc.* xv. 1859, pp. 176–186, pl. ix.

Description of some Remains of a gigantic Land Lizard (*Megalania prisca*, Owen) from Australia. *Phil. Trans.* 1859, pp. 43–48, pls. vii, viii.

On the Vertebral Characters of the Order *Pterosauria*, as exemplified in the Genera *Pterodactylus* (Cuvier) and *Dimorphodon* (Owen). *Phil. Trans.* 1859, pp. 161–169, pl. x.

On the Fossil Mammals of Australia. Part I. Description of a mutilated skull of a large Marsupial Carnivore (*Thylacoleo carnifex*, Owen), from a calcareous conglomerate stratum, eighty miles S.W. of Melbourne, Victoria. *Phil. Trans.* 1859, pp. 309–322, pls. xi xv.

On the Megatherium (*Megatherium americanum*, Cuvier and Blumenbach). Part V. Bones of the posterior extremities. *Phil. Trans.* 1859, pp. 809–830, pls. xxxvii-xli.

Report on a series of skulls of various tribes of mankind inhabiting Nepal, collected and presented to the British Museum by Bryan H. Hodgson, Esq. *Rep. Brit. Assoc.* 1859, pp. 95–103.

On the Orders of Fossil and Recent Reptilia, and their Distribution in Time. *Rep. Brit. Assoc.* 1859, pp. 153–166.

Monograph on the Fossil Reptilia of the Wealden and Purbeck Formations. Suppl. II. Crocodilia (*Streptospondylus*), pp. 20–44, pls. v xii. *Pal. Soc.* xi. 1859.

Monograph on the Fossil Reptilia of the Cretaceous Formations. Suppl. I. Pterosauria (*Pterodactylus*), pp. 1–19, pls. i–iv. *Pal. Soc.* xi. 1859.

On the Gorilla. *Proc. Roy. Inst.* iii. 1859, pp. 10–30.

Summary of the Succession in Time and Geographical Distribution of Recent and Fossil Mammalia. *Proc. Roy. Inst.* iii. 1859, pp. 109-116.

Address [to the British Association.] *Rep. Brit. Assoc.* (Leeds, 1858), 1859, pp. lix-cx.

Note on the Affinities of *Rhynchosaurus. Ann. Mag. Nat. Hist.* ser. 3, iv. 1859, pp. 237, 238.

'Megatherium.' *Stereoscopic Magazine*, No. xiv. 1859.

'Megaceros.' *Ibid.* No. xvii. 1859.

1860

The principal forms of the skeleton and the teeth as the basis for a system of Natural History and Comparative Anatomy. 8vo, *London* 1860 (Orr's Circle of the Sciences).

Memoir on the Megatherium, or Giant Ground-Sloth of America (*Megatherium americanum*, Cuvier). 4to, *London*, 1860. [A collection of papers which appeared in the *Phil. Trans.*]

Palæontology, or a Systematic Summary of Extinct Animals and their Geological Relations. 8vo, *Edinburgh*, 1860. 2nd edition, 8vo, *Edinburgh*, 1861.

On some Reptilian Fossils from South Africa. *Quart. Journ. Geol. Soc.* xvi. 1860, pp. 49-63, pls. i, ii, iii.

Notes on some Remains of *Polyptychodon* from Dorking. *Quart. Journ. Geol. Soc.* xvi. 1860, pp. 262-263. [Abstract.]

On some Small Fossil Vertebræ from near Frome, Somersetshire. *Quart. Journ. Geol. Soc.* xvi. 1860, pp. 492-497, figs.

On the Cerebral System of Classification of the Mammalia. *Proc. Roy. Inst.* iii. 1860, pp. 174-189.

Life of Lorenz Oken. 4to, 1860. [This was founded on an article in the 'Encyclopædia Britannica.']

1861

Essays and Observations on Natural History, Anatomy, Physiology, Psychology, and Geology. By John Hunter, F.R.S. Being his Posthumous Papers on those Subjects, arranged and revised, with Notes, &c., by Richard Owen. 2 vols. 8vo, *London*, 1861.

On a Dinosaurian Reptile (*Scelidosaurus Harrisoni*), from the Lower Lias of Charmouth. *Rep. Brit. Assoc.* 1861, pt. 2, pp. 121, 122.

On the Remains of a Plesiosaurian Reptile (*Plesiosaurus australis*), from an Oolitic Formation in the Middle Island of New Zealand., *Rep. Brit. Assoc.* 1861, pt. 2, pp. 122-123.

On the Cervical and Lumbar Vertebræ of the Mole (*Talpa europæa*, L.). *Rep. Brit. Assoc.* 1861, pt. 2, pp. 152-154.

On some Objects of Natural History from the Collection of M. Du Chaillu. *Rep. Brit. Assoc.* 1861, pt. 2, pp. 155, 156.

On the Psychical and Physical Characters of the Mincopies, or Natives of the Andaman Islands, and on the relations thereby indicated to other races of Mankind. *Rep. Brit. Assoc.* 1861, pp. 241-249.

On the Scope and Appliances of a National Museum of Natural History. *Proc. Roy. Inst.* iii. 1861, p. 360. [Title only.]

Monograph on the Fossil Reptilia of the Purbeck and Wealden Formations. Part V. Lacertilia (*Nuthetes*, &c.), pp. 31-39, pl. viii. *Pal. Soc.* xii. 1861.

Monograph on the British Fossil Reptilia from the Oolitic Formations. Part I. (*Scelidosaurus Harrisonii*), pp. 1-14, pls. i-vi. *Pal. Soc.* xiii. 1861.

Monograph on the Fossil Reptilia of the Cretaceous Formations. Suppl. II. Dinosauria (*Iguanodon*), pp. 27-30, pl. vii. *Pal. Soc.* xii. 1861.

Monograph on the Fossil Reptilia of the Cretaceous Formations. Suppl. III. Pterosauria (*Pterodactylus*) and Sauropterygia (*Polyptychodon*), pp. 1-25, pls. i-vi. *Pal. Soc.* xii. 1861.

Monograph on the British Fossil Reptilia from the Kimmeridge Clay. No. I, containing *Pliosaurus grandis*, pp. 15, 16, pl. vii. *Pal. Soc.* xii, 1861.

On the Cerebral Characters of Man and the Ape. *Ann. Mag. Nat. Hist.* ser. 3, vii. 1861, pp. 456-458, pl. xix-xxi.

1862

On the Extent and Aims of a National Museum of Natural History. 8vo, *London*, 1862, 126 pp., plans.

Replies to 'Essays and Reviews.' Ed. 2, 8vo, *London*, 1862. [Owen contributed a letter to Dr. Gilbert Rorison's ' Creative Week.']

Osteological Contributions to the Natural History of the Anthropoid Apes. No. VII. Comparison of the bones of the limbs of the *Troglodytes gorilla*, *T. niger*, and of different varieties of the Human Race ; and on the general characters of the skeleton of the Gorilla. *Trans. Zool. Soc.* v. 1862, pp. 1-31, pls. i-xiii. [A continuation of his 1857 paper.]

Description of Specimens of Fossil Reptilia discovered in the Coal Measures of the South Joggins, Nova Scotia, by J. W. Dawson. *Quart. Journ. Geol. Soc.* xviii. 1862, pp. 238-244, pls. ix, x.

On the Dicynodont Reptilia, with a Description of some Fossil Remains brought by H.R.H. Prince Alfred from South Africa, in November 1860. *Proc. Roy. Soc.* xi. 1862, pp. 583-585 ; *Phil. Trans.* 1862, pp. 455-467, pls. xix-xxv. [Contains also : (II.) On the Pelvis of the *Dicynodon.* (III.) Notice of a Skull and part of the Skeleton of *Rhynchosaurus articeps.*]

On the Character of the Aye-aye, as a test of the Lamarckian and Darwinian hypothesis of the transmutation and origin of species. *Rep. Brit. Assoc.* 1862, pt. 2, pp. 114-116.

On the Zoological Significance of the Cerebral and Pedal Characters of Man. *Rep. Brit. Assoc.* 1862, pt. 2, pp. 116-118.

1863

Inaugural Address . . . on the opening of the New Philosophical Hall, at Leeds, on Tuesday, the 16th of December, 1862. 8vo, *Leeds* [1863]. Another edition, 12mo, *London*, 1863.

On the Aye-aye (*Chiromys*, Cuvier ; *Chiromys madagascariensis*, Desm. ; *Sciurus madagascariensis*, Gmel., Sonnerat ; *Lemur psilodactylus*, Schreber, Shaw). *Trans. Zool. Soc.* v. 1863, pp. 33-101, pls. xiv-xxvi. [Also separately issued, 1863.]

On the *Archeopteryx* of Von Meyer, with a description of the fossil remains of a long-tailed species, from the Lithographic Stone of Solenhofen. *Phil. Trans.* 1863, pp. 33-47, pls. i-iv.

A Monograph of the Fossil Reptilia of the Liassic Formations. Part II. (*Scelidosaurus Harrisonii*), pp. 1-26, pls. i-xi. *Pal. Soc.* xiii. 1863.

Monograph on the British Fossil Reptilia from the Kimmeridge Clay. No. II. containing *Pliosaurus grandis.* Pp. 27, 28, pl. xii. *Pal. Soc.* xiii. 1863.

On the Osteology and Dentition of the Aborigines of the Andaman Islands, and the relations thereby indicated. *Trans. Ethnolog. Soc.* ii. 1863, pp. 34-49.

1864

Instances of the Power of God as manifested in His Animal Creation. 8vo, *London*, ed. 2, 1864. [Ed. 1, 1855.]

Monograph on the Fossil Reptilia of the Cretaceous Formations. Suppl. IV. Sauropterygia (*Plesiosaurus*), pp. 1–18, pls. i ix. *Pal. Soc.* xvi. 1864.

Monograph on the Fossil Reptilia of the Wealden and Purbeck Formations. Suppl. III. pp. 19–21, pl. x. *Pal. Soc.* xvi. 1864.

A Monograph of the Fossil Reptilia of the Cretaceous Formations. [Title-page, preface, and index, pp. i–vi.] *Pal. Soc.* xviii. 1864.

1865

An Address delivered at the Distribution of Prizes at St. Mary's Hospital Medical School, on Monday, May 29, 1865. 8vo, *London*. (Reprinted from the *Brit. Med. Journ.*) 1865, 16 pp. [Re-issued by the Hospital in 1868.]

Memoir on the Gorilla (*Troglodytes gorilla*, Savage). 4to, *London*, 1865. [A collection of papers from the *Trans. Zool. Soc.*]

On the Morbid Appearances observed in the Dissection of the Penguin (*Aptenodytes Forsteri*). *Proc. Zool. Soc.* 1865, pp. 438 439.

Contributions to the Natural History of the Anthropoid Apes. No. VIII. On the External Characters of the Gorilla (*Troglodytes gorilla*, Sav.) *Trans. Zool. Soc.* v. 1865, pp. 243–284, pls. xliii–xlix.

Description of the Skeleton of the Great Auk or Garfowl (*Alca impennis*, L.). *Trans. Zool. Soc.* v. 1865, pp. 317–335, pls. li, lii.

On Zoological Names of Characteristic Parts and Homological Interpretations of their Modifications and Beginnings, especially in reference to connecting fibres of the Brain. *Proc. Roy. Soc.* xiv. 1865, pp. 129–134.

On the Marsupial Pouches, Mammary Glands, and Mammary Fœtus of the *Echidna hystrix*. *Phil. Trans.* 1865, pp. 671 686, pls. xxxix–xli ; *Proc. Roy. Soc.* xiv. 1865, pp. 106–111.

Monograph of the Fossil Reptilia of the Liassic Formations. Part I. (Sauropterygia), pp. 1–40, pls. i xvi. *Pal. Soc.* xvii. 1865. [This and the parts under 1870 and 1881 form Part III. of the Liassic monograph, and a new title-page was issued in 1881.]

Description of some Remains of an Air-breathing Vertebrate (*Anthrakerpeton crassosteum*, Ow.) from the Coal-shale of Glamorganshire. *Geol. Mag.* ii. 1865, pp. 6 8, pls. i, ii.

Descriptions of Portions of Jaws of a Large Extinct Fish (*Stereodus melitensis*, Ow.), probably a Cycloid with Sauroid dentition, from the middle beds of the Maltese Miocene. *Geol. Mag.* ii. 1865, pp. 145-147, fig.

On a New Genus (*Miolophus*) of Mammal from the London Clay. *Geol. Mag.* ii. 1865, pp. 339-341, pl. x.

Observations on ' Recherches sur les Squalodons,' by Mr. P. J. Van Beneden. *Geol. Mag.* ii. 1865, pp. 405-411.

On *Macrauchenia patachonica*. *Geol. Mag.* ii. 1865, pp. 520-523.

On the Homology of the Tooth. *Archives of Dentistry*, i. 1865, pp. 309-311.

1866

On the Anatomy of Vertebrates, 3 vols. 8vo, *London*. Vol. i, Fishes and Reptiles, 1866, 650 pp. Vol. ii, Birds and Mammals, 1866, 592 pp. Vol. iii, Mammals, 1868, 850 pp.

Memoir on the Dodo (*Didus ineptus*, Linn.), with an Historical Introduction by William John Broderip. 4to, *London*, 1866, 56 pp., 12 pls.

On some Indian Cetacea collected by Walter Elliot, Esq. *Trans. Zool. Soc.* vi. pp. 17-47, pls. iii-xiv (1866) ; pp. 171-174 (1867).

On Dinornis (Part IX.) : containing a description of the skull, atlas, and scapulo-coracoid bone of the *Dinornis robustus*, Owen. *Trans. Zool. Soc.* v. 1866, pp. 337-358, pls. liii-lvi.

On Dinornis (Part X.) : containing a description of part of the skeleton of a flightless bird indicative of a new genus and species (*Cnemiornis calcitrans*, Ow.). *Trans. Zool. Soc.* v. 1866, pp. 395-404, pls. lxiii-lxvii.

On the Fossil Mammals of Australia. Part II. Description of an almost entire skull of the *Thylacoleo carnifex*, Owen, from a freshwater deposit, Darling Downs, Queensland. *Phil. Trans.* 1866, pp. 73-82, pls. ii-iv. [Abstract in *Proc. Roy. Soc.* xiv. 1865, pp. 343 344.]

Remarks on the Parturition of the Marsupials. *Ann. Mag. Nat. Hist.* ser. 3, xvii. 1866, pp. 382-384.

On an Upper Incisor of *Nototherium Mitchellii*. *Ann. Mag. Nat. Hist.* ser. 3, xviii. 1866, pp. 475-476.

On a Genus and Species of Sauroid Fish (*Thlattodus suchoides*, Ow.) from the Kimmeridge Clay of Norfolk. *Geol. Mag.* iii. 1866, pp. 55-57, pl. iii.

On the Genus and Species of Sauroid Fish (*Ditaxiodus impar*, Ow.), from the Kimmeridge Clay of Culham, Oxfordshire. *Geol. Mag.* iii. 1866, pp. 107-109, pls. iv, v.

Description of Part of the Lower Jaw and Teeth of a Small Oolitic

Mammal, *Stylodon pusillus*, Ow. *Geol. Mag.* iii. 1866, pp. 199 - 201, pl. x.

Evidence of a Species, perhaps extinct, of a Large Parrot (*Psittacus mauritianus*, Ow.), contemporary with the Dodo, in the island of Mauritius. *Ibis*, 1866, pp. 168 171. French translation in *Ann. Sci. Nat.* sér. 5, vi. 1866, pp. 88-90.

1867

Descriptions of three Skulls of Western Equatorial Africans—Fan, Ashira, and Fernand Vaz—with some admeasurements of the rest of the collection of skulls, transmitted to the British Museum from the Fernand Vaz, by P. B. Du Chaillu. From Du Chaillu, a Journey to Ashango-land, &c. 8vo. *London*, 1867 ; being pp. 439 460, 9 figures.

On the Osteology of the Dodo (*Didus ineptus*, Linn.). *Trans. Zool. Soc.* vi. 1867, pp. 49-85, pls. xv-xxiv.

On the Mandible and Mandibular Teeth of Cochliodonts. *Geol. Mag.* iv. 1867, pp. 59 63, pls. iii, iv.

On the Dental Characters of Genera and Species, chiefly of Fishes, from the Low Main seam and shales of coal, Northumberland. *Trans. Odont. Soc.* v. 1867, pp. 323 392, pls. i-xv.

Sur l'Anatomie des Edentés. *Journ. Anat. Physiol.* iv. 1867, pp. 35 37.

On the Argument of 'Infirmity' in Mr. Lewes' Review of the 'Reign of Law.' *Fraser's Magazine*, Oct. 1867, pp. 531–533.

Wayside Gatherings. *Gentleman's Magazine*, July 1867.

1868

Addresses on Medical Education. 8vo, *London*, 1868. [Before St. Mary's Hospital Medical School.] [See 1865.]

1869

On Dinornis (Part XI.) : containing a description of the integument of the sole, and tendons of a toe, of the foot of *Dinornis robustus*, Ow. *Trans. Zool. Soc.* vi. 1869, pp. 495, 496, pl. lxxxviii.

On Dinornis (Part XII.) : containing a description of the femur, tibia, and metatarsus of *Dinornis maximus*, Owen. *Trans. Zool. Soc.* vi. 1869, pp. 497-500, pls. lxxxix, xc.

Description of the Cavern of Bruniquel, and its Organic Contents. Part I. Human remains ; Part II. Equine remains. *Proc. Roy. Soc.* xvii. 1869, pp. 201-202 ; *Phil. Trans.* 1869, pp. 517-533, 535-558, pls. lvii-lx, 15 figures in text.

On Fossil Remains of Equines from Central and South America, referable to *Equus conversidens*, Ow. ; *E. tau*, Ow. ; and *E. arcidens*, Ow. *Proc. Roy. Soc.* xvii. 1869, pp. 267-268 ; *Phil. Trans.* 1869, pp. 559-574, pls. lxi., lxii.

Monographs on the British Fossil Reptilia from the Kimmeridge Clay. No. III., containing *Pliosaurus grandis, Pl. trochanterius*, and *Pl. portlandicus.* Pp. 1 12, pls. i.-iv. *Pal. Soc.* xxii. 1869.

On the Distinction between *Castor* and *Trogontherium. Geol. Mag.* vi. 1869, pp. 49-56, pl. iii, figs.

Description of a great part of a Jaw with the Teeth of *Strophodus medius*, Ow., from the Oolite of Caen in Normandy. *Geol. Mag.* vi. 1869, pp. 193 196, 235, pl. vii.

Note on the Occurrence of Remains of the Elk (*Alces palmatus*) in British Post-tertiary Deposits. *Geol. Mag.* vi. 1869, p. 389.

Notes on two Ichthyodorulites hitherto undescribed : *Lepracanthus Colei, Hybodus complanatus. Geol. Mag.* vi.1869, pp. 481-483, fig.

On Magnetic and Amœbal Phenomena.] *Monthly Microsc. Journ.* i. 1869, pp. 294 295.

Aperçu de la Géologie du Désert d'Egypte. *Comptes Rendus,* lxviii. 1869, pp. 625 628.

Milton and Galileo. *Fraser's Mag.* May 1869, pp. 678-684. [Letters bearing on the History of Science which passed between the above named, Louis XIII. and XIV., Cassini, Voiture, and Molière.]

1870

On Dinornis (Part XIII.) : containing a description of the sternum in *Dinornis elephantopus* and *D. rheides*, with notes on that bone in *D. crassus* and *D. casuarinus. Trans. Zool. Soc.* vii. 1870, pp. 115-122, pls. vii-ix.

On Dinornis (Part XIV.) : containing contributions to the craniology of the genus, with a description of the fossil cranium of *Dasornis londinensis*, Ow., from the London Clay of Sheppey. *Trans. Zool. Soc.* vii. 1870, pp. 123 150, pls. x-xvi.

On Fossil Remains of Mammals found in China. *Quart. Journ. Geol. Soc.* xxvi. 1870, pp. 417-434, pls. xxvii xxix.

On the Molar Teeth, Lower Jaw, of *Macrauchenia patachonica*, Ow.

Phil. Trans. 1870, pp. 79-82, pl. viii. Abstract in *Proc. Roy. Soc.* xvii. 1869, pp. 454-455.

On Remains of a Large Extinct Lama (*Palauchenia magna*, Ow.), from Quaternary deposits in the Valley of Mexico. *Phil. Trans.* 1870, pp. 65-77, pls. iv-vii.

On the Fossil Mammals of Australia. Part III. *Diprotodon australis*, Owen. *Phil. Trans.* 1870, pp. 519-578, pls. xxxv-l. Abstract in *Proc. Roy. Soc.* xviii. 1870, p. 196.

Monograph of the Fossil Reptilia of the Liassic Formations. Part II. (Pterosauria), pp. 41-81, pls. xvii-xx. *Pal. Soc.* xxiii. 1870.

Monograph on the British Fossil Cetacea from the Red Crag. No. I. *Pal. Soc.* 1870, pp. 1 40, pls. i-v.

Notice of some Saurian Fossils discovered by T. H. Hood at Waipara, Middle Island, New Zealand. *Geol. Mag.* vii. 1870, pp. 49-53, pl. iii.

Paloplotherium annectens, Owen. *Geol. Mag.* 1870, p. 143. [Letter.]

Observations sur les Caractères Cérébraux des Archencéphales. *Bull. Soc. Anthropol. Paris*, v. 1870, pp. 587-592.

1871

On Dinornis (Part XV.) : containing a description of the skull, femur, tibia, fibula, and metatarsus of *Aptornis defossor*, Owen, from near Oamaru, Middle Island, New Zealand : with additional observations on *Aptornis otidiformis*, on *Notornis Mantelli*, and on *Dinornis curtus*. *Trans. Zool. Soc.* vii. 1871, pp. 353-380, pls. xl-xliv.

On Dinornis (Part XVI.) : containing notices of the internal organs of some species, with description of the brain and some nerves and muscles of the head of the *Apteryx australis*. *Trans. Zool. Soc.* vii. 1871, pp. 381-396, pls. xlv-xlvii.

On the Dodo (Part II.) : Notes on the articulated skeleton of the Dodo (*Didus ineptus*, Linn.) in the British Museum. *Trans. Zool. Soc.* vii. 1871, pp. 513-525, pls. lxiv-lxvi.

On the Fossil Mammals of Australia (Part IV.) : Dentition and mandible of *Thylacoleo carnifex*, with remarks on the arguments for its herbivority. *Phil. Trans.* 1871, pp. 213-266, pls. xi-xiv, figures in text. Abstract in *Proc. Roy. Soc.* xix. 1871, pp. 95 96.

Monograph of the Fossil Mammalia of the Mesozoic Formations, pp. vi, 115, pls. i-iv. *Pal. Soc.* xxiv. 1871.

1872

On Dinornis (Part XVII.) : containing a description of the sternum and pelvis, with an attempted restoration, of *Aptornis defossor*, Owen. *Trans. Zool. Soc.* viii. 1872, pp. 119–126, pls. xiv xvi.

On the Fossil Mammals of Australia (Part V.) : Genus *Nototherium*, Owen. *Phil. Trans.* clxii. 1872, pp. 41–82, pls. ii–xi.

On the Fossil Mammals of Australia (Part VI.) : Genus *Phascolomys*, Geoffr. *Phil. Trans.* 1872, pp. 173–196, pls. xvii–xxiii, 8 figures in text.

Monograph on the Fossil Reptilia of the Wealden Formation. Suppl. IV. Dinosauria (*Iguanodon*), pp. 1–15, pls. i iii. *Pal. Soc.* xxv. 1872.

On Longevity. *Fraser's Mag.* Feb. 1872, pp. 218–233.

The Fate of the ' Jardin d'Acclimatation ' during the late Siege of Paris. *Fraser's Mag.* Jan. 1872, pp. 17–22. [Under the pseudonym of 'Zoologus.']

Serpent-charming in Cairo. *Blackwood's Edinburgh Mag.* Feb. 1872, pp. 169–175.

1873

[Address to the Fellows of the Royal Society on the questions of Income, Elections, Presidents, and payment of Secretaries.] 8vo [*London*, 1873], 8 pp. [Privately printed : a copy is preserved in the Zoological Library of the Natural History Museum.]

On the Anatomy of the American King Crab (*Limulus polyphemus*, Latr.) *Trans. Linn. Soc.* vol. xxviii, 1873, pp. 459–506, pls. xxxvi, xxxix.

On the Osteology of the Marsupialia (Part III.) : Modifications of the skeleton in the species of *Phascolomys*. *Trans. Zool. Soc.* viii. 1873, pp. 345 360, pls. l–lvii.

On Dinornis (Part XVIII.) : containing a description of the pelvis and bones of the leg of *Dinornis gravis*. *Trans. Zool. Soc.* viii. 1873, pp. 361–380, pls. lviii–lxi.

On Dinornis (Part XIX.) : containing a description of a femur indicative of a new genus of large wingless bird (*Dromornis australis*, Owen) from a Post-tertiary deposit in Queensland, Australia. *Trans. Zool. Soc.* viii. 1873, pp. 381–384, pls. lxii, lxiii.

Description of the Skull of a Dentigerous Bird (*Odontopteryx toli-*

apicus. Ow.) from the London Clay of Sheppey. *Quart. Journ. Geol. Soc.* xxix. 1873, pp. 511-522, pls. xvi, xvii.

On the Fossil Mammals of Australia (Part VII.) : Genus *Phascolomys* : species exceeding the existing ones in size. *Phil. Trans.* 1872 (1873), pp. 241-258, pls. xxxii-xl. Abstract in *Proc. Roy. Soc.* xx. 1872, p. 306.

The earliest discovered Evidence of Extinct Struthious Birds in New Zealand. *Geol. Mag.* 1873, p. 478.

1874

In Tom Taylor. Leicester Square. Sketch of Hunter's Scientific Character and Works. 8vo, *London*, 1874, pp. 420-433.

On the Osteology of the Marsupialia (Part IV.) : Bones of the trunk and limbs, *Phascolomys.* *Trans. Zool. Soc.* viii. 1874, pp. 483-500, pls. lxix lxxiv.

Note on the alleged Existence of Remains of a Lemming in Cave-deposits of England. *Proc. Roy. Soc.* xxii. 1874, pp. 364, 365.

On the Fossil Mammals of Australia (Part VIII.) : Family *Macropodidæ* : Genera, *Macropus, Osphranter, Phascolagus, Sthenurus,* and *Protemnodon.* *Phil. Trans.* 1874, pp. 245-287, pls. xx-xxvii. Abstract in *Proc. Roy. Soc.* xxi. 1873, p. 128.

On the Fossil Mammals of Australia (Part IX.) : Family *Macropodidæ* : Genera *Macropus, Pachysiagon, Leptosiagon, Procoptodon,* and *Palorchestes.* *Phil. Trans.* 1874, pp. 783-803, pls. lxxvi-lxxxiii. Abstract in *Proc. Roy. Soc.* xxi. 1873, pp. 386-387.

Monograph on the Fossil Reptilia of the Wealden and Purbeck Formations. Suppl. V. Dinosauria (*Iguanodon*), pp. 1-18, pls. i, ii. *Pal. Soc.* xxvii. 1874.

Monograph on the Fossil Reptilia of the Wealden and Purbeck Formations. Suppl. VI. Crocodilia (*Hylæochampsa*), pp. 1-7. *Pal. Soc.* xxvii, 1874.

Monograph on the Fossil Reptilia of the Mesozoic Formations. Part I. Pterosauria (*Pterodactylus*), pp. 1-14, pls. i, ii. *Pal. Soc.* xxvii. 1874.

Contributions to the Ethnology of Egypt. *Journ. Anthrop. Inst.* iv. 1874, pp. 223-254, pls. xviii-xxi.

1875

Preface to C. C. Blake, Zoology for Students. 8vo, *London*, 1875.

Note on a New Locality of *Dinornithidæ.* *Proc. Zool. Soc.* 1875 p. 88.

On Dinornis (Part XX.) : containing a restoration of the skeleton of *Cnemiornis calcitrans*, Owen, with remarks on its affinities in the Lamellirostral group. *Trans. Zool. Soc.* ix. 1875, pp. 253–272, pls. xxxv–xxxix.

On Fossil Evidences of a Sirenian Mammal (*Eotherium ægyptiacum*, Owen) from the Nummulitic Eocene of the Mokattam Cliffs, near Cairo. *Quart. Journ. Geol. Soc.* xxxi. 1875, pp. 100–105, pl. iii.

On *Prorastomus sirenoïdes* (Ow.), Part II. *Quart. Journ. Geol. Soc.* xxxi. 1875, pp. 559–567, pls. xxviii, xxix.

Monographs on the British Fossil Reptilia of the Mesozoic Formations. Part II. (Genera *Bothriospondylus*, *Cetiosaurus*, *Omosaurus*), pp. 15–93, pls. iii–xxii. *Pal. Soc.* xxix. 1875.

On Petroleum and Oil-wells. *Fraser's Mag.* Oct. 1875, pp. 437–449.

Review of H. Waller's 'The Last Journals of David Livingstone in Central Africa, from 1865 to his Death.' 1874. *Quarterly Review*, cxxxviii. 1875.

1876

Descriptive and Illustrated Catalogue of the Fossil Reptilia of South Africa in the Collection of the British Museum. 4to, *London*, 1876, xii., 86 pp., 70 pls.

On the Fossil Mammals of Australia (Part X.) : Family *Macropodidæ* : Mandibular dentition and parts of the skeleton of *Palorchestes* ; additional evidences of *Macropus titan*, *Sthenurus*, and *Procoptodon*. *Phil. Trans.* 1876, pp. 197–226, pls. xix–xxxi. Abstract in *Proc. Roy. Soc.* xxiii. 1875, p. 451.

On the Osteology of the Marsupialia (Part V.) : Fam. *Pœphaga* ; Genus *Macropus*. *Trans. Zool. Soc.* ix. 1870, pp. 417–446, pls. lxxiv–lxxxiii.

Evidence of a Carnivorous Reptile (*Cynodraco major*, Ow.) about the size of a Lion, with remarks thereon. *Quart. Journ. Geol. Soc.* xxxii. 1876, pp. 95–102, pl. xi.

Evidences of Theriodonts in Permian Deposits elsewhere than in South Africa. *Quart. Journ. Geol. Soc.* xxxii. 1876, pp. 352–363, figures.

On a New Modification of Dinosaurian Vertebræ. *Quart. Journ. Geol. Soc.* xxxii. 1876, pp. 43–46, pls. iv, v.

Monograph on the Fossil Reptilia of the Wealden and Purbeck Formations. Suppl. VII. Crocodilia (*Poikilopleuron*) and Dinosauria (*Chondrosteosaurus*), pp. 1–7, pls. i–vi. *Pal. Soc.* xxx. 1876.

1877

Researches on the Fossil Remains of the Extinct Mammals of Australia; with a notice of the Extinct Marsupials of England. 2 vols. 4to, *London*, 1877, 1878. [A collection of papers issued in serial publications, with some additional matter.]

On a New Species of *Sthenurus*, with remarks on the relation of the genus to *Dorcopsis*, Müller. *Proc. Zool. Soc.* 1877, 352-361, pls. xxxvii, xxxviii.

On Dinornis (Part XXI.) : containing a restoration of the skeleton of *Dinornis maximus*, Owen. With an Appendix on additional evidence of the genus *Dromornis* in Australia. *Trans. Zool. Soc.* x. 1877, pp. 147-188, pls. xxxi-xxxiii.

On the Rank and Affinities in the Reptilian Class of the *Mosasauridæ*, Gervais. *Quart. Journ. Geol. Soc.* xxxiii. 1877, pp. 682-715, figs.

Monographs on the British Fossil Reptilia of the Mesozoic Formations. Part III. (*Omosaurus*), pp. 95-97, pls. xxiii, xxiv. *Pal. Soc.* xxxi. 1877.

On a New Marsupial from Australia. *Ann. Mag. Nat. Hist.* ser. 4, xx. 1877, p. 542 ; ser. 5, i. 1878, p. 103.

1878

On the Relative Positions to their Constructors of the Chambered Shells of Cephalopods. *Proc. Zool. Soc.* 1878, pp. 955-975, pl. lx.

On *Argillornis longipennis*, Ow., a Large Bird of Flight, from the Eocene Clay of Sheppey. *Quart. Journ. Geol. Soc.* xxxiv. 1878, pp. 124-130, pl. vi.

On the Influence of the Advent of a Higher Form of Life in modifying the Structure of an Older and Lower Form. *Quart. Journ. Geol. Soc.* xxxiv. 1878, pp. 421-430, figs.

On the Affinities of the *Mosasauridæ*, Gervais, as exemplified in the Bony Structure of the Fore Fin. *Quart. Journ. Geol. Soc.* xxxiv. 1878, pp. 748-753, figs.

On the Fossils called 'Granicones ;' being a contribution to the histology of the exo-skeleton in Reptilia. *Trans. R. Micros. Soc.* i. 1878, pp. 233-236, pls. xi, xii.

Monograph on the Fossil Reptilia of the Wealden and Purbeck Formations. Suppl. VIII. Crocodilia (*Goniopholis, Petrosuchus,* and *Suchosaurus*), pp. 1-15, pls. i-vi. *Pal. Soc.* xxxii. 1878.

On the Solitaire (*Didus solitarius*, Gm.; *Pezophaps solitaria* Strkl.) *Ann. Mag. Nat. Hist.* ser. 5, i. 1878, pp. 87-98, 2 pls.

On the Occurrence in North America of Rare Extinct Vertebrates found fragmentarily in England. *Ann. Mag. Nat. Hist.* ser. 5, ii. 1878, pp. 201-223, 2 pls.

[Speech on 'New Guinea' at Royal Colonial Institute, December, 17, 1878.] Reported in *The Colonies*, December 21, 1878.

1879

Memoirs on the Extinct Wingless Birds of New Zealand, with an Appendix on those of England, Australia, Newfoundland, Mauritius, and Rodriguez. 2 vols. 4to, *London*, 1879. [Mainly a reprint of papers which appeared between 1839 and 1879 in the publications of the Zoological Society ; with the addition of a paper on the ' Anatomy of *Apteryx australis*,' a plate of *Notornis* (life size), and a geological map of New Zealand showing the localities from whence fossils were obtained.]

On the Association of Dwarf Crocodiles (*Nannosuchus* and *Theriosuchus pusillus*, e.g.) with the diminutive Mammals of the Purbeck Shales. *Quart. Journ. Geol. Soc.* xxxv. 1879, pp. 148-155, pl. ix.

Description of Fragmentary Indications of a Huge Kind of Theriodont Reptile (*Titanosuchus ferox*, Ow.) from Beaufort West, Gough Tract, Cape of Good Hope. *Quart. Journ. Geol. Soc.* xxxv. 1879, pp. 189-199, pl. xi.

On the Endothiodont Reptilia, with Evidence of the Species *Endothiodon uniseries*, Ow. *Quart. Journ. Geol. Soc.* xxxv. 1879, pp. 557-564, pl. xxvii.

On *Hypsiprymnodon*, Ramsay, a Genus indicative of a Distinct Family (*Pleopodidæ*) in the Diprotodont Section of the Marsupialia. *Trans. Linn. Soc.* ser. 2 (Zool.) i. 1879, pp. 573-582, pls. lxxi, lxxii.

Monograph on the Fossil Reptilia of the Wealden and Purbeck Formations. Suppl. IX. Crocodilia (*Goniopholis*, *Brachyocetes*, *Nannosuchus*, *Theriosuchus*, and *Nuthetes*), pp. 1-19, pls. i-iv. *Pal. Soc.* xxxiii. 1879.

Observations on the collection of skulls sent by Captain Burton to the British Museum, September, 1878. *Journ. Anthrop. Inst.*, vol. viii, 1879, pp. 323, 324.

Supplementary Observations on the Anatomy of *Spirula australis*, Lamarck. *Ann. Mag. Nat. Hist.* ser. 5, iii. 1879, pp. 1-16.

On the Occurrence in North America of Rare Extinct Vertebrates found fragmentarily in England, No. 2. *Ann. Mag. Nat. Hist.* ser. 5, iv. 1879, pp. 53–61, pl. viii.

Alleged Evidence of the Moa from Feathered Ornaments of Maori Weapons. *Ann. Mag. Nat. Hist.* ser. 5, iv. 1879, p. 169.

On the Natural Term of Life and of its Chief Periods in the Hippopotamus (*Hippopotamus amphibius*, Linn.). *Ann. Mag. Nat. Hist.* ser. 5, iv. 1879, pp. 188–190.

On the Extinct Animals of the Colonies of Great Britain. 8vo, *London* (R. Colon. Inst.), 1879, 23 pp.

1880

On the External and Structural Characters of the Male *Spirula australis*, Lam. *Proc. Zool. Soc.* 1880, pp. 352–354, pl. xxxii.

Description of a Portion of Mandible and Teeth of a Large Extinct Kangaroo (*Palorchestes crassus*, Ow.) from ancient Fluviatile Drift, Queensland. *Trans. Zool. Soc.* xi. 1880, pp. 7–10, pl. ii.

On the Skull of *Argillornis longipennis*, Ow. *Quart. Journ. Geol. Soc.* xxxvi. 1880, pp. 23–26, pl. ii.

Description of Parts of the Skeleton of an Anomodont Reptile (*Platypodosaurus robustus*, Ow.) from the Trias of Graaff Reinet, S. Africa. *Quart. Journ. Geol. Soc.* xxxvi. 1880, pp. 414–425, pl. xvi, xvii.

Monograph on the Fossil Reptilia of the London Clay. Vol. ii. pt. i. (*Chelone gigas*), pp. 1–4, pls. i, ii. *Pal. Soc.* xxxiv. 1880.

Demonstration on the Elephantine Mammals. Report of a visit to the British Museum. *Proc. Geol. Assoc.* vi. 1880, pp. 321–328, pl. ii.

On the Occurrence in North America of Rare Extinct Vertebrates found fragmentarily in England. No. 3. *Ann. Mag. Nat. Hist.* ser. 5, v. 1880, pp. 177–181, pl. viii.

1881

Descriptions of some new and rare Cephalopoda (Part II.) *Trans. Zool. Soc.* xi. 1881, pp. 131–170, pls. xxiii–xxxv.

On the Order *Theriodontia*, with a description of a new genus and species (*Ælurosaurus felinus*, Ow.) *Quart. Journ. Geol. Soc.* xxxvii. 1881, pp. 261–265, pl. ix.

Description of Parts of the Skeleton of an Anomodont Reptile

(*Platypodosaurus robustus*, Owen). Part II. The Pelvis. *Quart. Journ. Geol. Soc.* xxxvii. 1881, pp. 266–271, pl. x.

Description of some Remains of the Gigantic Land Lizard (*Megalania prisca*, Owen) from Australia. Part II. *Phil. Trans.* 1880 (1881), pp. 1037–1050, pls. xxxiv–xxxviii. Abstract in *Proc. Roy. Soc.* xxx. 1880, p. 304.

On the Ova of the *Echidna hystrix*. *Phil. Trans.* 1880 (1881), pp. 1051–1054, pl. xxxix. Abstract in *Proc. Roy. Soc.* xxx. 1880, p. 407.

Description of some Remains of the Gigantic Land Lizard (*Megalania prisca*, Owen) from Australia. Part III. *Phil. Trans.* 1881, pp. 547–556, pls. lxiv–lxvi. Abstract in *Proc. Roy. Soc.* xxxi. 1881, p. 380.

A Monograph of the Fossil Reptilia of the Liassic Formations. Part III. (Ichthyopterygia), pp. 83–134, pls. xxi–xxxiii. *Pal. Soc.* xxxv. 1881, iii., pp. 440–445.

On the Scientific Status of Medicine. *Trans. Intern. Medical Congress, London,* 1881, iii., pp. 440–445.

1882

Experimental Physiology, its Benefits to Mankind. 8vo, *London,* 1882, viii. 216 pp. [This contains the Address on unveiling the Statue of Harvey at Folkestone.]

In [G. R. Jesse], Correspondence with Sir R. Owen on John Hunter and Aneurism, &c., ed. 3. 8vo, *London,* 1882, 14 pp.

[Read Part XXIII. of his series of Memoirs on Dinornis.] *Proc. Zool. Soc.* 1882, pp. 1, 2.

On *Trichina spiralis*. *Proc. Zool. Soc.* 1882, pp. 571–575.

On the Sternum of *Notornis* and on Sternal Characters. *Proc. Zool. Soc.* 1882, pp. 689–697, figs.

On an Extinct Chelonian Reptile (*Notochelys costata*, Owen), from Australia. *Quart. Journ. Geol. Soc.* xxxviii. 1882, pp. 178–183, figs.

Description of Part of the Femur of *Nototherium Mitchelli*. *Quart. Journ. Geol. Soc.* xxxviii. 1882, pp. 394–396, pl. xvi.

On the Homology of the Conario-hypophysial Tract, or the so-called Pineal and Pituitary Glands. *Journ. Linn. Soc.* (Zool.) xvi. 1882, pp. 131–149. [**A.**]

Notice of Portions of the Skeleton of the Trunk and Limbs of the Great Horned Saurian of Australia (*Megalania prisca*, Owen). *Proc. Roy. Soc.* xxxiv. 1882, pp. 267–268.

Description of Portions of a Tusk of a Proboscidian Mammal (*Notelephas australis*, Owen). *Phil. Trans.* 1882, pp. 777-781, pl. li. Abstract in *Proc. Roy. Soc.* xxxiii. 1882, p. 448.

Address to the Biological Section of the British Association. *Rep. Brit. Assoc.* (York, 1881) 1882, pp. 651-661.

1883

Aspects of the Body in Vertebrates and Invertebrates. 8vo, *London*, 1883. [This publication consists of **A**, 1882, and **B**, 1883, with fresh title.]

Embryological Testimony to General Homology. *Proc. Zool. Soc.* 1883, pp. 349-352.

On Dinornis (Part XXIII.): containing a description of the skeleton of *Dinornis parvus*, Owen. *Trans. Zool. Soc.* xi. 1883, pp. 233 256, pls. li–lviii.

On Dinornis (Part XXIV.): containing a description of the head and feet, with their dried integuments, of an individual of the species *Dinornis didinus*, Owen. *Trans. Zool. Soc.* xi. 1883, pp. 257-261, pls. lix lxi.

On Generic Characters in the Order *Sauropterygia*. *Quart. Journ. Geol. Soc.* xxxix. 1883, pp. 133 138, figs.

On the Skull of *Megalosaurus*. *Quart. Journ. Geol. Soc.* xxxix. 1883, pp. 334 347, pl. xi, figs.

On Cerebral Homologies in Vertebrates and Invertebrates. *Journ. Linn. Soc.* (Zool.) xvii. 1883, pp. 1 13. [**B.**]

Evidence of a Large Extinct Monotreme (*Echidna Ramsayi*, Ow.) from the Wellington Breccia Cave, New South Wales. *Proc. Roy. Soc.* xxxvi. 1883, p. 4; *Phil. Trans.* clxxv. (1884) pp. 273-275.

Description of Parts of a Human Skeleton from a Pleistocene (Palæolithic) Bed, Tilbury, Essex. *Proc. Roy. Soc.* xxxvi. 1883, p. 136.

On the Affinities of *Thylacoleo*. *Phil. Trans.* 1883, pp. 575 582, pls. xxxix xli. Abstract in *Proc. Roy. Soc.* xxxv. 1883, p. 19.

Pelvic Characters of *Thylacoleo carnifex*. *Phil. Trans.* 1883, pp. 639-643, pl. xlvi. Abstract in *Proc. Roy. Soc.* xxxv. 1883, p. 163.

On the Answerable Divisions of the Brain in Vertebrates and Invertebrates. *Ann. Mag. Nat. Hist.* ser. 5, xii. 1883, pp. 303 307.

On an Outline of the Skull (basal view) of *Thylacoleo*. *Geol. Mag.* 1883, p. 289, pl. vii.

Notes on Birds in the Garden, Sheen Lodge, Richmond Park. *The Garden*, xxiii. 1883, pp. 303, 333, 349, 384, 402.

1884

History of British Fossil Reptiles. 4to, *London*, 1849-1884. [This book consists of a reprint of the papers which appeared between 1849 and 1884 in the publications of the Palæontographical and other societies ; it was issued from time to time, as a separate work to subscribers, and was finally bound and published as complete. Beyond a few notes, here and there, the 'British Fossil Reptiles' is identical with the papers in the Monographs of the Palæontographical Society, and these papers should always be referred to.]

Antiquity of Man as deduced from the Discovery of a Human Skeleton during the excavations of the East and West India Dock Extensions at Tilbury, north bank of the Thames. 8vo, *London*, 1884, 32 pp. 4 pls.

On the Skull and Dentition of a Triassic Mammal (*Tritylodon longævus*, Owen) from South Africa. *Quart. Journ. Geol. Soc.* xl. 1884, pp. 146-152, pl. vi.

On the Cranial and Vertebral Characters of the Crocodilian Genus *Plesiosuchus*, Owen. *Quart. Journ. Geol. Soc.* xl. 1884, pp. 153-159, figs.

On a Labyrinthodont Amphibian (*Rhytidosteus capensis*) from the Trias of Orange Free State, Cape of Good Hope. *Quart. Journ. Geol. Soc.* xl. 1884, pp. 333-339, pls. xvi, xvii.

Description of Teeth of a Large Extinct (Marsupial ?) Genus, *Sceparnodon*, Ramsay. *Phil. Trans.* 1884, pp. 245-248, pl. xi. Abstract in *Proc. Roy. Soc.* xxxvi. 1884, pp. 3-4.

Evidence of a Large Extinct Lizard (*Notiosaurus dentatus*, Owen) from Pleistocene Deposits, New South Wales, Australia. *Phil. Trans.* clxxv. 1884, pp. 249-251, pl. xii. Abstract in *Proc. Roy. Soc.* xxxvi. 1884, p. 221.

Evidence of a Large Extinct Monotreme (*Echidna Ramsayi*, Ow.) from the Wellington Breccia Cave, New South Wales. *Phil. Trans.* 1884, pp. 273-275, pl. xiv.

Description of an Impregnated Uterus and of the Uterine Ova of *Echidna hystrix*. *Ann. Mag. Nat. Hist.* ser. 5, xiv. 1884, pp. 373-376, pl. xiii.

Triglyphus, Fraas ; and *Tritylodon*, Owen. *Geol. Mag.* 1884, p. 286.

1885

On the Structure of the Heart in *Ornithorhynchus* and *Apteryx*. *Proc. Zool. Soc.* 1885, pp. 328-329.

Note on the Resemblance of the Upper Molar Teeth of an Eocene Mammal (*Neoplagiaulax*, Lemoine) to those of *Tritylodon*. *Quart. Journ. Geol. Soc.* xli. 1885, pp. 28-29, figs.

Notes on Remains of *Elephas primigenius* from one of the Creswell Bone-caves. *Quart. Journ. Geol. Soc.* xli. 1885, pp. 31-34, figs.

1886

On Dinornis (Part XXV.) : containing a description of the sternum of *Dinornis elephantopus*. *Trans. Zool. Soc.* xii. 1886, pp. 1-3, pl. i.

On the Premaxillaries and Scalpriform Teeth of a Large Extinct Wombat (*Phascolomys curvirostris*, Ow.) *Quart. Journ. Geol. Soc.* xlii. 1886, pp. 1-2, pl. i.

Description of Fossil Remains, including Foot-bones, of *Megalania prisca* (pt. iv.) *Phil. Trans.* 1886, pp. 327-330, pl. xiii-xv. Abstract in *Proc. Roy. Soc.* xl. 1886, p. 93.

On a New Perissodactyle Ungulate from Wyoming. *Geol. Mag.* 1886, p. 140.

1887

On the Skull and Dentition of a Triassic Saurian (*Galesaurus planiceps*, Owen). *Quart. Journ. Geol. Soc.* xliii. 1887, pp. 1-6, pl. i.

On Fossil Remains of *Echidna Ramsayi* (Ow.), Pt. II. *Proc. Roy. Soc.* xlii. 1887, p. 390.

Description of a Newly-excluded Young of the *Ornithorhynchus paradoxus*. *Proc. Roy. Soc.* xlii. 1887, p. 391.

Description of Fossil Remains of Two Species of a Megalanian Genus (*Meiolania*) from 'Lord Howe's Island.' *Phil. Trans.* 1886 (1887), pp. 471-480, pls. xxix-xxxii. Abstract in *Proc. Roy. Soc.* xl. 1886, pp. 315-316.

1888

Additional Evidence of the Affinities of the Extinct Marsupial Quadruped *Thylacoleo carnifex* (Owen). *Phil. Trans.* 1887

(1888), pp. 1-3, pl. i.   Abstract in *Proc. Roy. Soc.* xli. 1886, p. 317.

Description of the Skull of an Extinct Carnivorous Marsupial of the Size of a Leopard (*Thylacopardus australis*, Owen), from a recently opened cave near the 'Wellington Cave' locality, New South Wales.   *Proc. Roy. Soc.* xlv. 1888, p. 99.   [Title only.]

On Parts of the Skeleton of *Meiolania platyceps* (Owen).   *Phil. Trans.* 1888 (1889), pp. 181-191, pls. xxxi-xxxvii.   Abstract in *Proc. Roy. Soc.* xlii. 1887, p. 297.

1889

A Monograph on the Fossil Reptilia of the Wealden and Purbeck Formations. Suppl. IV.-IX. [Consisting of title-page, preface, and table of contents, pp. i-viii.]   *Pal. Soc.* xlii. 1889.

A Monograph on the Fossil Reptilia of the Mesozoic Formations. [Title-page, preface, and table of contents, pp. i-viii.]   *Pal. Soc.* xlii. 1889.

Monograph on the British Fossil Cetacea from the Red Crag. [Title-page, preface, and contents.]   *Pal. Soc.* xlii. 1889.

[N.B.—Professor Owen's Hunterian Lectures were generally reported in the *Medical Times*.]

LIST OF RICHARD OWEN'S HONORARY DISTINCTIONS

Member of the Royal College of Surgeons, August 18, 1826.

Apothecaries' Hall, January 7, 1830.

Correspondent, Academy of Natural Sciences of Philadelphia, January 28, 1834.

Correspondent, Académie Royale de Médecine, Paris, February 24, 1836.

Correspondent, Société Philomathique de Paris, February 20, 1836.

Correspondent, Regia Scientiarum Academia Borussica, March 1836.

Correspondent, Die Gesellschaft für Beförderung der Naturwissenschaften zu Freiburg, August 29, 1837.

Honorary Member, Societas Cæsarea Naturæ Curiosorum Mosquensis, April 27, 1837.

Honorary Member, Societas Physico-Medica Erlangensis, August 1836.

Wollaston Medal (Geological Society), 1838.

Honorary Member, Boston Society of Natural History, October 24, 1839.

Correspondent, Institute of France, February 7, 1839.

Corresponding Member, Académie Imp. Sci. St.-Pétersbourg, 1839.

Honorary Member, Hunterian Society, March 5, 1840.

Honorary Member, Royal Cornwall Polytechnic Society, 1841.

Honorary Member, Royal Geological Society of Cornwall, September 25, 1841.

Foreign Member, Königlich Bayerische Akademie der Wissenschaften, August 25, 1842.

Foreign Member, Hollandsche Maatschappij de Wetenschappen te Haarlem, 1842.

Foreign Member, Regia Scientiarum Academia Svecica, December 13, 1843.

Honorary Fellow of the Royal College of Surgeons of England, 1843.

Honorary Member, Academia Frederico-Alexandrina Erlangensis August 25, 1843.

Honorary Member, Manchester Literary and Philosophical Society, April 30, 1844.

Honorary Member, American Philosophical Society, January 17, 1845.

Honorary Fellow, Royal Society of Edinburgh, March 18, 1845.

Royal Medal (Royal Society), 1846.

Honorary Member, Société des Sciences Naturelles du Canton de Vaud, April 22, 1846.

Honorary Member, Naturwissenschaftlicher Verein in Hamburg, December 30, 1846.

Honorary Member, Naturhistorischer Verein für das Grossherzog-thum Hessen, August 25, 1846.

Honorary Member, Societas Regia Medico-Chirugica Londiniensis, February 9, 1847.

LL.D. Edinburgh, May 17, 1847.

Fellow, Academia Scientiarum Instituti Bononiensis, June 20, 1847.

Correspondent, Kaiserliche Akademie der Wissenschaften in Wien, August 1, 1848.

Associate, Société de Biologie, Paris, November 18, 1848.

Associate, Académie Royale des Sciences de Belgique, December 17, 1847.

Correspondent, Société du Muséum d'Histoire Naturelle de Stras-bourg, February 10, 1848.

Foreign Correspondent, Real Academia de Ciencias (Madrid), 1848.

Honorary Member, Royal College of Surgeons in Ireland, May 19, 1849.

Honorary Member, Royal Medical Society of Edinburgh, March 8, 1850.

Chevalier of the Order ' Pour le Mérite,' 1851.

Bronze Medal as Juror, Great Exhibition, 1851.

Honorary Member, Regia Scientiarum Societas Upsaliensis, June 25, 1851.

Foreign Member, Koninklijke Akademie van Wetenschappen, October 26, 1851.

Copley Medal (Royal Society), 1851.

D.C.L., Oxford University, June 23, 1852.

Correspondent, Natuurkundige Vereeniging in Nederlandsch Indië, February 18, 1853.

Gold and Silver Medals as Juror, Paris Exhibition, 1855.

Légion d'Honneur, 1855.

Correspondent, Asociacion de Amigos de la Historia Natural del Plata, August 22, 1855.

Prix Cuvier, Institut de France, February 2, 1856.

Honorary Member, Cæsareæ Leopoldino-Carolinæ Academiæ Naturæ Curiosorum, October 1, 1857.

Honorary Member, American Academy of Arts and Sciences, November 14, 1857.

Honorary Member, Royal Society of Edinburgh, July 21, 1858.

Foreign Associate, Institut de France, April 25, 1859.

LL.D., Cambridge, May 1859.

Honorary Fellow, Royal Society of Literature, 1859.

Foreign Member, Königliche Gesellschaft der Wissenschaften zu Göttingen, December 17, 1859.

Foreign Member, Kongelige Danske Videnskabernes Selskab, April 15, 1859.

Honorary Member, Musea královstoí České, 1861.

Honorary Member, Odontological Society of London, December 2, 1861.

Chevalier of the Order of St. Maurice and Lazarus, December 19, 1862.

Honorary Member, Zoologische Gesellschaft zu Hamburg, October 17, 1863.

Honorary Member, Anthropological Society of London, March 24, 1863.

Correspondent, Société des Sciences Naturelles de Cherbourg, December 12, 1864.

Silver Medal, New Zealand Exhibition, 1865.

Foreign Associate, National Academy of Sciences of the United States, January 5, 1865.

Honorary Member, Die Pollichia, ein naturwissenschaftlicher Verein der Bayrischen Rheinpfalz zu Dürkheim a. d. H. June 13, 1866.

Correspondent, Magyar Tudomanyos Akademia, January 30, 1867.

Knight of the Order of the Rose, October 21, 1867.

Correspondent, Reale Instituto Lombardo di Scienze e Lettere in Milano, July 2, 1868.

Baly Medal, Royal College of Physicians, 1869.

Foreign Member, Reale Accademia delle Scienze di Napoli, April 9, 1870.

Honorary Member, Societas Medica Londinensis, November 7, 1873.

—Commander of the Bath, 1873.

The Order of Leopold, July 9, 1873.

Honorary Member, Academia Medicinæ Neo-Eboracensis, May 21, 1874.

Foreign Member, Società Italiana delle Scienze, December 8, 1877.

W. B. Clarke Medal (Royal Society of New South Wales), 1878.

Honorary Member, Geologists' Association, 1878.

Honorary Member, Naturwissenschaftlicher Verein von Hamburg-Altona, 1878.

Silver Medal, Sydney Exhibition, 1879.

Corresponding Member, Reale Accademia delle Scienze di Torino, 1880.

Silver Medal, Melbourne International Exhibition, 1880–81.

Foreign Member, Reale Accademia dei Lincei (Roma), December 2, 1883.

Honorary Member, Essex Field Club, January 27, 1883.

Honorary Medal of the Royal College of Surgeons of England, August 9, 1883.

Correspondent, Accademia Valdarnese del Poggio, January 10, 1884.

— Knight Commander of the Bath, 1884.

Honorary Liveryman of the Leathersellers' Company, February 6, 1884.

Honorary Member, Hertfordshire Natural History Society, February 17, 1885.

Bronze Medal, Adelaide Exhibition, 1887.

— Linnean Medal (Linnean Society), 1888.

Honorary Member, Reale Accademia della Scienza di Palermo, January 6, 1888.

Doctor Universitatis Bononiensis, June 1888.

Owen was also a Fellow of the following learned Societies :— The Royal Society, the Linnean Society, the Geological Society, the Zoological Society, the Microscopical Society, the Entomological Society, the Palæontographical Society.

INDEX

PRINTED BY
SPOTTISWOODE AND CO., NEW-STREET SQUARE
LONDON

LIFE AND WORKS

OF

CHARLES DARWIN.

LIFE AND LETTERS OF CHARLES DARWIN.
With an Autobiographical Chapter. Edited by FRANCIS DARWIN,
F.R.S. Seventh Thousand. With 3 Portraits and Illustrations.
3 vols. 8vo. 36s.

CHARLES DARWIN: an Autobiography. With
Selections from his Letters by FRANCIS DARWIN. Portrait. 7s. 6d.

VOYAGE OF A NATURALIST: a Journal of Re-
searches into the Natural History and Geology of the Countries visited
during a Voyage round the World. By CHARLES DARWIN. Illustrations. Medium 8vo. 21s.; or *Popular Edition*, with Portrait, 3s. 6d.

THE ORIGIN OF SPECIES, BY MEANS OF
NATURAL SELECTION; or the Preservation of Favoured Races in
the Struggle for Life. By CHARLES DARWIN. 2 vols. 12s.; or post
8vo. 7s. 6d.

DESCENT OF MAN AND SELECTION IN RELA-
TION TO SEX. By CHARLES DARWIN. Illustrations. 2 vols. 15s.;
or *Popular Edition*, 7s. 6d.

INSECTIVOROUS PLANTS. By CHARLES DARWIN.
Post 8vo. 9s.

THE MOVEMENTS AND HABITS OF CLIMBING
PLANTS. By CHARLES DARWIN. Post 8vo. 6s.

EXPRESSION OF THE EMOTIONS IN MAN
AND ANIMALS. By CHARLES DARWIN. Illustrations. Crown
8vo. 12s.

VARIATION OF ANIMALS AND PLANTS
UNDER DOMESTICATION. By CHARLES DARWIN. Illustrations. 2 vols. Crown 8vo. 15s.

THE VARIOUS CONTRIVANCES BY WHICH
ORCHIDS ARE FERTILISED BY INSECTS. By CHARLES
DARWIN. Woodcuts. Post 8vo. 7s. 6d.

THE EFFECTS OF CROSS AND SELF-FERTILI-
SATION IN THE VEGETABLE KINGDOM. By CHARLES
DARWIN. Crown 8vo. 9s.

THE DIFFERENT FORMS OF FLOWERS ON
PLANTS OF THE SAME SPECIES. By CHARLES DARWIN.
Woodcuts. Crown 8vo. 7s. 6d.

THE POWER OF MOVEMENT IN PLANTS. By
CHARLES DARWIN, assisted by FRANCIS DARWIN. Woodcuts.
Crown 8vo.

THE FORMATION OF VEGETABLE MOULD
THROUGH THE ACTION OF WORMS. With Observations on
their Habits. By CHARLES DARWIN. Woodcuts. Post 8vo. 6s.

JOHN MURRAY, Albemarle Street.